JEWISH RENAISSANCE

A VOICE FROM THE CHORUS

VOLUME ONE | OBLIVION

VOLUME ONE | OBLIVION

Book One: A MIND IN CRISIS

Book Two: GROWING A NEW MIND

VOLUME TWO | REINVENTING THE PAST

Book Three: KNOW BEFORE WHOM YOU STAND

Book Four: REINVENTING THE PRESENT

VOLUME THREE | INVENTING THE FUTURE

Book Five: IS HISTORY A RIVER OR A THOUGHT

Book Six: END THOUGHTS ON A FLYING TRAPEZE

ISBN: 9781791328870

Edited by Malcolm Feuerstein

Cover, formatting and design by: Pnina Wolinsky, Kavnakee

WHAT PEOPLE ARE SAYING ABOUT
"JEWISH RENAISSANCE"

Prof. Emerita, Ellen Spolsky, English Literature, Bar Ilan University, Israel:

"Jewish Renaissance," enacts a renewal – encouraging, thereby, a renewal of readers' thinking about the inherited past. Jewish history is recounted in these pages not in chronological order, but as dreamed and reimagined. Feuerstein weaves events from recent European Jewish experience and from events during the Roman domination of Judea or from the Arab conquest of Palestine, with the lives of a cast of fictionalized characters in Israel in the 21st. century. Epic in reach, it is both ambitious and innovative. What is interestingly unique about the series is the way it tells the story."

Alan Stephens, Former Publishing Director, Martinus Nijhoff Publishers, The Hague and Boston:

Malcolm Feuerstein's new multi-volume work is a remarkable addition to Jewish-themed literature which is certain to win a firm place in the libraries, hearts and minds of all those with serious interests in Jewish-Israeli history, politics and intellectual life, be the readers Jewish or non Jewish. The books are however, much more than that, having a universal appeal which could be compared to the twelve elegant and erudite episodes of Anthony Powell's 'A Dance to the Music of Time.' Like Powell, Feuerstein has the gift for telling fascinating stories which compel the reader's attention alongside the examination in detail of intellectual, military and even medical issues; he is informative without ever becoming didactic. Nor will those seeking adventure be disappointed as the books do not neglect to engage and entertain their readers with incidents and exploits recalling the best of John Buchan and Erskine Childers. For all these reasons, Feuerstein's beautifully written work merits a wide readership.

Jonathan Hagin, Ex-Senior Cinematographer, Australian Broadcasting Corporation:

"Jewish Renaissance" is an epic tale that conjures up fantastic visual imagery. The dialogue and narration create a strong cinematic field in the reader's mind with characters that move backward and forward across a fluid lifeline. As a result, it is not only a page turner but also a thought-turner. In film, cinematographers call the time immediately following sunset the 'magic hour,' because of the afterglow of twilight. Reading "Jewish Renaissance" is reminiscent of this time of day when the lighting in the sky offers the best possible opportunity to reach for one's camera and capture each fleeting moment. Feuerstein does it in words.

Ariella Kaye-Hagin, MA in Writing for Television and Film; College Instructor of Academic Reading and Writing Skills, USA and Israel:

In the remarkable literary achievement "Jewish Renaissance," the writer uses deft strokes of an artist's brush to imbue his rich tapestry with the majestic and the mundane. In good literature, there are both works of art which one appreciates and enjoys, as well as those that leave an indelible impression in readers' minds. "Jewish Renaissance" embraces both. Nor is Feuerstein a stranger to the art of wit. In the midst of pathos and suspense, the tongue is never far from the cheek.

I highly recommend "Jewish Renaissance" to readers who like to indulge in the pleasure of beautifully written prose and a captivating story, as well as to readers seeking a deeper journey into the exploration of the human condition.

Ariella Merklin, MA Contemporary Design, University of Manchester/Sotheby's Institute of Art, London:

"Jewish Renaissance," is not just another novel. It incorporates elements of philosophy, dream and psychology with explorations into the conscious and unconscious mind, Jewish thought and Biblical wisdom. Feuerstein demonstrates an intimate perception of life in the ancient world and in modern-day Israel as he skillfully weaves into his story tales from the Talmud and paints an intimate picture of the diverse life of contemporary Israel from left-wing kibbutzniks to right-wing religious and an array of memorable characters in between. Feuerstein's writing is both intelligent and engaging. He deftly draws the reader into his imaginative and epic story.

Raymond J. Feuerstein, Master of Science, Doctor of Philosophy, Diploma of Membership of Imperial College of Science and Technology, Fellow of the Linnean Society, Fellow of the Royal Asiatic Society:

"From the first sentence I was interested. By the end of the page I knew I would keenly follow the storyline wherever it went. After a couple of pages I was hooked. This is a trilogy I will return to time and again. It links individual experience against a backdrop of a constantly changing world. Malcolm Feuerstein is my brother. He has been writing for newspapers, television and cinema for 70 years. This is his long overdue magnum opus. And what a magnum opus it is. Read it and you'll see what I mean."

THIS BOOK IS DEDICATED TO:

MY FATHER, **LEON FEUERSTEIN**, BORN IN CRACOW, POLAND, BEFORE WORLD WAR ONE, DREAMT OF A NEW LIFE IN AMERICA, THE GOLDEN LAND. BY SINGING SOLOS WITH HIS SYNAGOGUE CHOIR AT COMMUNAL EVENTS, HE EARNED THE FARE FOR THE FIRST LEG OF HIS JOURNEY, TO BERLIN. THERE HE BECAME A TAILOR. AFTER A FEW YEARS, HE EARNED THE MONEY FOR THE NEXT STAGE OF HIS JOURNEY, TO LONDON, WHERE IN A FEW MORE YEARS, HE HAD EARNED ENOUGH TO BUY A TICKET TO NEW YORK. BUT HE DIDN'T GET THERE.

AND TO MY MOTHER, **LYDIA**, (BORN GUMBINER) WHOSE FAMILY ORIGINATED IN RIGA, LATVIA, WHERE MY GRANDFATHER WAS A MASTER JEWELLER. THEY EMMIGRATED TO LONDON, THENCE TO NEW YORK, WHERE MY MOTHER WAS BORN, AND BACK AGAIN TO LONDON, WHERE SHE MET MY FATHER AND EFFECTIVELY BECAME THE SURROGATE FOR HIS AMERICAN DREAM. FOR THE REST OF THEIR LIVES THEY LIVED IN ENGLAND WHERE THEY HAD THREE BOYS, OSCAR, RAYMOND AND I, WHO WAS BORN IN THE JEWISH HOSPITAL IN LONDON'S EAST END, IN 1932.

THANK YOU, MUMMY AND DADDY FOR THE DEVOTED FIGHT YOU PUT UP TO GIVE YOUR BOYS A CHANCE, WHICH WE SEIZED WITH BOTH HANDS. YOURS WAS A FAIRLY TYPICAL IMMIGRANT STORY. BUT YOU WERE FAR FROM BEING TYPICAL IMMIGRANT PARENTS.

AND TO MY WIFE, **DR. MT**, WHOM I MET WHEN SHE WAS RUNNING A MEDICAL POST FOR THE UNITED NATIONS ASSOCIATION (UK) IN A SMALL TOWN ON THE BANKS OF THE UPPER AMAZON, BRAZIL, FOR HER IMPECCABLE ADVICE (SOUGHT AND UNSOUGHT) AND HER INDULGENT PATIENCE THROUGHOUT THE TWELVE OBSESSIVE YEARS IT TOOK TO RESEARCH AND WRITE THIS STORY.

I ACKNOWLEDGE A HUGE DEBT OF THANKS TO:

THE SIX PROFESSIONALS AND FORMER PROFESSIONALS WHO READ AND REVIEWED THE MANUSCRIPT AS IT WAS WRITTEN.

ALSO TO: **DR. JOEL RUTMAN**, FORMER EXAMINER ON THE BOARD OF PSYCHIATRY AND NEUROLOGY OF AMERICA, FOR MEDICAL ADVICE.

TO: **PROF. NORMAN A. BAILEY**, PH.D, FORMERLY WITH U.S. NATIONAL SECURITY COUNCIL AND OFFICE OF NATIONAL INTELLIGENCE, NOW PROF. OF NATIONAL SECURITY STUDIES, HAIFA UNIVERSITY, WHO RUNS THE BAILEY SEMINAR WHICH I ATTENDED FROM THE START. WE HAD DISAGREEMENTS BUT NEVER AT THE COST OF MY RESPECT FOR HIS SUPERB ANALYSIS AND PRESENTATION.

TO: **HAREDI RABBI"Y"** WITH WHOM I TOOK FOUR CLASSES PER WEEK IN JEWISH STUDIES FOR 15 YEARS, AFTER COMING TO LIVE IN ISRAEL. IF I WAS NOT REPUBLISHABLE AS AN ULTRA-ORTHODOX JEW, I EMERGED FROM THE EXPERIENCE A MUCH WISER ONE.

TO: THE MANY ACADEMICS AND EXPERTS IN VARIOUS FIELDS IN ISRAEL, THE UNITED STATES, AND THE UNITED KINGDOM, WHO ANSWERED MY QUERIES AND TO THE AUTHORS OF THE HUNDREDS OF BOOKS AND ARTRICLES I CONSULTED, A LIST TOO LONG TO CREDIT.

TO: THE MANY ISRAELI ARABS WITH WHOM I DISCUSSED THEIR LIVES IN THE CURRENT SITUATION, ESPECIALLY THOSE WHO AGREED TO BE INTERVIEWED IN DEPTH, OR WHOSE MEETINGS AND WORKSHOPS I ATTENDED.

TO: STAFF AT THE UNIVERSITY OF TEL AVIV'S SOURASKY LIBRARY, WHO WERE PRODIGIOUSLY HELPFUL DURING THE 50 DAYS I SPENT THERE, ON IN-DEPTH RESEARCH VIA SOURCES WHICH WOULD OTHERWISE HAVE BEEN CLOSED TO ME.

Imagine a glittering opera house. As the conductor raises his baton, a member of the chorus breaks ranks. He threads his way through the orchestra to the microphone and sings an aria from the famous opera about to be performed. He acknowledges a puzzled reception from the audience and returns to his place.

After the performance, a surge of reporters is waiting for him at the stage door. How did you have the gall to do that?" they demand. "I have been singing in the choir all my professional life," he explains. "In a short while I am due to retire. For once, I wanted to sing it my way." He hails a taxi and is gone.

Note:

The above scene occurs nowhere in the 1,000 pages of this trilogy. But metaphorically, it underscores every word.

Malcolm Feuerstein,

"A Voice from the Chorus"

Israel, 2019

VOLUME ONE | OBLIVION

Book One

A MIND IN CRISIS

Chapter One

Everything stopped, like a book slammed shut in mid-sentence. Would the end story ever be known? The next page, the next sentence, the next word? Consciousness and un-consciousness wrestled in his mind like Jacob and the angel. The last shards of clarity, like chinks of light, were overcome by a blackness that eliminated vision, internally and externally, and all thought.

The damage wrought by a single round from a Kalashnikov traveling at one kilometer a second that entered his rib cage and punctured his left lung like a party balloon, was life-threatening, but nothing a skilled surgeon couldn't handle if the patient reached him in time. The field medics had seen to that. He was evacuated by two stretcher-bearers to an armored ambulance and helicoptered to a Jerusalem hospital in forty minutes. Time was fractionally on his side. It was the head wound, caused by a ricocheting round, that mattered. It changed his life.

He shouldn't have been in the Arab village on the West Bank where an arrest was to be made. Colonels were not supposed to take part in operations. He had invited himself to join two squads of elite infantrymen commanded by a captain, a squad of Border Police and two Shin Beit operatives. He told no-one that he would be there, not even his commander.

***

The head of emergency services, Prof. Bondman, was waiting with an ambulance at the hospital helipad and in less than the three minutes it took to get the patient to the main building, he became certain that if his life was to be saved, two surgical teams, working simultaneously, would be needed. The colonel was rolling in and out of consciousness. His chest movements were unequal, one pupil had lost its luster and stared lifelessly, like a lightbulb switched off - a reliable prediction of no hope. As the patient was transferred from ambulance to trolley in the emergency wing, Ilana, the head nurse, was waiting. The professor briefed her on what had to be done. The patient heard his words. They stretched like rubber or a tape played below speed. "Not much of a chance," he heard the professor say. That meant death, he told himself. "With God's help," Ilana said, contradicting the professor, as they hurried to the lifts. "If you have any credit with the divine," the professor said to her grimly, "now's the time to cash it in."   For the third time in his life, Col. Yuri Pozner was supposedly in the hands of God. It was not reassuring. Could anyone hope to win three times in a row? In a mass casualty situation in which medical help would be given on the basis of triage, he would have been in the last category. Luckily there had not been a suicide bombing for a week. He had been upgraded, like a lucky passenger on a long-haul flight.

The injuries to his lung had to be dealt with before he went into shock. The swelling of the brain, an inevitable result of damage to the head, was an alarming but less pressing potential cause of death. To reduce blood flow into the brain which in turn would help to alleviate the pressure, Ilana passed a tube down his nostril into the lung. He was still conscious enough to fight the intrusion. She sedated him. Prof. Bondman opted for a chest X-ray and a CT-scan – the twenty minutes the latter would take was worth the risk, so that the surgeons would know exactly what to look for when they opened his head.

The chief neuro-surgeon agreed that immediate intervention was imperative. A general surgical team cut through his chest and inserted a large bore tube into the lung. More than a liter of blood, caused by internal bleeding, gushed out. The neuro-surgeons working on the head wound found that the ricochet in the skull had caused profuse bleeding. Pressure from the accumulation of blood had pushed the brain several centimeters off-center. It was in danger of being forced down its own stem. No-one survives that. The surgeons decided on a craniotomy. They removed six square centimeters of bone above the temporal lobe to give the brain more space.

In the recovery room, after five hours of surgery, the patient came to. His blood pressure had risen to ninety over seventy and his pulse was still weak and racing. He was disoriented and wanted to vomit. He imagined that a large grey bird was sitting on his shoulder impatiently waiting for him to die. He felt its hard claws on his flesh.

"Can you hear me? What is your name?" the professor asked, going through the basic neurological test. The patient nodded to the first question. Then he found words, but it seemed to him that it was the bird speaking. "My name is Yuri." The professor wondered why he didn't give his family name or rank. "Are you an officer?" "Yes, I'm a lieutenant ....." the bird said. At which point, the patient fell unconscious, the word "Colonel" stuck in the bird's mouth.

He came to as he was being raced down the corridor to intensive care. It happens sometimes with head-wound patients who are about to vacate their minds for weeks or for ever. The last splutter of an old car on a steep hill whose spark plugs are on the way out. Interminable hospital corridors encourage the mind to rewind. Patients in his condition are in danger of rolling off a mental cliff into fantasy or oblivion.

Penina Frydman, a twenty-nine year old clinical psychologist, was on her way to intensive care when the Colonel's stretcher trolley passed her, propelled at a run. She had time to glance briefly at the patient whose eyes were screwed tight, as if reacting to bright sunshine. Only his lips moved, as if he was sucking on a straw. Was he trying to speak?

She pulled out the pocket tape recorder she always had ready and ran alongside the stretcher holding it near his lips. When they reached the elevator she pinned her ear to his mouth. He seemed to be mouthing a single word, over and over, his face distorted with the effort, until it escaped like a barely audible scream which sent a chill down her spine. Zeydah!! Grandfather in Yiddish. She prized one other word from among the shattered syllables and broken phonemes of his speech: Zalman. It was a first name, once popular among Jews of east Europe, that had died out in Israel, where it connoted ghetto, stiebel, defenselessness, stuff to be left behind. One didn't hear of anyone being called that any more. She hardly had time to take in the information before he began to mumble something in whispered riffs of near soundless speech. But his lips did not synchronize and his lungs had lost power. She kept the recorder running at top volume. In intensive care she waited while they attached him to a forest of tubes. He was still mouthing words. She was impatient to capture them. They might be important. Unable to do so, she looked at him more closely. It was only then that she almost recognized him. The squat nose, broader than it was long, the drawn thin lips, which he periodically sucked as if they provided nourishment and the insignia of an elite combat unit offered clues to be read against the matted hair, the deathly pallor of his skin and swollen contusions to the forehead. Could it be? She wiped away a cake of blood from his identity bracelet and read: Colonel Yuri Pozner. Yuri! Her mind blanked.

When she looked down again, Yuri was not there. Instead, she saw her brother, Shimon, lying on his hospital bed. His wound, which stretched from the upper chest to his midriff, was held together by a row of black clamps. He tried to smile. The effort turned his face into a mask. Seconds later he was dead. That was her last memory of the man she had most loved. Pure sisterly love.

Memories of Yuri stirred slowly, like dead men rising. She saw him, a long decade ago, his face blackened, the Caribbean blue of his eyes concealed by dark contact lenses so as not to give himself away in the dark, an AK 40 across his shoulder, ready for a mission. She watched him disappear with his men into the moonless night to a chorus of aquatic birds in a nearby reservoir. Yuri was like a cat, everyone knew. He moved like one and he had nine lives. His men believed he was charmed against death. They held onto the belief like an article of faith. His invulnerability rubbed off on them. One of them, a young Druze, once said that if Yuri were killed in action, he would no longer feel safe anywhere, not even crossing the street.

Memory faded. Reality returned. Yuri was back on his bed. He looked an un-survivable mess. But somehow, Penina knew with unarguable certainty that he would survive. Things would fall together. Somehow. She never doubted throughout the forthcoming saga. The surgeons' strategies and their skills, the accuracy of the diagnosis, the synchronicity of every actor on the team, the faultless functioning of every piece of equipment, Yuri's own robust resilience and her belief in his determination to survive, would all cohere. That he would live was a matter of faith. Yet this was not enough. The force that glued everything together, enforcing outcomes, call it God or Fate or Luck or happenstance, or even the fearsome law of averages, was present, circling, warding off harm. She could almost see it. Yuri would climb out from the valley of the shadow of death. So why not her brother? Now we were talking about something other. He was one of the righteous. He had already won his place in the world to come.

You had to raise yourself above the ordinary to come to terms with his death. He had not, like Yuri, been granted nine lives, but one, which he lost at the age of twenty two, before he found out what he wanted to do with it. He showed none of the leader's charisma that Yuri possessed in abundance. He faced his short life with integrity and love. His charisma was not public, somehow it glittered in shadow. His love was not nourished by sex, but brought out the love of others, seeking no reward. One of her uncles, who had spoken at the funeral, wondered aloud why, with so few good men in the world, God had chosen to remove him. Wasn't he more needed here? His friends loved him and he loved them back. His family knew that he was someone special but tried to treat him as normally as possible. It didn't work. The most ordinary thing said to him, or that he replied to, took on a value that belied the casual. While he was alive, those few close to him and the many to whom he reached out, basked in a kind of love that none had previously experienced. She mused over her brother's abrupt submission to death and Yuri's likely conquest over it. In her heart, she asked her uncle's question.

She had known Yuri during her army service when he was a captain in Special Forces and she, a young conscript, still clutching her psychology degree, had been assigned to his unit. Alive to the world and its possibilities, welcoming experience indiscriminately, believing she could handle whatever life delivered at her doorstep, she quickly became involved professionally and romantically with the dashing captain. But what should have been a straightforward *boy meets girl* story was thwarted by a series of events, as if boy-and-girl were puppets in an Indian saga – he was sent on a top-secret mission whose objective was never revealed, then to fight in Lebanon for three weeks which turned into three months, where he narrowly missed having his left foot amputated. He had triggered a booby trap in a deserted Christian village near a command post, deep in Hizbollah territory. Since the Israeli troops in the area knew nothing of his presence, he had to wait for ten days to be rescued, living on a store of raw grain and oil in a bombed house. He got water at a slow drip from a leaking pipe which mockingly measured time. Gangrene set in. He watched its slow progress along his foot. When finally rescued and hospitalized, and told his foot would not be cut off, he experienced a delirium of thankfulness. To whom, or to what, he could not say. Recuperate, he rejoined his unit and was back behind enemy lines a day later. When he was returned to base, a spasmodic affair began, her first. It was not to last long. He was sent back to the fight behind enemy lines, with a small specialist unit, to help cover the Israeli pull-back from Lebanon. It was a heady time, when love and death were partners in a crazy dance, something like a tango, performed by exhilaration and despair. At war's end, a woman from his past swept back to occupy center-stage in his life and married him shortly before he was promoted to major. Penina had no chance. The woman was prodigiously beautiful and equally determined. Penina and Yuri had been on the edge of what she believed would be the relationship of her life. Years after, looking back, she mourned it as the greatest romance life was ever likely to offer, which never happened. At the time, she had every reason to believe her lover was serious. It took her a long time to recover from the scars.

Meeting him again, if one can speak of meeting a person who is barely conscious and hovering on the brink of death, the scars reopened. Was this a second chance, she asked herself? Or was life, the trickster, playing a game whose rules it alone knew? She had placed her faith in the cliché that she and Yuri were meant for each other. She never forgave herself for believing it and never forgave him for not.

Despite his condition, she still felt the deep outrage she suffered when he told her about Shira, his future wife and his wedding plans, as if a plausible explanation was all that was required. Not that their relationship, back then, had flesh. It was founded more on dream than substance, on romantic snatched moments rather than the slow growth of partnership and ended in a four-wheel vehicle parked near the edge of a cliff overlooking a spectacular view of the Mediterranean at dusk. Yuri did not share her dismay. He had been attracted to her certainly, more to her personality than her looks. Penina had to work hard to look passable. But she had a submerged attractiveness and a vibrancy that scored high in the sexual measurement we all use. To him, formally ending their relationship was like closing a little-used bank account. He broke the "news" without consideration of what it might mean to her. To explain all is to forgive all? No. That was too cerebral. Penina felt violated. Her personality had been raped, although her person had enjoyed the experience. Hadn't he realized just how hurt she would be? Hurt? Destroyed! She had wondered then, as she wondered now: how could he not have known? Her brother would never have acted in this way with someone who loved him. Such thoughts, trailing visual memories, came and went in seconds. Time had contracted to its shortest leash.

She reloaded the cassette and asked the charge nurse to record anything the colonel said. "I don't think he'll be saying a lot," he replied, his Hebrew laced with a strong Arabic accent. "Just in case," she said. He smiled at her optimism. He had seen it all before and believed this man would never leave the hospital alive. "Inshallah," he said – it's up to God. It made her feel better which is how it was intended. Nonetheless, wasn't it bizarre that an Israeli Palestinian nurse should be caring for an Israeli officer wounded on a mission in the West Bank, or its frequent corollary, that a Jewish-Israeli doctor might tend to an Arab suicide bomber, survivor of an abortive attack. She left the ward, walked at a fast pace to her office where she rewound the first tape on a larger machine and pressed play. Only a few scattered phrases were intelligible. The rest was as faint as hand-writing dried in the sun.

***

She spent the rest of the evening and much of the night in her apartment, rewinding and playing the tape again and again until she had traced every audible syllable. She worked urgently, as if she was rescuing words from a fire. Each one was painstakingly transferred to her computer. Many were utterances that made no sense or were just wild guesses at possible meanings. As she finished, she saw through her tiny window the lights go on in neighbors' houses, heard the engines of their cars purr into motion, became aware of daylight encroaching on the dark spaces of her apartment, and while the yellow streetlights went off in batches, she printed out her reconstruction of Colonel Pozner's speech, made herself some imported Italian filter coffee – the one luxury she could not do without – and settled into the only armchair that her small front room could accommodate to read what subsequently became known in the Colonel's voluminous file as PLE Tape One. It read as follows.

"... not far. you can..... I help, Zaydeh, I ...rest .... What if they catch .... No...........never leave.......I love you Zaydeh. (Subject's voice rises slightly in volume; vocal signs of distress). You have the coyach. You have! .... I can't ....worry. They will wait. Don't ...... will wait. Why Zaydeh? Why? I won't leave you Zaydeh You can! You can! My name? ... change? Yes. I heard. Yes, I heard, but...... All right. All right Zaydeh............My name is .... Zlatko.... born ...Warsaw. Why Warsaw? Mother ...wish. ...ather Russ... .....in prison. ...... to ....for a wedding. ....Rdom, Rdom...mother...gnant ...could not scape........ she ...to run for the Soviet .... I .... Safe there....... address .... Yes, uncle's .... Warsaw. Yes that's... Russians.

Germans... My name ....What? a Catholic. I live in .... Brest-Lit.... to Radom...... The church of .... My fath ...... prisoner ...... Officer ....cavalry. With my grandfather, but I can't find him.........to get home. Yes, for the ...mans.....

...Poles... I am a Jew from Widawa. Zalman Gains......to the Soviet border. Family...dead... the truth....the Poles the truth.... They ... know.......friendly OK. Do as they say.. .hostile...run. Better .. bullet... knife... your throat. "

Please..let...stay. God will...us. I ...never leave...Please...stay. ...not make...never. I...never. Please don't...love you!!!

Penina finished her coffee and observed with the affection of familiarity, the few movements in the street below – the two Hungarian sheepdogs, Buda and Pest, pedigreed members of a breed famous for devotion to their master, that prowled guard along the white gate opposite, their long, shaggy, matching white coats, heavy with overnight dew; a taxi pulling up at the Reinsteins', bringing visitors from Mexico; two young backpackers emerging, arms entwined, from a public garden – Europeans probably, doing the holy sites; the South African Moranis' Arab child minder letting herself into their house on the corner after a brisk walk from east Jerusalem; the bottle green car of Prof. Tabor pulling out of its reserved parking space and heading for the Hebrew University where its driver could grab a couple of hours of untrammeled concentration before the daily circus of academe opened to the world. Jews from Russia and Syria and Argentina and France lived in a sort of United Nations enclave, but the dominant social grouping was English-speaking, immigrants principally from the USA, Canada, South Africa and the United Kingdom. Penina knew all of her neighbors and their habits and why they had chosen to live in this mixed environment where all guarded their privacy while familiarizing themselves with the peripheries of other people's lives and always ready to help – when asked. It was a community and it wasn't a community. People had moved out because they found its social climate too cold and others, like herself, had bought in because it offered the bare modicum of emotional warmth she needed and a monied uncle had helped with the purchase. Not looking forward to the likelihood that it would make no sense, she returned to the text on her screen. She read it six times. Using knowledge culled from counseling Holocaust survivors who had fled east before the advancing German armies in the twilight year of 1940, plus a lot of guesswork, she made dubious sense of it.

***

On the tape, the Colonel was describing an incident in which a grandfather and his grandson, Zalman, were making their escape from German-occupied Poland to Russian-occupied Poland. The grandfather was too weak to go on. He urged his reluctant grandson to leave him. There were three main dangers the boy would face.

He would need a different cover story for each. The boy was made to rehearse them until he was word perfect. If the Germans picked him up he must pretend to be a Polish Catholic. He must say that his father was a Polish cavalry officer who had been taken prisoner. He was hoping to stay with a distant relative whom he would locate through some church in Radom in eastern Poland. It was his mother's wish. If he was caught by the Russians, he must tell them he was half-Russian, half Jew. His name Zlatko(witz). He was to say his father had been imprisoned by the Germans which might curry favor with the Russians. Only to the Poles must he be himself, Zalman Gainsburg, not because they presented no threat, but because, unlike the Germans and Russians, they wouldn't be fooled. If they were friendly, he must do as they say. If hostile, he must run for it. A bullet in the back was better than having his throat cut. What astonished her was that the action clearly took place in eastern Poland sometime about the start of World War II. Colonel Pozner was in his late thirties. Yet the events he described happened 25 years before he was born. Penina drank a deep slug of coffee. Why should he fantasize about events he could never have witnessed instead of fighting for his life? What purpose, if any, did such illusion serve? And why did he relate the incident in Hebrew, instead of the Yiddish or Polish he must have spoken at the time?

***

When she got to the hospital next morning, she presented the transcript to Natalie, the chief clinical psychologist, who scanned through it briefly and handed it back. "I've seen hundreds of these. There's nothing to get excited about," she said, returning to her screen.

"I've seen them too, usually from patients dredging up some painful childhood memory. But this is not a childhood memory. It's something he could not personally have experienced." "So?" "So there has to be a reason why he's doing it." "My dear Penina, if we're going to analyze every statement from the stream of consciousness that patients come up with, we'd never do anything else. If the patient pulls through, which doesn't look very likely right now, he's going to need a hell of a lot of help to recuperate. That's where you come in. How long did it take to do this?" "Half the night." "O my God! Penina get things in perspective!"

Penina had a complex relationship with her boss. They got on much of the time although they were opposites. Often they complemented each other. But Natalie believed in reports and research and case histories and her own considerable experience. Penina, accepted all that, but gave free range to intuition. She often rushed into cul-de-sacs, where she was often vindicated. The two women liked each other more as women than professionals. Without that bottom line, their relationship would have been stormy. Both knew they could not go on forever making allowances. One day an issue would arise which the shallow roots of their friendship would not be able to sustain.

Penina went straight to Yuri's bed. He was asleep on his back, breathing irregularly. She looked at the heart monitor which showed a series of periodic escalations. The patient's notes recorded he had had a disturbed night and had been in delirium much of the time. At the nursing station she found a tape with a note addressed to her from the charge nurse, now off duty: "Penina F. So I was wrong. He hardly stopped talking, if you can call it that. Couldn't make out any of it. Hope it will mean something to you. See you. Salih."

One side of a ninety minute tape and perhaps ten minutes of the second side had been recorded. "Almost an hour," Penina said to herself aloud, as she considered the task of decipherment. She was already late for her first patient but instead went back to her office. No-one was there. She played the first few lines which were barely audible and spun through the rest, stopping here and there, listening hard. The voice was not the same as on the tape she had transcribed. That was the voice of a child. On the new tape it was a man's voice. And although she did not get any real sense of time or place, she was sure that it was describing a different period and a different location to the earlier recording. There was an intensity about the few snatches she could decipher coming from a voice that was determined to be heard. It would take many hours to transcribe. Hours she did not have. On the way to the small pediatric post-surgery ward, she dropped by the technical workshop in the basement. Eliezar, a technician, who was a distant relative, said he would boost the sound and rerecord it.

"When I've finished it will sound like a football commentary. And Penina why don't you drop down one day when you don't have a technical problem. I finish at four. That's early for you, I know. I could always find something to do while I'm waiting. Maybe we could see a movie. I'm family, remember?" Yes, she remembered. Eliezer was a distant cousin on her mother's, the Sephardi-Moroccan side. She had visited him socially only once to wish him good luck and drink a l'chaim when he first came to work in the hospital. He was a striking looking young man about her own age who clearly had a personal interest in her, which is what had kept her away. She smiled to herself that he was so forward. Any male relative on her father's, the Ashkenazi side, who happened to be a technician would never suggest taking in a movie. He would think that since she was a professional with a second degree, going on her third, she was somehow above him, so he would lack the hutzpah – the cheek – to ask. But Eliezer did not stand in awe of educational status and did not recognize any distance between them. He might even have thoughts of marriage, if they got on well.

***

As she climbed the steps – to preserve her assets, not knowing how long she might need them – the incident brought a smile to her lips. It underscored her dual identity. From her parents, a Moroccan mother and an American father, she had inherited two worlds in which she could swim with ease. Despite the fact that her parents had divorced precisely because they found themselves, after almost thirty years of a marriage that seemed to change like the weather, finally incompatible. It was that incompatibility that had made Penina take up psychology. In fact, she was an unlicensed and unpaid, psychologist by the age of twelve, having observed her parents through torments, showdowns, reconciliations, renewals of love, rededications and emotional non sequiturs. It was like having a subscription seat in a private theater. Far from being embarrassed to argue or be affectionate in her presence, they used her, shamelessly, like an audience in a children's' theater – which gave them license to behave like children themselves. She loved them both, and tried to be as impartial as her childhood perceptions allowed. She long since passed the stage of wanting to hide when her parents lunged at each other like swordsmen with verbal foils. From the age of ten, she looked forward to such episodes, noting behavioral details, especially small things which had explosive potential. Her parents never seemed to be aware of the minefield buried beneath the domestic landscape and set off explosions regularly and seemingly inadvertently. By her mid-teens, Penina had become an accomplished mariner in choppy waters and learned to predict a casus belli or cause for conflict, taking her seat in good time for the next performance. When the final hurricane made landfall – over her father's serial infidelity, she was in her first year at university. For the course on common causes of marital breakdown, she had only to sieve through the discarded wreckage of her parent's marriage for research material. It was like having the course book inside her head.

Her experience as a child subsequently distanced her from "normal" people. She obsessively chose friends who were identifiable by psychological insecurity. Making friends was not a major part of her life. The core issue was analyzing them. Her friendships lasted only until she had learned as much as she thought she was likely to, or until the social circumstances that had nurtured them ended. No friendship lasted by virtue of its own impetus. They were almost invariably fed on outside pressures.

From an early age, she had been troubled by death. Not frightened, but inconsolable. Its inevitability struck her as inordinately unfair. That everything died was a cliché, she knew. But a cliché of numbing power. The thought struck her forcefully, in her early teens. Almost preposterously, it had taken shape after seeing a dead cat in the gutter, outside her home, that had been run over during the night. It was early, the street deserted. She approached the carcass warily on tip toe and gazed down at its misshapen body. Maybe it was a stupid cat that played dare with a car. Maybe the driver saw it and failed to stop. But it was not the history of its death that caught at her throat and forced tears onto her cheeks. It was the fact that something called death was the supreme reality. Perhaps the only one. The evidence was everywhere. It had come for the mother of her best friend, by way of leukemia; for a cousin, as the result of a careless road accident; for the only grandfather she remembered, through old age; for all those people one saw dead or dying on television, from war or disaster; for Israelis and Palestinians for whom death reached out with casual efficiency; for her two goldfish; her neighbor's parrot; her school's hamster; for the Shabbat flowers and for everything she ate. She had mourned all of them against a sliding scale of sadness, but never before had she put them all together in her mind to be viewed as a mosaic. She had seen dead cats before, but none had got to her like this banal casualty that some passer-by had cursorily kicked into the gutter. It was a couple of weeks after she first menstruated. Weeks in which she had thought of herself as a bearer of life. And now life seemed so fragile, so uncertain in its contest with death, a contest which death always won.

There was another form of death which she faced. Her parents' looming divorce. Wasn't that a kind of death in/of the family? Of love, of relationship and of responsibility. And she knew there would be other examples to add to her childhood countdown. Relatives she loved who were serving in the army, both young men and young women, or students from her school about to be recruited, patients in hospitals too sick to be saved, a swathe of cancer mortalities which removed neighbors and friends like pawns from a chessboard. Everyone seemed to be waiting in a queue for The End. In her mid-teens especially she saw death everywhere. Walking through a bustling market crowded with shoppers she might experience a poignant awareness that all of them were going to die. They might be laughing and seemingly unworried by anything at all, or acting up as they spoke on mobile phones more loudly than acoustics demanded, or slipping arms ostentatiously around each other's waists, or sitting on the edge of park benches enjoying the sun, or arguing or telling jokes, or kissing. But their fate would be the same. And none of them knew when. On family outings to historic sites, she refrained from running wild like the others, playing games amid the ruins, but sat and stared, imagining them peopled as they must once have been. Between pockmarked pillars, tumbled walls and truncated towers, she imagined the children who had once lived there. Children who belonged to the past, to history, to death. And a great sadness would descend on her.

She would hide and be patient with her sorrow until it went away. Most of the time she was a happy enough youngster until these bouts of melancholy and sorrow burst inexplicably upon her. She frowned more than she smiled. As she grew older, her face took on a serious cast, expressing her woebegone world view physiologically, especially about the eyes, which looked solemnly at the world, a solemnity sometimes relieved by an engaging, if guilty smile. She understood that her smile was an asset which dispersed the impression of gloom others had of her and used it deliberately to put them off scent. As she grew up she cultivated her smile until it became her best feature, to be used as a social weapon. She told no-one about her obsession, guarding it like a hand at bridge. She asked fewer questions than most children, preferring to work out her own answers and experiencing puzzlement and despondency when she couldn't.

***

Later, when she lived alone and needed intimacy, there was a slow succession of boyfriends, whom she discarded, once she felt she had read their minds. Like books, she returned them to the library of life and took out another. She was a fast reader. Yet she had a horror of being returned to the shelf herself. When a man ended their relationship, it exposed a lack of confidence in her looks and personality like a raw seam, conjuring up a paroxysm of self-communion. Penina persuaded herself, understandably, that she was ugly, whereas she was plain. She gave a lot of thought to her looks, inspecting herself minutely in the mirror, and was aware of her reflection on every surface, wherever she went. She was as self-aware as an up-and-coming model, but contrariwise, she sought her faults, not her good points. She possessed a fascinating plainness that could transform into surrogate beauty. Not the beauty of the wall calendar, but a kind of alternative beauty which stood to conventional beauty as alternative cinema relates to its commercial rival. Her interests and passions lit up her expressions and rendered her appealing to the type of man who was not a trophy hunter. When she looked into a mirror, she saw unenviable dullness, but she knew that her face could be transformed.

Although she could control this facility, it was most engaging when it happened authentically. Asked to smile, she could never gather her features into a harmonious composition. Consequently, few flattering photos of her existed. She believed she spoilt group photos and deleted them from her computer. She wanted no evidence of her visual deficiencies, neither for herself nor posterity. But under the right stimulus, her face might break into an unintended smile, seen by others as entrancing. She knew from her relatively few boyfriends that this quality gave its harvest when they made love. Unlike many attractive women, whose wholesome features are transformed by desire into a mask, hers were reassembled into an abstract of attraction. There were even moments when, men told her, she looked beautiful. She tried not believe them. She did not want to take the risk. They only said it because they pitied her, she thought, so believing would be buying into a lie.

Not until, in a psychology textbook, she ran across the concept of la belle laide, the ugly woman who possesses a transfiguring, hidden beauty, was she forced to reconsider. She had never heard of such a being. She read everything she could find on the subject, trying to relate it to the image of herself imprisoned in her mind, recalling remarks men had made, replaying half-remembered reactions which she compared with the written word, even reviewing the few old photos of herself she still had. It had always puzzled her why some good-looking men wanted to date her. Did it improve their image if they were seen out with an unattractive woman? Was it analogous to being known as a major donor to worthy causes? Surely, a man looked best if he had a beautiful woman at his side. Did escort services employ obese women or ones whose looks were irregular? Did a preference for the ugly imply perversion? Did la belle laide exist in real life or only in literature? Or did authors try to compensate for women like her, by claiming the virtue of beauty where there was none? You met the idea in novels, but where was it found in art? Did artists paint ugly women? If they did, surely it was to record ugliness for ugliness' sake. Where was the artist who found beauty in ugliness, who did not merely describe it? Her knowledge of art was far from comprehensive.

She had no answer. Nor, for a long time, did she try to discover one from close acquaintances who knew art history.

In moments of chronic self-doubt, she sought reassurance from her mother, who had breast fed four daughters and three sons, still clutched them to her shrinking chest in moments of joy or sorrow. Not Shimon, of course, whom she visited in the military section of the cemetery once a month, picnicking with one of her sisters and/or a daughter and one or two grandchildren in an adjoining park close to the grave, just beyond its enclosing stone wall. She did not know what to make of the afterlife, and was content to believe that her son lived on in her heart and in the hearts, or at least, the consciousness of those she brought with her. She would whisper the traditional prayer at the graveside, read psalm 104 that he loved most, recite a short prayer of her own, enjoy her picnic, peppered with the almost-identical stories she told about Shimon year on year and cook Shimon's favorite dish that same night. Penina was always touched and inspired to see how her mother's love was un-diminished by death. While she lived at home, she accompanied her mother as often as she could, but as she evolved into university student, army conscript and science-based professional, she grew away from religious practice, which seemed to her to carry diminishing returns for the obligations it imposed. She visited home less and less and when she did, avoided ritual, seldom appearing, even for festivals. Her absences were seen as a form of family apostasy by her more hard-skinned relatives who stuck together like a shoal of faithful fish. For them, only death or the need to live abroad were adequate reasons for not consorting with the familial group and participating in its cyclic rituals. The overthrow of her religious life fused well with the secularism of the majority of her colleagues, while the conduct of her personal relationships clashed incompatibly with the moral demands of a diminishing faith. At first, she felt like a passenger in a train misdirected by faulty signaling onto the wrong track. There was nothing to be done but wait for the inevitable collision. That it did not happen, surprised her. Over time, she concluded it never would.

***

Her father Mort's family, who lived in the United States, had never set foot in Israel, a land which meant nothing to them but embarrassment. Mort's marriage to a Moroccan Israeli was seen as an inexplicable act of insanity. Had he brought her to live in Philadelphia, it would have been seen as a young man's folly, which would end badly. But to go and live in Israel himself was extreme perversity. Unmoved by the "ought" of Jewishness, or even simple curiosity, Israel was beyond the horizon of their dreams, preoccupations and felt needs. At the first Thanksgiving following his return to the Land of the Free, after his divorce from Penina's mother, attended by almost forty members of his prolific family at the home of its most successful, Mort, a recently divorced father of six, after a procession of pre-prandial martinis and several glasses of Californian, was egged on to speak. He knew what they wanted. It was not far removed from what he wanted, which was to shake Israel out of his hair. "Boy, it's good to be back," he told them, to applause. "For a couple of decades or more, I've been living in toy town. Trouble is, they use real guns there." (Laughter, a pat on the shoulder and a few low whistles.) "Time went fast – it's only redeeming feature – but the result is that I feel I'm twice as old as I am. About a hundred, at least. I blame nobody but myself for the fiasco. And standing here I can hardly believe it happened. Israel is just not the place for a nice Jewish boy from Brooklyn. Once you're there, everything changes. It's like being blindfold and turned around six times and then let go. From then on, you haven't a clue. The papers all over the world are full of the place, the tv channels fixated. There are people I know in this country and elsewhere who can't eat breakfast in the morning until they've had their anti-Israel news fix." (More laughter and some cheers.) "It's so huge in people's lives. But you know, I once flew over the place. I'd been asked to escort a small group of lawyers from Europe on a fact-finding trip. Fact? They wouldn't know a fact if it climbed into the bathtub with them. We covered the whole country in fifty five minutes. From the Lebanese border to the Red Sea. And it was no jet we were in. It was a Cessna. You know, I got a rick in my neck from looking down on the country's narrowness. Fifty miles across at its widest point and about ten for most of the rest. Israel is all waist and no body. An anorexic dream. Wherever you go, after a few miles, you bump into another country. Usually a hostile one. Jews are generally pretty smart, so how did they get into this? I blame Moses. And God too. He gave the Jews the smallest country in the world in exchange for a promise to do everything he told them. Unfortunately, Moses wasn't a lawyer. Not one who'd passed the New York Bar exams, anyways. No smart lawyer would have bought a deal like he did. If the Jewish people had consulted me, I would have insisted that the first draft be mashed." "Which was exactly what Moses did with the first set of commandments," one bright young Frydman observed, to alcohol enhanced laughter. "And that is what Moses should have done with the second draft and the third and the fourth and so on, until he got a deal that walked on two legs. And you know what the most important clause would have been, if I was doing the final rewrite? That the Jews be led to some other place entirely. God owns the world, right? So what's so wrong with where we are now – Martha's Vineyard?" "We're on the verge of moving here," called out a female cousin. "There you go. Some Jews do get it right. Trust our family," Mort answered to rowdy applause. "So why all the fuss? Why is everyone so fixated on tiny Israel? Blink and you've missed it. You could pour the whole country into New Jersey and still have room for a small kingdom. There aren't greater obscenities to be solved in the world, to the magnitude of a hundred? It's unbelievable that this little strip of land can generate so much attention, publicity, outrage, hatred – and love. Yes, the love astonishes me more than the hate. Who cares, anyway? Not me, any more. All I can say is that I'm proud to be back in the Land of the Free. But seriously, I can't tell you how much I love you all. My cup runs over. No, really. You are my family. There's nothing like you. Israel is behind me. Times Square, here I come." He ended his remarks like an exhausted runner, breasting the tape. Intimidated by Mort's barely controlled emotion, which his banal humor failed to quell, his audience sat in abject silence for several seconds. "Who forgot to turn on the canned laughter?" he demanded, a winy grin mapping the sweating contours of his face. The family, realizing they were confronting a loveable but broken man, rose as one, in a standing ovation. He was hugged, kissed and embraced until his tears salted his wine. "Let me get you another glass," his host offered considerately. "What was it? Californian red?" "No thanks, Uncle Dave," he managed to say without sobs. "This is just how I like it."

***

After Thanksgiving, those present snuggled back into familial hibernation. Subsequent calls to celebrate family events would be responded to with declining enthusiasm. The Frydman great-grandparents had given the family mass. Over succeeding generations, their numbers had dipped dramatically, while centrifugal social and economic forces had spread the survivors across a continent. Distances were so huge that it was as if they lived in different countries. Without the double-edged benefits of technology, they would barely have been able to keep in touch. Only family members dwelling in the same, or neighboring states, tended to meet occasionally. The Thanksgiving turnout was exceptional. In part, it was a sad memorial of disintegration. Almost everyone invited, came. The Frydmans monitored eligibility with the fastidiousness of an exclusive club, disenfranchising distant family and those deemed to have crossed the Rubicon of right behavior. Barring totemic funerals, it was unlikely they would ever again gather in such strength. And there was only one funeral pending which merited full attendance. Mort's return was thus an ironical boost to the family ideal, precisely at a time when the ideal had lost its gloss, and was ready for the castoff bin. It was not that they ceased to love each other but that they had come to love other things more. Houses to be enjoyed, neighborhoods to be preserved, careers to be pursued, positions in civic society to be maintained, charity committees to be attended, arts institutions to be patronized, friends to be cultivated and loyalty to undemanding synagogues and beloved alma maters to be nourished. There was no such animal as an idle Frydman.

***

It took days before Mort was able to assess his new situation. The rugged coastline of golden and pale ochre cliffs that skipped like rams towards the sea made him feel melancholy. Its beauty hurt. The place was packed with tourists who curiously and painfully reminded him of Israelis. Loose-limbed, easy-going, disrespectful of silence, responsive, they had something to say about everything. He plodded around the six towns that overran the island, each in a different architectural style, as if they were going to a fancy dress party for townships. Two lessons could be derived from his Thanksgiving break, which included a trip on a relative's expensive yacht and a visit to an exclusive old-world winery, dating back to some when. First, that he was not in the same socio-economic bracket as the rest, nor even the least. He felt he had too hastily concluded that he had left his family in Israel to rejoin his clan in America. Now he realized that he had effectively left them both. Second, that he was a recipient more of pity than sympathy. Not being one to pity himself, he did not take it kindly from others. So he had not come home after all, except in the sense of having transferred himself bodily from one place to another. What did "home" mean, anyway? Going to live in Israel had been like having a heart transplant. And now he required his old heart back. Preserved in some imaginary incubator, it would have to be tested and replanted, he supposed, while trying to smile back at a group of friendly kids. Would his metabolism reject it, even though the organ was his own? After several days of carrying the question around with him through the pageant of tourist-packed towns, in one of which his cousin had single-handedly undertaken, among half-packed crates and screaming toddlers, the task of his renewal, he baulked. The thing that most disturbed him as he wended his way around the marina or the showcase farms, was that he had only two options. Either he must retire into self-abasement, or eccentricity. The latter chose him. When he said goodbye to his prosperous cousin, he meant it. He knew that not even she, the most heartfelt Frydman, would be able to condone the conclusion he had reached. It was to return to Brooklyn. Leaving the island, on the unpredictable ferry, was the best part. He could think about Brooklyn. His Brooklyn, where great-grandfather Frydman had worked in shoe sweatshops to support his constantly expanding family (both by procreation and immigration) after his arrival with a hastily-married and unloved spouse from Lithuania, two years before World War I. He progressed from laboriously cutting out soles and heels to making the shining uppers and then opening his own business which finally grew into Frydman and Frydman (his younger brother) Quality Shoes, with its own chain of retail outlets in five states. The family had long since left and forgotten Brooklyn and to return, particularly in less than modest circumstances, was crossing a line that would cut Mort off from the onward march of the clan. They were a little army, the Frydmans and he a deserter, twice over. His father, who had been chairman of the shoe factory part of the family business, had left him a sizeable sum in his will, which he had forbidden to be transferred to Israel. It had languished in the bank for over twenty years, diminished only by raids on its bounty whenever Mort visited New York, returning to Israel with his pockets stuffed with banknotes. His father had either forgotten or not seen fit to make access to the account dependent on residency, instead of transference. Without this inheritance, it is doubtful that Mort would ever have been able to realistically contemplate leaving Israel. He was eventually told by an uncle, a brother of his father's, that the testator had considered leaving him out of his will, but had made the money available as a potential lure that might one day bring him back. His father believed that the United States was the Promised Land for Jews – and everyone else who found haven there – and would have no truck with Israel, an inferior rival. Mort admired the tactical foresight that had left the door open enough for him to reinsert his foot. The short ferry ride from Martha's Vineyard to the Massachusetts coastline was like crossing an ocean in his consciousness. He made straight back for Brooklyn where he holed up in a cheap motel until he bought an inelegant apartment. It was in the same street where the family was living when he was born. Not the same building, which no longer existed. Nor, from the point of view of appearances, the same street, for it had been rebuilt several times and was now beyond recognition. But it bore the same name, and given that it had succumbed to widening, was more or less the same location where he had spent an unspectacular childhood, waiting for something to happen.

He needed to work and offered his services to a firm of attorneys with a demoralizing turnover of staff who represented low-income clients incapable of paying the going rate for legal advice. There was a lot of legal catching up to do, including the retake of some law exams. That was not a problem. He had a mind that the Talmud describes as a sieve. It absorbs everything, but nothing sticks (beyond its usefulness). Within a year he was handling some of the most difficult cases. It was an unexpected bonus for the partners to have at least one member of staff who was likely to be around from start to finish of a stubborn case. Eight years later and he was still there. But his work was such that it had to be left in its files when he went home, or it would have seeped into his private life – like gas from a faulty oven. He was a card-carrying workaholic. Spare time was his noose. The king problem for him was to find meaning apart from work. The answer came without him following his initial inclination and enlisting in interminable night courses or lecture series, or learning another language, or joining a film society or going dancing – ballroom – a skill he had never lost. Surrounded by sites on which childhood memories were framed like overpainted canvases, he found that when he looked at the present, he saw the past, as if the two periods had gone through some act of illegitimate marriage in a photographic laboratory. First it was buildings. Then individuals. Then whole street scenes. Then real-time incidents which he held in his mind's eye against analogies from earlier days. Greek prophets divined the future, but he prophesied the past. He worried if he was going nuts. He dubbed these experiences, cognitive accidents. They happened not only in the street, but in the office, in court, at the movies – there especially – and in bed. It was as if everything that happened, had happened before, or at least had a parallel. What challenged his interpretative skills – and almost his sanity – was when the same people – or as near as damn it – popped up in scenarios getting on for half a century apart. Not wishing to publicize this ability, curse, illusion or whatever it was, he confided in no-one except Trish, the Woman in his Life, and Penina, his Israeli daughter, during her spasmodic visits. He feared and rejoiced that he had entered a time-warp from which it was impossible to escape. His retrograde clairvoyance was uncontrollable, happening involuntarily, without warning. Trish reckoned he was haunting the past for emotional asylum. Penina worried that he was heading through the first stage of mental incoherence.

The downside was that the past haunted him back. It pervaded his life, slowly turning him into its tool. Often, it left him talking to himself. Trish could only take so much. Was it a sign of aging, perhaps of death? He debated this many times with himself. Family history, on both sides, charted a high proportion of early demise, with not a single example of venerable old age. He began to feel lonely and vulnerable.

The solution seemed to be to sub-let his apartment and move in with Trish. She was a middle-aged, once-pretty Jewish woman who could still paint and dress herself into a fetching article. Somehow – not even she knew why – she had remained in Goshen-like isolation, after the exodus of almost all the Jews from the neighborhood. Emerging from her rut, disturbed her. She and Mort did not have much in common, but what they had they shared like an inexpensive meal. They knew, that they were the last station on each other's tramline. Love did not enter their frame of reference, which was based on mutual support, mutual time-traveling and a veneer of affection that thickened, but never achieved, a qualitative emotional transformation. They had both had normal sexual lives in the past and still enjoyed the slackening pleasures of the flesh.

***

Penina had paid her father two longish visits, and several lightning strikes since the divorce. Once, when she finished her military service, she spent two weeks with him before launching herself into South America, and once again before she took up her present post at the hospital. She still loved him, the only remaining sibling who did, and had no doubt that her love was requited. It was the year before the tenth anniversary of her brother Shimon's death in the first Lebanon war. Unremittingly adamant, she cajoled her father into promising that he would come to Israel and visit the grave with her, without meeting the family, if he didn't wish to, for the anniversary. Trish couldn't believe anyone could be so focused. "Is this how her mother was?" she asked Mort in disbelief. "Her mother was worse," he opined. To make his promise to Penina, Mort had to break one he had made to himself, that he would never set his foot in Israel again. Penina tried to encourage Trish to join them but the latter would not consider abandoning her "societies" (choral and self-defense) in the middle of the winter season. "Oh, no! Oh really no. Oh really I just couldn't." Having made the disappointing discovery that Trish was Jewishly bankrupt, Penina accepted her refusal with relief. Had Trish agreed, Penina reasoned, it would have been a classic waste of time. It brought home to her, with undeniable emphasis, how much Israel was a mental construct. And not only for Jews. It was not some sun-drenched island which you came to sport on, without a historical or moral care, although those who did, lacked nothing. It was bald history, past and in-the-making, for which Trish did not possess the right mental toolbox. Her outlook was calibrated to Brooklyn and the other New York boroughs and she had no interest beyond their radius. 'If you already have the best, why try anything else?' she would say. She never missed a show, hardly ever a rated movie and occasionally read a book. The one thing, in recent years that she never missed was the acquisition of a new animal by the Bronx zoo or the birth of progeny to one of her favorite denizens, especially among the primates. All she would be aware of on Tel Aviv's beach front, if she ever made it there, was sun, sea and sand without Bauhaus, culture or history. Although Tel Aviv was rated by the National Geographic, as one of the six best-served beaches in the world, that was not the best reason for going to Israel. It was not that she was averse to new experience.

To the contrary. Unwilling to bestir herself, she had an insatiable curiosity, which she indulged through virtual travel. Glossy magazine features, television programs, promotional videos and a mountain of glossy brochures were the means, and especially reality shows. She never missed a second of castaway cares and couplings on remote desert islands. She talked about them indefatigably with her friends. When one of them happened to mention Israel, she went into temporary amnesia. Israel was an "ought" and she hated "oughts." Otherwise, she and Mort travelled virtually everywhere. There was not a five-star, nor a snazzy holiday village they did not check out, from Puerto Rico to Kuala Lumpur. Mort was like a passive smoker. He half listened, while she read out mouth-watering accounts of exotic dishes cooked by prize-winning chefs in Manila, while keeping one steadfast eye on whatever he was trying to read – usually an overlarge illustrated book about North American Indian history, a re-investment in a boyhood fad. Or, holding the book across his chest, he suffered his gaze to be directed at the twenty-four inch screen from which boatloads of tourist adventurers debarked onto un-pronounceable islands, where they were to dwell for a week or a year, or at armies of all-but naked sun-seekers disporting across sandy shores, which seemed to pop out of the sea, with monotonous regularity, between Capricorn and Cancer. Trish kept a log of favorites she discussed endlessly with clients at the fashionable hair salon where she was a top stylist, even with those who had actually been to the places she had visited electronically or on glossy paper. In such encounters, she often contributed more than her real-time rivals – apart from anecdotal revelations, whose necessary absence from her discourse pained her. She compensated by outlining what she would have said or done in this or that supposed situation and was thereby so engaging that clients borrowed thoughts and observations from her invented anecdotes to enrich their own travel litanies which otherwise paled by comparison. Mort was never dragooned into participation. He was left to please himself. Mostly, he pleased himself by pleasing her, while enjoying a degree of freedom of thought and movement he seldom knew when married to Penina's mother.

His onetime vibrancy had dissipated. Not yet sixty, there was little fight left in him. He took the world as it came, served up by Fate in monotonous doses. Placing himself in Fate's shoes, he was forced to admit he deserved no better. All ambition spent, he was left with a job that kept him busy, but no more. His colleagues wore their dissatisfaction like raincoats in summer. The clients he defended, were usually guilty as hell. The greatest part of his time was spent, in his eyes, working against true justice. He comforted himself in the belief that in defending the indefensible, he was at least helping to maintain the rule of law, or call it what you will. Judges decide. Lawyers prevaricate. Trish and American Indian history were his only supports. Thoughts about his family in Israel would occasionally flash into mind, but recollections of his early Zionist and liberal idealism had long before been self-amputated, while the smoke of battle still assailed his nostrils. The verdict, whenever he judged himself, was that he was a failure. He accepted this without protest. Most of the people with whom he came into contact were failures too, he guessed. Who knew? Nothing was certain. Trish had become his salvation. He never tired of watching her perform. Everything she did was performance, even when she sat, curled up on the floral sofa, before the television, watching others perform. She was infinitely watchable, like tropical fish. On spasmodic occasions when they went out, he felt proud of her and went to much trouble to present himself as best he could. Never able to answer the question – what did she see in him? – he enjoyed his good fortune, allowing himself to think she was the only prize he had ever drawn in life's casino. But that was wrong. Didn't he think he was the luckiest man alive when he married Penina's mother, Rebecca? He could not deny she was the most beautiful woman with whom he had ever had a relationship. And she came back to haunt him whenever he thought about his good fortune at finding Trish.

He had not known Trish as a vibrant nineteen-year-old, but he could not imagine she could ever have rivalled Rebecca's oriental beauty, which still drove him crazy in retrospect. When marital memories invaded an ill-lit corner of his mind, he hurriedly locked them away. Only for them to escape whenever he was appreciating Trish the most. It was as if he could not allow himself to enjoy his only remaining joy. Was he punishing himself, he asked himself? He received no reply. The best thought in which he found consolation was that his mental incursions into the past contrasted present-day Brooklyn with an earlier incarnation of itself and not with his time in Israel. That would have been emotionally unsustainable. He walked a narrow path through the valley of depression, flaring up at small things, while leaving the large ones to be taken care of by whatever forces worked upon them. He no longer cared. Trish, on the other hand, who hardly lived a more interesting life than he, was happier than she had ever been. With one divorce and one dead husband behind her, and no children, she was at last entitled to please no-one but herself. She loved her job. She loved the salon. She loved talking about everything that came into her head, including things she knew nothing about. She made nonsense seem plausible. She loved her clients, who loved her back. And in a wayward sort of way, loved herself. Above all, she loved taking a decade or, if lucky, a decade-and-a-half, off her real age each morning as she sat before her mirror. She still breathed occasional fire, like a middle aged dragon, at imperfections in her world of small concerns that she was passionate about.

Mort's best years, he now realized, had been in Israel. Life mattered there, which meant that each individual mattered. Dangerous, tumultuous, passionate, developmental, youthful years in which progress and mistakes alternated, like contending winds. Having consigned his Israeli experience to oblivion, he never revisited the land in reality nor voluntarily in memory, except for when an item of conversation or breaking news demanded. Yet he promised Penina he would return for her wedding. Over time, the promise had come to represent a threat in his eyes, but he continued to assure Penina he meant it.

Penina was the only sibling who kept in touch. Her older brother – the one who had been killed – had been buried within twenty four hours of his death, according to Jewish custom, not leaving time for the father to attend the funeral, which he would have done. Instead, he mourned in Brooklyn, reciting memorial prayers in the synagogue and sitting at home on a low chair, not shaving, receiving condolence visits, although none of these customs held any significance for him. It was a way of honoring the memory of the exemplary young man he had fathered, who had given his life for everything his father had given up. Penina's sisters had written their father out of consciousness, as he had done with them with matching zeal. The only times Mort, both husband and father, was ever referred to at family gatherings was as a negative example. Lacking the stimulation of shared memories, Penina sometimes forgot she had a father.

***

Penina's social life was as threadbare as a vegan's fridge. It consisted of loose social contacts with women and successive unsatisfying relationships with men, not all of them consummated – she did not give herself easily. Men often felt she was watching them all the time, as if through a keyhole. Only ultra-egoists took it in their stride. Since they habitually examined themselves in inexhaustible detail, they welcomed an accomplice. But that did not work for long, because Penina was a penetrating critic, seldom offering the complicit praise they sought. It was she who tended to terminate relationships, without rancor, on the grounds that they had 'sorry to have to tell you' grown cold, but when a man did so, he usually accused her vituperatively, with being cold by nature. She did not believe it. But disbelieving required all her faith. She craved the chance to prove her emotional sensibilities. She believed she was as full of feeling as a pomegranate of seed and that she had a treasury of emotional riches to invest in the right man. To date, that relationship had not materialized. The nearest it had come was with Yuri. She had been convinced that he was the one. In the years that followed his marriage to Shira, she slowly came to believe that life never dealt the same hand twice, so she would never meet another man like him. She devoted herself to her career which filled and emptied like a ventricle, with challenges and excitements. Her preference was for life's irregular rhythms. Constancy drove her mad. She expected to marry one day. But the thought that it would be to a man as right as Yuri, was abandoned like a broken down car in the middle of nowhere. As she would become a high-priestess in the temple of her career.

***

The day was routine, save that she could not get Yuri out of her mind. She saw patients from the last suicide bombing whose long term psychological wounds were becoming perceptible, like shapes in a dark room that materialized as the eyes acclimatized. She spent much of the afternoon with a girl of six who had lost a leg and suffered a stomach wound, in a suicide bombing and faced years of protracted surgery and rehabilitation. Penina was encouraging the girl to rebuild her image of herself, not as it once was, but by probing for a new identity. It was hard for a child who had barely reached her teens to adapt to the range of disabilities that now defined her. Two visits a week was all that Penina's schedule allowed. The rest of the time, the child ran a gauntlet of painful physiotherapy, constant monitoring and changes of medication, whose side effects were unpredictable. Penina was pleased to find that the girl could sit up. With effort she could reach for things, so she placed the girl's favorite toys at the edges of the bed and encouraged her to retrieve them. Penina admired a mini Teddy bear with a shiny brown coat and asked the girl if she would get it for her. The girl slowly sat up, reached for it, failed to get a good enough grip, reached for a fluffy cat, failed again, made another attempt at the teddy which she retrieved this time by clasping her two functioning fingers around its foot. Justifiably proud, she hauled it across the bed and handed it to Penina, who placed it on her lap. Pleased but exhausted with this extension of her powers, the girl fell asleep. Penina wondered how much of the world that the girl once inhabited was still retrievable. And how much of a new world would have to be created in her psyche. Rehabilitating child victims was not within the remit of her qualifications, but the preserve of the physio-therapists. She sometimes crossed the line to help her patients' psychological recovery. The physios, needing all the help they could get, welcomed her incursions. Guiding children, who had been blasted out of their normal world into one in which they had to learn to refunction, was the most rewarding part of her job. It was also the most draining. The children were the ones who kept her awake at night.

***

Eliezar was hunched over a large recording machine. He looked up when Penina came in. "Just running off a new recording for you. Be ready in two minutes. I spent hours taking the gaps and hesitations out. Must have cut it by fifty per cent." Penina would rather he hadn't. She would have preferred deciding for herself whether the hesitations had meaning. He checked a dial and when he looked up again his dark brown eyes were like glowing coals. Penina knew which way the conversation was about to go and rose to her full diminutive height.

"So what movie are we going to see tonight?" It was more statement than question. His enthusiasm had to be contained. "I don't think Ayal would like that," she countered. "Who's Ayal?" "A friend." "What's he do?" "He's a physiotherapist – I'm seeing." "That's what I should have been. Being paid to massage women! And here I am wasted among all this technological crap. I bet he can't massage like me, though. I didn't learn it from a book. I'm a natural. Women love it." "I'm sure they do," she said with a quick smile, intended to be polite, not encouraging. "All I have to do is put my hands on people and they feel better. You got any aches or pains?" "No. I'm just fine." "OK. Here's your tape." He held it up but did not give it to her. "So which movie?" "You've picked a bad night. I'm going to spend it going over the tape." "You're making a big mistake. The tape's interesting sure, but nothing like a good movie. That tape's not going to have you sitting at the edge of your seat. Who's the guy who dreams up all this stuff?" "He's a severely wounded Colonel whose chances of survival are not good, who seems to have entered some kind of dream world. It may be a psychological first. Sorry about the movie," she said, removing the tape from his hand and adding: "You know, I really appreciate this." "Sure you do," he said, a sour tone encroaching upon his mellifluous voice that implied she would have accepted his offer if he was a college graduate, or Ashkenazi. When she was gone he punched his palm with his fist. "She can't see through shit," he said aloud, alarming his next visitor.

***

She got through the rest of her schedule more quickly than expected. She must have been rushing things, she admitted to herself with a touch of guilt and for the second day in a row, left the hospital early. Within half an hour she was in the apartment she had bought three years earlier, after too many years of supine renting. Just big enough to match her moods, it owed its existence to the genius of the architect who had been forced by the lie of the land to design the four-floored building with an apex on its southern side seemingly too small to house anything other than a challenge. His solution had been to build two mini-apartments, each occupying two floors linked by a spiral staircase. Penina had the first and second floors. An irregularly-shaped kitchen, lounge and balcony off, occupied the first, and a small bedroom with a triangular bathroom en suite, the second. She had solved the problem of convergent walls by making a feature of the narrow apex on each floor. Daylight could be permitted to flood in through large windows or be checkered by shutters. Penina was happy here. She called it, affectionately, her coracle, after the one-man wickerwork boats she had seen in Ireland. Ideal for one person. Two would destroy the harmony.

Harmony was what she demanded of her environment, it being largely absent from her life. She had done courses in Feng shui and adapted it to her circumstances and needs. She did not follow the tradition slavishly as she failed to follow anything slavishly. The particular version of the system she adhered to, recognized five elements, which she symbolically interwove into her everyday life. Earth in flower pots on the narrow patio, which curved around the corner of the building like a boomerang. Metal in chime bells. Water flowing from a small fountain. Wood in a gnarled trunk that she once found washed up on Tel Aviv beach. And fire, amply supplied by the sun. They crossed her life at daily junctures – when she watered her plants, or the bells caught an easterly breeze, or listening with closed eyes, on warm evenings, while the fountain played a rhythmic cantata, or contemplating the criss-cross grains of wood which looked like the diagram of a torso in a medical textbook.

When she felt challenged, she aligned herself with the elements, meditating on each in turn until she achieved a state of trance, or equilibrium. Fire for the life force. Earth for stability. Bells for contemplation. Water for inspiration. Wood for creativity. Meditation was the key. She had spent a year learning the technique and practiced it as assiduously as a serious music student, until she could put herself into a trance-like state at will. It drove the images of shattered lives from her mind. But sometimes it incorporated them like transfigured icons. Whenever her fountain seized up, she listened to tapes of cascading water. She had another meditational drill based on Jewish Kabbalah. Feng shui was sensual. The Jewish drill, conceptual. You began with 'ayin,' the Hebrew word for nothingness, whose letters transpose into 'ani' the Hebrew for I. You become an 'I' in order to rule over the seven lower divine emanations: gevura or power to conquer yourself; tiferet, beauty, to see the beauty in everything even the 'ugly' (as God does); hod, majesty, which allows you see the wonder in creation; hesed, the love that you must share with all creatures; netzach, eternity, which celebrates the longevity of all life, even the fly that lives for a day; yesod, foundation, which encourages you to grasp how everything in the universe is linked like a chain; malchut, the kingdom, the world in which we live, over which we rule when we have transformed our nothingness and experienced our emanational self. Sometimes, she would be at a loss to know which meditation to follow. She would stand on her balcony, gazing into the night, aware of them both.

That afternoon there was no time for rituals. She opened the shutters to catch the last rays of the low sun and settled at her narrow desk next to the patio exit as she had the previous day. From it, she could see a city landscape of unwelcome tower blocks alleviated by clumps of fan and feather-leafed palms and low, wispy cloud. Her tape player took the disc she fed into it like a greedy fish. She pressed 'play' and settled back. At first, Yuri's voice sounded unreal. It was a man's voice, deeper than the voice of Yuri as she remembered it. After a while it became mesmeric.

"A Roman tribune is coming towards us. He is accompanied only by an army cook holding a harness bag. He takes pains to appear casual. He is close now. I see triumph in his eyes and blood baked by the sun on his tunic and arms. The blood of combat or massacre? Perhaps he has lent a deft hand at both. He stops about twenty meters away and scans our lines. "Well, Jews," he says, hardly projecting his voice. We listen intently. "I used to think you people were an intelligent race. Strange but intelligent. This campaign has taught me that you are strange and stupid. Did you really think you could take on the might of Rome?"

She switched off. She had expected to hear more about the boy at the border and was surprised to be transported in time to events that occurred around eighteen hundred years before. She supposed there was no logical reason why the Colonel should continue with the story he had begun on the previous tape. Nor was there any logic in his telling any story at all. If this was meant to be an historical dialogue, why didn't the Jewish protagonist speak Aramaic and the Roman, Latin or Greek? She reversed the tape and listened again. The two voices were identical, she noted on her pad. There was no attempt to "put on" a different voice for the Roman. But when was this meant to be happening? Was it the Great Revolt, sixty years into the common era, or perhaps the revolt of Bar Kochba, in the second century? She pressed play.

"You have already lost your Temple. You have already lost your place in the world. And you come back for more? Did you seriously think you could win? Did you think he could do it?" He opens a horse's harness bag and slowly draws out a human head. Holding it by its long black locks, he lets it dangle in the dying rays of the sun. Bar Kochba! Son of a Star. Leader of the revolt. Judea's last hope, whom some called Messiah. Even now the head caked in blood is proud, regal, dwarfing the Roman. In my mind's eye I see a hundred memories of our revered leader crouching like a leopard behind a rock and leading attack after attack. The coins in my

moneybag which bear this same head, burn against my thigh. The King Messiah! A group of Levites break into a dirge. "How are the mighty fallen, they sing. How grievously your children sinned to deserve this destruction. Forgive us, O Lord. Forgive us, our Father." Their lament, chanted by parched voices, echoes like a death knell. Their voices die down, overcome by despair. But a single voice continues. It is the feeble voice of an old sage, dry as bone. 'Hadaysh yomainu k'kedem,' he half chants, half shouts. 'Renew our days as in olden times!' It's unbelievable. We have just suffered the greatest defeat in our history and he sings about redemption! He must be mad. But deep inside me I yearn to share his madness. My lungs fill and I exhale the words with all my might. Others take it up, our voices echoing off the hills in the hot stillness. The wounded who can barely stand, help each other to their feet and find the strength to scream the words into the stifling air. Our defiance spreads like a brushfire in the summer heat. There must be a thousand of us who take up the cry asking God for renewal, asking God to turn back the sundial, asking God to grant us the final victory. A cohort of legionnaires rushes forward and draws a protective ring around the tribune. I see the interpreter hurrying to his side, ready to translate the words of our defiance. The tribune stops him with a gesture. He understands, without knowing their literal meaning. We keep it up for five minutes or more, until our parched throats crack. He waits patiently until every voice is still. He passes the head to an infantryman who raises it on the end of his lance in the shimmering air. "You are prisoners of Rome," he shouts. "Rome owns every bone in your bodies and the very tongues in your head. Every thought. Every act. Every hope. I say to you: accept the fate that Rome decrees. There is no choice." He looks around to see the effect of his words. Not a sound. He smiles a half-smile of satisfaction. His eyes fasten on me. The smile leaves his pock-marked face. He takes a few paces towards me. "Gideon ben Yehudah," he calls. "I had hoped to see your head at the end of a lance, like your failed Messiah. But I believe you would have preferred that to the fate that awaits you." He turns on his heel and walks away. After a few paces he half-turns and calls over his shoulder – "Your bride-who-was-to-be, is well, and under my personal protection, the Tribune Galinus." He nods his head in restrained mockery, as he introduces himself. "She is enjoying the best of Roman hospitality, as can be offered in the present circumstances." The voice is even, but the eyes drive his words into my head like pistons. I would die a hundred deaths to kill him now! He walks casually back towards the Roman camp with a feline gait. A voice from among us calls out in Latin so that he will understand. Jerusalem liberata!! Everyone takes up the cry, three times, filling the air with our shouting. The tribune spins round. He raises his voice which almost cracks with the effort: "Jerusalem capta! Jerusalem perdita! There will be no more Jerusalem." The cohort falls in behind him as if underwriting his words with their short victorious, close-combat swords, drawn, just in case.

Penina heard the player click off. For a full minute she did not move. How to explain Yuri's testimony? An army officer in modern Israel giving a first-hand account of the Battle of Beitar, which ended Jewish independence for almost two thousand years, until 1948. The end of the Jewish state. The end of the Jewish occupation of their land. The Colonel had spoken as if he was there, as if the events he described were happening around him. She changed tapes and listened haphazardly to the original recording which ran for two hours, stopping intuitively here and there. The gaps between words and events, which had been smoothed out in Eliezer's version, were most telling. Yuri's voice would go silent, sometimes for up to more than a minute, as he struggled to describe what he saw, or overcome the emotional effect. She filled a page with notes. It was after eleven. She dutifully returned a few calls from people who had left messages, but her mind was at Beitar, the bloody end of Jewish sovereignty.

***

Her last call was to Ayal, her current partner who, judged by the measure of past relationships, was long overdue for return to the library of life. He had spent a year in Taiwan after his army service as a dog handler, where he had learnt Feng shui, erotic massage and consumer-friendly Taoism. All of which he had introduced into her life. That is why she kept him. He taught her things she would otherwise never have known. He lived in an extension of his parents' home, on a moshav, a communal settlement, a twenty minute drive south west of Jerusalem. He stayed over with Penina on odd nights and she with him, usually over weekends. It suited him best to live in the countryside. It would be truer to say it best suited his dog. After three years with the army and another three with the reserves, his dog Bonnie retired at the age of 12. He volunteered to give her a home and the army, knowing she was going into good care, agreed. The pair of them had had a long list of adventures and shared a relationship that must be described as love. Penina never asked Ayal to live with her, knowing that if she did, he would not come. Bonnie came first. She had a whole moshav to roam in, with orchards, fields of maize, dog friends from way back, with whom she ran and barked and raided and not infrequently got into trouble. When she grew tired of the pack, there was a lake to cool herself off, and escape from the excruciating summer heat. When he could afford to buy a house on the moshav, or perhaps on a settlement on the West Bank, which would be cheaper, he would do so, so long as it was a place where Bonnie would have the freedom to run, play, sniff and explore. She was a highly intelligent animal with an IQ which, he used to say, if only it could it be measured, would recognize her genius. Now a physiotherapist at the hospital – after four years getting his professional qualification – he had spent the day alleviating people's back pains. At this late hour, he was in need of some alleviation himself, he told Penina. He suggested he came round. The best thing about their relationship, which was mutually acknowledged, was the amount of space they gave each other. Neither was expected to do anything with reluctance. So she was able to turn him down without argument, rancor, or disappointment. Neither had rights over the other. "OK," he said, "you stay on your island. I'll stay on mine." "Ring me tomorrow?" she asked. "Tomorrow I'm cooking fish satay with soya and peanut sauce. Come over."

"Friends?" "No friends. Just Bonnie and me. You know how much she loves satay." "Look," she said, "I'm not feeling sociable. Let's see how tomorrow goes. Laila tov." Ayal understood the subtext of her words. Every day in Israel, since the start of the intifada, was a new chapter, especially in Jerusalem. It was impossible to predict how it would end. "Bye, Penina. Laila tov." After ringing off, they both paused for a moment to think the same thought. Who got more out of their relationship? Or was it, as they intended, a draw?

***

After four hours of sleep, Penina's phone rang. The voice of the charge nurse in intensive care told her that the Colonel was talking again. Penina recorded the message in some mail box in her head and began to drift back into unconsciousness. Something made her rouse herself and peer at her watch. A quarter to three. The wrinkled blue sheets beckoned her to go back to sleep, but duty prized her awake. She got dressed on automatic pilot, unaware of how she looked. Not until she was driving through the chill, mountain night-air of Jerusalem, window wide open to keep herself awake, did she begin to assemble her mind, which returned to the recordings. How to explain the graphic detail and the heavy emotional involvement? Where did the Colonel get this material and why, she continued to ask herself, was it coming up now?

A picture of the little boy the Colonel had spoken of in the first recording formed in her mind. He was a wily youth in his early teens, Jewish in looks wearing a peaked school cap which hid his forehead and accentuated his brown, furtive eyes, dilated with fear. The boy stared at her, then looked away, then looked back again. He did this several times, holding her eyes longer each time he returned to them. Growing in trust? Why should he trust her? He had never seen her in his life. Where had this image come from? There was no description of him in the recording. She must have borrowed it from some archive of stills of Jewish refugee children, she told herself. She saw his father too, eyes shining with fever, saying he could not go on. He was about 50, a frayed shirt collar under his cheap brown coat, rubbing against a gaunt neck, the facial skin yellowing, perhaps with jaundice. Who were they, this pair whom she had created out of a few sparse words? How had they become incarnate in her imagination? Was she doing what Yuri did?

She was waved down at a road block and the images vanished. A black Border policeman in a green uniform, his hand resting lightly on the stock of a machine gun, peered through the car window. He recognized her and waved her on with a handsome smile. She had had several Ethiopian Jews under her care. They had a quiet dignity which, if lost, caused them to fold. But when preserved, it shone like a beam from a lighthouse. What a beautiful face, she thought, smiling back. One day, she would learn more about these Jews from Africa. It was one of the many items on her list of things-to-do that almost everyone in Israel has, without hope of ever reaching the bottom line. She switched the radio on to a 24-hour news service. Warnings of a suicide attack. Jerusalem was on high alert. She noted the blue flashing lights of waiting police cars near major intersections. The threat made the cool evening air seem sharper. She raised the window as much to shut out the crazy world as a reaction against the drop in temperature, as her car climbed towards the hospital lights

***

In the corridor leading to the intensive care unit she met Prof. Bondman on his way out. "He's stable. You can go back home," he told her. He looked exhausted. Penina had always admired his devotion. He was a man who could not have slept more than two or three hours a night for weeks. "Apparently, he said something. I'll just listen to it now that I'm here," she replied. The professor's tired blue eyes looked at her sympathetically. "Penina you really shouldn't have come. You mustn't let the Colonel take up so much of your time. The tape recorder will record, that's what it's for. Your other patients are your first priority. We can patch up the wounded, but post traumatic stress can ruin the rest of their lives long after the physical scars are gone. Go home." "Menachem," she said, calling him by his first name for the first time, "I haven't neglected anyone. I practically live here." The professor squeezed her wrist gently. "I know," he said, "but you must keep things in proportion. Out of proportion means out of control." "The Colonel is a special case," she went on, "his mind is trapped. He desperately wants to communicate. Does it matter if it's about an ancient battle or last week's football match results? He's passionate about telling us. If I can somehow get him to understand there's someone who's listening, it could turn everything around. I'm sure, in this case the mind is the clue." The professor's eyes closed involuntarily with tiredness. When they opened, they looked through, not at her. "When I was a young doctor," he said in an almost inaudible voice that made her lean forward to hear him, "I used to regard this hour as the hour of death. I was religious then. And sometimes, I could sense the angel of death hovering, hiding, as if unsure of himself, about two in the morning, waiting to take the soul of a patient. And I used to wonder why he was not more aggressive, why he did not just snatch his prey and be gone. And I realized that up to the last second something can still be done – the skill of a doctor, the prayer of a loved one, remission in the eyes of the Name. Man has more power than he knows – and far less than he deserves. They call it the human condition. I'm afraid your Colonel is slipping away, Penina. You know how a candle flickers before it goes out. I don't see a good outcome."

He refocused and engaged her eyes again. "Sometimes I almost wish I could believe again. Death to me now is the illogical proof of an unsolvable equation. Goodnight Penina." "Good night Menachem," she said meaningfully and daring to squeeze his wrist. He returned the intimacy with the briefest smile. She always felt he liked her but his inscrutable manner had kept her, like everyone else, beyond arm's reach. His personal view about death, was an invitation to familiarity, which he extended to few people, to step across the invisible line that separated him from the world. She felt touched and privileged. The professor's whole life was medicine. His wife, a doctor herself, and his three daughters knew that although they had first call on his love, they had second call on his time. He exercised his awesome responsibility over life and death like a general. Once he had believed that all was in the hands of God and that he was merely an instrument. But when he gave up his belief in God's providence, medicine became his religion, and like all substitutions, he transferred elements of what had been abandoned into his neo-orthodoxy. He believed in medicine, a religion without a God, whose priests were consultants, whose festivals were conferences and whose scriptures were textbooks. Prayer had become research. And there was no appeal for there was nothing to appeal to. God had failed to live up to expectations, so the professor felt absolved from his. As she watched him walk along the empty corridor, Penina realized, for the first time, how modest he was in size, how his shoulders sloped, how he stooped from the waist, as if battling a high wind, and yet how fast he was on his small feet. Scourge of interns and terror of stagers, he was an example of mind over body – and mind over soul.

***

On the way to the ward, she almost cried. She fought back her tears, scarcely able to believe what was happening. What the professor had hinted at, became suddenly clear. The Colonel was dying and there was nothing she could do. Go home. You have other patients. She was still in shock that the Colonel's life or death should have made such a breach in her professionalism, when she passed the Arab charge nurse, who had phoned her. She was fixing an intravenous drip on a young girl from Gaza, seriously hurt in a traffic accident. "Colonel Pozner has been talking for about twenty minutes, sort of," she said, adding with a grin: "Typically, he started up as soon as the professor went. He'd come here especially to hear your Colonel." "I'm really glad you rang me." "Penina," the nurse added, "if this girl gets over it, do you think you could see her. She's been taking things badly. Or do I have to go through Natalie?" Penina, almost out of earshot, gestured that she would. "She speaks some Hebrew," the nurse called after her. "No problem," Penina called back. "I'll draw my Arabic out of storage. And if it's not enough, try to be around."

***

The Colonel was on his back. He looked as if he was in peaceful sleep, exhaling as if he was doing light exercise. His eyes had been taped shut so they would not dry out. A digital display of waves flickered across a blue-tinted monitor screen indicating his blood and intracranial pressures and his EKG. He was wearing small grey headphones that fitted snugly into the ears, attached to brain stem response equipment, from which sound waves were transmitted to stimulate the brain and record if the stem had received them. The monitor recorded a flickering movement like a faulty lamp bulb. A white mask over his mouth was attached to a respirator which pumped humidified air into his lungs and maintained the medical fiction that he was alive. Without the respirator he would be dead in a matter of hours. And yet it was possible that this inert, unfeeling, unthinking, non-functioning body, kept going by machines that mimicked his physiology, would rise from the land of the semi-dead and live. Penina had not said a prayer since her teens – except once when her father underwent a triple by-pass in New York. Brought up in a traditional household, she decided, in her late teens, that prayer was irreconcilable with the lifestyle she had adopted. But now, despite the state of art technology available in this hospital and the state of art techniques that the medical teams dispensed, she could suffer no stone left unturned. It was not faith that brought her to prayer but doubt. Doubt that science was everything. To her surprise, she heard herself say: "Blessed are you, Lord our God, King of the Universe. May you grant a complete recovery to Yuri the son of Sara." Not knowing Yuri's Hebrew name, she used his secular Russian name and not knowing his mother's name, she used the name Sara, mother of the Jewish people. Finally, she added – "please don't let him die." Not quite believing that she had said it, still less convinced that it could have served any purpose, she collected the tape from the nursing station and took it to her office, switched on her desk lamp and, sitting in a pool of light, began to listen to Col. Pozner: Tape Three.

It was not easy to understand. Some phrases were repeated like mantras. Odd words scattered like seed. Sighs, groans, dramatic changes of voice levels. Marks of a spirit in distress. She had to admit, the material was largely impenetrable. Her eyelids lowered like shutters. She dozed for little more than ten minutes, but it was enough to blunt her tiredness. She turned on her computer, entered the code to visit a restricted medical site and ran a search on coma. The site came back within seconds listing over a million pages. Better too much than too little, she consoled herself. But the plethora of material was too much for a person in a hurry. She could find no precedent for Yuri's pre-coma revelations. That a patient who barely passed the most basic neurological verbal test, could recite at length and in detail events that occurred in the Roman Empire, the best part of two thousand years previously, in a state of semi-consciousness, was barely credible. But there was the tape, rewinding crazily, like a snake in an animated cartoon. She glanced at a model of the brain, atop her cupboard, a memento of her student days. What we didn't know about its functions would fill several of those huge textbooks that laid out what we did. Something in the brain had been freed, stimulated – created, she dared to add – by the wound to his head. It must have been the wounding rather than the surgical intervention that caused his revelations, because he had one before surgery. How could his long-term memory have been stimulated in this way? And long-term memory of what? Not for a moment did she consider that he might be recounting events that had happened to him in some murky historical past. That could only mean, in another life! Rubbish. Somehow he had collated all this material in his mind over many years, she deduced, and in all likelihood, he did not know that he had done so. Add a seminal imagination and you had the essentials for creating a window on the past. But why open the window now, when he needed all the mental resources he could muster? And how did he express what it was he saw with such verbal sagacity? Was all it needed a life-threatening head wound? Weeks, if not months of research lay before her. She told herself she was looking at a unique phenomenon. She searched diligently through key words, revealing hundreds of cases of PLE's, almost all recited after, not before, a coma resulting from a head injury. None showed the substance or detail of his. She decided that Yuri's experience was a unique psychological event. For a moment, her mind toyed with the idea of writing up Yuri's case history as a paper which she would present at a professional conference, or incorporate in her doctorate, but she quickly discarded the notion. Yuri meant more to her as a man than a case.

***

It was six a.m. She picked up the day's schedule which the head psychologist had left on her desk the previous night. She was assigned to burns victims. She braced herself. Burns always got to her. Dissatisfied with her own company, she took the empty elevator down to the staff canteen patronized at this hour by a few off-duty colleagues, in no particular hurry to go home. She took her filter coffee to a littered table where an intensive care duty nurse was sitting with a few colleagues. Half a dozen tables lit by the overhead neon were occupied. The rest of the canteen was in darkness. "Did it make any sense, what the Colonel said?" the duty nurse asked, drawing deeply on a cigarette directly below a no-smoking sign. "Yes, it was great," Penina answered, too weary to search for words. "You know Penina, you won't be able to keep this pace up. If you do you'll end up having to see a psychologist." Penina's dark brown eyes acknowledged the concern behind the humor. The charge nurse rose to go. "My lift will be waiting. Oh and there's one thing you should know. The Colonel's wife rang in. She's back from Australia. I had to tell her about the Colonel." "You really should have left that to me," Penina said. "Penina, she isn't the kind of woman you don't tell it all to. She gave the social worker a real hard time. She wants to know every last detail. You weren't around. She's coming in sometime this morning." The charge nurse drowned a newly lit cigarette in the remains of his coffee and left. "And have you heard?" a trainee nurse asked her. "They've traced some relative of the Colonel's. A brother." "I had no idea he had one," said Penina. "I don't think the Colonel did," said a head nurse, just joining them. "They were estranged. An older brother. Changed his name and has been living up in some commune near Tsfat. They haven't been in touch for years." A Brazilian charge nurse with whom Penina had established a good working relationship, got up at the next table. "Must go. Take it easy Penina and remember you're only one person." "I'll try," Penina replied. "You know, I've just been reminded that if you want to know what's going on at this hospital, ask the nurses." "And if you don't, ask we'll tell you anyway," the charge nurse said as he left with a bunch of colleagues for the short run to the Arab villages clustered in East Jerusalem. Only two young orderlies remained at a nearby table. They were speaking Georgian or some language of the Caucasus. One of them kept glancing at Penina. She knew he was looking for an opening. It was the last thing she wanted right now. Getting up, she walked through the area in darkness and exited by an emergency door.

***

Perched on a window bench opposite the entrance to the technicians' suite, she wrote a note to Eliezar. Could he please boost the sound of the enclosed tape as a matter of urgency? Could he make it the first job he did, when he got in? As an incentive, she added, that if there was a half-decent movie on that evening and he was free, she'd love to go. She wrapped the tape inside the sheet torn from her notebook and left it by the door, wondering why, on earth, she had suggested a movie. She could have changed the message but let it stand. In the burns unit staff room, two Ukrainian immigrant nurses were making tea. Without a word she lay down on an empty bed in the corner, and was asleep before they could ask her if she'd like a cup.

Chapter Two

"It's been a two-day march to Caesarea, the administrative capital of the Roman occupation. Many hundreds have died on the way. We passed through a procession of towns and villages that we had liberated during the revolt. For three years they had been governed by Jewish law. Our religion was practiced freely. The taxes that would have gone to Rome were spent on acquiring new land – and new weapons. The revolt that had begun here in these small towns unheard of in the imperial capital, might have liberated the whole of Judea and Samaria, Galili and across the Jordan and rocked the Roman Empire.

"Two of my brothers were killed. I saw one of them lanced through not ten meters from me during the battle for Beitar. It was after we pulled back and reformed around the citadel, which the Romans had no stomach to take for two days. One of the Sephoris volunteers, though wounded himself, brought me the helmet of my other brother, Aryeh. True to his name, true to his nature, he had fought like a lion and the Romans assigned a snatch squad to get him. He was hacked to pieces in a flail of short swords. And Tamar? Galinus will lust after her in his cups and beat her in his delirium. We had planned to be married on the fourth anniversary of the revolt, before we made our final triumphal march on Jerusalem, which will now never happen. Will my parents be safe in Sephoris? Will Rome's ever-vengeful arm reach them? Hundreds of Galilians had flocked to us before the retreat to Beitar, from Sephoris and Tiberius, Nazareth and Capernaum to fight our last fight.

"For two days we trudged through desolation. Only now do we see the extent of our defeat. Hardly a village stands, hardly a town is inhabited. Our enemy has systematically destroyed thousands of habitations, synagogues, markets, granaries, court-houses, spoiled the fields, fired the crops, ripped out the irrigation. This is no mere military campaign, this

is a policy of extermination. Places I knew which once bustled with life where you could buy a yearling kid out of five hundred on the eve of a feast-day, hubs of the surrounding countryside, are motionless, save for eddies of sand piling up against walls of mud or stone, making gruesome pirouettes into silenced courtyards, their onetime inhabitants massacred. No-one is left to stop the incursions of time. No-one to hold back the desert's embrace. No-one to redeem the land of the Jews. And the dead have been left to rot or become the food of animals. Burial is forbidden by Roman decree. They want us to behold our degradation. Everywhere are skulls and corpses and severed limbs. And the stink of death. Our land is an open cemetery, without graves".

The voice cracks. Penina holds her breath. Will he go on? She waits for several minutes before he speaks again, this time more quietly, the voice measured. She recognizes the tone of someone taking pains to remain calm. She turns up the volume.

"We are in Caesarea where their victory parade will take place. Most prisoners are being kept at the army barracks on the edge of town, but about a hundred of us, leaders of the revolt, have been herded into cages along one side of the hippodrome beneath the seats, where animals are usually kept for the games. We have been herded here to watch the Romans celebrate our destruction. For some time, the inhabitants of Caesarea – its non-Jewish inhabitants to be sure – have been pouring into the amphitheater to occupy the rows of seats, above us facing the sea, each of which runs for eighty meters from end to end. The first cohort, some three hundred men from the Syrian legion, march into the center of the hippodrome. A second cohort, of auxiliary troops recruited from the vicinity and the Greek port city of Dor, follow. The swelling cheers of the crowd rise and subside like a storm wind. The Jewish revolt has been crushed and they have come to pay their respects to the man who did it. I do not blame them. If we had managed to get the Romans off our backs, it would have gone badly for them. Bar Kochba, our leader, would have been anointed King of the Jews and there would have been no Roman procurator to favor foreign ambitions, to protect their trade, recruit for their legions, protect their idols and oppress the Jews. If we had won, we would have declared Jerusalem once more the capital of Judea, Samaria and Galilee, re-established Jewish law and practice and relieved this damned city of Caesarea of its false

claim to primacy. Caesarea? Who ever heard of Caesarea! Win or lose, the battle was for the highest stakes – our identity, our existence – and we lost. How was it possible? I watch them, assembled in their serried ranks, their shields at precisely the same angle, their helmets in perfect alignment. How did they win, these pagans who worship images in stone? Everything is in the hands of God, it's said, except the fear of him. These did not fear him and they won. Something beyond their ruthlessness, beyond their delight in massacre, their intense cruelty, rancor, avarice, and remorselessness, gave them the victory. They metamorphose into a machine with many legs and a single will. A machine has no heart, it does what it is built for. That is the Roman genius. But how do people who believe in so many gods achieve such unity? How do they blend their individual souls? Look at them. They are coming to attention now. Not a man out of place, not a sandal out of step. You would not get six hundred Jews to do that. We would form a crowd, or a mob, or a flock, or a procession or family groups, or bunch for an attack like leopards, or have a picnic, as the occasion demanded. We would be driven by our hearts and our fury and pray that God will bless us. But every man among the Romans knows exactly where he fits and what he has to do, from the engineer to the doctor, the cavalryman to the common foot soldier, the centurion to the general, like a host of evil angels. And how they train! Our sling shooters, especially from Galili, are unparalleled in their skills. But they could never put down a field of fire like Roman archers. We use skills acquired over a lifetime to take out individual soldiers as if they were marauding wolves attacking our sheep. We should have divided the best of our slingshots into heavy and light units and trained them to fire in devastating unison, so that each volley would decimate the enemy. There was no doubting our courage. They suffered great losses that only an empire could sustain. Our dagger men wrought havoc with their infantry, especially on terrain where they could not form a phalanx. But they were clever. They took us in small groups, attacking a hamlet, a redoubt, a fort. Destroying all as soon as it was taken. Remorselessly, for three years, shunning big engagements until the last when we were trapped at Beitar, destroying everything as they went, making starvation and devastation their allies. Perhaps we could have rolled our dice differently. Perhaps not. We could never have become a machine without a heart. We are spontaneous, not remorseless. We are fanatics for our small land. We do not have the professional military caste of an empire. We are governed by the heart and our history – they by their will and the machine. The machine does not know where the heart resides.

"I hear the roar of the audience. It builds up like a wave. It drowns the sound of the drums and the sea. Only the shrill note of the trumpets can be heard above the din, sounding a salute. I pull myself up, hanging onto the iron bars, so that I can see through the ranks of soldiers. A group of tribunes and senior officers walk along the esplanade and stop opposite the point where the two cohorts meet. They form a loose semi-circle, facing the parade, their backs to the sea. I can see General Severus, accompanied by his aide and escort walking slowly along the promenade acknowledging the thunderous applause of the crowd, followed by his chariot. He stops at intervals to face them and wave a regal hand. Each time he does so, the applause and shouts of the crowd reach a crescendo. The man who put down the Jewish revolt and destroyed the last vestiges of Jewish independence in our land is vastly popular among our pagan fellow citizens. He takes his place by the tribunes, mounts the chariot and raises his arms to quiet the crowd. A crowd of ten thousand is reduced to total silence, in a moment. Even the sea is momentarily becalmed. I have seen him before – in battle. He is inseparable from his uniform, a general to the core. We Jews respected him for his personal bravery – although there was no shortage of that on either side. But there was a callous side to his nature which he fostered with calculated cruelty, raising it to an art. We killed Romans to win, but he killed to deter, to terrorize. He had to make us writhe in pain – death was not enough. We wanted Rome out. He had to show that opposing Rome meant suicide."

Penina stopped the recording and sat back in her seat. She could not take the slow torture in Yuri's voice. Besides, she was late for burns. She remembered learning about the destruction of the last Jewish state at school, but not with such vividness, certainly not with such emotion.

***

The consultant and his team had already begun their rounds when she got to the burns unit. It wasn't like her to be late. The consultant glanced at her but said nothing. Two patients were to be discharged that day, with no more admissions until the next morning, except for emergencies. Although you never knew when there might be an incident, it looked like being a relatively quiet day. The consultant finished examining a patient who had been brought in three weeks before after a bombing in a coffee shop with third degree burns to his face and hands. "How would you like to go home?" he asked him. "Try me," said the patient. "I see no reason for keeping you here any longer. Dr. Abbas will give you some tips on what you should and shouldn't do and I'd like Penina Frydman to have a word before you go. Good luck." Penina returned to the patient after the round. The man's wife, a bright-eyed, plump woman was already sitting by his bedside. "One of the nurses told me he'd be coming home today," she said. "They always know before the doctors." Penina was not worried about the patient making a successful convalescence. She had observed him and his wife together almost daily and noticed how the wife always sat on the side of her husband nearer the scar, which covered half his face. She would run her finger gently across its contours, with fond gentleness, before the skin graft, while it was still black. Relatives usually sat on the patient's uninjured side, which Penina took as a harbinger of future problems, stemming from their helpless revulsion. But this woman, a secretary in a clothing factory, was able to see the man she loved through the scar. "I'm dying to get you home," she said, the sexual innuendo in her voice explicit. It was like balm to her husband's daunted self-confidence. They held hands and listened attentively to everything Penina told them. When he went back to work, Penina advised, he must behave naturally, never hide his face but look people in the eye, even if they looked away. "They'll do that," he said, "it's not a pretty sight." "What you have to remember," Penina told him, "is that when people look away, it's not necessarily because they don't want to look at you, but because they think you don't want to be looked at. They are protecting your privacy. Not always, but quite often. If you behave naturally, they will soon learn to be natural too. Children sometimes take longer. Sometimes it's like learning how to cope with a new daddy. But the rule applies. They'll get used to it if you do." His wife said: "I don't think it looks too bad at all, really." "You've got it," Penina said back to her, while thinking 'what a lovely woman.' She gave the wife the e-mail address of a burns' victim rehabilitation group. "Get in touch," she advised. "And make him go with you," she added. Turning to the husband, she said: "You might find at first that you will treat other burns victims like lepers. When you've learnt to accept them, it will be easier to accept yourself. Here's my card. If you ever need me, I'm here. You are both about to start a new life, so may your life be renewed."

The other person due for release was a flashing-eyed woman of twenty two, who had undergone serial skin grafts on her thighs. "My legs were my best feature," she told Penina, the prospect of her imminent release making her talkative. Most of the time, she read. "And my bottom end! That was a real asset. They've taken so much skin from it for the graft, I look like a plucked chicken. And those thighs – I'm going to have to give up short skirts and platform heels. That's for sure. And no more beach. I live in Tel Aviv and used to spend all my spare time on the beach. At weekends, I practically lived there. " She lifted one leg off the bed and studied it. "I'll have to become a recluse," she half joked. "Still, they haven't done too badly – when you think of how they looked when I came in. Gruesome!" Penina knew the woman was releasing less than half the text that was on her mind. The words were light-hearted, but the eyes were in pain. She had lost her mother in the same bus bombing and could not attend the funeral because of injuries. She seldom spoke of her mother, in fact she was often little more than monosyllabic when Penina visited. Not only had she missed the funeral, but had not been able to mark the ending of the shloshim, the three-month period of mourning. "I think you should do something to mark your mother's shloshim," Penina said. The woman grimaced, as if Penina had rubbed salt in a wound. "I recommend you visit the grave and spend some time alone there, just thinking about her. Things you used to do together. If there's any way you hurt her, tell her you're sorry. Out loud is better than inside your head. And the very next day, get down to the beach with a couple of friends. Don't choose a part where there are no people, if you can find one," she added with a smile. "Get into the thick of it. And behave exactly as you feel." "If I did that, I'd get arrested," the patient joked. Penina noted the pain level in the woman's eyes. It had subsided. "Thank you," the patient said. "I really mean that. You're the best thing that could have happened to me here." Penina smiled at her and kissed her on the cheek.

She passed on to a man whose hands and entire lower body had been burned. He did not have enough skin to cover all the area that needed to be replaced. They would have to find it from other sources. Meanwhile, they had done an allograft, using pigskin, so that the wound would be more receptive. The man was in great pain and mental distress. He loved his work at a school for disadvantaged immigrant youth from Russia and Ethiopia, where he was head of sports. It was more than a job – it was his life. Of good physique, never having had a day's illness, he found hospital routine more demoralizing than his wounds. Constant efforts to find out from the doctors how long it would be before he could start work again, had drawn vague answers. It was Penina's task to talk him through that. She sat down beside him and examined his hands that had received grafts five days earlier. He had been kept immobile for that time to allow the graft to take. "I'm no expert," she said. "But it seems as if it's coming along nicely." He looked at her with suspicion. "How long?" he asked. "You mean…?" "I mean before I'm back on a playing field," he answered sharply. "We're looking at about two years," she said, knowing that it might well be three. His eyes registered shock and anger. "Shit!" he said, his temples trembling. She waited patiently to be invited back into the conversation. There was no point in speaking until he was ready. "Well that's the end of it," he said. "The end?" "Of my life. You think the school is going to wait two years? There's nothing else I can do, or would want to, in this crazy world. I love those kids. Everything about them. They're perverse, ungrateful, unstable and crude. Some of them would steal their grandmother's false teeth for a fix. But they're great kids. Everything's against them, but they go through life chin first. No bowing and scraping. I teach some of them to box. Put them in the ring and they go for it at once. It's the only place where they don't foul. And you know why? Because it's the only place where everything isn't stacked against them. The only place where they meet the world on equal…" His chest heaved and the tears came, silently, falling down his cheek at sedate intervals. Penina got up. He was the kind of man who would come out of a good cry strengthened. In the meantime he was best left alone. "I don't remember the last time I cried" he said, as she was about to go. "I must have been a kid. You know what's the worst part of all this?" he added, with a tinge of self-mockery, "I can't wipe my own ass." "We'll take care of that as long as need be," Penina said with a discreet smile, "just make sure the battery to your buzzer is always fully charged." She was answered by the ghost of a grin.

Instead of eating with the medics from the burns unit, she bought two cheese and olive burekas and coffee and took them to her office. Her colleagues had broken for lunch. Munching a bureka, filled with goat's cheese, she slid the tape into her player and sat back to listen.

"General Severus is greeted by a storm of clapping, and stamping of feet. Thousands of lips whistle shrill encouragement. "Citizens of Caesarea" he begins, "of the Roman city of Caesarea!" They love him, these people. "It is a matter of irony that this magnificent city was built by a Jewish King – but King Herod was a Jew who knew how to serve Rome. Not the Jews of today who whine about our just taxes and rebel against our just government and disdain our righteous gods. Three years we have spent putting down their treachery. Three years at a cost I dare not count. The trouble with them is that they have never learnt their lesson – it's too simple for them to understand – that the choice is: serve Rome and prosper or rebel and suffer the consequences. And there will be consequences. This time they have gone a rebellion too far. I swear to you that the Jews will never rise against Rome again in this land or any other. Their revolt is their destruction. I have received instructions directly from our Emperor Hadrian to have Jerusalem ploughed over, to build a temple to Jupiter where their temple once stood, to rename the city Aeolia Capitolina and to ban Jews from living there forever."

A huge roar of approval greets each clause. The crowd is delirious at our planned disappearance from history. "It will be illegal to teach their religion. Circumcision is banned. And this ungodly mess which they call Judea, Samaria, Galili and the rest, from now on will be called by a new name - Palestine!" A great cheer mounts to the sky as if from one mighty voice, swelled by the troops who beat their swords on their shields and yell euax, euax until they are hoarse. Severus calms them. "Let us forget the Jews," he continues in a more relaxed key. "I wish to address a few words to the cohorts representing the legions that battled through this miserable insurrection. Soldiers have no time for words – we prefer action. But something must be said about the sheer determination, the sheer soldierliness of our men. I came here from the island of Britain, the farthest land to the west that the might of Rome has conquered, whose population is almost as troublesome as the Jews who you know only too well. There, as proconsul and a general of Rome, I put down a fierce uprising. Here I have finished putting down a desperate rebellion that took three and a half years of bitter warfare. Let it be known from one end of the Empire to the other, that no enemy can stand up to Roman power, be it Gaul, German, Briton or Jew. This Jewish war has been the toughest campaign of my life. Campaigns like these are not won by generals. We could achieve nothing without men like you. I am proud of you. I commend you. And I raise your pay by one tenth!" His words are greeted by a tumult of applause.

"But I have my reward also. Our divine Emperor, Hadrian, has appointed me pro-consul of the new province of Syria-Palestine – and this jewel of a city called Caesarea shall replace Jerusalem, at least until it is rebuilt as Hadrian's very own Aeolia Capitolina! The divine Hadrian promised to build a new city on this historic site just a few long years ago, an ambition which brought down the full fury of the barbarian Jews. But it is Hadrian's dream, not the Jewish wish, which has prevailed." The applause is thunderous. "I leave you now. I am to proceed to my new station in Syria. I can look any man in the eye and say: I love Rome with a full heart, as I know you do. I adjure you, citizens of Caesarea, of Palestine and of Syria. Seize the opportunity! Seize the day. This is no more the land of the Jews. Seize the opportunity! Seize the day! There is a new Jew-free land to be settled. Live and prosper under Rome's dominium!"

He acknowledges an orgasm of applause. Turning slowly from left to right, he raises his arm in an inclusive salute. Every single pagan feels the salute is meant for him. The Empire could not exist without men such as Severus. "Valete!" goodbye, he calls out a dozen times. "Reveni! Reveni!" Come back! Come back, they thunder in reply. His chariot makes slow progress along the embankment that leads towards the harbor of Sebaste, as citizens and soldiers cheer him out of sight. General Severus is a man, for those who love him, whose presence is as terrible as his absence is palpable – and whose legacy is the destruction of the land of the Jews.

***

The parade is dismissed by a senior tribune. He and several other tribunes mingle among the men. I spot Galinus and follow him with my eyes. He takes the trouble to talk to the ancillary troopers who speak Greek but little Latin. His Greek must be good or he could not banter and joke with them as he does. Behold the enemy at peace! They strut about the esplanade, kissed by spray from the sea. It cost them dear, though. Severus was forced to avoid major engagements until the bitter end. Our fury and our purpose were unbreakable. One whole legion – the Twenty Second, brought in from Egypt – annihilated, with huge casualties suffered by the remaining nine, and several ancillary units reinforced in large numbers to cover their losses. They find it hard that this was inflicted on them by Jews. But their contempt for us is tempered with the taste of their own blood. So they have won. They have achieved their ambition of destroying not just our people but our nation – at least for as far as can be foreseen. We may be destined to serve a long exile, but it will not be forever. I put the world on notice: one day we shall return!

***

The smell of food being cooked gets into our nostrils and allows us to think of nothing else. Even Tamar becomes a shadow in my thoughts. The acrid smell from log fires and hot juices is, to us, like perfume to a lover. After a while the soldiers queue for their rations and return to the hippodrome, carrying their food on their second shields, and squat down on the sandy ground. It's some kind of gruel served with strips of flat bread. The centurions sit apart and the officers sit on benches at a long carved table beneath a large canvas tilted eastwards to ward off the sun. We watch them, envious as crows. The men sit with their tent-mates in groups of eight, spooning the gruel into their mouths, quaffing water from flasks and wine from flagons. After a while a centurion selects a food detail from among the prisoners. They serve us from a rickety cart containing a few steaming pots. They progress slowly, pouring thin gruel into our bowls thrust out between the iron struts of our prison and toss scraps of dry bread onto the floor which we fight over. Those who do not have bowls open their mouths for the gruel to be poured between their teeth. A mouthful per man. It must last until evening. Much of it spills onto the floor stones, heated like an oven by the sun. Parched tongues lick them clean. Broad hands snatch tiny scraps of bread from weaker neighbors. The man on food detail who comes to feed me wears the hood of his burnouse loosely over his head, despite the heat, trying to cover the weeping sores which disfigure his face. He tries to hide between the folds of his head covering. The Romans deliberately chose a leper to serve us. I raise the thin strip of bread, tough as leather, to my lips and say the benediction, recognizing God's sovereignty over the whole world and blessing him for providing food from its soil. I dunk it in the gruel for a long time before my teeth can make an impression. I raise the bowl to my lips. I taste a tiny piece of meat between my lips. Instinctively I spit it out.

"What's wrong with our meat?" an educated voice asks in Latin. I look into the eyes of Galinus, the tribune, who has Tamar as his prisoner. I swallow the rest. The tiny piece of pork has landed at his feet. "Pig-meat is forbidden to us," I tell him. Some other officers and a centurion or two gather around him, puzzled that he should talk to a prisoner. "And why is it forbidden to you and permissible to us?" he asks, his question cadenced in a sneer. "Why does the tiger eat meat and the crane fish?" I answer. His expression changes from disdain to anger. "In the final count what good has your God and all his regulations done you? Look at yourselves. You're alive only because we got tired of killing you. But that can change." He steps forward and peers through the grating, placing his face close to mine. "And what is your God, who is so particular about pig meat, going to do about it?" The Roman is stooping towards me, his young face lined with contempt. I struggle to my feet and level my eyes with his. "What will he do?" I repeat, as if the question was too obvious to need an answer. "Our God will never desert us," I say in a hoarse whisper. The stench of my breath forces him back. "That is the difference between us, Tribune. If you are defeated, your gods are defeated with you. If we are defeated, God will yet redeem us. Invisibility is not absence. He is here, now, but he cannot be seen." Galinus snorts derisively and stands erect. His epaulettes glisten in the sun. "I am taking Tamar with me to Alexandria. You will never see her again. And when you are being sold in some Roman slave market, just look around at the might of that great metropolis, the heart of civilization and ask yourself if you and your pathetic band of brigands ever had the remotest chance of victory." There is no need of him to teach the lesson, I have been wrestling with that question ever since our final defeat.

He struts away, king of the moment. The food detail is coming back along the path. As the leper passes, he deliberately runs one wheel of the barrow into a rut. He makes some pretense of lifting it back, snatching the opportunity to mouth a message. Tamar is to be put on a ship for Alexandria this morning. She knows where I am standing and will salute me as she passes. She sends me a triple greeting – from the virgin she has always been, from the woman who yearns to bear me sons and from the bride she believes she will be to me in another life: love is eternal. At first, the words are meaningless. Slowly, they find a way to my brain like water seeping through rock. Tamar's fate is sealed. I cannot fight the pain. Better had she been killed at Beitar than suffer a life of humiliation in a Roman bed. But as soon as I have thought it, I shake my mind free. Perhaps she has some hidden destiny. Perhaps she will one day save her people. The sea shimmers like a sheet of Chinese silk unrolled by a merchant in a Jerusalem market. An intermittent coastal breeze stirs and stills the water making it break effortlessly across the esplanade.

***

A procession comes into view. Perhaps twenty women, each a rose of Sharon, walking in single file along the promenade, like dancers filing onto a stage. A small cart brings their simple possessions. A few of them wear Judean mantles with a design in the shape of the Greek letter gamma. They have been selected as concubines for senior officers or as gifts for Egyptian administrators. The rest are clothed in male togas – traditional dress for prostitutes. These are the best of the women taken in the campaign, to be sold in the up-market brothels of Alexandria. Something about the bearing of a tall woman in an ochre mantle grips the muscles of my stomach. I rise to my feet. It is Tamar. Even at this distance, and in these circumstances, her beauty is uncontested. The proud head and the outline of her body through the wraps of her garment make her stand out in this bevy of plundered beauty. She must have been told by the leper where to look out for me and as she passes, she turns her head slowly in my direction. I cannot see her full face against the deep blue haze hanging over the sea behind her. She raises her chin in pride and defiance. I raise my hands as high as I can and hold my fingers in the form of the priestly blessing. She has seen me. She bows her head momentarily, acknowledging the blessing, then continues, throwing back her shoulders and holding her head high. I understand her message. She will never be broken. A wave cascades over the esplanade. The women scatter, but Tamar keeps her pace, her wet cloak hugging her body. What awaits her in Alexandria? Will I ever see her again?

***

The sound of Natalie in loud discussion in the corridor made Penina switch off the tape. She sat still for a moment, adjusting her mind. Yuri's story had filled her brain with a thousand images. She had to force herself to return to present-day Jerusalem and the thought of Yuri in a life-threatening pre-coma, three floors below. How different his reality was. It was incredible that he could create these scenarios, as if he had prepared it all in his mind, print ready. She expected something less fluent, as seen through a glass darkly. She could not tolerate the notion that these were episodes from a life once lived. No, this was clearly some kind of mental construct describing events in real time – the present. It belonged to literature, not reality. But it also belonged to psychology. She had never had a patient who had visions of an unlived past. Fantasies, yes, and sometimes detailed recall of childhood experiences, real or imagined. Her thoughts were cut short by the door being opened by Natalie. She did not come in but continued her conversation in a raised voice with someone in the corridor. At first, Penina was too absorbed to listen. Then she heard the placatory voice of Natalie's interlocutor say: "There's no way of knowing if the hallucinations brought on the attack. The nursing staff just did their job. It's nothing to do with us."

Natalie entered the room. She was angry. She glanced at Penina, then at her watch. Penina was supposed to be in rehab. "Is that the tape everyone's talking about?" she asked. "Let me hear some." Penina began to rewind. "Oh, anywhere – it doesn't matter," Natalie said, stopping her hand. Penina pressed play. Yuri was recounting his argument with the tribune over pig meat. Natalie listened through headphones. "This has been cleaned up, hasn't it?" "Yes. Technical services did a good job." "I need the original. Why did you record it? As I see it, the Colonel has been having hallucinations, so what? I've heard sweet old grandmothers do it. But it never sounds like this. Listening to it, anyone would think he was making a keynote speech at a conference. All you needed to do, was put something in his notes saying the patient was having hallucinations. That would have been just one line. Finished. Now we've got to come up with a report about why we recorded him and what effect it might have had." "Effect? What effect? Did something happen?" "You mean, you don't know? The patient got very agitated over what he was saying last night and had an attack." "How can we be sure that was the reason?" "Good question. The professor seems to think that the patient was aware he was being recorded and that that encouraged him to spout all this. The emotional cost of these stupid outpourings was probably what drove him into having an attack." "Even if that's true," Penina shot back, "it doesn't account for the 'outpourings' themselves. I believe they are unique." "Very nice, Penina, but you've dropped me in the shit and it's not where I like to be. It's become a departmental issue, God help us." "There is only one matter of real interest here and that is what made him come up with all this stuff and why?" "Bless you, Penina, but that is not what the professor is concerned with. Look, I'm changing your schedule for this morning. I'll put someone else on your round. The Colonel's wife has arrived from Australia where she has been lecturing and needs to be put in the picture. Don't breathe a word about this inter-departmental balagan. Calm her down. When she left for her lecture tour, her husband was a senior officer in a prestigious combat unit and when she comes back she finds he's reduced to a – I know the term's not poli-correct – cabbage. She's at his bedside now. I've had a word. When you've finished with her, write me a report about why you thought fit to record the Colonel. I knew something like this would happen," Natalie replied, "once the hospital introduced peer review. Now everything has to be discussed and discussed until they can't tell the difference between silk and shit. Someone has been getting at the prof, probably a complaint from an ambitious medic. We're in for an era of denunciations, followed by show trials, no doubt. Unfortunately, it will be considered an advance by the people who matter."

***

The first thing Penina saw of Yuri's wife was her feet. She was sitting at her husband's bedside, the white curtain pulled round like a topless tent. Only her feet could be seen beneath its hem. They were long, slim and heavily-veined, sun-browned and adorned with sandals whose thin red and gold straps criss-crossed web-like, culminating in lemon pom-poms. The sort of thing you might purchase impulsively in an eastern bazaar but never wear. Penina had not seen anything like it in a hospital. Their inappropriateness, given that they adorned the feet of a wife visiting her severely wounded husband, made a kind of daredevil statement. Penina usually rationalized the behavior of people in an instant, but she could not see through this one. She pulled the curtain slightly to one side and found a bare-backed, thin-shouldered woman who looked up at her with the palest of pale blue-green eyes, made paler by the depth of her tan. She was wearing a mauve wrap-across top that hugged thrusting, eager breasts and exposed a fleshless stomach. Penina could not help being reminded of a medical clown. She did not respond to Penina's professional smile but stared back at her, waiting. Despite her grief, which hung on her cheeks like pearls in a jeweler's window, she was, Penina thought, a woman in total possession of herself. Even as clown, if that was her true identity. It was a relief. Otherwise, she would have been forced to think of her as an up-market eccentric. Before she spoke, Penina took in the intimate atmosphere which pervaded the small space. She felt she had stumbled into an exclusion zone. "Shalom," she said, extending her hand. "I'm Penina. Clinical psychologist." The woman stared back, reading the face before her, lightly enclosing Penina's brown-skinned hand in her own. "What are his chances?" she finally asked, as if Penina had passed some crucial test. "We simply don't know. Your husband is very difficult to assess. He seems to be in some sort of pre-coma state." She shrugged, in an admission of ignorance. "Is there anything I can do?" Yuri's wife asked. "Speaking medically, no." "And un-medically?" "That depends where you are coming from. For example, religious people pray." "I wouldn't know how. I was raised on a left-wing kibbutz. I still live on one. That's just not in my toolkit." "Well, there are a lot of people who believe they can help their loved one by talking, playing music, stroking their hair. Anything that might connect. Even in coma, which he has not reached yet." "Is that really true?" "Difficult to believe, I admit. But even patients who have been through long-term coma, sometimes say they were aware of people talking to them, or even casual conversations taking place between doctors, when they eventually come out. Medical orthodoxy rejects it, of course." "Dogmas don't grab me. I mean, what would you do in my place?" Shira asked. "Oh, everything I could think of. Pray, sing, read, reminisce, hold hands, ask questions, tickle, talk about family, friends, colleagues. Show photographs. Tell stories. Lots of stories. Dance, even." "Thank you, Penina. You've given me what I need." She released Penina's hand and turned possessive eyes on Yuri. What was there to possess? Penina wondered. The interview was over.

Penina pulled the curtain behind her, restoring the cubicle to its tent-like intimacy. She heard Yuri's wife's voice saying: "I'm back, my darling. In every sense of the word." Something in those words made Penina turn back. She parted the curtain enough to insert her head into the cubicle. "There's something I think you should know. I was going to let you settle back in before I told you. But there's no time like the present. First, let me ask you something. Does your husband speak in his sleep?" "Not really. The odd phrase maybe, when he is distressed." "Do you remember an example?" Shira was nervous about where the conversation was going and what she would have been told by the end of it. It inhibited her memory. "When he said anything, it was incomprehensible. I assumed it was about operations he had been on. Or his life in Russia." "Mrs. Pozner, I'd like you to read this. It's a transcript of things he has been saying since he came. They are voluble, I'd say, impeccable, accounts of events that took place in the Roman Empire, particularly around the time of Bar Kochba's revolt." She handed her the dossier. "He said all this?" Shira asked, turning a few pages of the document with incredulity. She began to put it in her bag. "If you don't mind, I'd like you to read it here." Shira looked at her in surprise but said: "No problem." "When you're finished, you can reach me on my bleeper. Just dial this number. You can write on the transcript, if anything strikes you. I have other copies." Penina gave her the number and left.

***

As Penina walked across the ward, she felt a deep loss. Not that she had had anything to lose, she told herself, but the feeling would not go away. Yuri's wife was back, in every sense of the word. What did that mean? It sounded as if she was asserting ownership. Surely that was her right. And just as surely, her doing so should have no possible effect on Penina's self-assurance. Penina could not compete with Yuri's wife's looks, nor by repute, with her mind. And her clowning? Was that her stratagem for getting out of holes?

She stopped in the corridor to glance through her notes about the patients on her schedule. But her thoughts returned to Shira like homing pigeons. She felt an urgent, perhaps irrational need to define the woman. Possibilities darted across her mind like falling stars. Then one appeared which held its position without a trail. Earth mother. Not in the conventional sense of sexual symbolism, although that was there. But in the sense that she grew out of deep soil. Not necessarily of the earth. It could be deep intellectual soil which had nurtured her. Penina measured her against the elements which she believed in. Soil certainly. She was fertile, perhaps intellectually only, perhaps physically only, perhaps both. Metal too. There was something metallic about her. She certainly had metallic determination. Fire, yes, it lit up her personality, not even a hurricane could blow it out. Air, yes, large lungs and a need for space. But water. Where was water, the catalyst for change? Looking back on their short encounter, Penina could find it nowhere. Finding no answer, she recapitulated on what she knew. An earth mother? That fitted. But an earth mother with pom poms? An earth mother disguised as a beach bunny? She had to rationalize this image before she could seriously return to her work. When the news came to her in Australia that Yuri had been wounded, Shira must have been relaxing by the poolside. Could she have got up, checked out of her hotel and caught the first flight, without even changing? Didn't she pack? Penina had to know. She went back to the ward. The curtain still enclosed the cubicle. She peered under it discreetly. No sign of luggage. She went to ward reception and asked the duty nurse if Dr. Pozner had arrived with a travel-bag. No, she was told. "She came in looking as if she was straight off the beach." Penina considered if that was possible. Would any woman pick herself off the beach and fly as she was, half way round the world to visit a wounded husband, even if time was at the highest premium? Had the person who informed her of Yuri's condition, scared the wits out of her? Didn't she have to get money from her room? Or change her clothes? Or pack? Or make a phone call? Or fix her makeup? The true answers did not matter, Penina reasoned. All that mattered was that it was possible to imagine that this woman was capable of doing so. And that made her formidable. By some sleight of mind, Penina managed to think of Dr. Pozner as if she knew nothing of her existence until that morning. Certainly, she tried not to think of her as the woman who had snatched Yuri from her bed a decade before. She kept the memory at arm's length.

She thought about the patient, who was fighting for his life. Why waste mental and physical resources on retrieving a "past" one? In no way could it help his survival. What was this burning desire to talk about the distant past, that overrode everything else? It was not natural. But it must be regarded as his supreme wish. Should she be true to his wish or to the predictable wishes of the ethics committee? As she decided to block a decision, for the time being, her beeper sounded insistently. Shira had finished reading. "This is really extraordinary, Penina, I mean extraordinary. You'll find me in the coffee station. What would we do without the coffee drug?" she heard Mrs. Pozner say, as she walked back to emergency. Suddenly, the decision came to her. She would be true to Yuri. The hospital corridors were deserted. The low-key lighting threw her reflection onto the glass wall, accompanying her as she walked. It must have happened many times in the past, without her being aware of it, but now her reflection supported the decision she had made. In her third ear, she heard Prof. Bondman's voice, as clearly as if he was walking beside her: If you thought the patient's supreme wish was to kill himself, would you help him? A good question, she told herself, a typical Bondman question, he had once asked. She dialed a friend who lectured in Roman history. When she told her about the Colonel's revelations, she agreed to look at the printouts and offer an opinion on their plausibility. "There's an enormous amount we still don't know about those times, but there's a lot we do. I should certainly be able to tell if it's credible." Penina arranged to drop the transcript on her friend's porch on the way home.

***

Shira was standing in front of the window, by a sandwich dispenser, gazing into the blackness. She did not move when Penina joined her. "Well, what do you think?" Penina asked, fishing for a coin to feed the machine. "It's formidable stuff," Shira said, still looking out of the window. "But where is it from? What does it mean? I didn't know I was living with a historian." "I was hoping you would clarify the situation – at least to throw some light on the question: where from? Could he have read all this? Sometimes, people read things in books or see movies which they internalize and later have these revelations as if they happened to them. Certainly that's what it looks from where I sit." "I wish I had the answer, but I have no recollection of him ever taking any particular interest in the Romans. In Russia, he had practically no knowledge of Jewish history. Fifty years of Communism had wiped out virtually all Jewish education, except for the underground networks. When he came here, he had never heard of the Festival of Chanukah, had never celebrated any other festival, did not know that the foundations of modern Israel had been laid by Russian immigrants in the nineteenth century. He did tell me that, as a boy, after he came to Israel, he read everything he could find about Jewish history. Maybe that's it. Maybe he internalized it as you say. But how much more is there?" "That's the point, Mrs. Pozner. When he was first admitted, he had some kind of revelation of an incident in Poland during World War II, long before he was born. I think there is a wealth of material from Jewish history, locked in his mind. When he came from Russia, he must have hungered for knowledge of the Jewish past, and what we are seeing is perhaps the regurgitation of what he discovered. Except that he has added a factor that wasn't present in the books that affected him so deeply. He has given himself a high position in the army of Bar Kochba. He has given himself a beautiful fiancé who is snatched from him by a Roman officer. He has given himself a place in history. Why? We all read books. I'm reading a novel, whenever I get some time, set in the States during the Depression. Why don't I have revelations about me as a sharecropper trying to feed a family of six on nothing? Or as a character based on any book I've read?" "But don't we do this all the time?" Shira asked. "Maybe we don't regurgitate it, as a first person narrative, but I'm certain we're affected by everything we read or hear or see. Particularly things that matter to us. We consciously internalize, at least what seems important. Or maybe it's involuntary. People talk about getting into a novel. It's not an empty phrase. At least while they are reading it, they are there. They are becoming part of the consciousness of the characters and vice versa. I teach literature. One of the reasons I do it is because I believe that literature changes people. It makes you see and sympathize with – or maybe hate – characters who are otherwise beyond your experience. And in time they become part of your experience, even though you are probably not aware of it. For whatever reason, my husband takes it a step further. He lives it internally and isn't just influenced by it, he recreates it like an artist repainting an old canvas. He makes it his."

Penina looked directly at her. "I want to hypnotize him. I don't know when. But at some point. I want to expose what is in his mind. I have to admit, I cannot tell you if there is anything potentially counter-productive in this. I do not believe there is. I can say that honestly. But I am very concerned that if we don't get this material out in the open, as it were, it may have some harmful effect on him later." "But why not wait until he is completely well? You can use hypnosis any time." "I'm sure Prof. Bondman has told you that we still don't know how physically and mentally well he will be. For my own part, I recognize the uniqueness of these revelations. They are here now, available. On tap. I cannot be sure they will remain so. It may be that when he recovers, they will sink like submerged rocks in his unconscious mind. They may trouble him in ways we cannot now fathom. It's the interchange between the conscious and subconscious mind that concerns me and I sense – that's as strong as I can put it – that it will be more difficult to use hypnosis once he has passed the stage of speaking spontaneously. There is no doubt he is suffering now because of these dreams, memories, fantasies, or whatever they are. It's like telling ghost stories in a haunted house. Let's lance the boil." "And you want my permission for this, is that what you're getting at?" Penina nodded. "What does Prof. Bondman say?" "I haven't asked." "Why?" "He would say no." "So it's up to me," Shira said more to herself than Penina. Penina said nothing. Shira looked through the window into the night time blackness, where things seemed clearer. She could see Penina reflected in the glass, coffee cup in hand. She spoke to Penina's reflection. "Is there a single overwhelming reason why you want to do this?" she asked. The reflection remained still, for a few seconds. Then she heard Penina's voice behind her. "Because it's great stuff." Shira smiled at her frankness. Penina's eyes waited for an answer. "It is great stuff. Let's have more of it." Penina exhaled deeply and handed her a sheet of paper. "This gives me your permission. Would you like to sign?" "If what you plan to do became known wouldn't you be in trouble, whether you have my signature or not?" "I would probably lose my job." Shira placed the page on the sandwich machine glass cover and signed. Penina left immediately.

She fed the six-digit code into the Hyundai's computer. The numbers were, by some barely credible coincidence, the date of her brother's death. Often she did so automatically, without thought. But tonight, tapping them out, reminded her of lighting memorial candles. Her forefinger hovered over the code buttons, as she took her time, as she visualized memories. She always, if fleetingly, commemorated his life, consciously or unconsciously, each time she unlocked the code. The date of his death was the key to her life. She turned the ignition on and drove toward the night exit, but fifty meters short, turned back and parked near a row of ambulances, donated by Jewish families from all over the world to commemorate lost loved ones. It was by now very late, but she had an irresistible urge to see Yuri, – alone.

***

As she entered the almost deserted ward, Penina noticed an ultra-orthodox man, dressed entirely in black, save for a white shirt and mandatory white tassels hanging from his waist, sleeping across two chairs. When she reached the Colonel's cubicle, she was greeted by Shira's large slim feet, this time shod in pretty black sling-backs. She peeled back the curtain of the cubicle, far enough to insert her head. Yuri's wife, now wearing a mauve shawl across her shoulders, was reading a poem to her husband. She must have gone home, changed and come back, since their meeting. Without looking up, Shira signaled to Penina to come in, nodding towards the chair opposite, and, without stopping to greet her, began a new poem. It was one of the shortest, by Amichai Yehuda, that likened the mental act of forgetting someone, to forgetting to turn off a light. "The light left on makes you remember the person whose light was turned off in your memory," Penina pitched in, with an imperfect quote. Yuri's wife smiled and stretched out a long, fleshless arm. Penina shook hands, but felt their handshake above the inert body of the Colonel, inappropriate. It made her uneasy. "You like poetry?" Yuri's wife asked. "It's the quickest way to what I feel, when I have time, which isn't often," Penina answered. "The one you were reciting, always got to me. Like so many of his poems, I think it is important, but I can't tell why. He's subversive. Like a mole." "He's Yuri's favorite. Among the Israeli poets." "Look. I'm sorry, I shouldn't disturb you." "You're not. Time's up, anyway. It's his brother's turn now. He'll stay with him until morning." "I didn't know he had a brother. You're the only next of kin we were told about." "Well, for better or worse, he has. And he's very much here. They haven't spoken for years, but he has suddenly materialized and wants to do his brotherly bit. We just don't get along. In fact I can't stand him." "He's not the ultra Orthodox man I saw when I came in, is he?" "You've got him in one. He also wants to read and talk to his brother, but what he reads and talks about and what I read and talk about come from different galaxies." "So you've arranged to take turns? Is it going to work?" "I've a heavy week teaching, next week so I couldn't spend every night here anyways. Maybe it's just as well that he keeps the ball rolling, at least when I can't come. Whatever he reads doesn't matter as long as Yuri's mind is stimulated – if that's possible." Yuri's brother's outline formed a silhouette on the white curtain. "I'd better go," said the Colonel's wife. "He won't look at me anyway. According to his scruples, I'm immodestly dressed. Carnal thoughts could be aroused if he sees more than my wrist or ankles. It makes me feel like taking my top off. With that, I'll be off. I haven't slept for forty eight hours. I came just as I was, straight from the hotel pool. In Australia, I mean. When I got the news, the next flight was leaving in two hours. I just made it." So, I was right, Penina thought. "Good night, Mrs Pozner." "Oh shit – I haven't introduced myself. My name's Shira." "Nice meeting you, Shira. If there's anything you need or want to know." "I know I can rely on you, Penina. I sense it. Be well." Penina was pleased she had made a good impression on Yuri's wife – and that she had been right about her. She liked strong women. They had less need to bullshit.

***

Shira had hardly gone when Yuri's brother took her place. He placed several heavy books and some thin pamphlets on the bedside table and looked at Penina as if wanting an explanation for her presence. "I'm Penina. Psychologist." "And what do you think?" he came back immediately, "Is it possible to reach him?" "I don't know. No-one does." "Unless the angel of death takes him, he is still in this world. And that means we can reach him, God willing." "I cannot deal with that argument. I am not religious." "Were you ever?" Penina would have been annoyed by his directness had his voice betrayed hostility. But both his voice and eyes showed sympathetic interest. His hands hung loosely at his sides, his head tilted sideways, waiting for an answer. For some reason that he knew best, the answer mattered. "I suppose I was once. As a child." "But now you have put away childish things? You face the world with adult bravery and no faith." He grinned as if he had made a joke. "You could put it like that," she said, seriously, but hoping to avert a discussion. "Interesting," he said, continuing to speak, as he sorted through his little library. "I thought I would read him some psalms. King David also faced the valley of the shadow of death. I am sure the twenty third Psalm will help him focus. Then there are the poems of the great Sephardi poets, not to mention the great selichot or penitential hymns."

Penina could not imagine that vivid cries of pain and vengeance by medieval Jewish scholars in response to brutal persecution, could be much help to anyone. He guessed her thoughts. "Selichot especially," he said, pulling out a thick blue volume with gold titling. "He is in darkness, where our people have been so many times throughout history. Don't you think that their tribulations are more meaningful to him than the chirpings of some modern songstress, like Naomi Shemer, or whoever?" "You do Naomi Shemer an injustice. Her songs are not only beautiful. They are for the mind as well as the heart. And almost all of them have a basis in Hebrew Bible or Talmud." "I am glad to hear it. I didn't know. But if that is a fact, is the best setting for them the concert hall or the club with its flashing lights and pagan dancing?" "It doesn't have to be done like that, but if it is, is it a sin?" "Things may not be sinful in themselves, but lead to sin. Why encourage them?" "Why, indeed. But I would need a better definition of sin than I've ever heard of, to make me change my mind." "Sin is doing what God has forbidden and not doing what he has commanded. Simple" "And throw in a few commentaries, no doubt," she replied, venting sarcasm. "A woman does not need to bother too much with commentaries," he said, more to himself than to her. He sat down and leafed through a diminutive book of Psalms. "I really should begin," he said with an inflected apology. "I have to drive back to Galili tonight." "I've been ready for bed for the last three hours," she replied, "I'm more than happy to go." As she left the cubicle, he began to move his body from the waist, rhythmically, to and fro, in time to the beat of the twenty third Psalm: "Even while I walk in the shadow of the valley of death, I do not fear evil," he was chanting. Long after she left the hospital, she could still hear those words. She knew many people who had lived them. Now, she was one.

***

We are waiting along the portside of Sebaste, Caesarea's port, best harbor of the eastern seabord. Another of Herod's creations. The rising sun has been beating down on our backs for two hours. No-one can guess what caused the delay, unless it is deliberate. The Roman has a secret fear – insurrection. He has conquered the world, yet he fears insurrection as a king with many concubines fears infidelity or as a barefoot child fears the scorpion. And he fears death. He is ready to die, but fears the consequences. He has no faith in the hereafter. He protects himself with armor and discipline and uses technology to kill without being killed. He wants to live for ever and knowing he can't, he kills without mercy, as if the death of ten massacred men will somehow make up for his own miserable demise. It is a powerful internal enemy that imperial man faces – the fear of being overthrown and the fear of death. All his achievements pale. I know the Roman. He has a civilization whose working parts coordinate like the rhythm of the heavens, from army to government, from art to commerce, from law to religion. But it has no soul as it has no heart. It's the price empire pays for success. The Roman laughs at the invisible God of the Jews. For him everything must be seen or felt, even his so-called mysteries are functions of the senses. There is nothing higher than the emperor, no command more compelling than an imperial edict. Compare him to the man of faith who believes God rules the universe. The man with whom God forged a covenant which gives him roots and ensures him a future. The man for whom defeat is victory and victory the fruits of defeat. He wants no more than to live under his date palm and does not fear death. The man who believes that all is in the hands of God, not those of the emperor's. We, who are that man, and thereby cannot be finally defeated, unless it be by God himself. No emperor, no army, no hatred, can utterly destroy us.

At last a centurion shouts at us to stand. Harnessed neck to neck with ropes, we rise slowly. At an order, we shuffle forward and begin to board the ship two by two, along the narrow gangway built for one at a time. Port workers and sailors cease work and gather in small groups to watch us make the precipitous passage onto the ship as it tilts and sways in the choppy water. After a few minutes, the incident they are waiting for, occurs. An older man loses his balance and falls, dragging the youth immediately beside him into the water. The tension of the ropes around the necks of those near them tightens unbearably, forcing them to fight desperately with their hands to keep the ropes a few millimeters from their throats. Then they do the only thing they can, to save themselves – they heave on the rope to pull the two fallen men back onto the gangplank. The fallen men scream an unearthly, high-pitched scream like demons in a chasm. Their legs work as if running a race, kicking the air. The port workers laugh raucously at the sight, but I notice the Phoenician sailors do not. They solemnly return to their work, making the ship ready to sail. Death is a bad omen before a voyage. A Roman soldier cuts the men loose and kicks the twitching carcasses into the swirling water. "You'll have an excellent catch of fat mullet round here in a day or two," he calls to the port workers, who do not all laugh, but glance at each other nervously. Neptunus, God of the Mediterranean, will be offended. For him only death by sacrifice or punishment is acceptable. The taking of life un-necessarily is a heinous offense.

We are at sea, huddled on the deck, tyed by neck and ankle. The waves have a rhythm few of us know. We are ill at ease. Some have thrown up, over themselves, for we cannot move. We keep our eyes on the heaving deck, not daring to raise our heads to watch the disappearing coastline as the ship rolls to starboard. The ship pulled away in a westerly direction from the shore but is now righting itself to take a northerly course parallel with the coast, heading for Tyre.

I raise my eyes to see the land I may never see again. I do not know what I expected, but the first thing I see, dominating all else is the huge temple in honor of Augustus Caesar on the top of a hill overlooking the port and city of Caesarea. The Romans had been involved in Judea, Samaria and Galili for nearly two hundred years but I never realized until now how severely we had been conquered. We did not lose the war at Beitar just weeks ago, we lost it over many years, with every new statue to a pagan god, every new temple and palace, every new amphitheater. Our casualties were not just the many killed in battle but those who were won over to Roman ways – my own family had too great a share of them. Anyone arriving at the port of Caesarea would think he was visiting a heathen country. We are now passing Dor, a huge pagan city a few miles north of Caesarea. I have been there several times to strike a deal for my father in one of the many wineries facing the sea, while Greek merchants haggle around me. I can see a synagogue near the shore, where the Jewish settlement is. A Jewish settlement in a pagan city, in what was once a Jewish land.

"I raise my eyes to the Carmel hills running parallel with the sea. The hills, where the Prophet Elijah hid from the soldiers of the apostate Jewish King, Ahab. They dance in the shimmering sun, curving and thrusting north and south, their forests spreading luxuriantly, the further away we get from the cities of Dor and Caesarea, which eat trees like locusts. I keep my eye on them, as I make a vow. "If I forget you, O Zion, may my right hand lose its skill." It is the pledge the Jews made when they were exiled to Babylon. Only after seventy years did they return to begin the restoration of the Temple. May I live to see the day repeated! And if not I, then my sons. And if not them, my son's sons. Or my son's sons' sons. I cannot take my eyes from those hills. They rise high above the sea and dwarf the foreign cities of the seashore. Cities come and go and statues of this god or that will crumble on their high promontories, but hills remain forever and they know their Maker.

"The sailors say the journey should be calm, but I notice how tense they are as they glance nervously from sea to sky. The death of the two men before we set sail, casts its shadow. We pass Tyre where most of the crew come from. The waters begin to stir. And the ship changes its rhythm like a dancer as the drums pick up the pace. It's beginning to roll on its axis. Never sell a god short, they say, if you want a peaceful life and Neptunus is second only to Jupiter himself in authority and fury. My last-remaining brother, Matityahu, who sits just behind me, presses his lips to my ear. "The crew are up to something. What do you think?" I look towards the prow where the crew has gathered. They are performing some ritual. A Roman augur stands near them, on hand if needed. The captain seems to be asking his advice. Three men detach themselves from the others and walk past us at a brisk pace. They are grim-faced. They walk purposefully along the bucking deck, broad feet spread wide. One of them carries a knife. Cold fear, running faster than thought, freezes my spine. From the stern, a scream pierces through every other sound. I hear it above the roar of the storm-driven sea, and the terrible creaking of ship's timbers, stretched to the limit. I hear another sound like galloping horsemen. The prisoners are hammering their heels on the deck in protest at the outrage that has taken place. I guess what has happened. I pound my heels like a maniac until they are cut. The sailors return. The hand of the sailor who holds the knife is crimson with blood. The next sailor carries a small piece of bleeding flesh in his cupped hands. Blood trickles through his fingers and leaves a trail across the deck. He hands the flesh to the captain who places it in a blue bowl and hands it to the augur. He, in turn, throws his head back in invocation, and tips the contents into the sea while those around him throw garlands of flowers and fruits. They rush to the rail to watch the sea swallow their sacrifice – a man's gall bladder which tastes of the sea. Neptune's tastiest tidbit. Many of us recite the twenty-third psalm. I do not know who has been killed to appease a pagan god's ghoulish appetite. And such gods, who do not even exist, rule the world? Where is the true God who made this sea, and all the lands around it and the heavens above? Why is he silent? I hear running feet and a squad of legionnaires spring onto the deck from below. They move up and down our lines screaming at us to be quiet, trying to subdue our rage, beating indiscriminately on the soles of our feet with wooden staves. But we are beyond control. We do not stop until our heels are too numb and bloody to hammer out our protest

any longer. A message is passed from mouth to mouth to pray for the soul of Reb Zecharia ben Yochai. I am shaken that he was their victim. I glance at Matityahu. His face is etched in despair. One of my earliest boyhood memories is of Reb Zecharia, leading prayers at the synagogue by the lake in the town of Capernaum, standing between two pillars, a Samson of the spirit in his white shroud, contrasted against the storm gathering above the distant hills. A premonition perhaps of the storm by which he was finally taken.

After half an hour the sea begins to calm. The Phoenician sailors look at us from the corners of their eyes with triumphant disdain. Why did God calm the sea knowing that it would reinforce them in their false beliefs? Why did he not create a huge storm and break the back of this vile craft and send us all to the bottom? Can there be a purpose in sending us as slaves to Rome?

As the storm abates, we feel empty, as if our internal organs have been eviscerated. We are beyond emotion, in a world that has been stood on its head, where meaning is rarer than fine gold, where man rules and man is mad. I do not need to look at my companions to know what they feel. We wait unthinkingly. And yet there are those among us who pray. Perhaps the future depends on them. Or perhaps the past. I dream of Tamar. Her face a mosaic floats below the blue sea. She knows I am looking at her. She opens far-seeing eyes and looks past me. I strain to see what she sees. Is it what time and distance will do to us? Yes, she is divining the future. Her mouth remains silent, her eyes resigned. A cloud comes to rest above me, severing the light from her reflection.

***

First light entered her room like a thief. Penina had forgotten to lower the shutters. She awoke exhausted, as if she had run a long distance. She had dreamt practically non-stop. But of what? She swung her legs out of the bed and, reaching for pen and pad, perched on its edge and poised to capture whatever scraps of memory she could recall, that had not moved on, like clouds driven by a brisk wind. Slowly, she realized that she had dreamt nothing of substance. She had been in the presence of some terrifying being which she could not identify. "Threat personified," she wrote, then scratched it out.

Whatever it was, had been invisible. Yet it was so powerful, it was as if she had seen it. Sitting, poised to write, she realized with a shock that she had seen nothing. She wrote the date, followed by: dreamt most of the night. Classical case of angst.

***

As a child she was taught never to let a dream pass without searching for its meaning. Whenever she ran to her parents' bedroom in tears over something she had dreamt, her mother would hold her tight and together they would find a meaning. Her mother would call in one of Penina's sisters to make up, with her father, the necessary threesome to annul the dream's negativity. "May the Merciful One change your bad dream into a good dream, as the dream of Balaam against the Jewish people was changed from a curse to a blessing." Her mother often quoted the first century rabbi, Hayesdai, who said that a dream not explained was like a letter unread. Penina's later studies in psychology supported the rabbi's dictum. Several colleagues had become dream specialists. It was an unsung province of psychology, but those who chose it, believed they had found the lost chord. In recent years she had accumulated a number of dreams which remained in her memory "unread," because she could not devote the time to interpret them. One day she would. She always remembered the details. But on this occasion, as she sat down to a breakfast of two cups of strong filter coffee, she felt compelled to draw whatever meaning she could from the shreds of overnight memory. The threat she had experienced was the threat of the little boy on the Polish border, she decided. She was living his fear.

The dream left her with a frisson of unease. She had tried to open the "letter" but too little of it could be understood. How could she, on whichever level of consciousness, feel the fear of that boy, as if it was her own? She had often confronted the demons of her patients' unconscious, but meeting her own, head on over breakfast, was like drinking iced water on a cold day.

***

For most of the time Yuri's eyes were closed. According to medical science, he thought nothing, remembered nothing, understood nothing and felt nothing. Occasionally his eyelashes flickered and although no-one knew why, it was taken as a sign of hope by those who loved him. The question throughout this period was whether he would ever come out of his present medical no-man's land. The options were, that he would die, survive, or descend into full coma. If the last, it would start all over again: would he die or survive? If he was to survive, powerful question-marks would remain. Would he make sufficient restitution of his physical and mental powers that could justifiably be called normalcy? Or would he be left in a state of helplessness? Or would he be reborn as a changed person? The chances were overwhelmingly against survival. A patient does not normally come out of this condition alive, and if he does, normality may remain light years away, if at all attainable. There is not much medical science can do for you. Modern medicine can sustain you while life and death debate your future. No-one knows if you will remain in that untouchable state for a month, a year or for the rest of a life – hardly 'your' life' – before being terminated by the grace of nature or the hand of man. It is a time when will or determination have no voice. If you recover, people say it is a miracle. If you do not, they console themselves with the thought that nothing could have been done. Fifty years ago coma was a death warrant – as it had been throughout history. Only fictional characters like Rip van Winkle escaped the draconian edict. Today, in hospitals all over the world, with the appropriate technology, aprons of opportunity are extended to thousands of individuals who are sometimes left for years, inarticulate, in limbo, awaiting a verdict based on unknown laws.

***

For much of each night and part of each day, he was attended by Shira, his wife and his brother, Akiva. They came bearing tapes and books and the conviction that their presence was effective. When they spoke or read aloud, they refused to believe they might be speaking to jelly. And when they played music, be it sacred or profane, they sensed that something stirred. Although they had begun in mutual dislike and ideological distance, the act of working for a common purpose brought them somehow together, if handicapped by mutual reluctance. They shared the same faith. Not religious faith, but faith in Yuri. He was not a cabbage. He would survive the coma and get well. That was their common credo. They abandoned their rigid schedule of dividing the time they were with him and began to overlap, taking some interest in each other's activities. Shira spent her time preparing her lectures, while Akiva read, or talked to her. At first they only heard each other, but after a while, they listened. Akiva, dressed in black, morning or night, sprawled in a chair, his tie loosened around his neck, long legs crossed at the ankles, turning his ear towards her like a radio-telescope capturing sounds from another planet, while his eyes watched the wall. In fact, he was familiar with much of what she read, at least the Russian part of it. Having lived the first twenty five years of his life in various parts of the Russian Federation, he had a good hold on Russian literature, art and music. So when she read a poem by Pushkin or Akhmatova, a passage from Tolstoy or Lermontov or a speech from Chekov or Bulgakov, he either knew it, sometimes by heart, or felt as if he had received a message from a long-forgotten acquaintance. He listened only briefly. To do more would be taking time away from his exploration of the treasuries of Jewish faith. He would thank her and open a heavy tome of the Talmud, which he cradled, like a child, on his knees and read to himself the central black text, constantly referring to the columns of commentary and notes, surrounding it on three sides. If he did not spend ten hours on studying the word of God and its interpreters, it was as if the day had gone up in flames. He was never without a book of Psalms stuffed into his pocket. When he drove, he listened to tapes of Talmud commentary, or one of the mystical treatises, or a sermon on ethics, or, if he was afraid of momentarily falling asleep, to liturgical music, or, if he was afraid of passing out, to klezmer. Occasionally, he brought his twelve-year-old son, but he would not let the boy listen to anything Shira recited, nor listen to the secular music she played. Father and son would sit in the corridor, the boy reading to his father from Rebbenu Jonah's commentary on "The Ethics of the Fathers," which he knew almost by heart, waiting for her to finish. Shira noticed that the boy never looked at her and kept his eyes down for those brief seconds, whenever she said something to him, and only replied if his father signalled to him to do so.

When it was Akiva's turn, he began with Talmud, the multi-volume exposition on the Hebrew bible. He read it in communion with thousands of Orthodox Jews all over the world, a page a day in a cycle that takes seven years. On commuter trains in and out of New York and many other cities, alone or in groups, in high tech offices and on park benches, in London and Paris and Moscow, in synagogues and colleges, in hundreds of small towns and villages across Israel, in Mumbai and San Paolo and Buenos Aires and Alaska, in Singapore and the Hague, Johannesburg and Berlin, in offices, in apartment blocks, in aircraft, on liners or at home, as well as in thousands of yeshivas, they pore over the vibrant, dusty meaning of the same page of text. At the end of seven years, huge and small celebrations are held to mark the event worldwide. At the last summation, 80,000 gathered at a stadium in New York to read the last paragraphs in unison. Similar celebrations were held all over the world. Shira had been taught at school that Talmud was an historical phase in Jewish thought, not applicable nor binding today. The door which opened into the world in which Akiva lived, was closed to her. Whatever lay beyond it, held no attraction for her, neither as a secular woman, nor a professional intellectual. Everything in her upbringing and education pointed elsewhere. The mutual tolerance she shared with Akiva, was based on common purpose, common sharing. Both had to constantly rein in their prejudices, as one might rein in a troublesome horse. Their relationship came to its lowest point when they contemplated each other's children. Shira practically mourned that the spirited little boy, who was Akiva's son, was being brought up in what seemed to her, a religious deep freeze. But Akiva despaired no less when Shira talked about her son by her first husband. It pained him to think of his lack of Jewish background, his ignorance of fundamental religious texts, his disinterest in any religious obligation, his disavowal of any emotional links with Jewish history. He saw the young man who was about to be commissioned as an air force pilot, as a victim, rather than a beneficiary, of secular education in which religion, in so far as it was taught, was merely another form of knowledge which you were either good at or not, and which laid no greater claim on your identity than algebra. Akiva assembled this hollow composite from Shira's remarks about her son, of whom she was inordinately proud.

Shira herself could not help liking Akiva's boy who physically resembled her own. She detected a physicality about him that made her want to liberate him, to turn him loose on a beach, to get him to run through the Megiddo forest, to rappel in the Judean hills, to hike through the mountains of Moav. What would her late husband have done with the lad! He'd have taught him to surf by the beach at Ashkelon, to ride a horse from one end of Galili to the other, before dropping down to the sea at Acco, to sleep in a tent in the desert and, when he was older, to become proficient in krav maga, Israeli karate. She knew that some of these things had not been absent from the life of his father. When she and Yuri were married, Stas, as Akiva was then called, had attended the wedding. He had not found religion yet, but said he was thinking about it. No-one believed him. She remembered the tall, eye-catching young man. Stas was lithe with piercing eyes that embarrassed women, who felt he was undressing them where they stood. Shira had never had a problem about eye contact with men, but she could only exchange the briefest of looks with Stas. She felt discomfort with his steady, piercing gaze that took in too much. She felt it inappropriate that her brother-in-law should look at her in that way. He danced all the dances from Israeli folk to American rock and Latin-American spice, and was proficient at them. After dancing with several women, he concentrated his seductive talent openly on a distant cousin of Shira's, with whom he disappeared before the event ended. Since then, she had seen him twice: at the funeral of the brothers' father and at the circumcision of Akiva's first son. He had converted the previous year to Judaism and taken on the name Akiva, the second century sage, who, like him, had become religious as a mature man – and subsequently became one of the greatest scholars in the rabbinic pantheon. It was the boy whose circumcision she had witnessed, who now accompanied his father, perhaps once a week, to pray for and sing to his severely wounded uncle.

Shira was responsible for the final split between the brothers. She hated the way their contact affected her husband. Akiva had been his

confidante and adviser, who held a treasury of memories of life in
Russia, particularly of their mother, who had been drowned in the
Black Sea when Yuri was eleven. The contact always upset Yuri. He was
a resilient person, but five minutes on the phone with Akiva, worse
still meeting him, undermined his self-confidence. Yuri was the most
positive man she had ever met, apart from her first husband. She hated
to see him enmeshed in a tangle of doubt and black nostalgia. It was
less what Akiva said than what he did not say. He was at a stage in his
life in which he was making great efforts to forget his secular past and
the thinking that invested it. Whatever he remembered, he covered
with a negative, often destructive sheen. He was killing the person Yuri
needed most. He refused to talk about their mother, or her death, about
his time in the Russian army, about their father's work or the decision-
making process that brought the family to Israel. His past belonged
to another person whom he was in the process of burying. It was a
long, silent funeral, without oration. Increasingly, all he was willing to
talk about was religion, which was hardly Yuri's most pressing need.
He had an opposite need. To remember, to make sense of tumultuous
years both in his family's history and the society around them. While
Akiva aimed to forget, Yuri strove to remember. Akiva's past was like
a self-amputated leg. Yuri's memories were too fragile to cohere. They
were pictures without captions. He needed an expert witness to sort
them out. It was a need that grew, the older he became. The deepest
sorrow was not knowing the exact circumstances of his mother's death.
On this, Akiva was cruelly silent, giving a distinct impression that
he knew more than he told. Contact between the two brothers was
particularly worrying for Shira when it occurred before an important
mission, for which Yuri had to be in maximal form. He would dream
of dark landscapes which the sun never reached, where stars never
rose. He wandered aimlessly in them, unable to reach his destination,
often not knowing what it was – the very opposite of what would be
required of him during the forthcoming mission. The following day he
would be disoriented. Shira was alarmed to see him reduced to a lesser
man. She knew that something relating to his mother's death haunted
him. It was the one subject he never discussed, except with Stas/
Akiva who answered in short bursts of evasion. These attempts upset
Yuri to the point that Shira forbade Akiva to make contact except in

an emergency. This Akiva adhered to in his own idiosyncratic way, ringing his brother before each Day of Atonement to ask customary forgiveness for anything he may have done, wittingly or unwittingly, to his detriment during the previous year. The conversation usually led to a stand-off in which both brothers forgave each other formally, without touching on the main cause of Yuri's hurt. Shira took this as another illustration of the hypocrisy of religious practice in which, it seemed to her, one went through the formalities of forgiveness, ignoring divisive matters which were never called into judgement. It was hurtful for Akiva too. Mastering his past, by way of forgetting it, was a consummate exercise in control which left his brother in the cold.

And here she was, consorting with Akiva three or four times a week, at her husband's bedside. One evening she got to the hospital a little early. Akiva and his boy were about to go. She watched the boy energetically stuffing books into his backpack. She had an almost uncontrollable desire to tell him to go out and play, kick a ball about for a bit. Akiva looked at her head on. His eyes had the old gleam, now framed by a graying beard and side curls and a large black hat. But they bore into her as they used to, not through her clothing this time, but through her mind. "I take him skiing you know," he said as if reading her thoughts. "He's quite good." She felt mentally naked. Akiva could tell what she was thinking. She remembered Yuri telling her that his mother, who was a fantastic skier, had taught the art to both boys. But Stas/Akiva was the star. Like his mother, he was a natural. Yuri was too young to achieve anything but promise. Stas took to his first skis like a new pair of shoes. She remembered Yuri telling her that his brother had been an officer in a sniper battalion attached to a mountain artillery regiment when the Russians were fighting in Chechnya. According to Yuri, his brother was also a great shot. Again, his mother was responsible. She loved to hunt, and being a good shot was her way of recognizing animal rights. One had the right to kill them, she believed, but only if done cleanly. To put a single killing shot into boar or deer or mountain goat or even a bison – which might take two – was acceptable, but needing several shots to put the beast away, or causing the unfortunate animal to slink off, wounded, and die in pain, was not. It was the first moral lesson the boys were taught and one memory that Akiva did not choose to conceal. He wondered if concern for the way an animal died which he learnt then, had funneled his interest into concern for animal rights that the Talmud propagated. He loved studying those passages and their commentaries. As a boy, he progressed well enough to be sent, every year, to a Young Communist skiing camp. When he reached the age of military service, he and most of his former campmates were posted to mountain infantry regiments. Not being academic, he did not go to university – which was the golden ticket to avoid the military. But he was eager to do his service. The army quickly discovered that he was also an excellent shot. He was sent on a sniper course and turned up at base-camp on the Russian-Chechen border with one bar on his shoulder, despite not being a graduate. By the end of a bloody campaign, he had added two more, boasted fifteen known kills in his record book, plus a bunch of maybes. Shira turned her eyes on the boy.

"And do you do any other sports?" "No," he said, studying his shoes. For once his father did not direct the boy's responses. Suddenly, the boy added. "Because it would take me away from my Torah studies." He said it as if he was reciting a well-rehearsed line that usually earned approval. "And what's your name? I keep meaning to ask and each time I forget." "Hillel Shmulik Hayim." "Well, Hillel Shmulik Hayim, keep ski-ing," she said. She caught Akiva's eyes for a moment. He had taken her remark in the right spirit. He was smiling. And did she detect for just a split second that old, penetrating look directed not at her mind, but her body? As father and son were leaving, Akiva said he wanted to bring his family to spend the Sabbath by his brother's bedside. The inference was that she should not come that day. "Oh that's fine with me. I was going to come but I don't want to impose. I think what I'll do is spend Friday here, until you arrive." Akiva looked at her earnestly. "Could you be sure to leave before Shabbat starts, with plenty of time to get home?" "Yes, I suppose I could." It was some time after Akiva and son had gone that she realized that as an Orthodox Jew, Akiva could not be responsible for another Jew breaking the Sabbath, which she would have done by driving home after the Sabbath had begun. It did not matter whether she ordinarily kept Sabbath rules or regularly broke them. What mattered was that he must not bear responsibility for the breakage. She was wondering at the unlikely fact that she had just been talking to a Hasidic Jew who had once been a Russian Army sniper. She could not integrate both images in her mind. And Hillel Shmulik Hayim? He would have but one image. He might as well have been raised on a south sea island, as far as any mutual understanding was possible. She felt a rush of sorrow for them both.

***

On the Friday in question, Shira left her kibbutz early and reached the hospital in time to have breakfast with her husband. That meant eating two peaches and half a papaya she had picked that morning, while a nurse filled her husband's intravenous feed bottle. "I think they're giving you the usual, darling. You must be really sick of it. I'll try to get them to think up something else," she told his inert body. "You, my darling, who liked to eat in a different restaurant every night – how have the mighty fallen. Well, a whole bunch of new restaurants have opened in south Tel Aviv and Jaffa. You wouldn't believe what has been happening since you went AWOL. And long before, apparently. We really will have to take our second city more seriously, when you get well. We've always preferred to go somewhere quiet and just be, and so we let Tel Aviv escape. Do you know they are beginning to call it the Miami of the Mediterranean? Not just the Bubble, anymore. You'll love it. It's not just the port and a few malls and a market or two and the marina and a bunch of cheap eats. Suddenly, everyone wants food. Of every kind. Middle Eastern, Italian, Mexican, Moroccan, Indian, Yemeni, Ethiopian, Greek, European, you name it. You'd think they had only just discovered the stuff. A few colleagues insisted that I go out with them the other night. So they take me to this place and insist on us all having the same dish. So I went along with it. I couldn't tell what it was, but it was delicious. Do you know what it turned out to be? Yuri oh Yuri, it was bull testacles. I ask you, darling. Good to keep up your testosterone levels, the chef said. But what good is that to me? You'd love it. They also do fatoosh salad. And their schug is the hottest I've ever had. We toured all over. Everything you could think of in as many varieties as it's possible to dream up. Not to mention the Yemeni neighborhood which is eye catching as well as being yummy plus. One of the oldest parts of the city. Beautiful at night. Cobblestones outside and everything you've never heard of inside, including foot soup. Yes foot soup. They cook the soup with bones, mostly animal feet. That's how it gets its name. I'll be having it when we go. I don't know if you can choose which feet you want, but at least you can choose the soup. Vegan restaurants abound. Someone said that a British newspaper had dubbed TA the vegan capital of the world. It's supposed to have 400 vegan restaurants. And apparently some of them are gourmet vegan. One is run by refugees from Sudan, waiting to be expelled from the country by the day. Shameful. There's a pizzeria which was started by two brothers from Congo with fillings you couldn't imagine. As for the Thais, they're everywhere. Of course, there are so many Thai workers in the country, they have a population base to support them. And suddenly a batch of Chinese restaurants has opened up or is about to. The whole area is looking like a cross between Marrakesh, Saigon, and an African market. And Jaffa, of course. I heard a tour guide tell his flock that if you can catch it, you can cook it, and if you can cook it, you can eat it. They say that some native species of wildlife in Israel are endangered because there's no limitation on what the Thais will eat. It's the only argument I can think of, in favor of keeping kosher – since the majority of animals are forbidden, if you are religious, you don't endanger anything. Only cows and sheep and chicken. I may be a bad example. As you know, I eat anything they put on my plate. But even I draw the line at snake, iguana and heron. The first two because they are aesthetically repugnant, the last because it is aesthetically pleasing. I don't mind shark – they would eat me, so I don't mind eating them. I feel the same about piranha. I haven't made up my mind about crocodile. When you're through all this, we'll celebrate at a new fish restaurant a bit nearer home, in Mahanei Yehuda. Beautifully cooked, and such portions! You'd have to help me. I'd never cope. What you've got to do, darling, is keep fighting. That should be no problem for you. They say that a wounded mind is like a maze. What you've got to do, is find your way out. That should be no problem. Remember those exercises you were so good at in the army? They used to drop you off in the back of no-where, on a moonless night, and you had to make your way back to base without navigational aids. You always got back first.

Keep walking, my darling – don't let your mind fall asleep and you'll find the way home. And if you still want me, I'll be waiting."

***

Akiva Pozner and family arrived in a rush. Their car, which looked as old as the prayers they recited, battered by a multitude of minor accidents and overworked by Akiva's commuting between his Galili mountain retreat and Jerusalem, had finally given up its ghost on a one-in-eight gradient hill. It had to be towed away. They – Akiva, carrying a heavy satchel full of books and a huge hat box, his wife, Lavinia Shraga, who was visibly pregnant, loaded like a pack-animal with family necessities, and their six children, four boys and two girls, who each carried a backpack and a sleeping bag – had just about made it to Jerusalem by hitch-hiking and three buses. They had been joined by Shraga's sister and her husband and their three children, who lived in the city. They too were Hasidim, but devotees of a different sect. Shira was still in the cubicle, saying goodbye to Yuri when the family arrived in the ward in a long string, like hikers on an arduous jungle path, in various states of distress and rapture, the youngest sporting backpacks that dwarfed their small frames. They stood in a silent bunch outside the cubicle, as if waiting for a family photograph – children in front, Lavinia Shraga's sister and her husband next, Akiva and his wife, who were the tallest by far, behind them. The quintessential ultra-orthodox family. In fact, Shira did take a photograph in her mind's eye, which she never lost. Akiva's wife, who was usually called Shraga, but sometimes, Lavinia, and quite often both, was an attractive woman with a deep frowner's furrow on her brow. But her whole face gave way, from time to time, to a beatific smile and, more rarely, a quick laugh. She contrived to be constantly busy, even when there was no cause. She had no pretension and little self-consciousness. "Take me as I am," she seemed to say, "I've no time for special effects." Shira responded to her immediately. If Shraga did not have a thousand things to do all at once, getting her disparate family ready for the advent of Shabbat, Shira would have liked to talk to her. "Excuse us, we will all have to get showered and changed,"Akiva said to Shira. Then to his son: "Shmulik, read to your uncle. Then it will be your turn Yael," he said to the oldest girl. "You can shower later." "Can I sing to uncle?" Hillel asked. "Of course. But not too loud. There are other patients. I'm going for my shower. Be good. " "Are you going to sleep here?" Shira asked Shraga in disbelief, as she watched the kids unfurl their sleeping bags and align them on the floor. "Oh no. The children are just going to have a little lie-down. We've been traveling since five this morning. The children are staying with a brother-in-law of my sister's husband's. They're eating there and sleeping there. It's less than half-an-hour's walk away. But Akiva and I will stay here all night to be with his brother. You know, Shabbat is holy time. Nothing is the same on Shabbat. If you can reach out to another soul on a common weekday, how much easier on Shabbat! We have brought food and we'd gladly ask you to join us, but you wouldn't want to stay here all night and that would mean that you would have to travel on Shabbat. You must visit us in Galili. We live very simply, but we make up for what we can't provide in material comforts with comforts of the spirit. You're very welcome." Shira was intrigued by this woman who rapidly took charge of every situation and could, no doubt, take charge of the entire hospital. She noticed that Shraga's intelligent forehead, when creased, made her look prematurely middle-aged. But she was endowed with a long slim nose, a pronounced chin, and pretty high cheek bones, which lent her a superb profile. An idle thought crossed Shira's mind: this woman could model hats. When she asked Shira to stay with them for some future Shabbat, her face lit up like a Chanukah candelabrum with all eight candles ablaze. Shira said it was an interesting idea, if they could get their dates right. But it was the last thing she would ever agree to. Spending the Sabbath with a religious family was like surrendering to the enemy.

Standing at the foot of the bed, Hillel Shmulik Hayim began to sing. An old Hasidic song in Yiddish, its plaintive melody exaggerated by his unbroken voice. Akiva returned, wearing an ankle-length, silken, black caftan and white socks. He opened the hat box, took out a long silk sash which he tied firmly around his waist, then he removed a large circular fur hat and placed it carefully on his head. He had the height to carry its breadth. If he could have been transferred to a painting of a seventeenth century ducal court in Russia, he would not have struck a false note. A few moments later, his wife came back with her sister and the smaller children, who placed their sleeping bags under the bed and were asleep as soon as their heads touched the floor. Shraga was transformed. She wore a long white dress with gold edging, a loose, multi-colored embroidered waistcoat and a white turban around her head which was draped over her shoulder. Shira had never seen an orthodox woman dressed in this way. Her face wore a look of serenity as if it had never hosted a negative thought. "Will you be home in time for Shabbat?" Shraga asked with concern. "Oh where I'm going's not far," Shira answered evasively. She quickly said goodbye and found herself returning their greeting of "Shabbat shalom," which means Sabbath peace. It was a slip of the tongue. No-one on her kibbutz used the expression and when her religious students wished it on her, she would return the single-word everyday greeting, shalom, in order not to give credence to the notion that the Sabbath had any special properties. As she left, an Arab nurse was handing Shraga a key. "Room 707," she said, with what Shira thought was a complicit smile.

So Akiva Pozner and the others, especially Hillel Shmulik Hayim, watched her go with regret. In no way could they have let her stay "for a while," because that would mean, according to all forms of orthodoxy, that they would be condoning her desecration of the Sabbath by being responsible for her driving after it had come in, an activity which came under the heading of prohibited labor, as defined by the rabbis. There was no room in the Pozners' rule-bound celebration of the day to allow her to stay for as long as she wanted. It was highly unlikely, they all knew, that she would stay for the entire Sabbath. They preferred her to go before it started rather than risk avoidable desecration, both for her sake as much as for theirs. As a non-observant Jewess she was, in their eyes, still obligated to keep the law.

So Shira Pozner, with a first degree in Modern Israeli Literature, specializing in Arab and Jewish women writers, a second degree in the History of American Literature, and a doctorate in Parallels Between Modern Israeli and Arabic Literature; fluent in English, Arabic, German and Hebrew; with a good command of Russian; conversant – and in some areas expert – in world literature across two centuries; who had read almost all major novels by non-Jewish and Jewish writers on three continents; widely-traveled; having spent months tracing the oral traditions of the Pequot Indians in the north-eastern United

States and the Toraja animists of Indonesia; a woman in her thirties who had served in military intelligence and was a genuine example of a cosmopolitan intellectual, could, under no circumstances, have accepted an offer to spend Shabbat with a religious family. Their religious culture was unwelcome, their religious sensibilities unattractive, the more sincere they were, the worse it would be. She had turned her back on the one opportunity she ever had of experiencing the Sabbath in the Jewish mystical tradition. She left, not learning about the rituals which would be celebrated over the next twenty four hours, not knowing the meaning of the rich garments her prospective hosts had donned, not hearing the songs and their message in several musical traditions that had been handed down from mouth to mouth for hundreds of years, not tasting the food which, to Akiva's family, had a special taste, the taste of the Sabbath eve, not hearing their prayers, nor communing in the certainty that the Sabbath marked the completion of creation and that on it even God had rested. She left, unaware of the irony written in the details, that a people who had known vicious persecution and lived in an atmosphere of naked hatred for millennia, spent one day a week, amounting to one seventh of their lives, in celebration of the creation of the world (a tradition maintained by some, even in Auschwitz) and proclaiming the beneficence of God's deeds. She would wilfully deny herself the opportunity to discover, in Sabbath rest, the deep root of Jewish longevity, otherwise called survival. She missed the emotional cadences of the day and the mesmeric beauty which sanctified place and time and personhood. Yet, had she been invited to spend time on a Sioux reservation, she would have leapt at it in awe.

***

She drove to a café-restaurant in the city center. One or two of her friends were already there. More would come later. They agreed to share a bottle of merlot-shiraz, vintage of one of the new boutique wineries that were springing up all over Israel. When asked how things were going, Shira described how she visited Yuri as often as she could, but made no mention of Akiva. Her friends would freak out, had she told them that Yuri had a Hassidic brother. It was too much to explain. A longstanding acquaintance, who misrepresented herself as an old friend, ambushed her in the rest room. "What are you hoping for, if Yuri pulls through?" she asked. "That he will take you in his arms and say: let's forgive and forget and start over again?" It might have been on the edge of acceptability if Shira had been asked the question by someone really close. She was saved from having to find a truthful answer, by not knowing what the truth was. "All I see with clarity, is that I must do everything possible to get him through this," Shira replied. "The rest is light years ahead." "I don't think it can be that far. I really do think you should think about it," the woman said. Shira smiled like an accomplice, who shared the woman's subversive view, although she didn't. She asked herself why. "I am afraid," she told herself. "I am afraid who Yuri will be, when he recovers. If he is not the same, there can be no going back." The woman did not see Shira leave. She was completely absorbed in the execution of an audacious hair, protruding from her chin, by means of a pair of golden tweezers. "How are you bearing up?" Shira was asked by another acquaintance as she rejoined the others. "I'm good. Doing well. I think Yuri and I will take a long holiday when all this is over," she replied with an optimism she couldn't account for. "Where do you suppose?" "Anywhere. The furthest place." "You've got guts, Shira. You always had." "We all have to do our best. What else is there?" Shira effused, before contemplating the chasm that seemed to separate her feet. Another friend raised his glass. "L'Hayim," he said, "to life and the gutsiest woman I know." She grinned back at them all, but found the paradigmatic status she was being awarded, for gutsiness, too embarrassing, not to say ill-deserved. Shira responded, by holding her glass high and studying the scarlet liquid as if it contained a message, before sipping and saying, "Exceptional. Where's it from?" She read the label aloud. It was a product of the Negev, the southern desert. "It's amazing" said one of the party, "what you can get out of sand."

Around the same time, Akiva and his family were welcoming the Sabbath, in the hospital synagogue. The small square room was filled to overflowing with Hasidim in fur hats and scintillating silk gowns, Haredim in black suits and wide black fedoras, patients in wheelchairs, some of them pushing their own drip stands, doctors in white coats, volunteer staff, soldiers and officers in khaki, their belts hung with small arms, visitors in loose-necked shirts, slacks and knitted skullcaps, if they were Israelis, and tourists in whatever garb was considered appropriate for

Sabbath wear in their many countries of origin. Women who presented an even more colorful display, worshipped separately, separated by a net curtain. Each could tell at a glance the group affiliation, and marital status of her neighbors by the wigs and cloche hats, the knitted snoods and silk scarves and turbans, or the uncovered hair of unmarried women and girls. Skirts and dresses reached down to the ankle, blouses or dresses were buttoned high. Apart from faces and hands, there was not an inch of flesh to be seen among the ultra orthodox women. They sang full-throated hymns of praise to the Sabbath. "Come, my Beloved, let us welcome the Sabbath," as it had been sung universally by orthodox communities across the globe for five hundred years, since its conception in the mountain city of Tsfat in Galili. As the first words of the prayer welled up, Akiva, eyes closed, straining every fiber of his third soul, contemplated the Midrashic account of how God gave the Sabbath to the People of Israel as a bride. He waited emotionally, as he did each week, for the Sabbath to join him under an epiphanic wedding canopy, where they would spend the next twenty five hours. Shraga, unable to see her husband through the curtain of demarcation, yearned for the sweet moments when she would surrogate for the Sabbath bride in her husband's arms. Through the spiritual tumult, she picked out his voice and sang her part in a split duet.

***

Penina was the go-between, conveying messages whenever Shira or Akiva found that their schedule had changed and new visiting times needed to be negotiated. But she also passed on information to each of them. It seemed to her that Akiva had two brains. One was what was left of the secular brain he owned before he became religious, which could still understand most messages from the outside world. The other was his new brain, filled with meticulous religiosity which commanded every aspect of his life. She wondered what horizons his son would encounter, with only one brain and no legacy from the world outside. He was a darling little boy, good-natured, loving and obedient. But, she detected an element of rebelliousness. Penina had had a religious education, having been raised in a traditional Moroccan-Jewish household and environment. She had done the diametrical opposite to Akiva. She had been brought up with religion and custom as central pillars of her life. Like a female Samson, she toppled the pillars of the temple when she became secular but never denied the intrinsic value of her religious heritage. Akiva, on the other hand, had had virtually no religious education and had been raised in a methodically anti-religious environment. When he became religious, he walked through the gateway of the tablets of the Law, and closed it behind him. Although Akiva detected more curiosity than animosity from Penina and still understood the secular world, in which she lived, he was scrupulous only to share with her the religious component of his mind.

***

Of the vast amount of literary inspiration that Shira could have drawn from her knowledge of Hebrew, English, Russian, Arabic and German sources, there was one poem she repeatedly reread during her hospital visits. Shakespeare's seventy-third sonnet, told it all. She had doubts that Shakespeare's sonnet was appropriate and suspected herself of reading it for her own needs, rather than those of her husband. They had read it together once upon a time, in the kibbutz, seated on a bench in a clearing, surrounded by mauve and red and yellow bougainvillea. It was an autumnal ritual in the heyday of their marriage, celebrating the autumn of death. They read it as an antidote to happiness, as if they needed to pull back from the brink of beatitude, which they might inadvertently cross. And what then? They read it, as the trees' shed leaves fell in an intricate, unrehearsed dance, choreographed by a petty breeze. Watching, they wondered how death could know such beauty, and asked how beauty could know such death? The thought sprouted at the back of Shira's mind, that if Yuri was not to survive, the sonnet's images might give him ultimate comfort. Let him be a leaf fluttering into oblivion like those they had once watched. Her thoughts reflected her ambivalence: to do all for his recovery, yet prepare for his end. And so, on more than one occasion, she read for them both:

"That time of year thou mayest in me behold

When yellow leaves, or none, or few, do hang

Upon those boughs which shake against the cold.

Bare ruined choirs, where late the sweet birds sing.

In me thou see'st the twilight of such day

As after sunset fadeth in the west;

Which by and by black night doth take away,

Death's second self, that seal's up all in rest."

Whenever she read the poem, she stopped there, censoring the triumphant hopelessness of the sonnet's final lines. Clothed in pathos, they delivered the reader to death's door. She saved them to read, if ever she lost him, over his remains. The moment for which, the sonnet mourns, we are headed with every step since birth. Death was not only our individual, but man's universal inheritance. Since the first time she read it, as a young student, she had been acutely aware of the poem's collaborative surrender. To bow before the inevitable, was also consolation. It had its own nobility.

No longer were she and Yuri sitting on the bench of their choice, but in the valley of the shadow of death, as Psalms has it. Then, just seven overflowing years ago, they had looked at each other, after reading the poem, in the fullest acknowledgment of their mortality, the coming to the end of things, condoned by love. In those days, death faced him constantly. The sniper's bullet, the chance ricochet, the well-crafted booby trap, the suicide bomber's payload, the cement slab cast from a rooftop, the poisoned knife, the training accident, death by friendly fire. She kept returning in her mind to that first time they had read the poem together. She remembered how the sudden epiphany of the impermanence of things held them in sorrow's clasp, as if they were sitting in a cold mist that reached the bone. It was the opposite of those deliriously manic moments, dominated by the pantheistic urge, in which they felt as one with the world, united with eternity. They took each other in their arms and hugged like frightened children, this six foot fighter and this petite woman, suddenly tasting a cheerless tomorrow, which had the taste of blood. "When I was a kid," Yuri had said, on the way back to the wooden house, where they lived, "and my parents took me on a long journey by bus or train or horse and cart or a borrowed car, I never wanted to arrive – no matter where. I wanted to go on and on and never stop. The view from a bus window, or a cart bench, was everything. That's our life, isn't it? We fill our days looking out of the window and try to forget that one day the journey will stop." He stopped to kiss her, she recalled, a gesture more of protest than passion. After that, she stopped taking the pill. When she told him, he said that he had hoped she would.

But nothing came of their efforts to form a child, progeny, a biological heritage, a baton held out to the future. Shira fell pregnant after almost a year and lost the baby at seven months. Yuri had swerved their four-wheel drive to avoid a child on a brand new bicycle, who shot out of a side street straight into their path. They hit a pylon. It was Yom Kippur. She was saved from major injury by her seat belt, but the fetus was not. The incident marked the beginning of their decline. The seventy-third sonnet held them in a trivalent embrace.

She let the tears take their course. At some point they would have to stop, she told herself. When they did, she rummaged in her bag and pulled out her book of sonnets by Shakespeare. Turning to the seventy-third, she began to read the lines she had withheld. She had made no conscious decision to read them, and could not have explained why she did.

"In me thou see'st the glowing of such fire,

That on the ashes of his youth doth lie,

As the death-bed, whereon it must expire,

Consumed with that which it was nourished by.

This thou perceiv'st, which makes thy love more strong,

To love that well, which thou must leave ere long."

Shira closed the book, kissed her husband's cold, unwrinkled brow with cool cosmetic lips. She was ready for his death, if and when it came.

She gathered her belongings which weren't many, and went to get the car. She was still within the hospital grounds when she received a call from an aunt. Her father had had a stroke.

Chapter Three

As she drove back to the kibbutz, she hastily made two compartments in her mind, to stave off panic, like two files on a computer. Sanity demanded she keep them apart. One for her husband. One for her father. Oh and her son. She put him in a separate document, sacrosanct, where no viruses could touch him. She drove very fast, despite the fact that her mind was not on the road. Her natural optimism, which would normally be looking forward to her father's recovery and to her helping him through whatever convalescence he would undergo, was dissipated by unremitting hopelessness, as if another hand was simultaneously painting over a canvas she was working on. If thoughts about her father seeped through into the compartment she had assigned her husband or vice versa, it would burst the dam of self control. Far from helping her father through convalescence, she feared he was already dead and that she may have missed the opportunity to go over things. There was so much she did not understand, so much that had never been said. He had become a controversial figure in the kibbutz movement and in Israeli society. But she knew little more about his views and the scathing critique he had developed about his homeland than a few articles by him that she had read and the voluminous and acrimonious criticism which shamed his viewpoint. As a small girl, she felt she was peripheral to his life. Repeatedly, she tried to penetrate his shield, but her girlish attempts were shattered upon it. His focus was always elsewhere. He did not seem to see her. It made her feel invisible. Only to be noticed when she did something wrong. He was an ideologue of the kibbutz movement which he lambasted, then of the state of Israel which he deplored, and finally of the Jewish people from which he separated himself. His family often figured in his writings, in which he bemoaned the world that they would inherit. But they did not figure much in his life. As she grew older, Shira read articles and statements about her generation in which he fulminated against its trivial pursuits, its misused education, its loyalty to the wrong ideals, its political criminality in pursuit of the Zionist enterprise, in which she fervently believed, which led him inexorably to completely de-legitimate the country she loved. She never had a discussion with him about any of it. He was a brilliant speaker, a rhetorician of the old school who could express his views with passion, and painstakingly explain his cherished beliefs again and again to ears that listened until they could hear nothing else. He was incapable of discussion. To debate with him was like stepping into the ring. He usually won. He had no respect for contrary opinions which he invalidated, scorned or shredded. But whenever he made his own case, unwaveringly convinced of its faultlessness, Shira was not persuaded. It reminded her of those interminable dormitory arguments about the existence of God or otherwise, which the atheist frequently wins on points, but far from creating more atheists, only serve to reinforce the believers' obstinacy. What could anyone do to gainsay him when he worked on his arguments all day long and a great part of the night and knew in advance everything others might say. He entered a discussion as if he was playing chess. Nobody devoted himself more to his cause except, perhaps, a gifted yeshiva student of whom he considered himself the very antithesis. As the serious yeshiva student spent ten to fourteen hours a day analyzing the word of God, he spent as much analyzing the Zionist state. And each time he drove the blade of his discontent closer to the hilt with some new publication, lecture, article or letter to a radical left-wing journal. His latest prognostications were immediately discussed by an inner circle of believers. Shira remembered that he was always reading or writing or on the phone or embarking on tortured walks among the orange groves in which he held his ground with some imagined adversary in long, stormy debates within his head, which he often vocalized. The physical symptoms of his internal turmoil were readily seen in the way he gestured with his hands, or stood still to make some salient statement or shook his head like a mastiff or even shouted out words and sentences which only she and the unpicked crop could hear. She had followed him more than once, hiding behind the cascades of rich yellow fruit, tiptoeing between the trees, guessing which way he would turn next. It was the closest physical contact they had. And he was completely unaware of it. Had he discovered her, he would have sent her packing or ordered her to finish her Arabic homework. She always felt he had something he wanted to tell her, but never had time. She also felt that, despite their failed efforts at communication, he was the only person who understood her. All too often he seemed only to notice her (in the form of her generation) in his writings – and then critically – but what he said about youth of her day was basically correct, she agreed, if at some cost to her personal integrity.

As she approached the kibbutz, she slowed down. All other cars in her lane overtook, while she assembled her mind. When she felt she was as collected as she was likely to be, she sped up and took the peripheral road, ignoring its speed bumps, to the far side of the settlement facing the sea. The house, unlike the others roundabout, had lights on in every room bar one. It looked like three sides of a Chinese lantern. As she turned off the headlights and ignition, and locked the car with her electronic key, she felt as if she wasn't acting independently, that she was a puppet, doing whatever she was supposed to do, whatever that might be. An uncle, her mother's brother, was standing outside the house with his son, smoking. "Is that you Shira?" his voice called. "It's Roy, your uncle. I'm so sorry," he added, coming closer. "I know it's come at a particularly bad time for you. You can be proud of your father. I was just telling Grant here – you remember your cousin, don't you – that he was a man of principle par excellence. He took everything to its logical conclusion, come whatever." "Thank you Roy," she said, kissing his cheek and that of her cousin. "I didn't know that he had…" "Oh, my dear. I'm sorry it was me that told you. It should have been your mother or Limor." "It doesn't change anything, does it?" She squeezed his wrist, smiled weakly and entered the house, hoping that at any moment the director of the scene would call: "Cut!"

***

Her mother did not see her arrive. She was entering the kitchen as Shira came through the open front door. Shira did not call to her. Instead, she found her sister sitting in their father's easy chair by the window. They hugged and cried. "It's all over," said Limor. "What do you mean?" "I mean he's gone. How can someone who was hardly here leave such emptiness behind him?" "The less you leave behind, the more it hurts, because now there is no way of finding out." "Finding what out?" Limor wanted to know, her eyes narrowing. She had stopped crying. Shira wondered if she dare answer her sister's question, truthfully. "If he loved us. Things like that." "Of course he loved us. He certainly loved me. I can only speak for myself, Shira. Don't you think he did you?" "No. I don't." "I know what you mean, Shira. But that's on the surface. I mean deep down." "I'm talking about deep down. I don't think he loved anything or anyone. I think he enjoyed certain things. And we were among them. He could have fun with us. But rarely. The world posed a great a threat to him. He wanted to be in charge of it and he wasn't." "You're confusing his work with his life." "His work was his life." "Look, we both know he was not the average father, give or take a decimal point. He had a vision and he pursued it. He didn't have time for a lot of things." "Like us." "I always thought it was you he preferred. You could understand what he was trying to say." "That has nothing to do with love. It's the respect an alert student earns from a lecturer." "I always envied you. It was always you he talked to. Never me." Limor's tears welled up again, like a pot on the verge of boiling. "Granted. I was a sounding board for some of his ideas, sometimes," Shira replied defensively. "But he could have used a tree instead. In fact I've seen him do it." "Oh, Shira, you don't mean a tree! You know, you're in denial. I think it's so awful you don't see that he loved you. It wouldn't be human if he didn't." "Limor, my sister, my darling, you're so full of love. You inhale and exhale it. You don't need oxygen. You got from Daddy what you needed. You loved him so much, you thought he loved you back. But for me it was like squeezing an empty lemon. No juice. A few drops, maybe." Limor controlled her mounting pain. "Shira. I know you always have to put everything in order, to be able to understand it. You don't understand things that don't add up. You know you're like Daddy in so many ways. This is a case in point." "How so?" "I'll tell you how in a minute. First answer me one question: did you love him?" Limor's question was like a threatening disturbance somewhere down the street. Her huge blue eyes filled with premeditated tears, knowing in advance what her sister's answer, if honest, would be. A corner of Shira's mind was in turmoil. "I never thought about it," she eventually heard herself say. "Well, there you are. If you don't even know if you loved him, how can you be sure he didn't love you?" Shira was used to being the strong one. The impotence to which Limor's questioning reduced her, made her feel a foreigner to herself. "He was so difficult to love, was Daddy. I'm not you, Limor, I couldn't." Limor encircled her elder sister, as best she could, with her short arms. The two hugged for a long time, without tears. They were standing on stone. "And how am I like him?" Shira asked, breaking the hug. "You live by your mind, Shira. As he did." "I'd have said by the heart," Shira countered. "No Shira, the mind. I think your heart kept knocking at the door, but your mind wouldn't open. That's exactly what he did." "But if neither of us opened the door to our hearts, how can you say that I loved him and he me?" "Perhaps love was left waiting outside, like an orphan. Perhaps it was let in occasionally to warm its hands on the stove, I don't know. But it was there, in waiting. Definitely a part of the taximony." "Don't talk biology Limor, I'm not sure it covers the case." "There's nothing more serious than biology, Shira, it's about how we're made." "I was always surprised that you went for it. I expected you to do something arty," said Shira, welcoming an unexpected escape from the previous discussion. "When you were a kid, your drawings were so imaginative." "Well, I've come to the end of that road," Limor announced. "I'm about to switch, I'm going to do a course on counseling for kids." "That's a big move." "Not so big as you think. If you know your biology, you know your kids. Because they are little animals, I suppose." "But why do you want to do this? Does it pay better?" "Worse, I think, if that were possible." "So?" "Call me an idealist," Limor said, her eyes twinkling. "I think that knowledge, like any form of wealth, should be shared. If you have a lot of money, you must give to those who do not. And it's the same with knowledge. You mustn't just keep it to yourself. And if you find some poor guy, you don't give him a handout, you should try to get him to stand on his two feet and eventually take care of himself. That's what I want to do with kids who have problems, especially those who have no chance. Point them in the right direction – and give them the hardest push I can." "A true child of the kibbutz," said Shira smiling. "Well, I may not live on a kibbutz any more, but I try to live as if I did," Limor said, looking down, but her spirit was high. "I'm

proud of you, Limor. And Daddy would be too. His chair suits you."
"Oh there's so much chair and so little of me." They sat looking out of
the window. It was a moonless night. They could not see the sea. But
they heard it, rolling up the sand beach and back, with its impeccable
rhythm, the more pronounced in the surrounding silence.

"Shira! You're here!" The high pitch of her mother's voice would have
sounded accusing in any other context. This was the moment of the
evening Shira was dreading. She stood. Her mother was half-hidden
behind two large plates of food. "You could give me a hand with
these," her mother complained. "Some people have come a long way.
They have to be fed. Here, hand these round." She passed a plate of
knishes for Shira to serve while she dispensed salty beigels from the
other. Shira had a series of short, almost identical conversations about
her father as she passed among the guests. "What a great man he was."
"What an original thinker." "How tragic it was that his views were
taken seriously only outside Israel." "He should be required reading
for everyone." As she finished, she found herself facing her mother,
who had circled the room in the opposite direction. "Don't I get a
kiss?" her mother asked, as if she was interrogating her. The plates in
their hands prevented Shira from doing more than peck at her cheek.
She was relieved that a more intimate gesture was not possible. They
placed their plates, almost empty, on the table. Shira was embarrassed
as her hand began to tremble. "When did it happen?" she asked.
"This afternoon," her mother said. "Where did they take him?" "He's
not in hospital. He's still here." "Why?" asked Shira, incredulous.
"Your father never wanted to be a cabbage. We talked about it many
times. He begged me, that when the time came, to let him just go."
"How do you know he could not be revived? Didn't you get a doctor?"
Her mother was silent for a long time as if she was formulating a
reply. Then she moved to an unoccupied corner of the room. Shira
followed "No," she said finally. "Why not, mother?" "We all know
that a doctor would have sent him to hospital. You know what they
do there. They would have connected him to a battery of machines.
You wouldn't have known where he began and the machines ended."
A picture of Yuri, strapped to his bed, shot through a screen in Shira's
mind. "So what did you do?" "I sat with him until he went. We held

hands." "It sounds like something half way between euthanasia and an execution," Shira said sharply. "If that's what you want to think, think it! But I know what I did was what he wanted." She held her daughter's eyes defiantly. Hers were red with pain and crying. Shira faced this once beautiful woman, small against her former husband's height, a serial adulteress, whose looks had waned with the years and who now resembled someone who had been shipwrecked alone on a remote island. "Is he in his bedroom?" "No, his office." "His office!?"

Shira entered the place which, for as long as she could remember, had been an inviolable fortress. An eagle's nest where only the eagle landed. A bed had been placed below the window, the desk moved into a corner. It was a worn trestle table rather than a desk, of the kind one erects for barbecues. Nothing else was big enough to accommodate all of his ongoing projects. Otherwise, the room was as she remembered it. Full of books in five languages, overrun with cuttings from magazines and newspapers, piled high with videos and DVD's, the walls festooned with maps. Dust from the ever-open windows had settled everywhere. Since he never allowed anyone to clean the room, except in hygienic extremis, for fear of something being moved and not replaced exactly in situ, it gave the appearance of a badly-run second-hand bookshop. As a little girl she used to creep in and look around when he was not there. It gave her a sense of purpose and daring. Now she stood quite still, observing the nostalgic scene before she crossed to the bed. A sheet covered his face. Shira gently inched it back. He lay there, eyes closed, facing the ceiling, his hooked Semitic nose dominating the face which seemed to have shrunk. The skin was white. He looked as if he was wearing a death mask of himself. She bent forward and dutifully kissed the taut forehead. It was hard as rock and cold as a cave. This was not her father. It was some lifeless ex-person, pretending to be him. His eerie coldness stayed on her lips. The taste of death. Not like Yuri's forehead which she had kissed little more than two hours before, which was not cold. It still had the taste of life. She perched on a seat beside the bed. Was this where her mother had sat, holding his hand as she waited for him to die? What did she think about, while she waited? What did he? Did they talk? Was there some kind of reconciliation, confession, accommodation regarding the past? Did he look at her and with one glance obliterate all negativity? Did he really want to go, to leave them all, to rob them of their duty to care for him? It was one thing, before the event, to request that nature be allowed to take its course, another to desire it when the time came. Had Yuri been asked in advance if he should be "let go," he would certainly have answered affirmatively. But when the time came, he would have wanted to take the chance. She was sure. He was a fighter. He would have demanded to be allowed to fight the last fight and suffer final victory or defeat. Wouldn't her father have wanted to do the same? If he would have, his death really had been an execution. Or at least euthanasia. Perfection was the difference between the two men. If her father could not have perfection, he would have nothing. Yuri would have said that perfection and imperfection were two sides of the same coin. It was impossible to predict on which side the coin would land. But for Yuri, it would have been impossible not to risk the toss. Was that why she had married him?

Her mother entered the room. Shira could tell who it was by the way she moved. Her mother had a ballet-dancer's grace. She sat on the remaining chair, like royalty visiting the sick. "Well. You've had time to think, Shirala. Do you still believe it was an execution?" Shira noted the use of the diminutive of her name. Her mother hadn't called her that for years. It was like a hand held out to help one cross a stream. "No, mother. That was a harsh, silly thing to say." "So what do you think now?" "I'm worried that he may have wanted to change his mind at the last moment." "Your father never changed his mind." "So where do we go from here?" "We will mourn him in our separate ways," her mother said. "And go our separate ways. There are enough ghosts. Do we want more?" "I'm not interested in ghosts either." "But you still don't think I did the right thing." Her mother's voice had quickened. "What possible benefit could there have been in doing otherwise?" she demanded. Shira lowered her eyes. "A selfish one, for me." Her mother went tense but said nothing. "I thought that if he lived a little longer," Shira began and after a small pause, continued, "we might have got on, he and I. Perhaps all of us. You know, when he was dying, he might have wanted to say something. Something he couldn't bring himself to say in normal circumstances." "That he loved you? Is that what you're thinking about?" Shira's body began to shake, her breathing grew shallow, but there were no tears. Her mother got up and held her daughter's head in her arms. "Oh Shirala, Shirala. That's what we all wanted. He did love us. He did. He loved the whole world. You just have to accept that we were only a part of his love. I too. Perhaps I, most of all, needed to know the answer to your question. But you. You must forgive yourself, my darling." "Forgive myself?" "That you could not tell him that you loved him. He understood. Believe me, he understood." Her mother squeezed her head and left the room. Shira sat in emotional limbo for several minutes, analyzing her mother's unaccustomed compassion. Gradually the solace began to peel off, like paint applied to a damp wall. She felt stifled. She sprang up, grabbed her purse and escaped through the back door her father used, to avoid unwelcome callers.

She ran to the beach, kicking off her shoes and, symbolically, the diminutive which her mother had substituted for her name. Holding her shoes in one hand, she waded into the low waves. With the other she scooped seawater to her face. The water was warm but felt cool on her burning skin. Her head, under her heavy hair, burned like an oven. "She's tricked you again," she said to herself. "The bitch has come out of it, clean as a mirror, but I am the guilty one for not telling him I loved him! And what about her? He thirsted for her love. That's what killed him. Like a man without water in the desert. He never knew whose bed she was in. I don't suppose she did. She had the worst reputation on the kibbutz. People said she drove him to his extremist views." She looked around at the view he must have gazed at, many times, in the early hours, when he patrolled the seashore, full of conjugal suspicion and loneliness. She began to wade out, until she was waist high in warm ripples. "His ideas were his refuge," she told herself. Among them he could choose what to love and what to hate. Through them he landed, shipwrecked, on a deserted island he might ultimately control, since he was the only person he would have to please. "Oh, Daddy! I used to think you lived in a fortress, but it was a hospice. Yes Daddy darling, you did die in a hospital after all." The sea breeze abated. As she walked up the beach and then the road, she had difficulty breathing. There did not seem to be enough oxygen in the air. The smell of ozone choked her. The house was still lit up like a lighthouse, signaling what? Danger? Rocks? Quicksand? The wrecked carcass of another ship? She quickly walked to her car. Most of the others were gone. How long does it take to commiserate? If she went back, there would just be her mother, her sister, her aunt, perhaps an uncle or two and perhaps a couple of ideologues, unable to remove themselves, men who stayed long after a meeting had ended, after a party, after a burial even, congenitally unable to accept that it was time to go home. She did not have the strength to spend more time in an atmosphere in which one could talk freely about anything, except the truth.

***

The funeral went exactly as Shira knew it would, except for the rain. No-one anticipated rain. She stood apart from the others at the graveside, in a bubble of ambivalence and sorrow. The cemetery was one of the most beautiful in Israel, bestriding two dunams of elevated ground that once housed an avocado orchard in the days of the collective's romance with agriculture. Ironic, in that the founding generation of the kibbutz, politically correct to the last dogma of their secular ideology, had no time for death, or at least for any religious symbolism that might be associated with it. They had made no preparation for the only certainty in life – that death would turn up trumps. Consequently, they were ill-prepared for the Great Reaper when he paid his first call. It was not that he was unexpected. There had been much debate about death and how to handle it, but no conclusions. The community was not ideologically mobilized for ceremonies that might carry a religious payload. They were worried that death might let religion and superstition – its synonym – in through the back door. Having their own cemetery might encourage weaker minds to dally with thoughts of an afterlife. Worst of all, it might provide an entry point for the rabbis who were personae non gratae, as much in death as in life. The kibbutz had at first shipped its inevitable dead to a kibbutz that adhered to a paler ideological hue, but later generations had come around to an acceptance of mortality without dogma and eventually built a cemetery on the only piece of land available – the former avocado plantation, with its spectacular view. There were those who opined that the site was better suited for a guest house, or hotel, while others countered semi-seriously, that a cemetery was a hotel of sorts.

For fear of missing any detail of the deceased's career or thought, the kibbutz secretary and an uncle read obituaries from soggy computer printouts. Neither Shira's mother, nor her sister spoke. Her sister told her afterwards that they had agreed that the focus should be on their father's work rather than on family pain. But Shira guessed that the reason why her mother did not speak was because she wished to avoid the sub-text that people would append to any feeling of loss she might claim. Her infidelities were common knowledge. Those who had been asked to eulogize the deceased, said much the same things with more or fewer words. Those who connected with his views called him a great mind, or a great man. Those with reservations, called him controversial or fearless. Those who opposed him were not asked. After the orations, when the body was to be removed from cart to grave, Shira realized that nothing had been said about the family's loss. She stepped forward and, standing at the edge of the trench into which the body was to be lowered, said in a low voice that mourners had to strain their ears to hear: "What my father contributed to society has already been said with justifiable eloquence. I just wish to add that he was also a father and a husband. He did not always find it easy to reconcile his working life with his domestic duties. At times they clashed. Not for some idle reason, but for the best of reasons. He was fired by the task he felt impelled to do. One of this morning's newspapers said that he flashed like a comet across our political skies. No-one can expect a comet to take the children to an ice-cream parlor. I am proud to have been his daughter. And I know that my mother and my sister share that pride." As she turned away, she caught her mother's eye. It reflected surprise and suggested approval. Only now did she notice that her mother had not foregone makeup. Each day she fought a losing battle with her mirror, but never gave up. Not even for her husband's final moment. Her customary bright red lipstick had been dethroned in favor of a paler shade, her thick blue eyeliner, whittled down to two thin crescents. Mother and daughter, Limor, had cuddled closely throughout the ceremony. Shira watched as the corpse was lowered into the ground and the first bucketful of earth was tipped on the remains of a man who dreamt of changing the world. She did not feel the emotion she felt at other funerals, particularly of those killed in battle. Her father wasn't in that disappearing white sack. He was in his books and op-eds. As she worked her way through the crowd, she thought she glimpsed a familiar face, partly hidden between a tree and a mourner's shoulder. An impression, not strong enough to distract her from her purpose which was to get away from the place.

***

Yuri was exactly the same as when she left him, but she wasn't. Her father's death and the reconnection with her mother, had left her pathologically restless. Sitting there and reading poetry, or whatever, seemed a dumb thing to do. She found a disc of the songs of Naomi Shemer in Yuri's drawer, put it into his CD player, put the earphones on him and pressed play. When the music started, she thought she saw a slight movement of his forehead. A one-ridged frown. How like Yuri! Why create more ridges if one will do? If she knew how to pray and believed there was someone to pray to, she would have said: "don't take him yet, Lord, I'm not ready." She watched her husband for a while, but her restlessness would not subside. She had to get away, for a few minutes at least. From Yuri. It was stifling within the cubicle. She left the ward, disoriented, and prowled the corridors, as if she was doing an inspection, poking her head into empty rooms, visiting three different toilets in a row, avoiding people or conversely displaying excessive politeness when she unavoidably ran into someone, constantly being reminded of meaningful things by meaningless things she saw or heard. She came to a long barely lit corridor. As she quickened her pace, her aimlessness abated. A triangular sign read: "Work in progress. Emergency lighting only. We regret any inconvenience."

***

Within its eerie quiet, she tried to focus on a world that seemed to be collapsing around her. She could not tell where she stopped and the world began. She felt she was wrestling herself in a mud pit somewhere in her mind. Her father's death, Yuri's coma, her mother's domestic revisionism, even the loss of her first husband on a secret mission, with which she thought she had come to terms, the sudden death of a young friend, a consultant, from cancer, combined with the disintegration of the kibbutz where she was born, presentiments of a new intifada, the threat of a new Holocaust – the ultimate catastrophe – and a host of shapeless threats that had no tangible provenance, combined in the darkness into a shapeless menace. Something within told her she must separate these besieging forces. By turning them into story. She could live with stories. One by one. Even Yuri had to be rendered into a story, if she was ever to leave this place whole. She confronted each, carefully removing its threat, as if she were drawing the fangs of monsters. She held her ground until she had accomplished her formidable task. When the poison was drawn, she walked back into the light, a stronger woman, but increasingly aware that the price she had paid for her salvation was severance from everything that had gone before. The ghosts had been laid. She had rendered them insubstantial. What now?

She went back to the ward by a route she had not used before and passed an office with its light on. She glanced at the illuminated nameplate. Penina's name shone back at her. She stared at it, not knowing what to do. Without making a decision, she knocked. Penina half-opened the door, clearly intending to ward off whoever it was. She seemed relieved when she saw Shira and invited her in. They sat opposite each other at Penina's desk. "I was sorry to hear about your father," Penina said. "I heard it on the radio." "You've heard of him?" "Of course." "He would have liked that. He felt too few people had. His life was about being known. Not so much him as his ideas." "I can't pretend I agreed with what he said." "Nor can I." "That must have been difficult for you," Penina observed. "When practically the whole country hates your father, it's not easy. Especially when you agree with them." "Is 'hate' the right word?" "Maybe not. But it's not far from the wrong one. Tell me, Penina, if you had to put him on a list of the people you would most like to meet, where would he come?" Shira asked. "Somewhere near the bottom." "Then you understand." "Correct, but I don't hate him." "That must be because you do not take him seriously enough. If you had, you would have hated him. He would certainly have hated you." "Whatever for?" Penina asked in shocked amusement. "Complacency. He would have tolerated you if you never heard a word of his message. But if you had got within a hairsbreadth, he would have hated you for not buying his whole package. The people whom he hated most, were the people who agreed with him but did nothing. Like missionaries who come to hate the people they are trying to convert if they will not listen." "You are in mourning, Shira. You have a great deal to work through." "Maybe I am, but I am also relieved that my father is no more – what a stupid way to put it! Put simply, he was a trial." "Then you must try to understand why that was. And come to terms with your feelings." "I think I did that just before I happened to pass your office." Penina, who had kept her eyes trained on her computer throughout their conversation, turned her face towards her. Shira noticed she had been crying. "What do you mean?" Penina asked. "Oh I found myself in a dark place and somehow all the negativity in me came out. It was frightening." "Did you feel something physically, see something?" "Yes, snakes. Not real ones, mental ones. Although they looked real enough. They were probably images of dark thoughts, like pictures that traumatized children draw." "What did you do?" "I knew I had to separate them before they became entangled permanently. I dealt with them one by one. First my father. I pictured him as Sisyphus – the ancient king of Corinth, who was condemned to push a huge rock up a mountainous track, only to see it roll down to the bottom, time after time. Remember? My father was a Jewish Sisyphus. Endless labor without success. Thinking of him this way helped me accept his death and his life. I no longer needed his love. Sisyphus had no time for love, anyway. And as far as my father is concerned, nor do I any more. Am I making sense? It was a hell of a lot clearer when it happened. I knew exactly what I had to do. Like finding an exam question you can answer. But Penina, it's the middle of the night. If you're still here, you must be working on something important." "I was just going through Yuri's file. This place is crazy in the daytime. It's like an airport terminal in Chelm. An hour in the daytime here, is worth twenty minutes at best. Please go on. Did you come to terms with what happened to Yuri?" "Yuri? Yes, Yuri. I had to find a box for him. Gift wrapped. You know how I saw him? It's so inane." "Tell me." "He was a very old man with a long beard and a stick, who had fallen asleep for seventy years.

Who do you think it was?" "Rip van Winkle." "Good try, but it wasn't. "You know the Talmud story about Honi M'agel?" "That takes me back," Penina smiled nostalgically. "Yes, we all learnt it.'" Well, that's how I saw Yuri. Remember, in the story, someone sees this old man, Honi, planting a carob tree. And, according to the story, it takes a carob seventy years to mature. I'm talking Talmud, not science. And this person asks him why is he planting a tree that can be of no possible benefit to him?" "So Honi says: 'The tree isn't for me. It's for my grandchildren.'" "Then Honi falls asleep for seventy years and when he wakes up he runs into his grandson, who is eating the fruit." "But it ends badly, doesn't it?" Penina said, creasing her brow. "Right. He can't convince anyone that he really is Honi, so he dies, a disappointed man. The moral is: don't expect thanks for trying to make the future a better place. Just do it." "My teacher taught it differently. She was religious," said Penina. "She said that in a midrash, God mysteriously takes Honi to heaven because he planted the tree not for his own benefit, but for future generations. She used to say that Honi was the first environmentalist. Of the hundreds of stories in the Talmud, it's my favorite. And when you packed Yuri into his box, did you feel better?" "Oh yes. It saved me from despair, I think." "Even though, in Honi M'gaal's case, he slept for seventy years and when he came back, no-one knew who he was?" "Oh that's just symbolic," Shira emphasized. "The point is that Honi came back, as Yuri will. So what do you make of all that?" "My first reaction, Shira? You've had a mini mental breakdown. Thank God, you pulled yourself through. By using myth. Mazal tov." Both smiling, they stood up and shook hands. An image on Penina's computer screen caught Shira's peripheral vision. When she focused on it, a picture of Yuri in combat gear, wearing the two bars of a full lieutenant, his face blackened, his pale blue eyes darkened by contact lenses, filled the screen. She glanced at Penina on whose brow a few globules of sweat slowly erupted.

As soon as Shira got back to her car, she put together a few scattered impressions. Penina had said she was working late because she was too distracted during the day. But why was she looking at an old photo of Yuri? And she had been crying. Did she get emotional about all her patients? Yuri was a lieutenant at the time the photo was taken.

That was before she and Yuri were married. Was it possible that Penina knew him in those days? She took a rough guess at Penina's age as thirty plus or minus. If she had opted to take an army-assisted place at university before doing military service, she would have been about 23 when Yuri was a lieutenant and could well have been posted to his unit. Did any of this matter? Shira did not know. What she did know was that she had to know. She rang the General. Dialing his number seemed conspiratorial in the darkness. "Hello Shira," a gravelly voice answered. "Not too late for you, Menachem?" "I always had time for you. Now I have all the time in the world and I don't know what to do with it. You know, now that I'm no longer with the service, I can refer to what I'm doing. I thought I would enjoy life now that I no longer wear a tape across my mouth. When I left the service, my mind ran wild like a dog let loose on the beach. I blathered about everything. I told people where I was going and when I'd be back and which flight I was on and what my hotel room number was and what I thought about this and that. Once, I had a reputation for being silent as a sepulcher. Everyone tried to prize small clues out of me. Now I've gone through a hundred and eighty degree turn, and no-one wants to know any more. Passing years, passing tears. I heard about Yuri. It made me sad. How is he?" "You remember the story about Honi M'gaal?" "Sure. Who doesn't?" "Well, he's Honi M'gaal." "You know, Shira, if I could choose to be anyone, I would want to be Honi. Are you surprised? It's simple. I'd wake up after seventy years and my grandson would be deputy head of military intelligence, or maybe head of it. And I'd say: what are you up to? And he'd say: I'm just reading this report of yours, granddad, about our retaliatory strike potential against Iran. We're hitting them tonight." "You always were an old cynic," Shira said, laughing. "Not true. Once I was a young cynic." "Don't you have any faith in the peace process, Menachem?" "Shira, my dear, I am one of its most fervent supporters. I believe in it like other people believe in the Ten Commandments. But you must not forget, what everyone seems to forget, that the peace process is a process. It's not a birthday present, or a pilot's wings. It has nothing to do with a president's term of office, or a political party's waning fortunes, or who is the bi-annual leader of the European Union, or some world bureaucrat tempted to get a paragraph into the history books, mentioning his name. A process goes on until it's resolved.

"Have you ever bought a carpet from an Arab collector?" he went on. "Once, yes. But it was more of a rug." "I'm not talking about rugs or shmugs. I mean a precious carpet of exquisite workmanship which the seller loves with obsessive love and the buyer would give his life to possess. An early nineteenth century Persian carpet. " "No, Menachem. That's something I haven't done." "So listen, you might learn something. Admittedly, it wasn't a shouk, but an exclusive house in Cairo's Heliopolis neighborhood. Both buyer and seller know that there is no other carpet like it. It is unique, a work of art. Priceless. How can two people ever agree on such a deal? In my case – I was buying for others – it took seventeen months and many meetings. The deal was on, then it was off. The price was right, then it was wrong. We got on one day, the next we couldn't stand each other. The asking price was well over a million dollars, in the days when a million dollars was a million dollars. We had explored every corner, had gone over the carpet's biography until we knew it better than our own cv's. We traced its various owners through history. We knew everything there was to know about the school of carpet-making in which it was created and even traced the carpet master who designed the original almost four hundred years back. It had become more than a carpet. It had become a metaphor. It was the Holy Grail. But in the end we agreed on a price. Were we happy? No. I had paid far more than I intended, and she believed there was no price that covered its value. "It was a woman?" "Yes. And what a woman. You know, quite a few Arab women are prodigious. Small wonder their men try to keep them out of sight. My point is that if it takes seventeen months of intensive negotiation for a carpet, how long must it take for a nation? Two nations, in fact. Process, process and again process.

"Did you ever read my favorite book – Kohelet? It tells us there is a time to love and a time to hate, a time for war and a time for peace, a time to cast away stones and a time to gather them. It doesn't say there's a time to negotiate and a time to prevaricate because the author, King Solomon, knew that if he put that in the book, when one party wanted to negotiate, the other would prevaricate and vice versa, and nothing would ever be agreed. When everyone wants peace, there will be peace. But Shira, my dear, you didn't phone me to hear about a once-upon-a-time carpet deal in a luxurious Cairo neighborhood, nor about King Solomon, one of the wiliest negotiators in history. How can I help?" "A small favor. I'd like you to run a check on a clinical psychologist called Penina Frydman. She works at the hospital where Yuri is. What I'm interested in is her army career." "Nothing else?" "Well, yes, everything else. Why not?" She heard his gritty chuckle. "I'll let you have something by morning. Just 'whats' and 'whens' but no 'whys.' Is that enough?" "I'm not asking for her full security dossier." "Always a pleasure talking to you, Shira. I'm sorry but I must go." Shira did not want the conversation to end. She spoke before he could cut her off. "You surprise me Menachem that you like Kohelet so much. So biblical. Not what I'd expect." "It's not as crazy as you think. It's a book about a journey through doubt, cynicism, disillusion and hope. Almost didn't make it into the canon. But they just couldn't keep it out. Nothing more suited to my work and our times. And it leaves the reader to come up with his own answers. So it's called the Preacher, or Ecclesiastes, as the world knows it. But this preacher is unique. He turns his listeners into preachers. In the end, the message becomes what each preacher wants it to be, magically held together by Kohelet. " "How can you say that? As I remember, it ends up smack on God's lap. I can't see the Menachem I know ending up there." "Highly unlikely, I agree. But the point of the book, is that everything seems to be going around in circles. But the movie's still running. Don't they have something in cinema parlance they call the end beyond the end?" "You mean the final twist?" "Is that what I mean? Well, what you call God's lap is the final twist. That alone makes all those circles meaningful. Watch this space, as they say. Shira, boobelah, I really have to go." He rang off before she had time to repeat her delaying stratagem. Nonetheless, she felt good. She would have felt better if she could have kept his attention a little longer. His voice and the things he said was like being massaged with long, bony fingers

***

She loved being alone in her box on wheels in the lateness of night, the deserted road head lit before her. Everything irrelevant was clouded in darkness. She was alone and not alone. She could call friends who, she knew, would still be up at this hour. These were people who came to life as the sun went down, who did not take sleeping pills and did not complain to doctors. They held down responsible day jobs, most of them, but their most creative, thought-penetrating moments came in the early hours in secluded apartments or rustic houses or soundless cars or while walking under an unpopulated sky, or drinking alone in low-lit clubs. Some had been raised on kibbutzim. Some had been raised in modern orthodox homes. Some were immigrants. Some were five or six generations Israeli-born. Most were Jews, but there were also Moslems, Christians, Druze, Beduin, Armenians and two Circassians in this nocturnal club, whose premises were where each member happened to be at the time he, she or you rang. Its members shared an ability to reach deep down into themselves, in the middle of black night, which stimulated them like strong coffee. They did not all know each other. There were networks within networks. Shira knew she could ring upwards of twenty people, across the country at this hour, and more abroad, who would be pleased to speak and discuss and all would have something to say.

She made a couple of calls for no particular reason, to people she knew to be serial chatters, finding one respondent, a professor of linguistics, in an all-night bar in Tel Aviv, frequented by high-tech insomniacs, and a second, a woman teacher and writer who was slowly fighting her way through the inhibitions of highly traditional Arab family life. She had won her dream to study Arabic literature at university, where she met Shira. She lived in Acco, in a house near the old city. It was comforting to hear their voices. The former, Prince, as he was called, having whizzed through the niceties about how Yuri was, quickly got to talking about his love-subject: getting machines to talk to each other. "I don't mean they'll be saying 'nice day, how are you?' They'll be passing ingots of information that the human brain could not absorb in a light year. They'll understand the universe, how it works, how it got here, where it's going. Ultimate fusion, we call it. Mind and fact in perfect marriage." "And will we understand what they are talking about?" "That's the problem – you've hit it. But we're working on that. You've heard the expression 'thinking out of the box.'

This is thinking out of your mind. The language of the universe! It will come," he assured her. She thought of Frankenstein terrorizing nineteenth century London, the Golem running out of control in Prague, Evil Genies of the desert and the many tales of man creating forces he cannot control. "You know, Prince, I think you're the best novelist we've got in Israel." "I'm no novelist. I'm rewriting the Bible. All Bibles. Except this time, we'll get it right." "Good night, Prince and good luck," she said, unsure if his obsessive assurance was not more alarming than comforting. "By the way, Prince. Are you working for some sort of start up?" "Start-up!" he almost exploded. "I've got at least five years yet to go hammering this out with a few friends before we'll be able to start anything. Startups are for when you've cracked it and all you need is some money to make sure you're right." Prince was certainly no fool, she reflected. With three degrees from MIT, Cambridge and Haifa Technion, he was free to choose whatever he wanted to work on. And he had chosen machine language. Or was it artificial intelligence? Shit, she wasn't sure. Although it sounded far-fetched and not a little scary, as she fingered Yasmin's name on the display on her dashboard, she felt reassured that people in a small country like Israel were among players and thinkers in the top league, in every field. When Yasmin answered, Shira guessed, from the way she tried to control her voice, that she was on a high. When she realized it was Shira, Yasmin immediately launched into a soliloquy on the joys of driving by night. Whenever ex-Israeli Arab relatives living in Canada, had to be picked up at Ben Gurion airport, which was where she was now headed, she had to do it alone. Only then did she feel completely in charge of herself, she said, in her dancing Arabic. "My husband suffers from night-blindness, so he could not drive, and besides, I could not bring him or any other male relative, as there would not be enough room for the visitors and their luggage. So I'm free. Sometimes, I have to bring a young nephew. But he would have to sit on someone's lap. This time it's a big family with children and there aren't enough laps to go round. I feel as if I am driving a space ship. I'm not on earth at all. It's about the only time I'm me." "I know what you mean, Yasmin. But there are many authentic 'you's, not just the one that's driving your mobile bubble in the middle of the night." "Yes of course, Shira.

"Funny that we got onto that. I've been writing a poem about "me". Or trying to. You know, about the number of 'me's we become in the course of a day. The reluctant 'me' that wakes up in the morning, thinking over the dreams of the night, and then the mother 'me' driving the family to school, not without breakfast, of course, and the 'me' who goes to college and pores over texts with my students, helping them to find their true 'me's' and then lunch and perhaps a meeting with my colleagues, Moslems, Christians, Druze and Jews – what a collection of 'me's, they are – and then home and mother 'me' takes over again, and then the wife 'me' has a quiet time with my husband – who is very busy being 'him' – and maybe, if we're not exhausted, we'll visit one of my sisters or brothers or one of his and talk 'me' talk for hours, or perhaps we'll watch the news, if there is a big story, as if we were eating hot soup, and I'll become the warrior 'me' or the peacenik 'me' or the 'who me?' or if there's a wedding, I turn into the public 'me' at my very best, the traditional 'me' that I want everyone to see, the absolutely gorgeous 'me' and if other people don't think so, it doesn't matter, because I'm just happy to be 'me' That's why, I say in the poem, that Arabs have so many children. It's because we love going to weddings. And after a wedding, what else is there to do but make more 'me's? Israel leaves us no alternative." "Yasmin, I know what you mean. You're so right. But please, please finish. You always have these wonderful ideas that you don't complete. You should be into your third book of published poems by now." "Inshallah. Mirtz ha Shem. What I want most is to find the essential 'me,' not the one who is so busy being 'me,' there is no time to find out who 'me' really is. I have written the first lines, do you want to hear them?" She did not wait for an answer.

"How many 'me's are there in me? I couldn't count them if I had twice as many fingers and toes. They wriggle, like snakes. Which raises the question: how many 'me's does a snake have?"

There must be one that's the real me.

Let's see. Not that one, nor that. Nor that one, nor that.

So where can it be – the real me?

Can it be that they are all me?

Impossible. I could not be all those 'me's,'

if I lived to be a hundred.

But even that would not be time enough for all the 'me's' I'd be.

"That's as far as I've got. What do you think?" "Oh Yasmin, my darling. Finish it. Or, I promise, none of my 'me's' will ever speak to you again. I won't read your e-mails. And I'll change my cell number. I'd be honored if you would send me a copy. Your stuff reminds me of someone. Oh yes, Shauki Abi Shaqra. Yes! Remember that opening line from 'The Silver Mouth': 'I always stretch my neck to see more of the giraffe?'" "Yes, I do, Shira. And then it goes on with two of my favorite lines in all of modern Arab poetry: 'the immigration officer stamps our backs. You are the journey.'" "Yasmin, darling, I've got another call. Damn it. If you don't finish your poem, the next time you make Burma Til Kedayif, may the kanafeh stick to your fingers and may you never get it off." "That's enough motivation for me, Shira. I can't imagine going around with dough on my fingers for the rest of my life. You'll get it soon, I promise."

***

Shira had barely cut the call, when her phone rang. It was Menachem. As usual, he began without a prelude. "You know what grabs me about Kohelet is the fact that I have done most of the things it applauds or condemns, lived through most of its contradictions or seen others do them. One minute, I reckoned it was great wisdom, the next it seemed like so much hogwash. It's something that gnaws at you over time. Does it always mean what it says? Does it say the opposite and expect you to work it out? It's the closest to life of any piece of writing I've read. Futility and nobility, not to mention joy and pain and nachas and trauma are in constant competition and convergence. To read it properly, you need a guide, someone who can tell you what's really going on. I've got the book here. Listen to this: 'A feast is made for laughter, and wine gladdens life, but money, is the answer to everything.' Isn't that a let down? A great book of wisdom telling you that money is the last word? I spoke to an army rabbi I know. Not someone who has never seen over the wall of a yeshiva. He's been through two wars and many incidents. He knows what it is to see men blown to bits or become paraplegics. I asked him if Kohelet was telling us that, in the end, money was king. 'You cannot read Kohelet without knowing the codes, he said. 'Would you go into battle without checking the scale and contours on your map?' He went on that in Kohelet, common words are often used to define principles. For example, whenever the word 'waters' is used, it refers to the Law, which is deep like the sea. Likewise, when it refers to the power of money, it means tsedakah, which the world translates as charity, which it isn't. So it's saying: sure, go ahead, have a good time at parties, if that's your idea of fun, but tsedakah is a must. We also know from the Talmud that charity is equal to all religious commitments put together. Even our parties must have a charitable purpose. It's telling you to live a full life, not a hollow one. If you want to party, then party, but never forget your obligations – you still have them, no matter, whether you're dancing the tango, or whatever they dance now." "Menachem, is this really you speaking?" "Shira, don't worry, I'm not going to throw on a prayer shawl and run to the nearest synagogue. I don't even know where it is. But in three-and-half thousand years of history we have produced a wonderful literature, easily among the world's best. So why ignore it? Because much of it is religious? OK, let it be religious. But it's ours. And it doesn't belong only to the rabbis, no matter how much they pretend it does." "I'm nearly home," she said. "Let's leave it there, Menachem. And thanks. You always make me feel good." "That's nice! It means the treatment is working," he said. Then the line went dead.

***

"Are you all right?" was the first thing Yoram asked. "Not entirely," Shira answered in a shaky voice. She was sitting in her father's office, opposite the place where he used to sit, when she brought her homework to be vetted. Piles of papers and manuscripts lay on the table before her in rugged heaps. "What's wrong?" "This," she said, passing him a printed book. He glanced at the title: The complete works of Hayyim Nachman Bialik. "He might well be Israel's national poet, if we had one," he observed. A few lines had been highlighted. "What am I supposed to do?" he asked. "Read." He read aloud:

"I know a forest and," Oh, come on, Shira, I know this by heart. Everybody does. Well, more or less. And there's a small pond in the forest." He put the book down and continued from memory. "There's a shady wood that's cut off from the world," his memory racing, as he paraphrased.

"And, wait a minute, there's some girl sitting in the shade of an oak, spawning fish, golden fish, I think. But all the time she's actually dreaming of an upside down universe. And no-one, but no-one has any idea what's in her heart. And there's a lot about storms and lightning. It's the best thing Bialik ever wrote. The whole class loved it. Even I did. And poetry wasn't my favorite flavor."

"It's beautiful," he said, holding the book out to her. "Did you see what's written in the margin?" Shira asked. Yoram glanced at a penciled note opposite the last line. "Shira," it read, followed by two exclamation marks. "So?" he asked. "My God, Yoram! Here is a poem by Bialik of all people, about a mysterious girl who lives by some pool in some upside-down world that's cut off from everywhere, spawning, God help me, golden fish. And no-one but no-one understands her. And my father saw me as that girl! Beyond understanding. Beyond reach. Which also means, beyond love! If there were two things I knew about my father they were: one, that he was a genius; two, that he alone understood me. Now the second has gone up in flames." "OK, Shira, you're not going to like this but you were a strange kid. Something of it is still in you. You lived in a world that no-one could touch. You were always in the woods or by the sea. Or the fish ponds. Yes the fish ponds. We other kids wondered what you did there. Sometimes we followed you. But you never seemed to do anything you couldn't have done anywhere else." "Except be alone." "OK, if that's what you wanted. But maybe that's what struck him when he read Bialik. He realized he did not know what your heart was saying. The irony is that neither of you knew what the other's heart was saying. His loss was the greater. What he expected of you and what he got were two different lists. It was a bitter disappointment to him when you enlisted. You could have got out of the army if you'd wanted to. He told my father he was hoping you would refuse to serve. He practically went into mourning when they put you in military intelligence because you had such good

Arabic. If he had been religious, he would have said the prayer for the dead. The irony was, he always encouraged you to learn it, thinking it would project you into the heart of the peace movement." "He never said a word about this to me. How do you explain that?" "Of course he didn't. He saw problems as if they were made of crystal glass. And he was convinced that anyone who did not have blinkers, must see what he saw. With your education and his tuition, he believed you would follow him, repeating his mantras, to the ends of the earth. Everything was collapsing around him. The kibbutz, the State of Israel, as he saw it – his marriage – I have to mention it – and then you. He hadn't gone through a lifetime of ideological warfare, and his father before him, so that you could help run spies in Gaza for army intelligence. He was very proud of your excellence at Arabic. At bottom, he wanted you to be the son he didn't have." "Shit, Yoram. You're making this up." "He wanted children who'd carry on the fight, into the heartland of the enemy, which in the circuitous end turned out to be his own people. That was the split in his nature. He was a revolutionary in politics and a reactionary in relationships." "That's maybe how you saw it, but it's far from…" "The truth? OK. I won't pretend two truths can be nailed together like planks. But it approximates." Shira did not answer. Yoram continued. "This might hurt, Shira, but it's got to be said. All that stuff about what a genius he was – sure he was a clever man who crashed through a few political road blocks – was simply your way of explaining why you two were not close. And it was his defense too. He was always too busy saving the world to notice if you wanted to play, to talk, to cry, eat ice cream, or even be saved like the downtrodden he ranted on about. That's why, although you had violently opposing views, you kept putting him forward as a candidate for some sort of Nobel Prize for Genius. It was a crude attempt at explaining why he had no time for you, nor you for him."

"Nonsense, Yoram. You make it sound as if I was the only one who saw what he was worth. Lots of people thought he was a genius. These articles prove it." She pushed the pile towards him. "The writers of these articles had their own reasons for wanting to celebrate him," Yoram continued, picking one up to glance at the author's name, then the title. "The greater the genius, the easier it was for you to justify his hands off approach to his family in general and you in particular. He was an embittered old man. As for love: either he was an emotional miser who couldn't give his love away, or an emotional pauper who had none to spare. My father was much the same, except that in his case, I can't use the genius excuse. Everything was pure thought for them both. Human relations were a conceptual problem. They were mathematicians of the soul, except they didn't believe such a thing existed. Pity, because that's the only part of the human personality they might have understood. They liked to play chess with real people instead of wooden ones. An unusual breed! Nineteenth century humanists, who did not find enough oxygen for their over large lungs in the ideologically thin atmosphere of the twenty/ first century. Their parents had believed that ideology makes the world go round. And in a week we'll be laying to rest the great socialist experiment they devoted their lives to – and mistakenly tried to force everyone else to do the same. I don't believe in life beyond death, obviously, but I think there'll be life beyond the grave for the kibbutz movement. They are not all going private. Quite a few are still as socialist as they once were. We haven't yet heard their last word."

"You get six out of ten for trying, Yoram. I'd give up to half of my kingdom, as the emperor said, to put my finger on what went wrong." "Nothing went wrong," Yoram argued, "it was doomed from the start." "That's what my father would have said about the Zionist dream." "I get your meaning, Shira. But just as the Zionist dream will never be washed up, the kibbutz idea will never bite the dust. It's had a few throws, but it isn't finished yet, neither in this country, nor overseas. It could still help save the world." "Perhaps that's true but there are two obstacles." "Go on." "First, the world has got to want to be saved. And second we've got to work out what went wrong." "That's why you should come to the general meeting next week, Shira. It's going to be uncanny, I warn you – like sitting through your own funeral, but come." "More like sitting through a horror movie. It's not my genre. Tell you the truth, I was thinking of giving it a miss." "You can't afford to, Shira. None of us can. Look, Shira, I desperately need to talk to you. The day of the meeting perhaps?" "Perhaps. But there'll be so much else to think about."

She watched Yoram slip through the back door and walk at a military pace towards his office. She felt an ambivalent affection for him. He was of her generation. Same education. Same values. Born on the kibbutz two years before her, he had gone through the same experiences she had. He went out into the world after his army service in Logistics – his father too had not wanted him to serve – travelled India, toyed with that nation's divine pluralism, come home to the kibbutz, off again to Zurich to do business management, returned to Israel, this time to a shared apartment in Tel Aviv, to head a government-aided start-up, the idea of some army buddies, two of them from his own kibbutz movement. With astonishing speed and surefooted efficiency, they turned it into a highly successful concern, quoted on the Tel Aviv stock exchange. Just a few years later, they opened a subsidiary in the United States, which was eventually quoted on the New York Stock exchange. It was finally sold for a princely sum that landed like a craft from outer space among the five comrades, four men and one woman, who had pioneered the enterprise. Each received enough to make them think they were kings. At the celebration after concluding the deal, in one of Manhattan's smartest restaurants, one of the quintet proposed an alcoholic toast to "every person a king." All knew that it was the slogan of the right-wing Jewish ideologue Ze'ev Jabotinsky, whose name was never pronounced, except to be reviled, in left-wing circles, but they lifted their glasses high. Once they would have considered anyone who did so a traitor. The headiness of success cut them off, at least momentarily, from their kibbutz roots. Truth to tell, they had been living like rampant capitalists for more than a decade. For two of the five, success launched them in totally new directions.

One remained in the United States, went into real estate, married "out" and, as the cliché would have us believe, never looked back. Another, Gal, opted for Germany. There was no foreseeable peace to be had in Israel and he was not prepared to witness the death or maiming of any more close friends in combat. He made a brief attempt at settling first in Sweden, a country that had known nearly two hundred years of untrammelled peace with no external threats on the horizon, whose high principles and long-legged women, held him in thrall for two years. Eventually, he re-sited in Germany, where his grandparents came from. After playing a leading role in bringing about two world wars in which over eighty million people had perished, the Germans were in post-traumatic shell-shock and extremely unlikely to attack anyone, he estimated, for at least four or five generations, while their nation's sheer economic size and warrior reputation would staunch any hostile moves against it. Just the place to raise a family. Above all things, he wanted peace. German security was good enough for him. As for Germany's recent genocidal past, he saw no tension between it and the evolving present. Not to be ignored, but neither should it be over-emphasized. Today's Germans were not yesterday's. Speaking the language and comfortable with German culture and the secular, entrepreneurial mentality of contemporary Germany, he integrated fast, but applied the brakes well short of full-scale assimilation. He married a curvaceous Ukrainian Jewish immigrant who was in quest of a tradition she had only heard of, instead of her rival, a more striking German post-Christian intellectual, who had tasked herself with integrating mind, heart, body and career into a proficient modernist working model, with no maternal ambitions. Motherhood, indeed multiple motherhood, was an ideal that his Ukrainian choice was devoted to, as long as it could be achieved in modest luxury and not play havoc with her figure. He threw himself into a high-profile job in high-tech, simultaneously helping build the renascent German Jewish community, mainly of Russian provenance, and devoting himself tirelessly to furthering economic and cultural ties with Israel.

Shira remembered him as an unimpressive, over-quiet youth, who never had much to say for himself, but who had unexpectedly enlisted in a combat unit and served in some of the bloodiest episodes of the second Lebanon war, rooting out Hezbollah gunmen and their lethal rocket bases, deliberately planted in heavily populated civilian neighbourhoods, mostly Christian. The army began the process of bringing him out of himself, but he always remained a loner. From what she'd heard, he had shed his introversion in New York and subsequently remodelled himself as a public figure in Berlin. People on the kibbutz, used to think that Shira and Gal were similar and should become a couple, because they both preferred silence to raising hell and their own company to others'. But her silence was not his silence, nor her introversion his. He was marking time, awaiting the stimulus to overthrow his shyness which had served as self-defence in the collective ethos of the kibbutz, which finally surfaced five thousand miles from home, ten years later. It had happened among the skyscrapers of Manhattan, which he worshipped with neo-pagan idolatry. Shira, on the other hand, was waiting for nothing, other than to burrow deeper into herself. Inward-lookingness was the pathway her mind took, naturally. It was not a stage on the way to somewhere. When she first saw Manhattan, she assimilated its wonder in her psyche. There was no need to live in it, or to see it again, or marvel about it in breathless conversations. It existed in her mind as a glorious series of images, which she could conjure up at any time. Nothing had ever brought her completely out of herself, not ideology, nor sex, nor war, nor career, nor fear, nor marriage. Even when motherhood came, she told herself constantly that the wondrous being she held in her arms had originated in her. She all-but assimilated her son, paying lip service to his separate existence, regarding him as if he was an extension of herself. Even now that he was an adult, about to earn his wings, she felt that they were umbilically linked, as if he still fed from her body.

***

Yoram, restrained by a sense of duty, returned to Israel from the honey trap of Manhattan, viewing dismissively the alternative options that were available. He knew full well he could beat a path through the financial thickets of the New World. But Israel was his home, and opportunity was not the target, but the means. There was no need to divide his talent and his psyche. Thanks to some astute funding by the Israeli government, the arrival of almost one million immigrants from Russia, many of them with sound scientific background, careful nurturing of the best by academe, the input of the military and the defence industry, and the generally accepted belief that if the country did not stay ahead of the game, there would be no game to play, opportunity was opening up in Israel for spectacular growth. He could easily have fed himself into Israel's emerging international scene, in which one's personal address was a meaningless detail. He could earn a more than comfortable living. He was invited to join one of the biggest public companies, where he was to be groomed for top management in some distant corporate future.

While he and the company were still mulling over the details, his father and the then secretary of the kibbutz, requested an urgent meeting. Although he was spending his time psyching himself up to fight in the entrepreneurial trenches of a large Israeli corporation, he reckoned that a lunch was the very least he owed the kibbutz movement. Although he believed that the kibbutz had inevitably followed the dinosaurs into evolutionary extinction, he suffered the guilt of a young sailor at having abandoned his first ship. He took them to a small café cum restaurant off Rabin Square where he felt they would feel comfortable. His father, fearing to raise his son's hackles, said little. The secretary, fearing a vacuum, spoke volubly, floating his sentences like dumplings in a pot of oil. Yoram obligingly pulled them out, as they were done. He had supposed they wanted his advice on a business plan to stave off bankruptcy and had rehearsed some sage advice. But the secretary delivered a monologue, tracing the kibbutz's history from its inception. The facts were well-known to all present, so their recitation was more like the catechism of a lost faith.

When he finally came to the main purpose of the meeting, Yoram was astonished. It was not his advice they sought, but him. They had brought a proposal, in writing, which they were sure the kibbutz general meeting would ratify, that he should take on the role of watchdog over the industrial output of the kibbutz after its privatization. He would have full authority over the executive running of the entity which, as yet, did not have a name. But whatever it was to be called, Yoram would make the decisions. Naturally these would be discussed at general meetings which would in effect, rubber stamp them, functioning only in an advisory capacity. It would be up to him to decide what changes were to be made in order to save what could be saved from the present morass and guide the kibbutz like a holed ship through the rough waters of the new economics. Most of the members were expected to opt to stay and make the best of the new circumstances, clinging to as much of kibbutz communality as could still be rescued. The secretary offered to resign and take leave of absence for a year, so as not to become a focus around which opposition could grow. Yoram would be free to hire his own staff in or out of the kibbutz, and act in all matters, like the chief executive officer of a company. The secretary handed him the paper.

Yoram held it between thumb and forefinger and stared at it for a while, before settling it in his bag, unread. "It was like accepting the surrender of a defeated army," he told me in the kibbutz's onetime tractor garage, already going through conversion into a private pub. He knew what it meant for the two men, sitting opposite, who were born on the kibbutz, had devoted their lives to its ideals and were now waiting to attend its funeral. His father was staring blindly out of the window. Yoram was even more astonished by his own reaction. With refusal on the tip of his tongue, he heard himself say he needed time to think it over. Why the hell did I say that, he asked himself as soon as he said it? His father and the secretary looked at him unbelievingly. He had been their last best hope and they had already resigned themselves to the inevitability that all hope was dashed. They all got up at the same time. A waiter, who had just come on duty, asked them what they had had. None could remember. The secretary and Yoram each laid some notes on the table, but Yoram's father pushed their money aside and settled the bill with a 200 shekel note. "This one's on me," he said, "it was my idea, for better or worse. Just don't keep us hoping too long," he told Yoram. "Someone once said: he who lives on hope will die fasting. Don't ask me who. My mind's a sieve, these days." Yoram noted that this was the only observation his father had made. A man who could express himself volubly in four languages, he had remained silent throughout. The saber of change had severed the thin relationship between father and son. Yoram was sad to see his father reduced to silence. But was it the silence of the grave, or the chrysalis?

***

On the day when Shira's parent's kibbutz voted on privatization, she returned dutifully and sat reading the proposal of dissolution at her father's desk. "I admire what you're doing. From what I hear, you are going to make this place buzz," she told Yoram as he came through the door, assessing him, not for the first time, as a potential partner, more out of curiosity than intent. He had done the same with regard

to her, on many occasions. He was an impressive looking man, she
reflected. If he had been a young university professor and she had been
free, she would probably have wanted to take the matter further. At
least to test it out. But having grown up together from babies' nursery
where, in more ideological days, babies were raised communally,
away from their parents who could not be trusted not to instil in
them unacceptable, non-socialist, social values, on through a host
of agricultural jobs in sun-baked summers and mud-ridden winters,
through the petering joys of communal living, through joint meals
in the huge dining room where the entire membership ate daily and
celebrated religious holidays degutted of the trappings of religion, in
order to render them politically correct, through twelve years of the
kibbutz school system which hammered into them a doctrinaire take
on the world and themselves, through meetings and demonstrations
and music lessons and their uniformed youth movement's character-
forming summer camps, and in later years, through the feeling of
sliding down a precipice into the valley of despond, where everything
one had been brought up to believe was questioned and overthrown
by circumstances beyond control. What had happened to that faithful
phalanx of people pointing the way, the way towards the "just society,"
whose principles could be passed on to others around the world, like
an Olympic torch. Suddenly the flame was snuffed out and only a
small minority was able to see in the dark. There was no-one to say
"this is how we do things on a kibbutz," or "this is not the way we do
things." To see everything that you believed melt like snow, leaving
only rivulets of murky water, was a blow at personal integrity and
responsibility, which, more than dogmatism, had lent color to their
lives. Her thoughts about Yoram were thus mired in the mud of shared
biography. In the days when they lived in a political idyll, when they
were considered examples of and advertisements for the communal
life, they were too iconically self-aware for emotional adventure and
since the collapse, too chagrined to find comfort in shared plight.
That was how she explained to herself how a man whom every woman
would register the moment he walked into a room, was so distant on
her horizon.

As these thoughts passed through her mind, she did not listen to what he was saying. Suddenly he got up from his seat, lent across the desk and gave her a non-invasive kiss. She neither responded nor broke away, but laughed. "You sound like a geisha," he said, pulling his head back to look at her. "Sorry, Yoram," she said, touching his arm with the tips of her fingers. "All that did, was remind me of those days we spent shoveling cow-shit together. Our lives are too enmeshed." He lent forward and kissed her again, pressing his tongue against closed lips. "That reminded me of getting in the maze harvest," she said. "Well, that's an improvement," he calculated, moving his lips towards hers a third time. This time she turned away. "I'm not on the market," she explained. "Think of me as a book that's out of print." "Look, Shira, I know you're not free now. I admire your loyalty. But let's face it, the chance of Yuri coming back is slim. That's what everyone thinks. Together perhaps we could make something of this place – and out of other kibbutzim too. The kibbutz movement is not dead, it's changing. I'm not expecting you to give up your lecturing. I know what it means to you. I mean I want someone with me who will understand what I'm trying to do. Who will be there." "Are you proposing marriage, a business partnership or a long-term shack-up, Yoram?" Her eyes were serious but her lips curved in an impudent smile. "Shira, let's leave it for the moment. Let the air clear. Then you can join me as wife, business partner or long-term geisha. The choice is yours." "You have no preference, one way or the other? She asked, teasingly." "I think you know what I want. Look, Shira I'll be late for the meeting. We don't always go for what we most want, but what we think is best. I think we could turn this place around and save some of its idealism into the bargain. First, we must save what we can of the kibbutz for Israel's sake. Then we must extend ourselves to create a kibbutz system that will help transform developing economies and bring a solution to life in the urban mess that is distorting the new mega cities. We hold the solution to the world's problems. I'm not just talking about Mobileye and Waze and drip-irrigation, and desalination, the myriad of new technological answers we've come up with for a better technological response to world problems. Israel has so much to give. I want to be in the front of that. And I want you to be beside me." She looked at him quizzically.

"I know we could do it, Yoram. But I live elsewhere. I'm married, yes, but I'm also a geisha to my job. Every lecture is a tea ceremony. And with every author I teach about, I have an affair." "Even the dead ones?" "Especially them. I don't think you could live with that." "Did Yuri?" "Yes he did. But he was as married to his job as I to mine. He married the army. It gave him all he needed. The army was a surrogate wife who gave him as many children – otherwise known as soldiers – as he could handle. I never gave him that." "And the marriage?" "It had a few loose panels, but it worked." "I want something better than that." "I hope you find it." "I'll find it when you stop hiding," he told her. "Come to the meeting, Shira. It's just fifty meters away." She watched him leave through the seaview door. How long had he felt like that about her? Was it recent, the result of the new uncertainties in his life? Words her father had written in the margin of Bialik's poem, drifted back to her: "Like Shira." She felt lonely, as if Bialik and her father were right. She was the solitary girl by the pond.

***

She had intended to go to the dining room for the assembly's last meeting before the vote, and even speak, but, at the last minute, changed her mind. She was superstitious, a mental habit she had learned from her mother, of which she unwaveringly disapproved. But there was nothing she could do about it. She believed, despite herself, that bad things happened in threes. Her father's death was now being followed by the funeral of the kibbutz. She feared that if she attended, Yuri would pass away shortly after. She had intended to check the origin and reason for the belief, which was probably buried in some Bohemian folk-world, but had never got round to it. Self-consciously, she turned on the ante-diluvium television set and settled down in her father's chair as if to watch a private movie on a closed circuit channel. "Death of a Kibbutz," was the title she gave it. There would be no award ceremony, she reflected.A few speakers, mostly pensioners, spoke against the motion. No-one, other than the proposer, bothered to make the case for the proposal. The screen showed veteran faces and bony farmers' hands holding the microphone shakily, while they reminisced about the good old days which rose before their eyes like images in a treasured family album. The camera respectfully framed them in non-intrusive close-ups. The winning side could afford to be magnanimous. Everyone knew that the ballot vote being conducted at the other end of the hall, would be overwhelmingly in favor of privatization. The old guard had insisted on making a final appeal to stave off the evil decree, but their words floated to the ceiling, joining the balloons, hangovers from less troubled days.

***

"May I join you?" The voice was familiar. Yoram's father was standing by the internal door. "There's nothing much to do at the meeting. It's so predictable." "That's the worst of it," Shira replied and went on: "This kibbutz, built with such ideological passion, should have gone out like a Shakespearean tragedy – with everyone stabbing everyone else." "Shakespeare's days are over, Shira. "Today they stab you in the pocket," he said. "You mean economics ruined this place? I don't think so. Its spirit died. Economic decline was the consequence," Shira ventured. "You mean the spirit could have withstood cancer? I've two minds on that." "I'm sure the spirit was lost first," Shira continued, looking out to sea. "Capitalism won because it was on an up," Yoram's father replied. "Marx said, it's inherent in the capitalist system to lurch from the heights to the depths. We happened to live in a holding period for capitalists and a downfall for the rest of us. The capitalist knows how to cushion the blows. The worker doesn't. But it'll change. For now, each of us has to find his own solution. Your father advocated the most extreme." "You think my father advocated a solution? He was a brilliant critic of the world's problems. But not in solving them." "Yes he did. Not on principles I could endorse. But I understand how he got there." "If you really do, explain it to me." "That's far from easy. I need ten minutes or ten weeks." "I haven't got ten weeks," she said seriously. "You're lucky. I've got all the time in the world, now. O.K: your father in ten minutes." He took off his watch, the only luxury he possessed, which contrasted with his frayed blue cuffs and historic jeans, and laid it on the table in front of him.

"To understand the man, you must be conversant with several lost worlds," he began. "Their social plumbing alone would take a lifetime to figure out. You really want to know about it? It's not my favorite subject." "Why not?" "Because the landscape is barely passable. You have to read the stars and walk by the light of the moon, wade rivers and slither down mud slopes. You need a sixth sense and a well-padded ass. Your father began his journey in Germany. To recapture the mood of Germany, in the late nineteenth century, is almost impossible." "The nineteenth century? He wasn't born yet." "No he wasn't, but his father was. His father was the greatest influence on his life. To understand your father, you have to go at least four generations back, but I'll spare you that. Let's start with your grandfather, a lawyer in Potsdam. One of the few Jews allowed into the university, where he ran into a wall of personal and institutionalized anti-Semitism and no-go areas for Jews. It was like living in a bad smell. You know how the Yarkon River used to stink before they cleaned it up? He used to say that his father had graduated with one hand held high in surrender, the other holding his nose. Whatever Germany demanded of him, he complied with. He renounced everything Jewish, and reached out for everything German. It's culture I'm talking about – and identity. His family had lived in Potsdam for as many generations as their Germanic neighbors, but that earned him meager tolerance. He was a liberal – of his day, of course – who believed that liberalism would eventually liberate the whole world, which by some miracle, would include him. His son, your father, who was another lawyer, had no such illusions. The humiliation, the compromises, the prejudice, the racism, which allowed no escape from the dhimmi status of the German Jew, caused him to flee in a different direction. He, your father, took his liberal inheritance and an inevitable measure of self-hatred, joined a labor Zionist youth group and prepared for emigration to the only place where the Jewish people were in charge of a reasonable portion of their fate. Palestine as it was then. He was going to help rebuild the nation which had not existed territorially for almost eighteen hundred years. He was going to help create a nation of "new Jews," starting with himself. The Jew who was not subservient to others, who was not powerless, who did not live in the shadow of the ghetto, the Jew who could look anyone in the eye as an equal. Even more, as a comrade. Who would march forward with all the peoples of the earth toward one or another socialist Utopia. My father, who did not have your father's advantages, but was a self-educated intellectual – a breed that has been wiped out by the pandemic of universal education – more's the pity – joined him in a left-wing Zionist youth movement, which trained in Bavaria, for an agricultural life in Palestine.

"They arrived at Jaffa in 1933, a month before Hitler became Chancellor. He and his nineteen colleagues, also mostly German Jews and a sprinkling of Sudeten-landers, needed no greater proof they had made the right decision. Almost half of them were lawyers, the others academics and musicians. Their Zionist youth movement sent them to found a kibbutz that would be part of the world leftist revolution, that would not only rebuild an ancient civilization that had been off the political drawing board for millennia, but by the same act, create a beacon that would usher in an age of worldwide equality, responsibility, fairness and opportunity. This birth of socialism in an ancient land by an ancient people would be an exemplary lesson for the world. What inspired a whole generation in those days, is precisely what bores their descendants to tears today. I said that your father was heavily influenced by his father. But negatively. He despised him. He despised the way his father took insult and prejudice without a fight and, even more, the way he took upon himself the fraudulent role of a believing Jew, in the privacy of his own home. If your grandfather was at home for the start of the Sabbath and not at a concert or dining out, he donned a white skull cap with gold edging and performed the motions of being a religious Jew. Not that he believed in Judaism. But at least he knew what he did not believe. And that was how he defined himself. He was not a German Christian, he was a German Jew, even though he had pruned his Jewishness to proportions barely measurable – in order to get through the lowliest door of acceptance. And because he was not a Christian, he over-compensated on the Germanic side. He strove to be more culturally German than his German colleagues. But it did him little good. His voluminous knowledge of history and the arts, especially the maze of modernist literary and artistic movements, was resented, not appreciated. Anti-Semites, whose grasp of their own culture, was simplistic, if not meager, felt it was improper for him to know what they did not. In the eyes of those he wanted to impress, he was still a Jew. My father once told me, that your father had once told him that on one personally famous occasion, he had "disinherited" his own father." "How, Mr. Koenig?"

"Well, his father had gone off to Bayreuth to see Wagner's Ring with a group of fellow non-Jewish lawyers. (There were some.) For three days, he enjoyed the pagan worship in its medieval revivalism. Wagner's famed anti-Semitism could not detract from the artistic experience, in which he desperately wished to participate on equal terms with the rest of the audience, who saw the composer's Jew-hatred as an expression of his Germanic genius. Wagner, it was said, hated Jewry because he loved Germany. Your grandfather returned to Potsdam, chastened, even broken and never again played the pious Jew, except to take a day off work once a year, pretending he was sick and making a brief appearance at the Yom Kippur service. For half an hour, at most. The rest of the day he walked the streets, without eating, bemoaning who he was and bemoaning who he wasn't. In an ironical way, he was keeping the fast more profoundly than many of the people in synagogue who only fasted because that was the day when Jews fasted. At least he was taking meaningful stock of himself, even if his self-assessment was pathologically wrong-headed. His son, your father, didn't even do as much. But as an undeniable witness to his father's hypocrisy, he morally disinherited him in a short-winded ceremony somewhere along the Unter den Linden, close to the Brandenberger Gate, to be precise, which was his father's cane-swinging, favorite walk. Your father determinedly chose his own invitational gateway to the future, which was to be constructed in Palestine, now Israel. It led directly to the kibbutz (communal) way of life, which would, in time, become the instrument that would change the world. It was missionary, prophetic, socialist, and just. From each according to his means, to each according to his needs. Could anything be fairer, simpler, less compromising? Who, of his persuasion, of that generation, needed more? Who wanted despised, residual Judaism, when there was a brave new world for the brave new Jew to be built – in concert with the brave new everyone else. His generation never looked back but had their eyes trained on some bright socialist future, both for his own sake and for the sake of mankind. It was a vision. It shone like the full moon. But, like the moon, it waned.

"After almost half a century of physical and intellectual investment and a large measure of success, the bubble burst. What was he to do? At this point, his father's pessimistic ghost rose from the grave to reclaim the son. The father had hated himself for being a Jew. Instead of fighting people who hated Jews, he joined them in hating them even more. Slowly, but inexorably, the son followed, pointing out – metaphorically, of course – that it was the Jews, once again, who had failed. They were exactly as their accusers depicted them. The kibbutz failed because the Jew could not succeed as an idealist. Narrow-minded self-interest always got in the way. The constant anti-Semitic besmirching campaign, designed to persuade non-Jews of Jewish calumny, seeped at his shallow roots. He became as anti-Semitic as his accusers, blaming himself for being who he was, and Jews in general for being what they weren't. So what was he left with?

Nothing much. That did not preclude him from having an audience, both in Israel and abroad. In Israel, your father reheated his own father's strict diet of anti-Semitism. On lecture tours to the new Germany, he fed it to hungry mouths which, consciously or not, thirsted, nostalgically, for their ancestors' diet, spiced with its addictive genocidal peppers. Your father's own knowledge of Jews, Judaism and Israel was as bare-boned as his father'. All he thought he needed was to rebut the few skeletal arguments of the anti-Semite, readdressed to meet new contingencies. But that, as it turned out, was not enough.

"With a rejected religion, a failed politics and a falsetto social standing, he was naked in the world. Some Jews in that situation rush to find the nearest fig-leaf, but he yearned for a new belief system, something to cover the whole of him, not just his private parts – and found it in the new utopianism that looks on the past, every nation-state's past, as a series of colossal, unmitigated mistakes, and outmoded ideas, much as his father had looked upon his own Jewish heritage. There is an almost delicious if grim irony in the fact that the anti-Semitic denial of genuine people hood to the Jews is now, by extension, being applied to the very peoples who bred, or adopted, the theory. I tell you, Shira, we hear about Jewish self-hatred ad absurdum, but never about non-Jewish self-hatred. And I'll tell you something else. Without non-Jewish self-hatred there would be no anti-Semitism. I've learned this by observing your father and reading. The anti-Semite hates some part of himself and he copes with his hatred by projecting it onto the Jews. It is as true today as it was throughout history." "I understand what you are saying," Shira cut in. "Anti-Semitism as the self-hatred of the anti-Semite? Fascinating. It fits the description of every anti-Semite I have ever encountered like Cinderella's slipper. As for self-hating Jews, there are very few of them in the taxonomy of Israel. I once had a discussion with a group of parents, including Holocaust survivors, who claimed that one of the many joys about living in Israel was that you had to explain to your children what anti-Semitism means. The children found it astonishing to hear that it existed – because they harbored no parallel hatred for other people in the world. That is one of the best arguments for the existence of the State of Israel that I know. But we're veering off course. You were speaking about the new utopians. How are they going to break up society as we know it? How will they ever rule?" "You will have to find your way into your father's book for the answer. I believe, and this is only what I've gathered from remarks he made, that he thought that Islam was the only force that could pull it off." "Trust him to come up with an idea that not one in twenty sane people would buy into." "I don't think he thought it needed more." "I'll come to that when I read his book," Shira promised. "But I just love your idea that anti-westernism, as espoused by guilt-ridden westerners, is anti-Semitism come home to roost. That explains a lot. The irony is shattering.

"The new utopians are predictably refugees from the collapse of the left. Why did they bolt, Mr. Koenig?" "They did not bolt. They temporarily abandoned their dream. They believed that socialism destroyed itself because it was symbiotically attached to the nation-state which could never rise above self-interest. If Germany was for the Germans, as was France for the French, as were Russia and Britain for Russians and British, there was no way forward. Socialism failed because nationalism and its outcrops – colonialism, imperialism, racism, globalization and anti-Semitism, strangled it. The answer of the new faith is in world government and world institutions, which by-pass parliamentary democracy – which Karl Marx proclaimed a farce. But one which could be used as a stepping stone to world dominion. And the new utopians – academics, bureaucrats and politicians, opinion-makers, work towards undermining the nation state to the point of collapse. From its demise, they believe, will rise the perfect society, like Horus from the underworld. And who will rule all this perfection? Why, them, of course, from their academic towers and their edifices of missionizing bureaucracy and their political HQ's. They don't expect to be popular, which is why they will have to be protected, and the rest of us suppressed, by a world army. To, achieve this, they will have to overthrow every nation-state and replace it with a mixed multitude of ethnic entities. Multiculturalism, their watchword, demands that races become so mixed that shouts of Germany for the Germans or France for the French, or even Luxembourg for the Luxembourgers, will be emptied of meaning, hollow shouts in the night." "They cannot do it by themselves, "Shira interrupted, "so who will be their allies? They can't do it alone." "You are going to gawp at this, but think about it. Their allies, according to your father, will be a hodge podge of people who think they are utopians – usually the most unlikely groups – and Islam." Shira laughed. "Nothing could be more unlike some post-socialist utopia, than an Islamic theocratic caliphate," she commented. "Correct. It would have to be a shotgun wedding between the new utopians and Islam, but it would be a marriage nonetheless." "And they will live happily ever after? I can't see it."

"You are right. I'm not talking about a love marriage, but one of convenience. Basically the utopians have no more respect for Islam than Islam has for the west. When the Islamic caliphate finally seizes control, the utopians will begin to undermine their authority exactly as communist parties undermined their erstwhile leftist and liberal allies across Eastern Europe after World War Two. It will be very like the cannibalistic feast the Bolsheviks made of the Mensheviks in Russia. Got it? The Utopians know that most people will hate Moslem supremacy and will eventually rise up against it, as they have against every form of imperialism. By then it will be too late. Utopia will be here. A socialist Utopia redeemed."

His voice trailed off. He glanced at his watch. "That was eleven minutes. I'm sorry, it took longer than I thought." he added apologetically. "How little we know about our past," she said, in awe, "about each other, about the world we think we live in." From that point, there was nowhere to go. They turned their eyes to the television. The secretary of the kibbutz was at the podium making an appeal for those who had not yet voted, to do so. "I had better do what he says," said Yoram's father. "A good many people have found reasons for not being here today. It's like a visit to the dentist. But if you have a rotten tooth, what choice is there?"

***

Left alone, she felt the room change. This no longer felt like the office where, as a little girl, she would sit by the coffee table in the corner, doing her homework in the last rays of the dying sun, waiting for her father to notice her. Sometimes, as the sun dropped below the horizon and the room turned from a golden haze to ambivalent twilight, he would cease his eternal scribbling and look at her for a few minutes. Aware of his stare, she would sit it out, like a supporting actress waiting for the director to find her something to do, until he either spoke or switched on his desk light and got back to work. That was her signal to leave. She was not welcome in the evenings. No-one was. Her father was a creature of the night. He worked until the early hours and wrote off mornings almost completely, unless he had to see the doctor or attend a meeting. His health was not robust. He attracted viruses and everything contagious, but his constitution went unchallenged until the last years of his life when he developed high blood pressure, atrial fibrillation and asthma. They killed him, in concert with his forgetfulness about medication and a flippant disregard for common-sense safeguards. Some people said he was trying to kill himself, but no-one listened. The doctor tried to ward him off another source of danger. Anger. He was warned that if it did not kill him, it would seriously contribute to his demise. This only encouraged him on his wayward course. The notion of dying in anger, better still, rage, was the most ethical exit from the human condition he could envisage. The doctor recommended meditation or a cruise. To which his patient replied that he did not wish to meditate about the world, but change it. Nor would a cruise be sufficient. What he wanted was a revolution. Book him a revolution and he would be there. On such occasions his blood pressure, driven by slow-burning ire, would bring a ruddy glow to his face, his pupils would dilate and his breathing impair, so that the doctor, fearing a death in his surgery, would hastily change the subject. But now, at midday, the atmosphere in his sometime office was heavy, as if it were night. Shira remembered how much the room's mood was influenced by her father's presence. When he wasn't there, it was just an untidy space, too small for its contents, bursting between the seams of untidiness and chaos, totally eclipsing, in authenticity, those reconstructed offices of the famous dead, you find all over the literate world. But when he was present, the room took on a presence reflecting him and his will. Everything had a purpose and every stitch referred back to him. His office was a ship in rough seas. And he was the captain.

***

She moved around the office, collecting memories from book titles, and the way things were arranged in an irregular regularity that only he understood. There seemed little purpose in just hanging about for old time's sake. She was about to leave when she saw her father sitting at his computer. He was lifelike, not at all the ghost. He did not seem to notice her. She watched him breathlessly for a moment or two as he un-necessarily switched on the desk light and began to pound the keyboard with long forefingers, his thinning brown hair and the blotched skin on a broad forehead, all she could see of his face. The scene was so real, like something that had happened many times before, that she had no fear. Her father went through his daily rituals with literal clarity. Slowly, he raised his head and looked at her. She saw his face. The skin was an incandescent white without a trace of color. Now she was afraid. Her spine chilled. She felt as if she was standing in the path of an icy wind. The face looked at her questioningly. Whatever question it may have intended to ask, remained unspoken. A few seconds went by, then a speckled hand switched off the computer and the ship's captain disappeared in a slow fade. She immediately regretted not having noticed if the keys of the keyboard indented when her father's ghostly fingers pressed on them. He had recognized her, she was sure. The illusory encounter might have made her want to flee, but something emboldened her. She sat down in his seat, without a thought that it had, moments before, been occupied by her father's ghost and switched on the computer. There were files on everything under her father's purview and that meant everything. Press reports, academic essays, articles gleaned from the Internet, letters and abstracts. Files on nature and science and politics and history, and religion. A good deal of space was devoted to world government and multi-culturalism as well as his own writings. Among them, she found what she was looking for: a file of 12,000 kilobytes titled: "An Introduction to the End of History as We Know It." There was another file, encrypted, which she could not access. She pressed print, waited what seemed an unconscionably long time for the elderly machine to cough up less than twenty pages, flung them into her bag and made for the door, where she stopped to survey the room, for what she took to be the last time. Everything was in place. But the reading lamp on his desk was lit. Did she switch it on when she sat down? Why should she? It was broad daylight. She fled.

***

What next? She was due to lecture in two hours. She felt a hunger to see her son. Her conscience told her she should be with her husband. At some point, she knew she would have to visit the military cemetery where her late husband was buried. The anniversary of his death was the following day. She knew she would not be able to make it then. Apart from all this, she experienced a strong urge to take herself to some quiet place and read her father's introduction. First, she had to get away from her parent's kibbutz, like a new born emerging from a dying mother. She sat in the car for a few moments, measuring time against her incompatible obligation. She made up her mind without realizing it, because when she drove through the kibbutz security gate, she took the road that led to the hospital.

On the way, she rang Menachem. "Did you find out anything?" she asked. "Not a lot but enough," he replied. Hearing his slow voice was comforting. He spoke as if he measured words with a medicine spoon. That was his style. He might raise his voice to a moderate shout, but had never screamed in his life. "This young psychologist," he went on, "did serve in your husband's unit. He was a captain at the time. She, a lieutenant." "Oh, so she did," Shira interjected. "She must be a real hard nut, "the General went on, "A woman psychologist, attached to a combat unit, sleeping rough, or not sleeping at all, constantly on the move, no privacy, maybe even having to share a tent with males. She'd have had to convince them she could do it, not worrying too much about personal cleanliness, kissing makeup and perfume and a daily shower good bye, being ready for foul language and lewd songs and maybe the odd grope. That's why they used to put women soldiers on office duties or at most in artillery, where they can live in a hut with other women on a base and not in a field. They would never have selected women for an elite infantry combat unit. Not then. Now, it's different. We've got a combat unit that's half female on the Sinai border facing off the Islamic State. Nowadays women are forty per cent of the military and are heavily represented in combat units. Your Penina must have volunteered. The question is why? Is she butch?" "No. I'm beginning to wish she was." "Sounds as if you've got competition, Shira. This one's a tough cookie, I warn you." "So am I." "I know that. But what kind of competition can she be if Yuri's in a coma? If that's what's worrying you." "He won't be in a coma for ever. If he doesn't come out of it, they'll pull the plugs." "Will you go along with that?" "Yes. I've thought about it enough." "Shira, I take my hat off to you, as the English say. But what's she like, this woman?" "She's not what you'd be looking for, Menachem. You probably wouldn't notice her, if you were both in the same room." "And this is your competition?" "I didn't say that. There's no reason to suspect her motives. It's just that because a few things have happened, I've had to stitch my impressions together. She's no threat to my past or my future. But she does have some involvement with my comatose spouse and I just want to know if they were connected in the past and how far they went. There's no denying she has something. She can actually look quite fetching. When she smiles, her face transforms. She fascinates. Highly intelligent. Professional. But that's not it. There's a kind of latency about her that I can't explain." "You mean, as a woman?" "Ah, the sex factor. It's never buried very deep in men's thoughts." "Sex is like Rome," the General observed. "All roads lead to it. Is she sexy?" "I think she might be for some men." "I see, but tell me in one word." "In one word? Ugly." "Wow, Shira. You haven't forgotten how to hit the target." "OK, maybe, plain. She's not unlike a monitor lizard. At first you think it's ugly. But people can get hooked on them. Even think they're beautiful."

"Une belle laide, do you mean?" "You're astonishing Menachem, you've got it. I never thought of that. But that's exactly what she is – trust the French to have the right word – ugly beauty. Yes! There's a gallery of belles laide in literature, particularly French. Some Americans too. The most famous case I know about, in the real world, is Edith Piaff. Thank you, you've got her perfectly." "So what are you going to do?" "I don't know. Keep an eye on her, what else? When we got married, Yuri told me that he had grown fond of someone and that it would be difficult to make the break. From her point of view, he meant. I think. Could that have been Penina? Dozens of small things tell me that she has an emotional relationship with Yuri. It could hardly have happened if she had only known him since he's been in coma. Even I find it difficult to relate in the present situation. All's in the past." "So whatever relationship they may have had is dead and buried?" "What happened once, can happen again." "I can't imagine that, if Yuri had to choose between this lady and you, he'd chose her." "I must tell you something, General. Before all this happened, I mean before Yuri was wounded, we weren't getting on that well. We got married on an impulse. And impulses don't last. We decided to think it through and, when I got back from Australia, we'd talk. So if he ever gets out of this coma, I don't know how he'll feel. Not even who he'll be." "And what did you decide in Australia?" "That I wanted him. I want to be with him." "Now I understand your interest in Penina." "Look, General. When I say we married on an impulse, that's half the story. We had a short crazy affair. We both felt we were being forced. An exterior force, coming from outside ourselves. It was like an arranged marriage in some primitive society. I wasn't pregnant. I can't say we were in love either. We married because we needed something badly from each other. God knows what."

***

She found Penina sitting on a chair next to Yuri's bed, asleep. The sight angered her. Sleeping next to him, even on a chair, was too close. She gave the curtain a harder tug than was necessary. Penina woke up.

"It's been quite a day," Penina said, putting one hand to her forehead. The two women exchanged hasty looks, barely taking the other in. "I'd like a few moments alone with my husband," Shira said, giving Penina no option but to leave. She got up, un-necessarily checked Yuri's notes and left with a curt smile. She sensed Shira's antipathy and wondered what had caused it. She very much wanted to maintain a good relationship with Yuri's wife. Shira regretted she had been antagonistic. She should have kept her new impression of Penina to herself, instead of holding it up like a portrait for the sitter to see. A young Arab nurse came to rub Yuri's backside with salve to prevent sores. Shira helped her turn him onto his side. She was glad to have something to do. Yuri was heavy, a dead weight in a white sheet. Shira had a premonition of him being lowered into a gaping hole in the ground inside a funeral shroud. "I haven't seen you here before," she said to the nurse, needing to divert her mind. "It's almost the end of my second week," the nurse said, in a voice not much above a whisper. "It's a bit nerve-wracking. In this ward, anyone can die at any moment. Not all the nurses get sent here. So it shows they have confidence in me. They say it's a good career move." "I'm sure you'll make a good job of it. I'm very happy for you to be looking after my husband." "Oh, is he your...? They say he's touch or go." "I'm sure you will do all you can to make it 'touch.'" "We've got a new patient," the girl said, her voice quickening. "Over there. Moshe. He's Kurdish. Was once a famous singer in Iraq. Now he's in a sort of coma. He sings sometimes. A bit scratchy, but quite nice. When he's not singing, he chirps like a bird." Shira noticed that Yuri's head was tilted towards the newcomer's bed. She speculated that his new neighbor's arrival might be therapeutic. "Practically, the whole family speaks Arabic to one degree or another. The grandmother's Arabic is better than her Hebrew. I like talking to her. I think she perfumes her breath. You're bound to see them, they come at all times." With Shira's help, she turned Yuri onto his back. He fell asleep at once.

Shira was smiling a goodbye to the nurse, when two small girls appeared at the end of the aisle. "I must be a prophet," the nurse said, "here they are." The two girls were quickly joined by three older girls, then by a few boys and they, by a group of young women, followed by older women, followed by a much older, diminutive woman, who wore the lines and folds in her small face like tokens of authority. She was dressed in a black gown, edged with gold and a white scarf around her head, edged with silver. Despite the fact that she used crutches, she walked with self-conscious regal dignity. Shira thought of the Queen of Sheba, as she watched the party take up its position around the bed of the sleeping patient, settling, like a theater audience, in a row of chairs to one side of the old man's bed. A chair with arms was found for the old lady, who gently prodded the patient with a crutch to wake him. Two, smooth-faced young women came forward to help, with soft-voiced exhortations. The man awoke, looked around, smiled, composed his face, and perhaps his memory, and began to sing. His voice sounded like a venerable fiddle with a broken string or two. But the song was permeated by a dull beauty and a mood of slow-moving mystery, like a thicket in mist. A younger man, perhaps in his late-teens, arrived and immediately produced a mobile phone, which he held close to the patient's mouth. "Never heard this one before," he remarked, when the song was finished. "Daddy must have reached deep down to find that." "What was it about?" the old lady asked. "I didn't get all of it, grandmother. But I did get the bit about the Temples which were destroyed, but they can never destroy the Temple in our hearts." "He loved the Temple, your father," she said. "I pray that when the Lord takes him, he will dwell in the Temple above." The old lady fished a book of psalms in a silver, metal casing, out of an embroidered bag and began to read to herself in a barely audible, supplicatory voice, emphasizing what she wished to emphasize. There was nothing automatic in her reading, a notable characteristic of those over-familiar with a text, despite the fact that she must have read those same psalms many hundreds of times. Shira, mesmerized by the scene and its actors, talked to them whenever opportunity allowed, as she put together a mental album of their story.

Of five grand-daughters, one in particular, a vivacious girl of about 16, had that mysterious beauty which western men find so attractive in women of the east. Shoulder length black hair, smoldering brown eyes, a brown skin that glistened as if it had just been oiled, a walk which was almost a prance – all fed into an image which was no less impressive for being a stereotype and no less appealing for being self-conscious.

Moshe was a man of about fifty who had suffered severe head injuries in the suicide bombing of a packed bus, a few months back. Head injuries were less common in such incidents than injuries to the stomach, back and chest because most bombers were seated when they detonated themselves and the nails and shrapnel with which their bomb belts were rigged, ripped through the mid-body of the passengers around them. Moshe was bending down at the crucial moment, and took the blast in the head, mitigated to a certain extent by the torn and mutilated limbs of other victims who sat between him and the bomber. After three months of surgery and constant monitoring, he had recovered the power of speech but not communication. He spoke in fast spurts, but incomprehensibly, holding an interminable conversation with himself. He laughed from time to time, but most of his speech was delivered in earnest to invisible interlocutors. Sometimes he moaned or wailed for an hour on end. Or perhaps he was praying. Was he praying for a refuah shalemah, a complete recovery, in some gibberish that even God would find it difficult to understand? Although the Colonel could not explain it to himself, it was important to him to know what the man was saying. Later, Yuri reported that the Kurd was the only one, among patients, visitors and staff, to whom he felt he could relate. But Moshe's incomprehensible rhetoric gave nothing away. Sometimes he sang in a thin voice peppered with pathos, the voice of despair. If he happened to start on a wrong note, he persevered, never finding his way back to the right one. While he always spoke in Hebrew, he always sang in Kurdi. He had been brought to Israel as a baby from northern Iraq, a small bundle wrapped in a sheepskin, during the exodus of Jews from that country, to live in the old-new land of the Jews. Now he was returned to the helplessness of a newborn. His extended family watched over him by turn. There were seldom less than two at any hour, sleeping at night, on chairs around his bed or on stretchers in the corridor, eating their homemade food, each portion wrapped neatly in napkins with a main bowl of Kurdi salad, from which they all partook. The entire family were musicians in the Kurdi tradition. Each played an instrument, or sang, or both. Moshe had been the main composer for a small group of Jewish and Moslem musicians in Mosul, as well as its star singer and player of the halil, the Kurdi flute. He did his best to recreate a group in Israel, but few had the skills and he was not a patient teacher. His removal from the life of the company thanks to the suicide bomb was a severe blow both to their morale and their options. His teenage son had learned almost every existent Kurdi Jewish song from his father, who had been a noted singer and performer in Mosul or ancient Nineveh, before bringing the eighteen members of his extended family to Israel in the early 'fifties.

They posed as Moslem Kurds in their seminal, hazardous journey part hiking, part bussing, even hitching, through Iraq, Syria and Turkey and, at the Greek port of Thessalonika, boarded a ship for Cyprus and then Haifa. Approaching the city through an early morning summer fog, which blotted out the lower town, they were still a mile offshore, when the sun burst through the slate-grey sky and picked out the golden dome of the Bahai Temple, which must rank as one of the most beautiful examples of domed architecture in the world. The head of the family's mouth fell open at the sight. In a short while it was filled with impromptu song – a song about what he was witnessing, told in words that came from Prophets and Psalms and his own gift. In a mystical epiphany, he mistook the Bahai Temple for a vision of the third Jewish Temple that the Messiah will build. Many of the songs of the Jewish Kurds were impromptu, created on the spot for a particular occasion, at which the singer-composers, some of them itinerants, were adept. This time, he excelled, capturing the full emotional thrust of the biblical and personal meaning for a Jew returning to his ancestral land and to the temple which one day will be restored there. It was the best song he ever composed, people said – and the only one he refused to record. "It was born from my heart. It will live in my voice," he insisted. He sang it, each year at the saharani feast, the Kurdish Jewish festival, where it soon became part of the liturgy. His son, Gavriel, who now watched him mumbling his hours away, had spent his entire childhood and youth learning the songs from him by rote, missing school when his father suddenly remembered a long-since forgotten classic, learning it word by word and note by note, not always understanding the literal meaning and disconsolate that many cultural allusions were lost on him. But he persevered, becoming a popular, part-time singer and balladeer among the 80,000 Kurdi Jews, members of a once flourishing community, who made it to Israel. The knowledge of how far he fell short of his father's art, gave his performance a tinge of fruitful melancholy, which added to his reputation. Audiences experienced it, both as sadness and as a redeeming nostalgia for a tradition that was waning like the moon. It was not uncommon for them to sing along and cry along at his concerts.

The Israeli Kurds unwaveringly clung to their distinctive past, retreating into their deep history, much older than Islam, recalling ancient memories, if imperfectly. The generation that had been born in Kurdistan had mostly passed on, and the remainder did not have an informed idea of how much the tradition had been eclipsed. Now that Gavriel's father was out of circulation, like old currency recalled, singing to himself in a travestied version of a once-noble tradition, Gavriel was forced to find other sources to learn from – low fidelity recordings, made on the cheap in Turkey, old radio archive material, performed on Israeli radio and scraps of song remembered by members of his family or members of the community of Kurdish Jews in Israel. He came to the hospital as often as he could, usually around eight in the morning, since he had to be at his job as a waiter in a kosher Kurdish restaurant by 10.00. If his father, tempted by the morning light, happened to break into song, he reached for the tape recorder in his back pocket, opposite his cellphone – he was always pressing the buttons of one or the other. His eyes shone, when his father sang a few bars of a song he didn't know and darkened as the singer stopped at a note which he repeated over and over, like a flickering lamp. Sometimes he, and sometimes one of his sisters, sang to their father. The old man's 16-year old granddaughter was his favorite. She could rise to the highest notes like a bird to the highest branch. Yuri always seemed to tilt his head in the direction of the Kurdi's bed whenever she sang. Was he listening? The medics said no. But the occupants of the nearest beds and their guests all strained to hear. Her voice was a reminder of the multi-purpose paths that Jewish history has taken.

It sang of survival, and of the myriad shimmering jewels of Jewish cultural identity.

***

Shira was determined to finish her marking, before she left for the cemetery. She was pleased with the essays she read. They were the first creative efforts of the course and the standard was high. Almost all her students had done three years military service, for men, and two-and-a half for women, had travelled Asia or South America for a year or more and absorbed cultures and ideas that had broadened mind and character, so that by their middle twenties they had experienced more, read more and thought more than the average student elsewhere. Some of their essays or stories were fit to be published in modest literary magazines. In the middle of the heap, she found a poem. It was by a girl from Laos who had missed a number of lectures and sat in silence through the rest. Shira had tried to draw her out, but she remained intractably attached to her shell. Shira had planned to spend time with her once she had submitted a piece of work that was discussable. Could this be it? It was short, but Shira did not mind. The girl was trying, that's what mattered. She read:

"A Poem To Shira, Who Is A Poem:

"Only the roar of tears did I hear,

inside my head,

when grief's river burst its banks,

and bore me on its tidal back,

and drowned me in the tears I shed.

Then nothing, Blessed Nothing."

Shira froze. Still holding the page in her hand, she read the poem twice more. She was deeply moved. The poem was dedicated to her. It was highly personal. But why? What was the writer saying? Its meaning came to her slowly like a lantern lighting up a room in darkness. It was sharing the grief that the writer knew Shira must feel about the death of her father. Blessed nothing. The nothing that remains after the death of a loved one. Blessed, because the agony is over. Perhaps the writer too had lost someone dear to her. A beautiful poem on mourning and death, Asian to its core, a haiku of mourning. "Exquisite," she wrote in the margin. "I look forward to your further work. And thank you." And below that she wrote: "90%." The highest grade she had given for some time.

***

The military cemetery was in darkness. The main gate was locked but the pedestrian gate stood open. An armed guard asked for her ID. When he compared her photograph with her face, he kept his eyes on her a few beats too long. As a rule, when men showed an interest – it happened with monotonous regularity – she took it as a form of flattery. But she felt invasiveness in the young corporal's surveillance. She wanted to keep her mood in tandem with her purpose, but that was now in tatters. She pocketed her identity card and strode away, feeling violated and condemning herself for feeling so. Why a guard on a cemetery, she wondered. Wasn't that taking security a stage too far? The yellow glow of street lights lit up the paths and the edges of the first rows of well-tended graves. Soon she was surrounded by them. Awesome serried ranks in the yellowing light. The cemetery seemed deserted. A kind of eeriness hung over the site, like light mist over water. She felt very aware of herself as she listened to the rhythmic click of the heels of her boots. It was not comforting. Her skin tautened. In the distance a tall, manly figure was coming towards her. He seemed to be in no hurry, as if out for a stroll. She walked more firmly, making a clatter with her heels. As the figure passed, he nodded slowly. His dark brown eyes, held hers with a look of complicity. There was only one reason why anyone would be here at this time. Shira wondered at whose grave he had come to mourn. Graveyards were a memory bank of stories, barely hinted at on headstones, bearing military insignia and topped with stars of David. A son, a father, a comrade? These graves told the story of the nation. Its wars, its dreams, their price, more fluently than a book or a movie.

She was startled when her phone rang. It was the General. "My Delphic oracle tells me you're in a tight spot," he said, his voice slightly edged with seriousness. "If I remember correctly," she answered, thankful it was him, "the Delphic Oracle spoke in maddening puzzles which you analyzed until you came away with the message you would have eventually thought of if you hadn't gone to consult the oracle in the first place." "So am I right? Where are you?" "In the cemetery where Joel is. It's the anniversary of his death." "Remember me to him." "I will. He'd like that." "Don't cemeteries scare you, this time of night?" "Not at all," she lied. "In that case, I have the perfect story for you. Want to hear it?" "You're going to tell me, whatever I say, right?" "Right. Once upon a time, there was a young girl who was late going home. So, against her better judgement, she took a short cut through the cemetery. It was late at night. It was misty. She was scared. She was ready to turn back, when she saw a little old man coming up behind her. 'Excuse me, sir,' she said. 'Do you mind if I walk with you?' The old man agreed, with a smile. They walked right through the cemetery without incident. When they got to the farthest exit, the girl said, with considerable relief: 'Thank you sir. You see, I was terrified of being alone.' 'I understand,' replied the old man. 'I used to feel like that, when I was alive.'" Shira smiled and shivered, despite herself. "General," she said, "you're a beast." "I just want you to know, Shira, when you're in a fix, you can rely on me." He rang off.

She glanced around to see if the visitor she had spotted was still in sight. At first, there was no sign of him, until he stepped out of a swirl of mist, not thirty meters away. Momentarily, she stopped breathing. There was something ethereal about the figure. Something not quite right. She could not help think about the ghost in the General's story. Whatever will be, will be, she told herself, as she turned off the main path and headed for Joel's grave. "Hello, Joel. It's me. Is it only a year, since I last came? It's more like ten. Are there two people anywhere who lived so fast? Ring seats. Two wars – you in the sky, me on land, never out of each other's minds, never out of danger. Lebanon – the beauty and the beast. We were made for each other, Joel as you were always saying. Identical backgrounds. Identical foregrounds. We agreed about almost everything. People asked: don't you ever row? And then, disaster. Perhaps it was the only way it could end. I never got to the bottom of it. I know you wouldn't want me to. You would say:

'go along with what they say. If they say it was an accident, it was an accident. They know best.' I know they do, but I have to admit that each year I have a greater need to know the truth. Were you on a secret mission? Did they shoot you down? Or was it, as they said, a technical fault? Perhaps one day the authorities will make it public. Either way, I lost you. Does it matter how? I thought it didn't, but it does. I can't help feeling that if it really was an accident, then the rest of my life has been an accident. My marriage to Yuri. My career. Everything, except our son, of course. Some malfunction of the plane or freak weather or human error. I can't bear that to be the reason. If you were on a mission over northern Syria and you got hit but made it to the sea, where your plane came down, but you parachuted out and survived for a while in a dinghy, that would be something I could live with. Even if you were fished out of the water by the Syrians and are still confined in some forgotten hell like other Israelis they captured. It's not worried me before. But now it hangs over my mind like a cloud that never rains. A cloud of unknowing. Where did that phrase come from? Something I read, probably. Perhaps because I'm under pressure. Like the high velocity training you did that distorted your face and made you black out. Yuri's in a coma and his chances of survival are slim. Am I to lose him as well? But if you were still alive, I would not be married to Yuri. So I tell myself, it wasn't an accident. I tell myself, life is not just a game of snakes and ladders. I tell myself, that your death had a purpose. And that, if death has a purpose, life must have one." She looked around for a stone. She found a nice rounded one, smooth and gray, with streaks of-white, under a tree and placed it at the foot of the grave. An ancient custom, still current among Jews, dating back to when the Jewish people were desert nomads and buried their dead in the sand. They homaged their burial sites with stones. Which also kept wild animals from ravaging the grave.

***

When she got home, Bristol was not in his room. She found him sound asleep on the sofa. A wave of love and compassion swept over her as if she had been doused by seawater heated by a hot sun. She stroked his face, but not hard enough to wake him. All her worries that nibbled like rats in the recesses of her mind vanished in an outpouring of affection.

At breakfast, she could tell that Bristol wanted to tell her something. It wasn't until he got to his second cup of fresh mint tea that he spoke. "I said a prayer for Yuri last night." "What do you mean, a prayer?" "Well, I just said that I hope he gets well." "That's not a prayer. That's a wish. A prayer is something you ask God for. But there isn't a God. So there's no point. You must have been doing something else." "But I can wish, though." "Oh, yes, my darling. I wish for many things. With all my heart." "Where did you go last night, Mum?" "To the cemetery." "Why didn't you take me?" "Sometimes, I need to be by myself. I talked to your Dad for a while. I was really talking to myself. It was like my private time." "I really want to go. I'd love it, if you could come too. What about tomorrow?" "If you really want to." "Yes. I really want to." "Why?" "Don't laugh – I want to show him my wings." "That's beautiful, Bristol. Sure we'll go. He'll be so proud." "You know, Mum, when I'm flying, I sometimes feel as if he's right there, sitting next to me, but I feel even closer to him in the cemetery." "Me too."

After Bristol had gone, she opened the fridge, gazed at the contents and shut it. All she wanted was water. As she poured a glassful, then another, a chemist's brew of river, aquifer and desalinated, she thought of the General telling her that in Kohelet, water was a symbol of the Law. The literary hutzpah brought a thin smile to her lips, but no comfort. "I don't mind dying from starvation, but not thirst," she told herself, as she sat at her computer. She had hardly attended to it recently, just picking out staff notes, and student concerns from the never-ending flow. Dredging through the 'unanswereds' she came across one from an Italian university. Would she be willing to give her paper on the third day of their conference on "The Utopian Novel?" Her reaction was that it must be a mistake. Then, she remembered. In the race-by days before she went to Australia, where she heard the news that Yuri had been severely wounded in action, she had been invited by said university to participate in a literary conference. She had knocked out a proposal, had not had time to let her department have sight of it, planning to explain all when she got back from Australia, and sent it off a day before catching her flight to Sydney.

That was the last act she performed while she still held her life in her own hands. And the last time she thought about the conference. She hunted about her computer for her proposal and while trying to locate it, found a notification, over a month old, informing her that she was on the list of speakers. When she glanced through her piece, she was dismayed. It dealt with not one, but two of the most prestigious novels of modernity, with allusions to a third. Was she mad? She read the proposal from end to end, wondering at each sentence if she had gone too far.

***

"As one reads through European literature, one meets many Jews. It is not an exaggeration to say that most of them are symbols of unscrupulousness, and if not always, but often, of evil. But there are two novels, by two of the greatest novelists of their times and beyond, neither of them Jewish, which heralded Jews as exemplars, as benign symbols of universal truth. Two utopias which rely on a Jew for their outcomes. In neither case do we know why the authors, George Eliot and James Joyce, both intellectually brilliant, at the height of their creative genius, with but a threadbare knowledge or experience of Jews until they contemplated writing novels about them, requiring enormous research and consideration of the Jewish condition, chose to promote a Jewish hero. Eliot researched her Jews bookishly in nineteenth century England; Joyce, socially, among Jewish intellectuals, who befriended him, in between-the-wars Trieste, adding some mitigated stereotypes from contemporary Irish prejudice. We do not know, because they did not specifically tell us. We can, of course, guess. Neither recruited their Jewish heroes out of casual or easily-satisfied need. Their exhaustive investigations gainsay this.

George Eliot advocated two forms of liberation in her final work, "Daniel Deronda." Of Women, who must free themselves from their dependent inferiority on men. And Of Minorities – in this case, Jews – who must be freed from their dependent inferiority on the nation state. In the latter case, the cause of dependence is clear. It is due to a historic wrong, which denied the Jews a country of their own, where their homemade history and culture could re-emerge. She created a hero, who, when he discovered his true identity, found the desire to consummate self-discovery by going to live in Palestine. I shall argue that her argument for his cultural independence can be legitimately extended from Deronda to the minorities in Britain today. Not to return to their countries of origin, but like those Jews who did not take the Zionist option, to further their dual inheritance, combining British culture with the culture of the countries of their provenance. The message of "Daniel Deronda" is as relevant to the Pakistani, the Punjabi, the Sikh, the Moroccan, the Chinese, Somalis and Nigerians living in Britain, as it was to its eponymous hero. I shall argue that George Eliot deliberately used two distinct styles in the same novel, to tell her tale of liberation, a stratagem often decried and widely misunderstood, but which she found mandatory. My argument runs against some distinguished critics of the novel, who protested that the two tales it told were mutually exclusive. One eminent British critic recommended excising the Jewish part of the story from the rest and confining it to the literary dustbin. A distinguished Jewish critic suggested performing a similar exercise in reverse, saving the epic Deronda chapters by detaching them from the struggles of the spoilt English heroine to find an environment in which to exercise personal freedom. I shall argue that both critics were right, within the parameters of their vision. They did not and perhaps could not be expected to see what Eliot saw – two forms of discrimination that had to be resolved before England could move forward. She understood the critiques against her book, insisting it was an integrated whole, and exactly what she wanted to say, by employing two distinctive styles to tell two interlinked stories. Who knows better – author or critic?

James Joyce also employed stylism to create the impressionism he desired, for Ulysses. In his case he used a different style for almost every chapter, not as a pyrotechnic literary display, but to suit his theme to the action. To call his novel utopian, will raise eyebrows, if not ire. I shall argue that it was a double utopia: Joyce took Homer's classic story, which served as a lost utopia, already, in classical Greece, and turned it into what he saw as the pedestrian utopia of his own day. It was reductionist, and enormously ironical. He was saying, this is the utopia you perceive, if you look around. This is what is left of the great

Greek saga. How have the mighty fallen! But he did not display disdain. He did not unsmilingly parade the weird customs, banal attitudes, unchivalrous deeds, religious and political inadequacies, pornographic longings and small-time failings of his fellow countrymen. He was understanding, jocular, commiserating, observant, didactic and above all compassionate towards his contemporary utopians. This is what heroes and gods and goddesses have come to. This is how love and honor and reputation are worn today. And for his hero he chose – a Jew, a business-suited, advertising salesman. A middle-class, assimilated, Jew to stand in for Ulysses, the helmet-glinting Grecian hero? It was part of Joyce's compassionate reductionism. The Jew, seen as an irredeemable outsider by many of his fellow Irishmen, as the "other" writ large, neither to be trusted, nor understood, was the one Joyce chose to navigate the Scyllas and Charybdisses of modern life. The liver of life in a lower register. In the hands of a run-of-the-mill anti-Semite, the faint-hearted Harold Bloom, with his lurid predilections, unpardonable manners and gluttonous appetites would have become a wicked caricature. But in the hands of Joyce, he possesses an inestimable nobility in the miniaturized mold of the Greek hero. Ulysses, the wily wanderer of antiquity, becomes Harold, the universal wandering Jew. I shall attempt to demonstrate the interdependence of this pair of nomads – Ulysses crisscrossing the eastern Mediterranean through almost twenty tumultuous years, Bloom crisscrossing Dublin in the space of an average day – by placing each in the other's circumstances: I shall briefly consecrate Bloom as King of Ithaca and Ulysses as Dublin's Bloom. How would they behave if their roles were reversed? Allow me to share another thought. Ulysses' odyssey began after the Battle for Troy, the decimation of the greatest heroes of the Greek warrior pantheon, the battle to end all battles, at least for a time. Bloom's peregrinations took place after World War I, the greatest period of carnage known to man up to that time. Ulysses went through many hells and delights in order to return to the ordinariness of Ithaca. Bloom, buffeted constantly by metropolitan gales, and experiencing its questionable pleasures, clung to the ordinariness of Dublin with his fingertips. Isn't the ordinary, the thing we value? Isn't a modernist utopia discoverable in the bustling streets of between-the-wars Dublin? It is, if, like James Joyce, you have the compassion, insight and love to notice it."

***

Shira would have to leave for the conference at the weekend. She was extremely nervous. The agenda she had given herself was impossible. It would be academic self-immolation. At a staff meeting, she made uncharacteristically impoverished contributions, attempting to hide the fact she had nothing to say by saying it at length. Behind her apathy was a feeling of dread. It accompanied her everywhere, as if she dwelt in a haunted castle. She described the sensation to her sister, as like the brain being slowly barbecued. She could smell the smoke. Work offered no redress. Writers whom she glorified, grew pale, passages that normally fired her imagination, went cold. And what about Yuri? She attempted to reach Professor Bondman repeatedly. "You must be the busiest man in the world," she told him, when she finally got through. "Correct. And you must be the luckiest. I'm only taking calls about emergencies within emergencies," he replied. When she explained about the conference and her worries about being away from Yuri, he unequivocally advised her not to miss it. "If I had the authority to order you to go, I'd do it. The conference is what you need. Shira, we're not going to do anything drastic while you're away." "And if he gets well, or...and I am not there?" "That's a chance you must take. But remember, exciting as it is when he opens his eyes, he is not going to play chess the first day."

***

She was reading the goddess Circe segment in "Ulysses," when she took a call from the head of her department, still suffering from a virus. "I think you should know that one of your students died last night. Actually, she committed suicide." "My God! Who?" "I thought you might know." "Yes, I do. Of course I do. I suppose it was the girl from Laos. What a waste!" She thought of the silent student who had sent her a poem. It could only be her. "She wrote a suicide note in the form of a poem," he went on. "Evidently, when she finished it, she took enough sleeping pills to keep her sleeping for ever." "For ever! Oh my God. She dedicated a poem to me. Was that it?" "Yes.

Sorry I had to break it to you." "But why? Why? Oh Norman, there's no way I can explain it. She showed no indications that she was in distress like that. A bit withdrawn, yes. But I really do think she was beginning to come out of herself. I thought the poem was a letter of condolence." "What for?" "When my father died. Like the note you sent me. Like most people did." "Do you have the poem?" "Yes, it's right here, somewhere." "Read it to me." Shira fished it out of its file and began: "'nothing but the roar of tears inside my head.'" Norman heard her gasp and break down in tears. She could not go on. "Shira are you all right?" "Oh my God! Oh my God," she replied. "I didn't notice. I didn't get it! She wrote: 'Inside my head'. And you know Norman, Oh my God. I read it as: 'Inside *my* head'. I thought she was personifying me, in my grief. But it was not about me, it was about her and the anguish she was in. It was a scream for help. A final alarm. And I failed her. I didn't hear it. I perverted her meaning and made it my own. I was so caught up in the meaning of words on paper, I was deaf to the living word. I've failed as an educator and as a human being. When is the funeral?" "They are talking about flying her back to Laos." "Relatives?" "Divorced family. Neither parent living in Israel. The father, originally an Israeli from Belgium, lives in Atlanta. He's on his way here. Mother's a Catholic. She's flying in from Vientiane. You'll be hearing from the Dean of Students and possibly the police. Thought I'd warn you. There was a suicide letter too, apart from the poem. In fact there were several screwed up attempts by her to say what she meant." "Do you know what the letter said?" "Only what I've been told. It was a farewell to someone she loved." "A love letter?" "You can say that. "They were all addressed to Shira. She must have written them, then killed herself." "But how did she get the poem into my heap?" "That must have been before." "If I'd only read it sooner and acted, I might have been able to do something. Save the poor child, somehow." "I don't think so, Shira. In one of the letters she wrote that since her love cannot be returned, she had no choice but to take it with her." "Are you saying she thought she was in love with...? And I didn't even know. How tragic." "Look, Shira, you must understand, there was nothing you could have done." His words provoked a cold flush of guilt. "Such an inspirational girl. Jet black hair and vivid coal black eyes. I love my Asian students." "But not in the way she wished," he corrected her. "Not as she would have wished," Shira repeated, tasting each word, trying to understand. "I have a favor," said Norman, "that I want to ask." "Go ahead, Norm." "The girl was a poet. I think that is clear. They found other poems among her things. I want to write a poem called 'Death of a Poet.' It's about a Filipina – I'm changing her nationality because I know about Filipinos, there are so many of them in Israel – who falls in love with her poetry professor and kills herself, taking an untold wealth of unwritten and half-written poems with her. In the poem, I'll try to imagine the poems she hasn't written and include most of the ones she has." "Oh. It's a beautiful thought. Please." "I'll show you, when I finish. Are you all right, Shira? Really?" "Don't worry, I'm fine. It's just that people are dying all around me. It's like having a lethal contagious disease."

***

She had hardly put her mobile down when the first bar of Mozart's "The Marriage of Figaro," heralded another call. It was a colleague and rival from her department. "Shira, I was so sorry to hear about your student. I know you well enough to know that you will inevitably blame yourself. I just thought I'd tell you – if you don't already know – that the philosopher, Martin Buber, had a similar experience." "No, I didn't, Ronit. I've only just heard. I'm still in shock." "I don't remember all the details, nor whether it was while he was still a professor in Germany, or after he settled in Jerusalem. Anyway, there was a student who was feeling hopeless and went to see him. Buber was working on something important and didn't give the student much time. Certainly, he did not touch the young man's problem. He did not pick up that his visitor was existentially desperate. The student had gone to see him as a last resort and when he found he didn't get the help he needed, he committed suicide, which he might have done in any case. Buber blamed himself and never forgot. What was the point of struggling with the meaning of some philosophical text and missing the meaning of his young visitor? He struggled with himself. After that, he always found time for his students, particularly those with problems. They say the incident led him to develop his I-Thou philosophy which sets out his categorical imperative – that we must treat and love the Other like ourselves. He borrowed heavily from Leviticus, of course.

His book "I-Thou," was studied in every philosophy department in the western world." "That's really interesting, Ronit. Thanks for telling me. It helps. I read your article on the modern Hebrew novel. It was great." "No criticisms?" "Let's meet." The caller laughed. "You know, Shira, what's important about a tragedy like what happened, is not so much that it happened, but what you do about it." Nice words, Shira thought. But there was no absolution in them.

Shira placed the phone beside her on the glass table-top where it blinked in three colors as a text message passed across its screen. She watched the letters flit by, without reading them, as she might watch rain clouds glide across troubled heavens. More about the suicide, no doubt. Like the fourth child, at the Passover table, she did not have the capacity to ask, or be asked questions. She remembered the despair in the girl's poem, the reaching out with her eyes in class, the contrariness that would blow up like a freak storm, the time she joined a line of students waiting to see her and impatiently left before it was her turn, the way her work was always handed in late and sometimes unfinished, sometimes brilliant, sometimes incomprehensible, contrasted with the tranquility with which she would sit through lectures, looking alluring and unreachable, like a desert island in a high sea. Was anything getting through that jet-black haired head? She had wondered. What was being said by those piercing dark eyes? Or was she sunbathing in her own reflection? How could she have been reached? Shira came to the comforting conclusion that there was nothing she could have done, save send the girl to a campus psychologist. Yes, the girl had needed professional help. Only that could have saved them both. But she had not even done that. She had seen and done nothing, and a lonely young creature was dead. A feeling of inadequacy overwhelmed her. How much guilt could she bear? The eminent German-Jewish Professor Buber might have come up with an answer, but she was bereft. Then it hit her – she would never let it happen again.

***

When the time came to pack for Italy, she had no guilt and no regrets about what she was leaving behind. Neither a husband who might suddenly burst into life, or death, nor students who might kill themselves, nor a kibbutz that might be swallowed up by the earth, she allowed nothing to lay claim to her unadulterated attention. She was animated by the double thesis she had opted to present. She had placed herself in an uncompromising position with regard to the two writers she intended to cast in new light. Her views were not conventional and, as she threw a backless black dress – the only designer item she had – for the end-of-conference dinner, into her wheelie, she wondered why she had not been more circumspect with her argument. All that stuff about Daniel Deronda being relevant to minorities today and the utopianization of Dublin was akin to wearing a low-cut front. Low cuts had their place, but not at academic conferences. Doing a quick finger count, she found more opposition in the department to her paper, than approval. One doctrinally unmitigated opponent, a professor approaching retirement, who was expert in four literatures, told her unequivocally, on the way to a lecture he was about to give, that what she planned to say was opinion, not scholarship. "Scholarship has taken us as far as it can, she replied. It was time to make classic works relevant to our own day. Opinion is all one had." "You prove my point," he observed, before attempting to disappear through the swing doors. She wouldn't let him go until she had finished. "I think it was John Locke, 1632 to 1704, who said something to the effect that 'new opinions are always suspect for the very reason that they are not yet popular.'" She quoted the speaker's chronology to give her parting shot some gravity. But she was toying with the wrong opponent, who replied: "'People buy opinions as they buy milk, because it's cheaper to buy milk than to keep a cow,' – if my memory does not do violence to an observation made by Samuel Butler, (1835 to 1902), not that other Samuel Butler, (1612 to 1680), who said something you, if not all of us, should take to heart: 'Life is the art of drawing sufficient conclusions from insufficient premises.' It's a hard world, my dear. But good luck, anyway," he added as the door swung shut behind him.

***

Bristol was sitting on a wooden bench, with a clear view of his father's grave. He had placed, on the gravestone, an imitation pair of pilot's wings, which reflected shafts of sunshine, whenever the clouds stepped back. Shira watched him, from a distance. His lips were moving. Was he talking to himself? Or to his father? She began to walk towards him, but he looked round and when he saw her, stopped speaking and waved. She cut through a lane between the graves to find a quiet spot and dialed a number. Yasmin's voice answered. "Shira, is it?" Shira could not speak for a beat or two. "Shira?" Yasmin repeated. "Yes, it's me." She could not think of anything to add. "Is something wrong, Shira?" She did not answer. "I wasn't sure it was you," Yasmin continued, "you always ring at night." "It is night," said Shira's voice. "There is something wrong, isn't there?" "Do you know what day this is?" "No. I mean, sure, it's Thursday." "It's two days before I fly to Italy to further my beautiful career, leaving a husband who could die any moment. What do you think of that?" "Do you want me to come to wherever you are? I'm teaching in a few minutes for an hour, then I can come. Where are you?" "In the cemetery where my first husband's buried. I don't feel like hanging around. It's lovely of you to offer, Yasmin, but it's not necessary. I don't know why I rang." "Because you wanted to talk to someone. OK, I'm someone." "You're a very dear someone, Yasmin. But I'm really sorry, I don't know why I'm wasting your time." "If you rang, there must be a reason, Shira. I expect you know what your Jewish friends would say. You want to know what I would say. Right, I would say that you're in the best possible place to think things out. What's a cemetery after all? It's a huge caravanserai, the last one on our journey. A beautiful place. It's a place where speech is meaningless. That's why you can't speak. Our everyday thoughts are meaningless. That's why we must think of things that are not. In a cemetery, we are balanced between our world and paradise. I know that Jews and others think that a cemetery is an awesome place. Your priests must tread carefully, when they go there. You wash your hands when you leave to get rid of impurity. But we see it, how shall I put it, not like a five-star hotel, no, but, yes, like a caravanserai, a beautiful inn which is the gateway to heaven. My mother used to take us to the graveyard when we were children, just to walk about and to know that death comes to all of us and that we must be prepared for it. It's not scary. My father, like many Moslem men, women too, has always visited the graveyard, not just for funerals or to pray in someone's memory, but to wander about and think of the wonderful place we are finally going to. It's like standing on the edge of paradise. It lifts you up, whatever problems you have. I strongly rec…" Shira heard her friend's voice crack. Then tears. Fearing tears of contagion, she said: "I must stop you there, Yasmin….I have to go. Speak to you later." She forced her own tears back and walked quickly, to collect Bristol. "This is going to sound terrible, but I must say it. Why does it have to be Daddy down there? Why can't it be somebody else. Why not Yuri?" he asked. Shira tightened her grip on his upper arm, as if it was her answer. She loved the way that her son – a grown man: feel that bicep – purposefully became a small boy again, when she needed him to. She needed him to now. Reassured, she looked around at the well-swept graves, the headstones inscribed with minimal fuss, stretching as far as the eye could see, the uniform slabs of marble or stone in sober rows, offering an alternative narrative to Nature's. Visitors in single-minded sorrow, or huddling in groups, lay flowers or pebbles in memoriam, with geometrical precision. Somewhere, out of sight, a funeral was going on. The volleys fired in honor of the deceased by his comrades, told her so. Another cruel death of a young soldier, male or female. Paradise? She could not see this place as a gateway. Not unless the deceased was in such agony of mind or body that the ending of life was a euthanasical kindness. A line wrenched from Shakespeare's one hundred and forty sixth sonnet, fought its way into her mind: 'once dead, there's no more dying.' She couldn't accept Yasmin's's thesis. If Yuri were to die, it would be the end, not some new beginning.

***

Only when, at ten thousand feet and climbing, she beheld, through the El Al Airline window, the narrow slither of land that was Israel, did she realize the enormity of what she was undertaking and the mess she was leaving behind. She sucked her lips hard until she tasted her lipstick. The world she was leaving, she told herself, would have to do without her and the world she was visiting would have to put up with her. That was it. Then as the seatbelt signs were turned off, she saw him, just a few rows down. A tall, lean-bodied man with a high neck and dark brown hair, embroidered with grey, no doubt one of those people who belied their age. He had got up to rescue something from the luggage compartment. The first thing she thought of was not the impossibility of him being there, but the fact that he had once been called an ectomorph by the kibbutz school psychologist and had to endure months of name-calling by the other students. The illusion lasted little more than a blink. He was not Joel, her first husband, come to haunt her. Damn close, mind you, but this man, who could have been Joel's brother, was alive. She pulled her shawl across her shoulders. In recent weeks she had experienced a wave of memories of her onetime husband. His presence was vivid in her dreams. And occasionally, as now, she thought she saw him, while awake. It was as if he was taking over her mind. Competing for her attention. Wooing her. One image, in particular, repeatedly invaded her daydreams.

Once upon a fairy tale, she and Joel had been holidaying in Ireland. They had hired a coracle in a boatyard by a lake in Donegal. He had been trying to read her copy of Ulysses which she lugged with her wherever they went. "Sorry," he said, "I'm not getting on with this. The English is too hard and there's no story." He made as if to drop the book overboard. She grabbed for it. He held it above his head. She stood, grabbed once more, lost her balance and plunged into the water. He tried to block her fall and fell in after her. "My book! My book!" she screamed, thinking it must by now be sinking to the bottom of the lake. "Excalibur!" he yelled, holding her copy of Ulysses, still dry, high above his head with one triumphant hand, while swimming with the other. "Well, that was more exciting than anything in the whole damn book," he said as they crawled up the bank. "But not as exciting as what's to come." Taking his meaning more from his look than his words, she hastily scanned the empty landscape and edged back her skirt.

***

After the rituals of passion, he dozed off. She remained awake wondering why Joyce had chosen to tell the story of Ulysses the way he did. As she recalled Joel holding the book high above his head, as if it were the magic sword from the Tales of King Arthur, a thought struck her. The magical arm that emerged from the lake, in the legend's telling, had grasped the sword in order to preserve it until it was needed. Wasn't that what Joyce had done? He had plucked it from its watery repository and cut through the Gordian knot of modernity to tell a saga of ordinariness. The heroism of the Ordinary. Out of the Aegean of antiquity, Joyce conjured a Lilliputian Dublin. By mockingly substituting a tattered paperback for the emblem of chivalry, Joel had opened for her a new outlook on Joyce. She barely thought of the episode again until, years later, she received the flyer advertising a conference on utopianism in the novel. She immediately thought of her revelation on Joyce and combined it, in her proposal, with a review of "Daniel Deronda" which she had once taught in class. So Joel was still with her, projecting himself into her life, guiding her, not letting her go. But how could that be? It must be that she was projecting herself through him. Why? Why the appearances in dream and daydream? Why the feeling of closeness, almost of things as they once were? Why the imaginary sightings, as in the case of the man a few rows down on the flight, for this was not an isolated incident? It was perhaps normal, immediately after a loss. But was it normal a decade later? Was it at Yuri's expense? How could it not be? And here she was on her way to present an academic paper, suggested by Joel's inspired tomfoolery. Was she falling in love with her first husband again? Did it matter that he was no longer alive? She had loved him with all the emotional resources she had. She had never stopped loving him. Then, in what seemed like a televised newsflash, he was gone. Was that the end of love? How could it be? Had she possessed a spiritual inclination, she might have found it easier to come to terms with her thoughts. As it was, she wondered if she was going mad.

***

Two days after Shira touched down in Rome, the Head of Literature Department, at the university was going through her proposal. It had some good ideas, he thought, but it likewise contained some bad ones. He angrily highlighted the section on George Eliot, which contained an allusion to the relevance of the novel for minorities in England today and to the suggestion of reversing the roles of Ulysses and Bloom, placing each in the other's context. He was debating with himself what Shira could possibly mean by suggesting it, when his mobile rang. Not recognizing the caller's number, he almost did not take it. "Is that Norman Zangfield," a voice enquired. "Yes, how can I help you?" "I'm Menachem Bondman. I am Head of ..." "Ah yes.

You're at the hospital where the husband of one of my colleagues…" "Precisely." "How is he?" "That is what brings me to ring you. I would like your advice, although I may not be able to take it." "If I can be of help, no problem." "The point is that during the night, the patient went into full coma. That means, he is not functioning at all. It also means, he could be in that state for a very short or a very long time. Mrs. Pozner is attending a literary conference in Italy, as you know. The policy of the hospital is to convey news of this kind immediately to the next of kin, unless there are substantial grounds for delaying it. I will have to make the decision, of course. In this case, I feel an extra burden of responsibility, because I urged her to go. I am considering not telling her for a day or two. Just so that she can deliver her paper." "Oh, definitely. I think that is the thing to do." "With all due respect, that is not what I am asking. What I want to know is, would it be disastrous if she did not deliver her paper and flew back immediately, which I am sure she would." "A disaster for her career, you mean?" "Yes, for her career. I believe she relies on it a great deal for her general wellness. Being the wife of a man in coma is one of the greatest tests a woman can face. She is going to need all the self-confidence she can muster." "What she has chosen to do, in my view, at the conference, is stick her neck out, like the proverbial tortoise. It could make or break her. But she's pretty tough, you know." "Yes, she's tough. But dare I rely on that? Thank you for putting me a little more in the picture. I'm very thankful for what you told me."

***

Forty eight hours later, corresponding with the day after she was due to present her paper, Professor Bondman sent the following message to Shira: "I am sorry to inform you that your husband has gone into full coma. This could be a merciful intervention. The future is unpredictable, which may well be a blessing. My very best regards, Menachem Bondman."

VOLUME ONE | OBLIVION

Book Two

GROWING A NEW MIND

Chapter One

Penina snatched a few hours of sleep, before her mobile rang. She answered with her eyes still closed. She heard the voice of the head nurse. "This is an emergency. All staff to return to the hospital immediately. I repeat: this is an emergency. All staff to return to the hospital immediately. This is an emergency. " Penina was fully awake in an instant. She reached for her mobile and switched to a news station as she got dressed. She knew by heart, what the headlines would be. She needed details. A suicide bomber had blown herself up on a bus in the city center. It was the height of the rush hour, a favored time for bombers, when roads would be packed and it would be more difficult for emergency vehicles to get through. First reports were twelve dead and many injured. Relays of ambulances were taking the injured to Jerusalem's hospitals. On the newscasts, survivors and witnesses were being interviewed. She heard a frantic woman telling a reporter that she had tried to get on the bus with her sister but there was not enough room. Her sister had boarded and she had waited for the next one. Less than a hundred meters down the street, the bomb went off in the bus her sister had taken. The witness was one of the first to reach it. She tried to climb inside but the metal parts were too hot to be touched and the stench and smoke made her want to vomit. She walked around the bus, hoping to see her sister or recognize her clothing through the windows, but she could see nothing except a mass of twisted metal and contorted bodies and hearing people's screams. Penina was by now in the driving seat of her car, fingers spinning the radio dial. She heard reports by survivors, police, ambulance men and eyewitnesses, on every station, as she drove to the hospital, foot hard down. Her mind deftly interpreted the information into its long-term meaning. The traumatic experience of the woman looking for her sister – even if she found her alive, albeit in shock and lightly hurt, would stay with her for years, perhaps filling her with a fear of the dark and the unexpected. And if she found a body part, or piece of clothing she recognized, the pillars of her world might collapse, taking her mental status with it. A student who had been waiting for the bus at the next stop said he was looking to see if the number was the one he wanted when it blew up. "A bus is such an ordinary thing," he said. "You don't associate tragedy with the ordinary. I keep on seeing it, over and over." Penina remembered a young computer wizard who had seen his comrades blown up by a landmine during the Second Lebanon War and had gone to India after his army service to escape the trauma, only to see it repeated on the waterways of Kerala. Her own mind was filled with images past patients had described, mixing with images created from the reports she was listening to. Her mobile rang. It was Ayal, the physiotherapist, wanting to know where she was and wishing her well, over the next couple of days, which were going to be tough. He was phoning from the hospital. "I've canceled my patients for today," he said. "I thought you would be here by now. It's a pretty nasty one. You're going to be in demand non-stop. Listen to me, Penina, give yourself a break between patients. I know you too well. You'll go through the day like a forest fire. Take sixty seconds. It's all you need. Just empty your head as if it was a rubbish bag and breathe as I taught you. Then do it all over again. Three times. There's no time for meditation, or anything like that. Try to pace yourself for once, Penina. It's the only thing you're lousy at. Catch up with you later." His measured voice was reassuring. As she approached the hospital, she readied her mind, not only for the immediate problems that would confront her in the wards, but pictured the aftermath of tragedy, the pain and suffering and uncertainty and fear that would affect concentric circles of individuals fanning out from the victim. She also knew that time could be a friend as well as an enemy, and that her work could make a difference. As she walked through the hospital doors she knew what was expected of her, and was ready.

***

The first casualties had arrived by private car, before the rescue services could get to the scene, or the radio and television stations had mobilized their crews. A storekeeper, on his way to work, who was traveling behind the bus, brought in the first casualty, a woman whose torso, covered in blood, had been hanging partly out of the bus window. A taxi-driver brought in a man he found sitting on the pavement who showed no sign of injury but whose face reflected the white pallor of death. He was lucky to be brought in among the early victims – the rescue services, exercising elementary triage, would have given priority to cases with better chances of survival. One of the worst effects of bus bombings is blast damage. Within the narrow confines of a bus, the explosion bounces off the vehicle's framework, causing internal injuries. Victims may look unharmed, but multiple blood vessels may have burst and the victim's blood pressure reduced to zero.

The hospital lobby was filled with patients and the first wave of what would become a human tide of relatives, searching for children, parents, brothers, sisters, and friends. Photographers, from the photo unit, were moving from stretcher to stretcher, recording faces for identification. One of them, Raphael, whose pony tail bobbed this way and that as he set up his shots, noticed Penina crossing the lobby. He called her over. Without stopping to get the best shot he could, of the jewelry of a woman who was otherwise unrecognizable, he shouted: "Penina, there's a woman I think you should look at. Her sister was on the bus and she can't find her. She's getting hysterical. Over there. The one having an argument with the nurse. Sorry, but I thought you should know. " Penina saw the back of a tall, thin woman, shaking with anger. "Can I help?" she said, on reaching the pair. The nurse was palpably relieved, and beat a retreat. The woman turned her eyes on Penina. They were the palest blue she had ever seen, suffused in misery like twin lakes in fog. "My sister, was on the bus," she began. "There was no room for me." "I know what happened," Penina said in a calming voice. "I heard you on the radio." The mist cleared for a moment. "Was I on the radio? No-one knows where she is," she went on. "How can that be? My God! Perhaps there was nothing left?" She burst into tears. "That doesn't happen," Penina said. "Don't be afraid. We'll find her." "We'll find her, we'll find her," the woman echoed mockingly. "They all say that. But I demand to know the truth! What have they done with her?" The woman was shouting. Penina knew that her last sentence was not a question. It was an accusation. "Not all the patients have been identified. We're going to Information. They keep a record of everyone who has been admitted here, and at other hospitals." The woman's eyes filled with disbelief. "An ambulance driver told me that the injured from the rear end of the bus were brought here. Did you hear me? Here!" she screamed. Penina noted the distorted slant of the woman's mouth and the way she held one shoulder lower than the other. "Give me her name and a brief description," she said, raising her voice above the woman's. "I'll see what I can do." The woman calmed down and seemed, at least superficially, normal. "Ellie Lagerhorn. Aged twenty six. Tall. Nordic looking. A natural blonde. She was so beautiful." She began to cry. Her anger had fled. Without it, she seemed lifeless. Without anger, without hope. The woman had described her sister in the past tense, finally convincing Penina that she was not looking at a relative, but a patient. "Come with me," Penina told her, taking her arm. But the woman snatched it back. Penina led the way to Information, the woman trailing behind her. The clerks stiffened as they saw them approach. "This woman has lost her sister. Is there any record of an Ellie Lagerhorn." "We've already told her that we have not identified anyone of that name. We've checked the other hospitals. We'll inform her the moment we have some news." The woman let out a piercing scream that rose above the surrounding chaos, which stopped momentarily, as if a referee's whistle had sounded. Then she crumbled and rested a trembling head on Penina's shoulder. One of the clerks was going through photographs of people who could not be identified, while the woman monitored them with one eye, her head still on Penina's shoulder. A pair of shoes was shown her, the only identifying mark of some victim. They were Roman-style sandals of a type that many Israeli women wore. The long arm of the woman shot out and snatched the photograph. "These are her shoes!" she shouted, trumping all doubt. "She must be here! Where is she? You're hiding her. Now I've caught you out." "These belong to a woman with a very different description," Penina said, reading the notes below the photograph. "I don't think she can be...." "Why are you keeping her from me? Something terrible must have happened to her. I demand to see her!" the woman said in a voice of iron. One of the clerks tried to whisper something to Penina, but the woman was becoming agitated and Penina led her to the ward for burns victims.

"This woman has recognized her sister's shoes," she said as she showed the picture to a senior nurse. "Not another one!" the sister answered. "She's in the last bed. I'll have to leave you to sort it out." Penina found four people sitting by the bed of a woman whose head was swathed in bandages. "Are you relatives?" she asked. "Yes. This is my sister, Orit" said a middle aged man, indicating the bound figure. "But these people think she's someone else." "That's right. She's my mother," said a young woman, adding sarcastically, "I think I should know my own mother, injuries or not." Penina looked at the tall woman to gauge her reaction. The woman's brow was furrowed with deep lines as if she was struggling with something she could not comprehend. "Who are these people?" she demanded. "This is my sister beyond doubt. You can tell them all to go home." She kissed the patient tenderly in the middle of her bandaged brow. "If only I had caught the bus instead of you, my darling sister. Why do these things happen?" The other claimants became agitated. Penina gathered her professionalism around her like a cloak. "This can't be your sister. Your sister is tall like you and blonde. This woman is shorter than me and the traces of the hair she has left are quite dark. You said your sister was thirty, while at a guess, I'd say this woman is in her mid-forties, at least. They can't be the same." The woman stood perfectly still, seemingly without breathing, wrapped in thought. "What are you talking about?" she shouted at Penina without looking at her. "This is my sister." She addressed the figure in the bed with compassion. "Why do these things happen? What makes them happen? Are you dead? Get all these people away!" She sank to her knees beside the bed and howled like a wolf. Penina tried to raise her but despite the woman's exhaustion she pushed her away with ease. Penina made the shape of a syringe with her thumb and forefinger to a passing orderly, who returned a few minutes later with Ilana, the heavily-built Head Nurse. "I know about her," Ilana said as Penina started to explain. "I've had several reports from staff." She placed her hands under the woman's armpits and raised her gently but firmly to her feet. She took hold of one arm. Penina took the other. The woman's howl turned into a low-pitched wail, then silence. She let herself be led into a small cubicle and offered no resistance when Ilana sedated her, as if she understood it was time for temporary oblivion. As Ilana injected a sedative into the woman's arm, Penina noticed the two watches Ilana always wore in a suicide-bomb emergency – the first set on normal time, the second, synchronized to time zero – when the bomb went off. This watch told her to a second, how long patients had sustained their injuries. "I hate having people sedated," Penina said as Ilana removed the syringe. "I know it must be done, but it's a defeat, every time. What if her sister is in another hospital, or even here, in all this chaos? What if she dies, while this woman is under sedation? I'd never forgive myself." "If we had a hundred psychologists, Penina, you could say that," Ilana said. "You've nothing to reproach yourself with." The Head Nurse smiled the blunt smile of one to whom smiling does not come readily and hurried to the next crisis. Penina watched her broad Russian back disappear among the press. Ilana knew the secret of how and when to be tough. It was a gift, aided by a compliant desire in most of us to be taken under control, just as we feel we are losing it.

"Where, in God's name, have you been?" The voice was Natalie's. "Just walk in and choose a patient? Like pick and mix in a candy store? Don't bother answering. Just let me tell you what you are supposed to be doing. As luck would have it, we have had three clinical psychology students, about to take their finals, assigned to us for a week, as from today. It's the best and worst time for them to be here. The bomber did not notify the medical school that she was going to rid the world of herself – and, tragically, a whole bunch of others – this particular morning, so their medical school was unable to cancel. I've assigned you as monitor. You're to show the students how the department works and how we deal with crises. Push them into the chaos, with both hands. Just remember they aren't allowed to take decisions. You'll find them hiding in my office. They've never dealt with anything like this. They are terrified, but eager to get started. Good luck."

Penina supervised her students all day and well into the evening by which time, they were friends for life. Her medical colleagues, she told them, had X-rays, catscans, INR machines, and physical evidence such as injuries, to guide their expertise, but clinical psychologists, although they also made use of the above, often had to judge the pitch of a voice, the use of a word, the expression of a thought, or the use of body language to get on top of a case. At really difficult moments, she confessed, it was like reading tea leaves. And it could mean the difference between achieving normalcy or victimhood.

She did not even think of the Colonel. His ward had been evacuated, its patients transferred to other wards, or assigned to corridors, previously fitted with power points, to take medical hardware, in order to leave space for victims of any new emergency. He was not conscious of what was going on around him. Penina passed by his bed several times, but did not recognize the patient in it.

***

That a patient who barely passed the most basic neurological verbal test, could hold forth at length and in detail on events that occurred in the Roman empire the best part of two thousand years previously, in a state of semi-consciousness, was barely credible. But there was the tape, rewinding crazily, like an animated cartoon. Clearly, the part of the brain that contained these memories was not the same as the part involved in everyday speech. She glanced at a model of the brain, atop a cupboard, a memento of her student days. What we didn't know about its functions would fill several of those huge textbooks that laid out what we did. Something in the brain had been freed, stimulated – created, she dared to add – by the wound to his head. It must have been the wounding rather than the surgical intervention, because he had one revelation before surgery took place. How could his long-term memory have been stimulated in this way? And long-term memory of what? Not for a moment did she consider that he might be recounting events that had happened to him in some murky historical past. That could only mean, in another life! Rubbish. Somehow he had collated all this material in his mind over many years, she thought, and in all likelihood did not know he had done so. Add a seminal imagination and you had the essentials for creating a window on the past. But why open the window now, when he needed all the mental resources he could muster? And how did he express what it was he saw with such verbal sagacity? Was all it needed a head wound? Weeks, if not months of research lay before her. She told herself she was looking at a unique psychological event. Once (again) her mind toyed with the idea of Yuri's case history leading to a paper, which she would present at a professional conference, or incorporate in her doctorate, but she quickly discarded the notion. She could not face benefitting from his ordeal. Just for now, he was in full coma. Ever further removed.

***

The clinical psychologists' room was empty. Penina sighed with relief. The last thing she wanted was to run into a colleague. Since Yuri had gone into full coma, she had lost speed. Not in commitment, but in effort. She felt that a tree had been felled which left a hole in her personal environment. She was sitting by her computer, unable to recall her code. She had to search her address book. She fed it in, clicked onto 'receive messages' and waited. If pressed, she would have had to admit that she was waiting for salvation. For a message from the gods that said: "This is what you must do." There were eleven messages, not one from the gods. She scanned the list for anything of importance. At the tenth entry, she stopped and stared: it was from her American cousin, Lauren, whom she had not seen for years. They kept in desultory touch by passing greetings via friends or colleagues who traveled from Jerusalem to New York or vice versa. She was used to strangers on the telephone telling her that they had been asked to send her cousin's love and occasionally suggesting they should meet. The latter approach usually meant that Lauren was playing the shadchanit, the marriage broker, and had whetted the appetite of some supposed marital candidate with exaggerated tales of her Israeli cousin's intelligence (that came first in Lauren's book) followed by her character, and what an interesting person she was. Her looks, she was sure, were not mentioned. Lauren was a genuine beauty, without the aid of Revlon, Max Factor or Gucci, et al. She used them, yes, but to proclaim her status rather than enhance her looks. Penina was enviously aware of Lauren's effect on men: she transformed them. A 45-year-old bachelor, who counted his conquests on one hand, would be transformed into a raving Don Juan in the bask of her smile. Penina had seen it happen. The meek were transmogrified into hunters, the plain-looking, art-brushed into confident escorts, and the clinically depressed became impulsive utopians after five minutes of her attention. The men she sent only existed in that form in her presence. In a short while, they changed back into diurnal dreariness, like Cinderella, programed to turn into a pumpkin at the stroke of midnight. By the time they rang Penina, jetlagged and unconfident, they were already albatrosses around their own necks. No, she told herself, she could not stand another of Lauren's suitors. Not now. Not with a war on. Yes that was the answer, she'd use. There was a war on and she was in the middle of it. And she could not meet anyone. Taking a decision about a hypothetical situation, made her feel better. Uncertain if she was right or wrong, she cajoled her computer mouse to bring Lauren's message onto the screen.

"Dearest Pen, guess where I am! London! For a psychiatric conference which was damn interesting for once. Also managed to eat in some really fine restaurants and caught some great shows. And the Embankment at night! I expect this is nothing to you. You must have done it all when you were studying here. How I envy! Actually the conference ends today. Thinks: why not get Pen to come over for a few days. We'd have a proverbial ball. Drive up to Scotland! Take the tunnel to Paris! Don't think about it. Just come! This is one of my best ideas. We've so much to catch up on and I need to get conferencitis out of my bones. Sending all the love you could wish for, Lorrie."

The message was so different to the one she anticipated, Penina was in shock. She read it twice, to make sure it was no joke. The gulf between Lorrie's expectations and her own situation was unbridgeable. Did Lorrie really think she could drop everything and fly off to London? More likely, some plan of Lauren's had fallen through and she had come up with a new one, regarding meeting her. Evidently, nothing had daunted her notorious impulsiveness, which she drove to the ultimate point. Penina was slightly annoyed that such a good idea should be proposed at so impossible a time, and replied immediately.

"Darling Lorrie,

What a wonderful idea – but how can I? I am up to my neck in a war. There's no way I can leave. People are being killed and maimed. I appreciate the thought – it is one of your best – but not right now. Glad to hear the conference was worthwhile. You make me nostalgic about London. I had a great time there. There's an alternative to me coming to London – why don't you come to Jerusalem? It would be a much-needed therapy just to see you. Think about it. All my love, Pen."

She read it through, refrained from making any changes, pressed 'send' and began to scan the rest of her mail. There was one from her father in New York, complaining that he had not heard from her in weeks. She wrote back, using her work load as an excuse. As she pressed 'send,' her incoming mail icon flashed 'receiving mail'. She brought it to her screen. It was a reply from Lauren who must have received Penina's message while she was at her computer or phone. It was short and businesslike. "Hi Pen. How about Cyprus? Love. L." Penina replied at once: "You're moving in the right direction. Keep going – east. Love P."

After that they exchanged messages as if they were talking in the same room. "Pen. I've never been to Israel and wouldn't know what to expect, apart from possibly being blown up. Where else is there? Jordan?" "Lorrie. Nowhere else. P." "Pen. Someone told me that Petra, wherever that is, is a great place. Is that easier for you? L." "Honey, if we're to meet up, it's got to be Jerusalem. I must be honest. I can't give you a lot of my time. But Jerusalem is a beautiful city, packed with history. You've never had a problem finding your way around. I'll warn you where not to go. I've got some heavy cases right now. Example: a Colonel who is in coma and had some PLE's, from Roman times and God knows when else. Give it a try. Love, P." Penina waited a few minutes but no answer came. Her cousin was probably inquiring about a trip to Dublin. Moments later, the receiving icon indicated that a new message was coming in. Penina was sure it was from Lauren and guessed at its contents: "Decided on Paris (or Edinburgh or Venice, or Helsinki). Let's get together another time when there's nothing else to think about. Love. Your cousin." She clicked on the new message. She was right, it was from her cousin. It read: "Arriving Ben Gurion airport early tomorrow morning. Please don't pick me up. Remind me of your address and I'll take a cab. Funny you should have a Colonel with previous life experiences – that's what the conference was about. Hope I'm doing the right thing, coming to Israel. I'm a graduate coward – with honors – when it comes to being killed for no good reason. Dying (may the pun be averted), to see you. Leave the key anywhere,

I'll find it. Lauren." Apart from the pleasure of seeing her cousin, Penina predicted a useful outcome. Her cousin – a highly respected psychiatrist in private practice in Manhattan – who devoted a lot of her time to impecunious Medicare patients – could surely be used to sharpen Professor Bondman's interest in the uniqueness of Yuri's case and perhaps allow the use of hypnotism which needed departmental permission. She replied to her cousin, saying how excited she was and telling her not to take a cab but to look for a driver displaying her name – probably misspelt – when she got to the arrivals lobby.

***

The fragrance of expensive perfume awoke her. Her eyes slowly took in Lauren's tall, elegant figure as it slowly materialized, like a developing print. She leapt up, arms extended and the two women embraced. "I've been spying on you," said Lauren, speaking through red hair. "You know, even when you're asleep, you look professional. I always wondered at that – you even looked like a professional person when you were peeling potatoes in the Catskills. When most women do that, they look as if they never did anything else." "Maybe, Lauren, but you have the edge. Whatever you do, even if it's taking the rubbish to the bin, you always look beautiful." "A blessing and a curse," Lauren replied. "What are you doing in my office, anyway?" Penina demanded, with mock crossness. "You're supposed to be in bed, in my apartment." "A lot of good it would have done me if I'd gone there. Do you sleep here because you can't afford the rent?" They held each other at arms' length, reading the inventory of their faces, investing in memories. "Now that you're here, Lauren, there's something I'd like you to look at. Just a sentence the Colonel came up with before he went into coma. I was listening to it before I fell asleep." "He's comatose?" "Yes yesterday. In this instance, he's talking about the land of Israel." She handed Lauren a print-out on which was written: "The blessed land. Let its stones cut my feet, yes, let its stones cut my feet. Its cuts are like caresses." "I couldn't hear the rest," Penina went on. "I could only stay with him for a few minutes, that time, but he didn't say anything else. He was very up-tight. When he relaxed his hands, I noticed deep nail marks in his palms. "Let its stones cut my feet," she repeated with wonder. She felt the challenge of Lauren's skeptical gray eyes. "I don't know what to make of that, Penina. Was he quoting? Reading? Writing, perhaps?" "Or was he remembering?" Penina put in quickly. "But people don't remember like that." Lauren said. "It was poetry. It was something thought out, after the event. Perhaps long after, like recently." "But it is based on what he felt at the time. Perhaps he put it into poetic form later, maybe years later, but it was the direct result of experience – of the experience of having his feet cut by the stones on the way to Caesarea."

""Oh, come on!" said Lauren, "what we are talking about is memory, or rather, how we remember. But Penina darling, don't drag me back to the conference. I had a week of it." "Oh, I would have loved to have been there. Look, 'how we remember' is something I've been working on. Do you mind, if I try a theory out on you?" "OK. But just remember I'm not an expert. Just an interested gal," said Lauren. "Sure. I'll try to remember that. The question is: when we look back on events in our lives, don't we remember them as the conclusions we came to, rather than the events themselves? We remember events as we assimilate them, not necessarily in their pure state. Listen to this," Penina said, searching among the files on her desk. "This is a young officer, who was blown up with his tank, a few years back. He's talking about what happened. "A bus was taking schoolkids back to their settlement when it was fired on by terrorists. We were called out to give the kids cover and engage the enemy. The attack took place only a kilometer from our position. We got there in perhaps 10 minutes and immediately pulled into a firing position. They were still shooting at the bus, with automatic weapons, from a house less than fifty meters down the road. Through the telescopic site, I could see the kids screaming, the driver looked dead. Let the bastards have it, I ordered. As the gunner leveled the cannon, there was a huge explosion. The tank is off the ground. Have we been hit? Did the canon backfire? Was it a malfunction in the ammunition compartment? I must have been thrown against the tank's roof. We're falling to the ground. I am flying through flames. It's all I remember. When I came to, I found out that we had lost two of the crew. Three children in the bus had been killed. How they destroyed our tank is a mystery. It was an Israeli-made Merkava, said to be the best in the world. They had planned the incident with professional precision. The whole incident was a baited trap. They wanted to get a Merkava, to prove a point." Lauren was about to say something, but Penina stopped her with a gesture of her hand. "What I'm reading was taken from his interview with me, soon after he was admitted. That is how he remembered it. But this is what he said, later, under hypnosis. There is one major discrepancy." She skimmed through a thick transcript in Hebrew while Lauren watched with polite curiosity. The letters on the page seemed to her bleak, without beauty, not like Chinese or Arabic. "Here. This is what he says. 'The driver is probably dead. I can't see any children, but I can hear them. There is blood and what could be brains on the bus windows. Enemy fire is coming from a white house fifty meters away. Why ambush a bus from a house? No sense. Let the bastards have it. I give the order: Take aim. An explosion. My God! The tank is rising. We are off the ground. They must have got us with a mine. Flames everywhere. Nothing. I am nowhere.

"They planned the incident with professional precision and had chosen a precise point to attack the bus, making sure to kill the driver first. They had calculated that we would send a tank in response, exactly where we would take up our firing position, and had planted enough explosives on the spot to sink a battleship. We didn't stand a chance. Later we leveled the house, to the usual chorus of world disapproval, which was not extended to the murdered kids." Penina looked at Lauren for any sign she had seen the point. "Very interesting but so what?" she said in an adversarial tone. "In the first account, he has no idea what caused the explosion. A malfunction, he supposes. Or a hit. He describes events as they appeared at the time. In the second, he has become aware of new facts and built them into his memory. He now says that it was a landmine. Which was true. We do that all the time. Our memories develop and change." "About everything?" "Yes, I believe so." "What you're saying," Lauren pursued, "is that the officer had two memories of what happened. One, his original memory from the time of the relevant experience – which is apparently no longer consciously available to him – and one, a later, multiple memory, a mixture of what he remembers of the experience and information that he has gathered since. He now knows that it was a mine. He has forgotten he once thought it was an explosion within the tank, or a hit of some kind. OK. Suppose years have passed. He's now an old man and you hypnotize him. Which memory will you get?" "One of any number – if he has had good reason to develop them," Penina said, confidently. "I can't buy that," Lauren countered. "If you are using hypnosis, you will always get the original. Hypnosis, Penny, is the truth drug. Well, kind of. If he has had reason to change his mind, he will hold secondary information in another part of his brain. There can be a second, a third or even a fourth version. But these are hybrid memories." "So how do you account for the fact that in the tank story, he came up with a hybrid version, as you call them, and not the original, under hypnosis?" "There has to be some local reason, depending perhaps on the way he was hypnotized, or perhaps two parts of his brain were transmitting information simultaneously, or perhaps he was misunderstood." "I don't have the records available right now, but just you wait. This is something I've been working on. Put simply, I believe there is a hierarchy of memory. We pull out the one that suits us at the time, according to received knowledge." She began to pack her things.

"On another plane altogether, I've got to do my rounds now, Lauren. Do you want to get some rest, take a look at Jerusalem, or stick with me?" "If you don't mind, I'll stick." "That," said Penina, "may have been a bad decision – I've a list of hard-core patients as long as my arm. It's going to be a sad morning."

***

She led Lauren towards the first patient on her list. A few feet from the bed she asked her cousin to stay back, until she had established contact. Then she moved briskly forward, noting the eye movement of the patient who had taken in her presence but pretended she had not seen her. When she reached the foot of the bed, the girl was looking down at her clutched fingers. She quickly read through her notes: Enat Barad, 15, of Mevushelet near Jerusalem, severe lacerations from bolt and nail missiles to the lower abdomen, upper left breast, lower face and left eye – 40% loss of vision, recovery of up to 70%-80% possible. Severe PTSD. Father on the critical list. Grandmother in serious condition. "Hi Enat, I'm Penina." Enat said nothing and continued to look down. "Is there anything I can get you?" The girl did not reply. "Do you want to sit up?" Enat shrugged her shoulders. Penina walked around the bed and raised her as much as she could, readjusting the cushions. Enat made no effort of her own. "That's a lot better," Penina commented. "How are you sleeping?" The question seemed to prompt a struggle in Enat's mind. "The nights can be long in a place like this," Penina added, giving the patient a possible lead. "I don't sleep," Enat said, curling her lips, as if words had a bad taste. "Not at all?" "No." "What do you do all night?" "I think." Seeing that there was the possibility of a conversation, she signaled to Lauren to join them. Lauren stood at the foot of the bed. "Lauren, this is Enat," Penina said, switching from Hebrew to English. "Hi, Enat, my name is Lauren." She smiled broadly at the girl, displaying a row of expensive white teeth. The girl was immediately taken by Lauren's resemblance to a model in a tv commercial. "At Americay?" she asked in Hebrew. "She wants to know if you're an American," Penina translated. "That's right. I'm an Americay," she said with mock solemnity, holding her right hand across her left breast as if taking the oath of allegiance. Enat tried to smile. Her right cheek swelled with the effort, but the cavity in her other cheek became more cavernous. "My family is half American and half Israeli," Enat volunteered, breaking into accented English. "Two of my uncles and half my cousins are Israeli and..." she suddenly pulled herself up, as if she had said the wrong thing. Penina guessed that the girl was censoring herself. She was no longer a vivacious and confident teenager, boasting about her mixed background. She was working on a new image of herself, which took account of her new situation. One day, if all went well, the two images would encounter each other – and dwell in peace. It was Penina's job to set her on the path, so that the overlap would include as much of the original as possible. She decided to bring the girl back to the present. "What do you think about all night, if you don't sleep?" Enat clutched her hands and looked at them. "I think about my Dad," she said finally. "How is he?" Enat drew her body in, making herself seem smaller than she was. "He's dead." Penina wasn't sure what to make of that. It wasn't in her notes. "Who told you?" "No-one told me. I just know." "You can't just know something like that, Enat." "They won't tell me because they think I'll be upset." "And wouldn't you be, if you really knew your father was dead. You'd be crying. You're not crying." Enat turned molten brown eyes upon her. "I'm crying inside!" she tried to shout, but without enough breath to achieve the desired volume. Everyone in the ward glanced towards them. "You're crying because you fear he will die. And you're trying to protect yourself from that possibility by pretending the worst has already happened. It won't protect you, Enat." "Can I speak to her?" Lauren intervened. "Will you translate?" Penina nodded. Lauren leaned over the bed as far as she could reach. "Enat. Have you ever ridden a horse?" Enat did not understand why she was being asked what seemed to her, a frivolous question and did not answer. "I used to a lot," Lauren went on. "A horse is a large and very strong animal with a will of its own. There is no reason why he should do as you say. So, if you want to go anywhere, you have to control him. You do that by using the reins. If you know how to use them, controlling him is fairly easy. But, Enat, my darling, the horse you are trying to ride is a fantasy horse. The trouble is that you can't control it. It'll do what it likes and will take you with it. You may think you are in control, but you are not. A real horse will go where you want it to. You must take control of the real horse, Enat. Take the reins. Go on. You will get better if you do. Do you understand what I'm saying? And one day, when I come back to Israel, we'll go for ride. Perhaps in the desert. I've never ridden on sand. I've always wanted to." As Penina translated the last words, Enat's face became a mask of pain. Tears poured down her cheeks, disappearing on one side like rain into a hollow. Penina put her arm around the girl's shoulders and let her cry herself to sleep. "You've opened her mind, Lauren. Thank you."

It was a depressing morning. The emergency room, psychiatric ward and corridors were full of patients who, apart from organic injuries, presented a classic range of psychological trauma from PTSD to denial, anxiety, fear, avoidance, lack of control and every nuance of depression. Among visiting relatives too, there were clear signs of disturbance. A girl of eleven insisted on seeing her father, even though she had seen his name listed among the dead. "But where is he now?" she demanded? No-one could tell her; a once-self-assured computer programmer worried constantly that a bomber would walk into the hospital and detonate himself right by her bed; a taxi driver, whose face had been shredded with flying glass, had nightmares of billions of glass projectiles approaching the earth through space. One case after another reminded Lauren of 9/11. Her practice was a few blocks from the Twin Towers. In the weeks after, she saw many survivors. In Penina's company, she slowly became aware of the same ripple effect, like a layer of volcanic ash, which slowly encompasses every thought and every act and every horizon after an atrocity. Israel had not experienced a single cataclysmic event on the scale of the United States, but suicide bombings and drive-by murders can produce a similar toll on the individuals involved. The long-term results of such tragedy will be carried across lifetimes, mitigated, perhaps, by time and therapy and human resilience, and, in some cases, passed on to the next generation, as the traumas of the Holocaust often were.

In the afternoon, Penina took her guest to meet her colleagues in the psychology department while she finished her rounds. Lauren spent a lot of time discussing similarities and dissimilarities among 9/11 victims and the rising tide of suicide bombing cases. She formed the impression that her Israeli colleagues were dedicated and highly competent at their job, if a little over-reverential to the textbook. "The Palestinians must be having a terrible time of it too," she observed. "Definitely," said a senior psychiatrist, who introduced himself as Mohammad. "But there are differences for us. We have low expectations. We do not believe anyone will help us, so we expect nothing. I'm talking about the man in the street. They either slowly pull themselves together or they slowly fall apart, or they put all their energy into revenge and hatred of Jews, which conceals their symptoms until they do something irrational. They are not going to get the psychological or psychiatric help they need. If they come here, they will get what we can offer. But the damage is not so much individual, as societal. We can't cure an entire population's psychology. Only peace can begin to do that. They are in despair. On the other hand, Israel is largely a western type society and its Jewish population have high expectations. They want the quick fix. They want to be patched up and sent back to the psychological front line immediately. Israeli Jews believe they should have a personal psychiatrist each, on call twenty four hours a day. And if they don't get one, that's another cause for anxiety." Lauren knew she was swimming in waters that hid strong currents, but she had no intention of leaving Israel as ignorant as when she arrived. "Let's say you are partly right and partly wrong." The voice came from behind her. It was one she had not heard before. Turning, she saw a diminutive man in his mid-fifties, with a lined face and mischievous green eyes, standing next to Penina. "We haven't met," he said, extending his arm. "I'm Prof. Bondman. The point about the suicide bombers, stone throwers, so-called martyrs of the knife, etcetera, whose work we deal with almost every day, is that they are not in despair. On the contrary, they are euphoric, ecstatic, triumphalist even. They are dedicated to destroying the Jewish state, and each bombing or knifing, or lethal rock-throwing, is a piece in the mosaic of conquest. If they have despair, you might say they suffer from a transcendental form of it. True, the society in which they are rooted is in despair. But what does that mean? Many people would think that it was the result purely of the Israeli occupation and the daily injustices and humiliation that, admittedly, go with it. That is the conclusion people would jump to, because that is what they have been led to believe. And it is part of the truth. But what I call Palestinian transcendental despair is also born of the abysmal leadership they have had for a century, the terrible corruption that the regime stinks of, the injustices of a police state, the appalling unemployment, the total absence of progress and the hate machine run by their leaders against us, which substitutes revenge for hope and even more importantly revenge for the malfunctioning of their own society. Revenge and hatred are as lethal to the metabolism as smoking and heroin, pollution and cancer. In their obsession to kill us, they are killing themselves. Each bombing, each attack, is as much directed against their own leadership and their own society, as against us. It is also directed against the terror activists themselves. The fact that they so often blow themselves up is an indication of their frustration with their own lot as much as with ours. They know there is a way out, but they refuse to take it. That is the true seat of their despair. I would say that we, I mean the Israeli Jewish population, suffer from a similar type of despair, except that we use other means to extricate ourselves. Both they and we know, there is a way out. But neither is prepared to pay the price. Cold-blooded murder and horrific injury, inflicted on the unfortunate people you have been seeing this morning, cannot be explained by despair. It is an obscenity which cannot be given justification, because it leads to the path of Auschwitz. Once you concede that the deliberate murder of innocents can be justifiably used as a weapon in order to spread terror into the hearts of others, you have taken a flying jump from the moral high ground and landed just short of Armageddon. I have the greatest sympathy for the Palestinians, and no small amount of respect – we have a lot of them in this hospital as patients, not to mention staff, but they are immobilized, as we are. Both sides seek to solve their dilemmas by cognitive dissonance. We both pretend it is the answer. It is not. It's the problem." Prof. Bondman had a quality of discourse which gave the impression that, when he had finished saying what he had to say, the conversation was over. His colleagues nodded and got on with their business, making phone calls, scanning their computers and leaving the room. Lauren, whose American Jewish liberal instincts had been scratched by some of the things the professor had said, was about to continue the argument, but Penina spoke first. "Prof. Bondman has said he'll see us tomorrow morning after he has finished his rounds." Bondman's merry eyes looked up at the American who stood a head taller. "I believe you did your MD under Prof. Ricardt," he said. "He is a good friend of mine – and a good friend of Israel. I look forward to our meeting tomorrow. But now, if you will excuse me." He held Lauren's hand in his for a few seconds longer than propriety demanded, before he made for the exit. "I've done as much as I can today," Penina said, watching him go. "At last I'm through. We can go home." Lauren looked at Penina's face, its lines deeper than this morning, stripped of its vivacity. Her skin was matt.

***

Penina drove back to her apartment, dropping off for some basics at a tiny mercolet. It was a democratic institution whose limited stock had been voted onto its shelves by the ever-changing demographics of the neighborhood, which recently had become a haven for religious young couples starting families, or trying for their fifth, or sixth child. Weaving through the group of Orthodox women gossiping outside, whose excitable children spilt dangerously onto the road, Penina and Lauren reached the shop which they half-filled. The other half was occupied by an Orthodox man and his wife debating the merits, relative to cost, of a large plastic Sabbath tablecloth. The plump, dark-skinned owner's wife, who was unrolling it across the counter, smiled brightly at Penina, whose hands delved deftly among the items on the shelves which had been left in untidy heaps by other customers and their children. She introduced Lauren as her cousin from America. "B'rachim ha Ba-im, welcome," the woman said in a sing-song voice. She added: "You like Israel?" "I only arrived this morning. It's too early to say," Lauren said quickly. Penina could tell she did not like being asked. As they left – and were immediately replaced by two impatient customers from the volatile band of young to youngish women, besieging the premises – Penina heard the owner's wife say to the Orthodox couple: "In my opinion, Jews should love Israel before they come. Why does she need to look around? Is she a cop?" Penina knew exactly what the woman meant and why Lauren would not have understood what the words implied.

"I hope you have somewhere else to go to when you shop, Penina. That place would drive me crazy," Lauren said as they climbed the steps leading to the upper level of a small hill into which two short rows of apartment houses had been cut and faced with Jerusalem stone.

"Don't worry, we have malls and big stores, but you have to drive there and park and go through security. This is so convenient. Besides I was brought up shopping in shops like that. It's like reliving my childhood." "But those women. And their kids. As soon as one is old enough not to need the pushchair, the next one is already climbing into it. Maybe sooner. Did you notice? They each had a bunch of kids around their feet, and they were all pregnant! It was like a tv commercial for childless marriage." Penina's face projected an un-convincing smile. She had no plans for being swamped with kids herself, but to be married and have two or three little monsters, seemed to her, at age 34, more like a receding mirage, although still a desirable one. "You're not into children, Lauren, I get the feeling." "I'm neutral. Show me the right man. Ask me at the right time. Yeah, I'd have a kid. I just never seem to get my paradigms right."

"What do you mean, 'the right man'? You're married to Robert. You're halfway there." "Something less than halfway. Robert and I are splitting." "I'm so sorry." "There's nothing to be sorry about. It just didn't work out. Besides, there's someone else on my horizon." They had reached the light-blue-painted door of Penina's apartment, accessed through a small patio, littered with pot plants and a small almond tree. A weathered, all-wood bench lay against the railing. "The patio is my lung," Penina said, fumbling for her key. "In the summer it can be really oppressive inside. The air conditioning is the answer, but only if you have it on at gale force. I come outside and sit in the breeze and eat water melon and feel like a real person. B'rachim ha Ba'im," she added, as Lauren entered. "Welcome."

"Wow, so many colors! A rainbow of an apartment. I was wrong. I always thought you veered toward the staid, Penina." Penina frowned and opened the shutters. The late sunlight filled the room with pale gold, picking out the reds and blues in the Persian carpets, adding a veneer of mystery to the pictures, mainly reproductions that adorned the walls. Lauren stood back and looked at the pictures one by one. "Robert has a passion for pictures which he conveyed to me. About the only passion he did. But now I love art. We go to openings almost every week. We went, I meant to say. Must get used to the grammar of marriage." "Marriage has grammar?" "Sure. When you fall in love you use the future tense. When you're married you use the present. And when it all falls apart, you use the past." "Except that not all marriages fall apart." "Yes they do. It's just that some people aren't bright enough to notice. But even if they survive the slings and arrows somehow, they all end. It's called death." "Does that scare you?" "Now don't you get professional on me," Lauren replied, with a flourish to her smile which was like adding chocolate chips to cream. "I've heard every possible answer to that question. So have you, I guess. For my part, I've nothing to add," Lauren wound up in a descant voice." "I always feel that the answer tells me almost all I need to know about a person," Penina observed.

"You're not going to stop, are you, coz? Well, all right. I can't pretend that death is something you should file away and forget. After all, it's one of the things that most interests me – your Colonel's colorful past lives and, by implication, his past deaths. From what you said on the phone he walks through death like a ghost through walls." "I want you to know how much I appreciate your coming, Lauren." "Look, to be honest, I wanted to have major time away from Robert and see you again, of course." She reached out her hand, which bore a narrow-band golden wedding ring, affectionately. Penina took the opportunity to place a glass of mixed Israeli Shiraz and Merlot in it. The cousins grinned at each other. "L'haim, to Life," said Penina raising her glass. Lauren clinked hers against Penina's. They both held their glasses well down the stem, causing a high octave ping as the rims met, as if announcing the next round of a life cycle. "And I also had," Lauren went on, "some interest in seeing Israel." "Only some?" "Aw come on, Penny, it's you who was brought up at the Zionist end of the family. We didn't know the difference between Jerusalem and Jerseyville. My father wanted us to be essential Americans of the kind he was, with zero sum allegiance to anything else. He was a patriot, a Legionnaire, a flag-waver at the drop of a hat, who marched in every march he could march in, and I don't mean protest marches, I mean he marched for Glory, Glory Hallelujah and he always kept a black list in his mind of fellow Americans who only found time to protest. No counter attractions. Not to Israel, nor to the Pope, nor to Mecca, nor to foreign political agendas, nor to the old countries that people left in order to build something better. No looking back. 'Remember what happened to Lot's wife,' he used to say. 'The choice is a pillar of salt or the Statue of Liberty.' You know, he even included the Puritan heritage and WASP sensibilities in his list of what was unacceptable. If there was an office of High Priest of the Melting Point, he would have run for it. Another thing he used to say was that Wasps should not be outside the pot, just stirring it, they should be right inside, swimming like the rest of us." "Do you go along with that?" Penina asked enthusiastically." "I suppose he's right in theory. But in practice you'll never get rid of privilege. Sure, everyone should be in the pot, but the Wasps will see to it that they'll all be wearing life vests. You can be sure of that. Besides, it raises the question, who is minding the pot? If no-one is stirring, the stew will burn. That is the insidious problem that has bugged America since the beginning. Can the pot cook itself? It's a minefield, I know. My Dad just walked through the mines and never once got blown up.

I admire you Pops," she said, raising a glass of Israeli wine towards the mellowing horizon, "what you lacked in ideology, you made up for in conviction. I'm proud to be your daughter!"

"Food?" Penina suggested. "I was beginning to wonder when you were going to ask." "Let's have dinner out tomorrow when we're both feeling human. If there's not another bombing, we'll be on top of things at the hospital by then. If you're feeling pecky, there's a good takeaway suchi place near here. I'll order some. Will that do for now?"

***

The following day was scheduled to be routine but busy. She did not hear from Lauren all morning. At about four, she rang to find out how she was doing. Lauren's voice was more high-pitched than she had yet heard it. "You'll never guess where I've been," she said, laughing. "Mea Shearim. Me! In Mea Shearim." Penina was as surprised as Lauren meant her to be. "You're still alive, so you must have known to wear a long dress, cover your hair and everything else." "Oh yes, I was well-briefed," Lauren answered. Mea Shearim was the most orthodox quarter of Jerusalem where both men and women were required to dress according to extreme canons of modesty. "Did you manage to read the transcripts?" "Yes, I did. Aren't they something!"

Penina was delighted that Lauren seemed to be so taken by them. They had agreed it made no sense for her to come to the hospital again. She should spend it looking around Jerusalem. Penina would be back between seven and eight, and after a shower and a change, they could go out to dinner.

Penina had been involved in several counseling sessions during the afternoon with families of terror victims. One had been a particularly grueling conversation with a family whose son had sustained general injuries when a suicide bomber blew himself up at a restaurant where he'd stopped for lunch a few days before. The surgeons had pulled him from the jaws of death by a series of operations, but he had spiraled into depression and was in danger of losing the ground the surgeons had won. The battle now to be fought was for his mind, and she was being asked to perform in psychological terms what the surgeons had accomplished physically, but without an operating theatre, without instruments, without a clear map of what had to be done. It would have been helpful if the family had some form of belief, but in their world outlook, God's will had no remit. This was a secular family, for whom there was no solace, only recovery or loss. Had it happened in battle, they would have quickly adapted themselves to the situation through patriotism, but there was no reconciliation with the ultimate in victimhood. While the boy's mother had no God to lean on, she placed all her hope in Penina's skills. It was a huge weight for Penina to bear. In the absence of belief in the deity, the mother seemed to treat Penina as all-powerful, all knowing, all wise. Her tearful eyes beamed pleas at the clinical psychologist that should rightfully have been addressed to heaven. She clung desperately to the belief that Penina would find the golden formula that would restore her son's will to live. Penina realized she had two patients to attend. The mother was as much a patient as her son. She never left her son's side, except to remonstrate with the nurses or accost a doctor. Penina realized that this woman would have a huge influence upon her son's recovery, if there was to be one. As long as the mother saw hope, there was hope. To reassure her, Penina had to assume a semi-divine role. Nothing less would do. It was not one to which she felt suited. (Away from the ward, she laughed at the part she was required to play.) At her third visit she broke through the cocoon of self-pity that had enshrouded her patient. "When you go home," "when you get well again," "when you are out of here," were terms she had threaded through her monologues with him. When, suddenly, he asked: "how long will I be here?" she knew instinctively that he had picked up the message and rounded the bend. She told his mother, who threw her arms around him. As she withdrew, leaving mother and son in an umbilical hug, Penina unobtrusively removed her halo.

***

By the time she got back to the apartment, around eight, she was without her mantle of composure. "Is something wrong?" Lauren asked, the moment she saw her. "Nothing that some good Arak won't fix," she answered, throwing her backpack onto a chair and relieving the wine wrack of a bottle of Kentucky, the first bottle to come to hand. "I think," she said, holding up a generous double, as if making a toast, "that the Colonel is finally getting to me. L'hayim." "Well he's got to me and I've not had a tenth of your exposure. What in particular?" Lauren asked. "I won't be ready for that question, until I'm sitting in a restaurant I like and the first course is on its way. Do you mind a non-meat place? I'm an occasional vegetarian and today is one of my occasional days."

Penina managed to book a window table at a restaurant that had one of the best views of the old city. Lauren was stunned. "It's like looking at living history." "Living history is supplying me with an unending stream of clients right now. I can't watch it from an aesthetic point of view any more. But you can – so enjoy." Having inadvertently introduced a discordant note, she was eager to change the conversation. "Tell me about the adventures you've had today." "Right. They tie up with your Colonel. First, I must explain. You probably don't know, but I have another cousin in Jerusalem, on my mother's side. I only knew vaguely that he existed until I met a mutual friend at a wedding in New Jersey and she told me about him.

"I gathered that he is a mystic and very Orthodox and lives, I think I told you, in Mea Shearim. So I rang him on an impulse this morning, after I'd read the transcripts and he said come over. Even the taxi driver found it hard to find. A lane within a lane, within a lane. Thank God, I'd been warned how to dress. I looked as dull and unsexy and uninteresting as it's possible to be. When I looked in a mirror I looked like an extremist Amish. Even then, when I asked the way to the house, a woman neighbor went running indoors and rushed out with an awful shawl which I had to put over my head. I was already wearing a really nice one that I'd bought in Harrods. I felt a hundred per cent shmuck." "Whenever I have to go to an ultra-orthodox district, I feel so sexy," Penina countered. "I imagine I'm turning guys on all the time. If these guys are not allowed to see any female flesh, what a premium flesh must have." "He even left the door open throughout our meeting and people kept on drifting in and out for no apparent reason, pretending to look for things. Such lousy actors. It was because he mustn't be left alone with a woman, even one like I must have looked this morning. We never managed to work out what we are to each other. Something like second cousins once removed, perhaps. Do you remember those interminable conversations over those dreadful black and white family albums during those summers in the Catskills? In shot after shot everybody stared at the camera as if they were suspects on an identity parade? And Grandma used to say: "this is your third cousin twice removed." Even she didn't always get it right – and she knew them all. But this guy this morning, he was something else. For some reason, he could not get my name. He kept introducing me as Miss Spoorka, something like that. I kept telling him my name was Lauren. His English wasn't great." Penina couldn't keep back her laughter. "Oh my God, Laurie, he was introducing you as family. Mishpoorcha is Hebrew – and Yiddish – for family. He was telling people you were related." Lauren's face beamed like the sun. "Isn't that just it? On the flight, I learnt twenty useful Hebrew phrases from the flight magazine. That wasn't one of them." "You flew El Al?" "I wanted to immerse myself in the experience. Why start learning about Israel when you land? Why not start when you board?"

"Tell me, honey, what did you and your long lost cousin manage to talk about? I'm intrigued." "Ha. Ha. Did you know that Jewish mystics believe in reincarnation? He didn't bat an eyelid about the Colonel. He said the Colonel's here to work off some legacy from a past life and if he does it successfully, he won't need to come back again. Look, I'm not into this stuff. I can't see any basis for it. Talking to my cousin is like talking to a flat-earther. His total certainty is unbelievable. Not a square centimeter of doubt. And certainly no room for debate. He holds opinions as if they were laws of thermodynamics. Even so it's totally fascinating. Do you know what they believe?" "Not in detail." "Well, you're going to have the opportunity. He wants to meet your Colonel and he wants to listen to the tapes. I told him you would have to decide that." "Me and a whole committee."

"You know what I think," Lauren continued. "I could never accept what the Colonel says. I'd want a small army of classical scholars to check this stuff and if they say it is historically impeccable, that would have to be taken into consideration." "Of course," said Penina, "a historian cannot confirm or deny that in a past life, someone did a particular thing on a particular day, but the general situation he talks about certainly fits the historical bill. There was a battle of Beitar, the Jews were defeated, hundreds of thousands were sold into slavery, Rabbi Akiva was martyred and the Jews had to wait nearly two thousand years before a new Jewish state was born. We have no record, in the sources, of the victory speech by the Roman General Severus, but we do know that what the Colonel reports him as saying, was, in broad outline, historically true. Jerusalem was ploughed over, it was renamed Aeolia Capitolina, Jews were banned from living there and Rome did rename the country Palestina, meaning the land of the Philistines, the ancient enemies of the Jews, as a direct slap in the face to any future Jewish claim. Was the Colonel actually there in some other life, did he really hear General Severus, or did he put all this together in his head from sources readily available?"

"What interests me, Penny, is the apparent connection between his description of things and creative writing, of which it is, I think, a function. Just as the novelist or the dramatist or the poet travels in his own imagination, empathizes with people and the events that shape them, so the Colonel creates his own story which is as real to him as the present time. In other words, he projects himself into a past which he creates in his own mind in the present." "Based on what? Where is all this erudition coming from?" "Not from past lives, certainly," Lauren maintained, "but from prior knowledge and his own creative ability. It has to be based on stuff he has been taught in school, read in books, seen in films or imagines. What he does is to build it into a coherent picture with himself at the center. He becomes the lead actor in his own play. That is the part that really interests me. I want to know why should anyone want to do that, rather than if it is possible. The man is a dramatist, possibly one of the best in the country. If he had a one-man show in an off-Broadway theater – it'd be a sellout." "One thing could ruffle your argument, Lauren. If there was a piece of knowledge about which he could not possibly have known from the sources you have mentioned – that would be an effective challenge." "Indeed. But have you found something like that?" "No. I'm just positing. In principle that is what we should be looking for, if we're talking about some sort of scientific test." "And where should we look?" "Text and sources. It's all we've got."

"In the anomalous claims literature," Lauren answered, "there are many examples of supposedly special knowledge. Things that no-one else could possibly know. Yet there is frequently, a mundane explanation. I read whatever I could lay my hands on, before I went to the conference in London, and I spoke to all types of experts there. There is a huge following of people who believe that this phenomenon is authentic, or might be. Even some psychiatrists. There was one at the conference who accepts it hook, line and sinker. But in the vast majority of accounts of alleged past lives, including some famous ones, there is often a mundane explanation, based on the subject's deception or self-deception, innocent or otherwise. In one case, I've forgotten the name, a woman described a previous life in an Irish village during the potato famine, in a plethora of detail. It was checked against the historical record and shown to be accurate. The woman, an American, spoke under hypnosis in a broad Irish brogue, and even spoke some Gaelic. She took the Reincarnationists by storm. Her story of a pre-life in Ireland, was published and became a best seller. No-one could find fault with the amazing detail she came up with. Just a few years later, it came out that as a girl she had lived near a neighbor who came from Ireland and who used to tell interminable stories about her life there. Apparently, the woman had simply sublimated her girlhood memories, personalized them and regurgitated them as recollections of a previous life lived in another age. At school functions she had delivered Irish monologues in a heavy Irish brogue. As an adult, some psychological trigger opened this storehouse of memories which were so vivid, she believed they were her own. Since they clearly did not belong to life in America, she supposed they were evidence of a life somewhere else, a life she had once lived. Deception? Self-deception? More likely it's an example of the dynamics of the brain. It makes you wonder how much of other people's experience we assimilate and treat as if it were our own. Do we collect other people's experiences and build them into our psychological identity as one might receive a physical transplant? Is that what enables us to understand the motives and actions of people very different from ourselves – the child abuser, the rapist, the suicide bomber? Or do only some of us do that, the ones who claim past life experiences?"

"I want to be fair, Penny, but I think you have a sneaking desire to prove the Colonel right and medical science wrong. You're putting your personal feelings before science." "How can you say that?" Penina cut in angrily. "I have a sneaking desire to come up with the truth. I'm working in a perfectly scientific mode. You test new information against existing theory. If there is no match you find out if the information or the theory need adjustment." "I just have the feeling, Penina, that you would welcome science to be wrong, regardless of the consequences, whereas I would be totally dismayed. Everything I believe in would be shattered. My career would no longer have meaning. And it's the same for you, except that you seem to will it. Why?" "Why do you think?" Penina asked, wanting to tease out the nuances of Lauren's thought." "Only you can know the answer. It could be a disenchantment with current medical practice or philosophy, or with the stranglehold of medical bureaucracy – or within yourself. But I sense in all this a desire for the deluge, a sort of professional death wish." "All right, Lauren. You're both right and wrong. I am disenchanted, as you put it. But it is with the inadequacy of the means we have at our disposal to deal with problems that keep coming up. If past lives theory could be made kosher, it would give us such an important tool to deal with much of the misery I see daily. At the bottom of every victim's heart is the question: 'why me?' I can try to patch up their lives psychologically as a surgeon patches up membrane and tissue. In many cases I can give them a new outlook, a way of grasping the world anew, a way of relating to their families, their loved ones. I do it all the time, or at least I try to. But the question 'why me? 'is beyond my remit and that, deep down, is what they want to know. I can't talk to them about the law of averages or probability. They won't buy it."

"Look at it this way. A suicide bomber gets onto a crowded bus. He – or she – has to sit somewhere. The bomb goes off with the usual carnage. The person who happened to be sitting next to the bomber stands no chance. Others are severely or lightly injured. If you are severely wounded, you want to know why it was you who was hit, and if you walk out of the scene lightly wounded or not wounded at all, you want to know equally vehemently why you survived while others had their lives destroyed. With all the professional counseling in the world, I can't reach down that deep. Sure, I can point out that there was only one seat left next to you and that was taken by the bomber, or that you got up late that morning and that's why you didn't get your usual bus etc., but people think there is a reason for everything and want to know what it is. People search for meaning in their lives. It's a very powerful instinct. It's what makes us human. I cannot explain it to them. I don't know, myself. So it's not that I am disenchanted with medical science – although I am not enchanted either – it's that it does not, in certain cases, the ones I'm involved in, come up with a healing answer. And it is dogma that stands in the way." "Not dogma. Fact!" "Not fact. Fear!" The two women read each other's eyes for a long time, vainly seeking concession. "Believe me, I understand what you've been going through the last few years," Lauren said finally. "We had 9/11. But solace and healing can only come from what we know to be true. You can't import an illusion because it might be useful to some people to survive their trauma. True healing must be based on truth. We're not Plato. We can't just tell people what we think is good for them, regardless of the truth. Illusion is what I spend all my time stripping away from my patients' minds. It's like stripping off old paint so that I can add a new color. I'm not letting delusion in by the back door. No, sir!"

Lauren thought she glimpsed the suspicion of a smile play subliminally on Penina's lips. Penina opened huge eyes and suggested they talk about something else. Lauren gestured with her hands that she was willing. "You know," Penina said, "I've been looking forward to you coming as much for your professional insight – and I do hear what you say – as much as to hear where you're at. So what happened between you and Ron?"

Lauren balanced a profiterole on the edge of a long spoon with the precision required in a laboratory experiment. "The short answer is that it's all over with us," she said addressing the profiterole. "And the long answer?" "The long answer takes all night but the last sentence is identical with the short answer." "What went wrong?" Penina asked, wondering when Lauren was going to exhaust her interest in balancing the chocolate coated ball on the tip of her spoon. "Nothing," was Lauren's answer. "So why?" Lauren looked directly at her cousin. Her eyes were in neutral. "It wasn't right from the start. It just went on being less and less right." "Don't tell me you were never happy together, I don't believe it." "Yes, we were, in quotes, happy. In the sense that we got on well, we did things together, he had his career, I had mine, we always took an interest in each other's work, we had the same tastes, or similar, in art, in music, in movies, in people. We had a large circle of friends across the board, highly intelligent people. We have a town house which we made into really something. We argued over what should go where, but respected each other's opinions." "Sounds a touch too cosy. And in bed?" "It was a draw, neither of us was champ." "Sounds like a commercial for marriage, not divorce." "It's a marriage of the predictable. It's a marriage that could have been planned during those overlong summers in the Catskills and probably was. 'They are so suited.' 'They would make such a nice couple.' 'Did you see the way she looked at him.' 'I think something's going on.' 'Is she Jewish' – we met when families still asked that question. 'Yes. Thank God.' 'Don't push, don't push.' 'Let things take their course.' 'Keep your fingers crossed.' 'If she's a shiksa, do you think she'll change?' You must remember all that, Penny!" "I remember. But not Ron. Did he really come to the Catskills?" "Of course not. I met him years later. But he could have been some guy staying in the next cottage whom I might have met on the way to the grocery store. At first, marriage seems a game. You play until one day you realize it's not a game, it's for real and it's not the reality you want." "What do you want?" "Not that. You don't come out of yourself. You keep adding same to same. You forget your potential." "The tumultuous saga of the Jewish woman," Penina observed. "Too right. The Jewish woman has traveled light years in just two generations, maybe three. And the Jewish male is still a peddler at heart, just as the non-Jewish male is still a hustler. They're both looking out for how to make it. No matter if they work on the fiftieth floor on Wall Street, the non-Jew still plays with his gun, and the Jew chases the nicest available non-Jewish woman with the biggest boobs, and if he gets her, he thinks he's made it. They are like retarded children. When are Jewish men going to catch up?" "With what?" Penina questioned. "With the new Jewish woman. We're not looking for comfort any more. Don't bring us diamonds." "What has replaced diamonds?" "Scalps. We want scalps to hang around our waist." "Whose scalp?"

"Don't you know? Jewish men's for a start. After that, you can really get going. The scalp of poverty. The scalp of abuse. The scalp of starvation. The scalp of racism. The scalp of political correctness. Jewish women aren't waiting in line any more for the great Melting Pot, where we get stewed until we resemble a badly cooked goulash. Nor do we want to spend our lives cooking up answers to anti-Semites. Screw them! We must engage with the world. And do you know who the real enemy is?" "Let me guess: anyone who tries to stop you." "You've got it by the balls."

"But tell me, Lorrie, is all this good for the Jews or bad for the Jews?" "Oh, it's the one and only good for the Jews. Trouble is, our men are still trying to work it out. How much longer can we get by on gefilte fish, Haman taschen and Bar Mitzvahs? That's culture? That's a contribution? For how much longer can we iterate and reiterate the "firsts" that we created? The belief in a Creator who lends purpose to life? The notion of a regular day of rest for man and beast? The idea that all men are equal because they are created in the image of God? The idea that love for your fellow doesn't stop at your ethnic boundary. I could go on. But I don't want to go on." "Let me add a first that I've only recently been made aware of. It's something Shira, the Colonel's wife, has been working on. She says that our early scriptures introduced prose fiction into historical writing for the first time. Before that, holy writings were myths written in epic language. Man was entrapped both in the myth and the language in which it was preserved – as in the creation stories of Marduk. In them mankind was created to serve the gods as slaves. By freeing man from mythical language, he/she was offered, for the first time, the possibility of development as an independent character. A human being. Not a human slave. To see himself as a free agent. And even, as we know from the story of Adam and Eve, to disobey God. That was a first which still applies, and how!" "I've never heard that one, Penny. If it's true, it's tremendous. But it doesn't change anything for me. I'm fed up reciting lists, debating the argument, trading on the past. Every time a real conversation comes up, I need a Bible which, I admit, I don't know that well. So when are we going to talk about the present? When are we going to do something? When are we going to be relevant? I don't mean in high tech and arms peddling. I mean, about today!"

"Lorrie, you're not going to like this, but you should live here, in Israel. You want to be a Jewish woman, this is the place. You want to make a difference, this is where making a difference starts. All those things you talked about, our past glories and the creation of present ones, and others in the future are only truly relevant here. Only here can they be related to today. Our way. Our day. And they are being. Slowly, yes slowly. But it's happening. The history of the Jews is the inverse story of the cuckoo. We lay our eggs and place them in other peoples' nests, and they go ahead and make them their own, without even a thank-you. Call it a melting pot, call it pluralism, call it democracy, call it stupidity. But they hardly ever acknowledge the provenance of our contribution. If you could patent ethics, we could sue for billions. Meantime, Jews outside Israel are living in cloud cuckoo land."

"I won't deny a word of that, Penny. But from what I hear, this country isn't ready for the new Jewish woman, like it's not ready for the new Mizrachi or Reform or Palestinian woman. They are all seen as off-Broadway. A sideshow. But we're not. Why make things harder for ourselves? In America, at least people know what we're talking about. Here they don't even know that. Why have enervating run-ins with antediluvian males, who think history stopped way back? That's another of our firsts. An ironical one. Our rabbinical gurus were sure history stopped centuries before Fukuyama came up with the idea. Why waste your energy confronting men who think that females who 'step out of line' are little better than witches? This is "Crucible" thinking. Arthur Miller, redux, remember? Today the Israeli Chief Rabbinate is a woebegone replacement for Deputy Governor Danforth. There is vast energy among American Jewish women. It is a salvific energy. We want to change the world. We are prophets. And we can deliver. But here we are fought off like a pack of wild dogs. That's what coming here would be about. Women want to have public prayer services at the Western Wall? Terrible. Women want to read our holy books in public? Nerve-racking. Women want to bless the congregation? Disgusting. Women want to be rabbis? Unforgiveable. Women want to be women as they define it, not as men define it? An abomination! Who knows more about what being a woman means? An ante-deluvian male, with the thickest shell in the shop, or women themselves?"

"I must be honest, Lorrie," Penina cut in. "I don't want any of that. Nor do most women I know." "Don't tell me you think progress comes from abstinence, Penina! Does healing the world – now there's a great Jewish idea, going way back to the Talmud – come from sitting on your tush, while watching over the meatballs? " "What about you, Lorrie? Do you think it comes from politically fired feminism which is right on equality but blind to difference? Vive la difference, the French say. Long live the difference. I haven't forgotten it, even if they have! We and men are not the same. I won't have my difference sacrificed on the altar of liberal or feminist politics. I cling to it. It's dear to me. I want to be the cleverest, the sexiest, the best informed, the most volcanic Jewish woman in the world." "You are not conscientized yet, Penny. You'll never win the fight against reaction until you face the reaction inside you." "OK, Lorrie. Let's suppose you're right. Let's say that Jewish women have an incredible amount to give the world, both Jewish and non-Jewish. But the best, I'd go so far as to say the only, place to do it is here, Israel. It may be a fiercer struggle, but in the end this is where it matters. This where the Jewish buck stops." "That's too ethno-centric for me," Lauren protested. "If you do it in some other place," Penina warned, "it'll get dissipated. It'll get cuckooed. Maybe distorted. Whatever. If it's the Jewish woman's reach, you wish to extend, this is where it must happen. This place is fit to bursting with ideas. With opportunities. With new horizons. Only from here can Jewish ideas be exported and keep their "copyright." If we're talking about a Jewish contribution, first make it work in Israel and then put it forward as a working model for whoever is interested elsewhere. Take the Scandinavian countries. They have some of the best socio-political arrangements you can have in the contemporary world. Did they run around seeing how everybody else did it? Sure, they borrowed a few ideas, including a few Jewish ones, available through their Christian biblical tradition, but basically they looked into themselves and asked what kind of a society they wanted – and went ahead and built it. Of course building the just society in the core of the Middle East is not the same as building it on the northern periphery of Europe. That's what the Scandinavians don't understand. Something tells me they would never have succeeded on the narrow strip of land we occupy, with everyone around them, trying to kill them. But we will. The Swedes have had almost 180 years of peace. If I were to envy anything in this world, I would envy that. Our modern state has been around since 1948 and generationally, we've known only war. Everything depends on its circumstances and circumstances depend on their time. That's a universal law."

"I hear what you say, Penina, but just as you won't sacrifice yourself on the altar of political feminism, I won't sacrifice myself on an altar of a 2,000-year-old religious logjam. I've a better idea. Let us work things out in America and then export them, as you put it, to the rest of the world." "But the rest of the world isn't the United States of America. What you work out may not fit. Too often, it doesn't. Better leave it to the locals. Give them help when they need it. Support the good. But don't try selling worldwide Redemption. It's not like selling beef burgers at McDonalds. No two peoples will agree what it is." "You know, Penny, I'm glad I came. I'll go back with a different mind set. This place is getting to me. So are you. And so is my outrageous cousin in Mea Shearim. You know the old saying – ask five Jews and you'll get ten opinions. I've learnt something, in the short time I've been here: each one of those opinions is right. " "Honey, when I think we might have driven up to the Highlands or taken the tunnel to Paris! Very nice. But so what?" "You know something?" Lauren asked, rhetorically. "If there was some way we could separate the 'so what's' from the 'what are really importants' in our lives, we'd be on the winning track."

"So what's with you and Ron? Something tells me there is someone else on the horizon." "Right. But the two aren't connected. Ron and I were finished anyway." "I hardly know anyone who told me the last relationship was not finished before the new one began," Penina observed. "This time it's true. His name's Steve. He's a senator. Married, of course. For the second time. Children from both marriages. Middle height. Well built – takes care of himself. Ruggedly good-looking. You'd think he was a film star. A refugee from the land of Forty-something." "Meaning?" "He's fifty-one and feels he hasn't impacted. "He's one of those guys who show great promise in their Twenties, make rapid progress in their Thirties, bottom out in their Forties and when they hit fifty, panic because their promise was not fulfilled. Often they get married again to a younger woman to keep them feeling young, so they can have another try." "At marriage?" "No. At making an impact. And that's what he's going to do. He has so much to give. He really has. Of course he's bogged down in a second marriage, which turned out more disasterous than the first. He's got to cut and run. He's not the kind of man a woman can own. Or children can twist round their chubby fingers. He has a public life. He has a wider constituency. He needs to make up for lost time. And he needs me." "You'll marry him?" "He's a senator, come on! He can't just leave his family and shack up with another woman! He's not just up against 'what will the neighbors say,' he's up against what the ballot box will say." "You think it will last?" "It'll last as long as it works. No marriage should live longer." "Children?" "I don't expect him to add to his present pool. I don't need that to fulfill myself either." "What do you need?" "I need to know, at the end of the day, that I've fulfilled myself. That I haven't just done my job, got by, been understanding to my patients, maybe having presented an intelligent idea, or two, at a conference. I want to make a difference." "Healing patients doesn't make a difference?" "Sure it does. But it's a micro-difference. I want to be macro." Lauren finally masticated her profiterole in a slow, digestive process that owed as much to ritual as appetite. "And marrying your senator will make you macro? Does he have a name, by the way? Yes, it's Keystone." "Keystone! And he's a senator?" "He certainly is." "How can anyone be called that!" "Easy. His grandfather was one of the creators or financiers of the Keystone Cops. He made a fortune out of them, which was the basis of all the other fortunes he made since. So in gratitude, his parents named their third child Keystone. And you know, he says it's been a great help in his career. He's strong on law and order – and his name makes people think he was born to it. They take it as a joke, but a serious one. And they vote for him. Isn't that incredible? At school the kids gave him such a hard time, he wanted to change his name. It would have been a tragedy." "Where do you fit into this, Lauren?" "I'll run his diary, his schedule, grant or not media interviews, mark up what he should read in the newspapers, what to watch on tv, keep an eye on committee reports and hearings and social media, have an ear to the floor of both houses, make friendships with people in the Administration, buy what he needs to wear – both his wives were rotten at that – see he goes to the right parties. In general, run his life!" "So you'll be the ghost in his machine. Is that enough?"

The flow of Lauren's speech ended abruptly. Her hands which choreographed the air animatedly as she spoke, settled reluctantly on her lap. Her vibe count subsided. "That's the one question I ask myself," she said in a sober voice, staring at a yellow pickle stain on Penina's side of the tablecloth. "I haven't downloaded the answer yet. But I'll let you into a secret," she said, her eyes glistening, without removing their attention from the stain. "I may go into politics myself. I could learn so much from Keystone. And the contacts I'll make! I've been thinking about it. It's not at the front of my head yet, but it's there, moving slowly towards the beleaguered center stage of whatever brain I have left, after twelve years of domestic soap. I've decided not to hide my light under a bushel at meetings, parties, discussions, talking with tv producers, party managers, anchors. I'll make sure everyone knows who I am and what I believe. It may mean upstaging Keystone sometimes, but that's just in-demand necessity and one day – one day – someone significant is going to say, 'Lauren, you should be in politics, not just holding Keystone's coat.' That will be the start of my campaign." "A Democrat presumably. But which house?" "Oh I think Senate. Yes. But not a Democrat. Keystone's that. I'll be Republican." "You'd go over to the enemy? Everyone votes Democrat in our family. Even your Dad." "I must make a clean break, from our blessed family and from Keystone. If I follow the family's vote pattern, I'll never stop being the granddaughter of immigrant Jewish grandparents. If I follow Keystone I'll remain no more than his protégée. I'll choose an issue that's in the wind that I can speak on as a woman and ride on it." "What kind of issue?" "Some bandwagon issue that comes from way outfield and grows into a major political debate. It doesn't matter what. Something people didn't anticipate. It's all I need to launch me, plus the media flutter over changing my party base, plus the fact that I won't exactly have gone unnoticed until then. Plus the fact that I'll keep myself in tip top condition physically and mentally. The camera loves to love. And anchors love to dive." "How do you expect Keystone to take that?" "Keystone will have got up to ten years of devoted service from me as wife and coat holder. Enough already. Do we all have to go way past our sell-by date? By then we'll both be ready for a new brand." "You're thinking two decades ahead. That's awesome! Where do you want to end up?"

Lauren raised her eyes and fixed them on her cousin in a judo lock. Penina had seen troubled patients do this, when they were going to say something epically outrageous. "I want to be in a position of ultimate power," she said, relishing the surprise on her cousin's face. "I want to wake up in the morning and make decisions that affect the whole world. I want to be President of the United States." After an imponderable pause, both women began to laugh. Penina, in relief at what she took to be the intended absurdity of her cousin's remark, Lauren, in the surety that her cousin had taken her serious confession as a joke. "How typically Lauren," Penina said to herself, while insisting on paying the bill. "President or as damn near," Lauren continued, as Penina decided which bank card to charge it to. "Yes, I'd settle for Secretary of State." As she rose, Lauren studied her image, momentarily, in the glass above Penina's head. Full lips with a red-brown gloss, photogenic to a fault. Red for passion. Brown for depth. "A slightly browner base in future, I think," she said to herself, sub-vocally. Lauren was no Narcissus – who fell in love with his own reflection, in perpetual self-love. She remained unmoved by hers. Her looks were less a part of herself, than an asset, a means to an end, a windfall. Like being born with an enviable bank balance. She concealed herself behind her looks as politicians do behind their power. Ultimately, they were the same.

***

Shira delivered her conference paper and flew back the same day, reliving her journey home from Australia, when she did not know if she would find her husband alive or dead. There was a certain symmetry to life, she reflected, sometimes cruel, sometimes bliss. She had been in the grip of its cruel pincer for too long. She needed a break. What kind of a break, she had no idea. Maybe a visit to an experimental farm in the desert, which represented the cutting edge of agricultural technology for the future. Yes, young Jews, of many backgrounds, with idealistic minds and pliant goodwill, contributing to tikkun olam, or mending the world. Purpose and effort in the unlikeliest of places.

***

She went to the hospital. Her husband was in a bed marooned at the end of a corridor. The emergency ward was still overflowing with victims. He was asleep, the monitors around him, immobile, constantly checking for signs of life. How long would they and she have to wait? Her mobile rang. It angered her. She held it to her ear but said nothing.

"Shira? Can you hear me? Have you seen Yuri yet?" "I'm with him, if that is humanly possible, Menachem." "You've gone through too much, baby. Yuri is in the shadow of the valley of death. You must be shattered. You're working like a slave and I bet you're not eating. The least I can do is get you to the nearest trough. Besides, I want to talk to you."

"What about?" "Your whole situation." Shira didn't answer at once. She had been trying to assess her "whole situation" for weeks but could not get sufficient distance. Perhaps the General might have some insight. "When? That's the problem." "Tonight. When you're through." "Impossible. I'm coming back to the hospital after I've been to the department. Yuri may be awake. I don't know what to expect any more." "And after that?" "I won't be able to leave till God knows when." "God knows when, is my kind of time. Ring me when you're ready. We'll go to a pizza house that's open 24 hours. There's one condition – you've got to eat." "I can't promise I'll come, still less eat," Shira said, inside her head. The General had rung off.

***

As she walked towards the restaurant, she spotted the General at a window seat, speaking to a waitress. He settled back in his seat and began to read the first edition of the morning papers. He looked as if he was sitting in an illuminated box in the blackness of the night. When she met him in the past, he always projected authority, but now unaware he was being looked at, he appeared an ordinary guy – thickset, overweight, casually dressed, middle aged, unremarkable. She could not remember seeing him in civilian clothes. They didn't seem to suit him. The image was discomforting. She would have preferred him to appear authoritative, even authoritarian. Yes authoritarian. Someone who could tell her what to think, to do, to hope for. He rose when she entered and his persona seemed to engulf him, as if he had flung a prerogative cloak around his shoulders. The face tightened, the eyes became alert. He seemed glad to see her, but didn't smile. To her surprise, the place was half full, despite the hour. A mixture of truck drivers, policemen between shifts, a few army personnel, drivers breaking their journeys and scattered among them, a collection of night-owls and insomniacs. Everyone looked the hour. They ate slowly and in silence, except for a group of heavy goods' vehicle drivers who kept up a boisterous conversation, joke-filled, which broke the fishbowl atmosphere. The waitresses, sitting at a table with nothing to do, stared at the non-stop cartoon show on the television screen with the sound turned to zero. "I can't believe I'm here. What is it?" She looked at her watch. "My God, it's 2.35." "I can't believe you're here either," he said, with a mite too much feeling. She was mellow with fatigue and smiled back conspiratorially. She looked around for the waitress. "Don't worry, I've ordered. I saw you pull up." "I only want coffee." "People never want to eat when they need it most. It's called exhaustion. I got you tehina. They make it here. It's the best." The tehina with pitta was served in the shape of a crater, with a small lake of olive oil in the middle, seasoned with hyssop, surrounded with hot peppers. A collection of 'additions' was placed before her on small plates, plus a large cup of coffee. Shira gulped at the coffee and attacked the tehina, with well-baked pitta bread. "I have to admit, food was a good idea," she said, glancing at the General who looked back like a keynote speaker about to broach a bold idea. She encouraged him with her eyes, while she got on with the food. "Have you thought enough about what you're going to do if Yuri, God forbid, doesn't come out of this?" She would have parried the question, had she not been so tired. "I spend a lot of time trying not to," she replied. "Shira, listen to me. You have to face it. Or it will counterface you." "There has to be a proper time for doing things," she replied quickly. "There has to be a time when one's ready." "The number of times I've thought that," he told her. "In ops, you always think you need more time, more training, more planning, more intelligence. One is never ready.

But someone shouts 'go' and you damn well go, and you find you're as ready as you'll ever be." "I'm not. I'm simply not." "Go!" he barked, as if giving an order. People at neighboring tables looked at them. A half-asleep night-owl sat up with startled eyes. "Now! At this moment! In all your unreadiness, and uncertainty! What are you going to do?" Shira was startled into clarity. "There are two ways of coming out of a coma. One, you die. The other, you have some kind of life," she told him as if she was lecturing a class. "If it's the first, I'll have to go through what so many army widows go through. For me it won't be first time. Doesn't mean I'll be able to handle it any better. But my first duty will be to my son. I come next. If it's the second, I may find I'm tied to a man with severely limited functions. In that case, he will come first, my son second and I, third. What bound all this together in the past was us – Yuri and I. But the 'us' will have been blown away. We will exist as two separate people with separate needs, separate solutions, separate functions, living in separate worlds. What I have feared, almost all my life, will finally catch up with me. I'll have no place to hide." "Why must you hide?" "Because it's the only place where I'm not afraid." For the first time in her life, Shira had lowered her guard to the ground. She had not done so with either Yuri or Joel. It was a superb moment of clarity. Her arms suddenly felt heavy. She could hardly lift the remains of the coffee to her lips. Then tears. She did not fight them. She needed her remaining strength to stop herself from crying aloud. The tears ran down her cheeks and flooded the corners of her mouth. The truck drivers burst into histrionic laughter. One of them had finished a funny story. "Let's go," said the General, rising and taking her arm. As they left, the night-owl at the next table looked at her with huge, sad, brown eyes. Their expression was contagious. She felt like a clown in a circus, winning over her audience with a face painted in sorrow.

As they drove, she felt she was too much the center of attention. She had to turn the conversation. She asked the General what he was going to do now that he had retired. "I've found a think tank, or it found me," he said, "all I've got to do from now is think. At least no-one is going to get killed." "I thought you'd take things easy." "There's nothing so difficult as taking things easy. Besides, it's not in my nature. The think tank pays well too. Funny, I always avoided tanks in the army" "You are worried about money? I thought you'd have a handsome pension." "True. They say the older you get, the less you need. I find the opposite." They reached the main road. Instead of turning left, back towards Jerusalem, he slipped into a Tel Aviv bound lane. Shira noticed but did not question herself or him. Everything that happened was predestined. She was not just a passenger in a car. She was a passenger, period. "I was being driven around in a Mitsubishi until last month," the General said. "One of my many lost perks." He glanced at her. "Shira, you need a good rest. It'll turn you 180 degrees." A large, blue road sign with an arrow pointing to Tel Aviv, shot by, like a visual command. Yes, she must go to Tel Aviv. No choice. She must go where the General took her. She fixed her eyes on the constant stream of oncoming headlights. The General put on a tape of fast Klezmer music, led by a weeping clarinet. She felt she was in a cocoon, content, protected, oblivious of the necessity that, at some point, she would have to become a butterfly. "How did your Italian diversion go?" he asked. "I had to come back early, as you know. But I gave my paper. Some liked it, some didn't. I liked it. I also learned a lot." "Namely?" "That literature can mend the world." "You mean something makes politics stop. Greed stop. Conflict stop. And instead we all read novels?" "It would be a wonderful first step." "You're talking about what they used to call bildungsroman?" "We were discussing that at the conference. But there's a difference. Bildungsroman – trust the Germans to have a word like that – was typically about some old guy looking back on a misspent youth and bemoaning where he went wrong. Dickens' 'Great Expectations,' is a good example. But what we mean is a young man reaching out for the good life, meaning the moral life, by endorsing the principle of 'mending the world,' not waiting till the end of his run before he sees the light. It's not introspective. Its purpose is to reach out to help others and find yourself, oneself, on the way. The moral is at the start, not the end. Without a better world, there's no way of saving oneself." "Too true," the General said, easing into the fast lane.

***

They reached the Tel Aviv waterfront, still insanely over-active. The early morning twilight subdued the glitter of the serried lights from hotels along the beach front. She made no protest when he pulled into a hotel parking lot. He checked them in and led her to the elevator. She felt she was sleepwalking, as if she would awaken at any moment. When they got to their room, the General led her to the small balcony overlooking the sea. She took the view in slowly. Three quarters of a waxing moon; ragged white lines of white headed waves; ships' lights in the distance; a few aircraft sitting in the sky, waiting to touch down at Ben Gurion airport; an intermittent breeze, teasing the sea. She breathed in deeply, filling her lungs. The ozone worked like glucose on a dehydrated patient. She stretched her arms above her head. "It's beautiful here," she said, turning to the General. He was standing very close. She had barely finished the sentence when she felt his lips. She allowed him to kiss her for a few moments before responding. Then she put her arms around his neck and teasingly drew her nails across his naked scalp. His body was tense, without the electricity of younger men. That was reassuring. She wasn't looking for electric shock therapy. "Let's go in," he whispered. "Oui, mon General," she said. As they got into bed, she wondered if this was really happening. A voice in her head said to her: "Come on, Shirala. You know what you are supposed to do. So do it." "If I can remember what I'm supposed to do, I will," came an answering voice.

***

They did not wake up until almost eleven. "Oh shit! I've missed the departmental committee meeting. I'm supposed to be speaking," she said reaching for her phone. The General pulled her back. "How was last night?" he asked, smiling possessively. "Unforgettable," she told him, with a matching smile. She didn't know why she said that. The previous night no longer existed and the Shira who had slept with him no longer existed. She felt like a migrating bird that had landed at a stopover for a short while, and now had to find its wings to continue the journey across continents. She remembered being laid on her back and then his full weight upon her She did not resist but did all she could to bring matters to a speedy conclusion. For her, it was a purely physical act, enjoyable, like warm rain, but lacking emotional sustenance. "I've imagined this so many times," he said. "You're constantly on my mind." Shira smiled a glistening smile and swung her legs in a balletic curve before perching on the edge of the bed. She found her phone and dialed. She felt really smashed, she said to whoever was listening. She thought she was going down with flu. But she could be there in an hour and a bit. Had she missed the meeting? "Really? What luck!" She stood up. The General's eyes studied her body, as if it were a sculpture in an experimental gallery. "I'll just get a quick shower," she reported. He began to stir, meaning to join her. "You stay there," she said in a voice of soothing command. "Have a rest. You certainly deserve one."

***

Penina reached Shira half way through the day. Could she come to the hospital that evening? Shira had managed to keep Yuri out of her mind, since the General took the lane turn to Tel Aviv. She didn't know how. She struggled with the thought of going to the hospital and, unavoidably , her husband's bed, so soon after vacating the General's. Had her husband's condition deteriorated, while she was "sleeping" with his ex-commanding officer? "It would be really be tough to get there tonight. Is something wrong?" she asked. Her pulse was racing. "No. There's nothing new to worry about. It's just something I need to discuss with you." "Does it have to be tonight?" "Preferably." Against her better judgement, Shira agreed. For the rest of the day, her act of disloyalty followed her around like a stalker.

***

"I'm sorry if I disturbed your plans," Penina said. "But thanks for coming." Shira waited for her to go on, but she sat at her desk, studying her rose tinted fingernails as if they were the next case in a bulging schedule. After a while, she spoke. "Something may have happened this morning, which, if it really did happen, is most strange. I can't say I'm on top of it, yet." She stopped, her eyes still on her nails. "What exactly is it?" Shira asked vigorously, as if helping to get a cartwheel out of a rut. "I was near Emergency, so I popped in to see Yuri – oh he's back in the ward now – and I was just fussing about, I suppose, when he spoke." "Spoke? Really? What did he say?" Shira asked, electrified. "He said: is that you…?' "Shira? Did he say, Shira?" "No. That would have made sense. He said: 'Julia.' 'Is that you Julia?' Do you know a Julia who is close to him? A relative, perhaps?" "No," Shira answered, as if denying a false accusation. "He's never mentioned anyone of that name. Did he say anything else?" "Yes. He said 'Beatrice was right.'" "Who is Beatrice?" Shira asked. "I've no idea," Penina admitted. "So what happened? Is he still talking?" "No, he is exactly as he was. The readout records no brain activity at any time today." "Which means what?" "Which means that I'm losing my mind." "My poor darling," Shira said. "Did you see him speak?" "Not when he said 'Julia.' I had my back to him. But when he talked about Beatrice, I was watching him like a falcon. His lips were moving." "Were his eyes open?" "No. Shut." "Did he show any other signs of life?" "No. None." "Did you report this to Professor Bondman." "Of course." "And?" "He thinks I imagined it. That's the likeliest explanation. Otherwise, all this multi-million-dollar technology would have to be towed away. "So where does this leave us?" Shira asked. "With my reputation badly tarnished. I had to tell you tonight," Penina said, looking up, directly, at Shira, "because it's quite likely that my boss will take me off the case first thing tomorrow." "What a tragedy. Can I do anything about it?" "Thank you, Shira, but there's really nothing." Shira squeezed her wrist and left her office. Bracing herself, she walked towards the ward.

***

"I betrayed you last night, Yuri. With the General" Shira told the comatose figure. She was standing at the foot of the bed. "I don't know why. I think I just wanted to know if I could still function. I'll never betray you again. Not with another man, and not with your revelations, or whatever the world will call them. Yes, the world. Do you remember all those discussions we had about making literature your own, when you were my student? You seem to be doing that to perfection. I am prepared to do anything, including lying through my teeth, to allow you to tell your story. I know that, above all, is what you want. Penina is on your side. Trust her. There is another thing I never told you. Perhaps I should have. When I slept with the General, it wasn't the first time. He didn't know that. He'd forgotten. But when I came out of basic training and was posted to his unit he made a great play for me. I'd been warned about him, but I was young and stupid and reckoned I would have been more offended if he had taken no notice. I dreaded not to be seen as sexy, desirable. If a man with his awful reputation wouldn't have been interested, how could my self-esteem have survived? We didn't break up, one day it just stopped. It was then that I applied for a transfer to the Military Police. To get rid of me, he gave me a ludicrously positive recommendation. It was so good, another branch of Intelligence picked me up and I ended up liaising with his department from the next block and seeing quite a lot of him. By then, he had some other stupid recipient for his enlarged ego. He treated me respectfully and we became good friends. Much later, when you were doing your stint in Intelligence, he became your commanding officer. I dreaded that he would remember and might want to renew the relationship. But he had forgotten all about me. There were so many women in his life. It was like a shooting gallery. How many bullseyes can you be expected to recall? I just thought you should know." She had kept her head bowed as she spoke. Then she looked up. Her husband seemed to be asleep, but there was a movement of the lower face that could be interpreted as the glimmer of a smile. "That's one of the things I love about you, Yuri," she said, "your perverse sense of humor."

***

For Penina, relearning the brain's mechanism was an exercise in frustration. She had not studied the great muscle since she was a student. Then it had been presented as multiple systems which served discrete functions, linked by some unnamed over-arching principle. Its various parts and their functions, their breakdown and recovery, could be learned more or less precisely – if you had a "mind" for it. Cause and effect. Breakdown and cure. The gamut of human behavior, told in cellular reproduction, synaptic bridges etcetera. Learning was shadowed by the unknown. Lecturers never shied away from gaps in our knowledge. But grades were not awarded for what you do not know. The cumulative effect of four years getting her clinical psychology degree and three more for social psychology, was that you knew what you knew. There was a body of knowledge to be learnt and you learnt it. The darkness beyond that, had subsequently to be explored with the torch of personal experience and the results of neuroscientific research as they mincingly unraveled. Over the years, she had collated her own approach to things, her own answers, based on the cases she encountered, which slowly but reassuringly turned into a personal canon. She was unaware that this is what she had been doing. Yuri's case was the catalyst of her self-evaluation. The greatest obstacle to his recovery, if he ever came out of the coma, would be restoration of consciousness. Consciousness, the least understood phenomenon of phenomenal man. "Since we must admit that we really have no idea how consciousness arises," she told Shira, "it is even more difficult to ponder how it works. Hence repairing or retraining a damaged brain is an uphill struggle, at an almost vertical gradient." As a practitioner, she was left dangling over a precipice. It reminded her of an incident, years back, while she was backpacking in Peru. In Cuzco, the ancient mountain capital of the Incas. She had been marching about mindlessly, at seven thousand feet, as if she was in Tel Aviv, which is at sea level and flat as a pancake. Predictably, she had an attack of nausea. She hurried to an empty table at the back of a small cafe. She knew she was going to pass out. A black cloud at the back of her head was moving across her brain, as a raincloud slowly blocks the sun. The last thing she remembered was the dusty, cracked shoes of the waiter, who stood ready to take her order. Then she lost consciousness. Height sickness. When she came to, she did not know where she was. Looking around, she found she had been moved. She was lying across two chairs, one supporting her shoulders, the other her ankles. She had no idea how long she had been left in that position, but the moment she realized that she was not supported in the middle, she fell, tush first, to the floor.

The memory now revisited her, challenging her professional balance. Until she realized how little she knew about the mind, both from her learned and personal experience, indeed how little was known about it at the highest levels of scientific enquiry, her balance was as it had been when she was supported by two chairs. The impossibility of being able to predict the outcome of Yuri's coma, was the catalyst. She felt she was falling between the evolving canons of neuroscience and her own canon of experience, twin chairs that could no longer support her weight. Prof. Bondman assured her that the brain would surrender all its secrets in time. The meantime must remain the meantime, unbearable as it was. That was too messianic. It was how men traditionally explained away ignorance – by believing in a golden future. Yet now, she had no better choice than to turn to a messianic option of her own. Yuri would stomp back and she would be the major catalyst in restoring him to normalcy or in helping create a new him.

She joined internet chat rooms, where survivors of coma and families of people in coma, gave support to each other. She assiduously followed the exposition in learned journals of the latest research, corresponded with families who had loved ones in coma, who had come out of it by recovery or death, read through hospital records, confronted neurologists and psychiatrists in canteens, in hospital corridors and car parks. It was at one of these brief encounters that Shira found her, talking to a professor of neurology who took Shira's arrival as an excuse to end the conversation and drive away with a conciliatory wave. "Shit!" said Penina, watching him disappear in a box of deep blue metal. "You know, Penina, you're going to wear yourself and everyone else out. I admire your commitment. But don't you think you are overdoing it?" "The fact is," she answered, holding Shira's eyes, "that I am going through, let's call it, a personal crisis." Shira lightly squeezed her arm. "I've always felt comfortable with what I knew. I always felt that I could help, be useful, even mend and cure. But suddenly I've come to believe I am living an illusion. How ironic that the case of a man living in a coma, who, in the recent past, would have stood no chance of surviving – which is in itself an outstanding triumph of today's medical science – raises the level of our ignorance as surely as it raises the level of our knowledge. The more you know, the less you know. I'm sorry Shira. You're the last person I should be saying this to." "There's a verse in the Book of Proverbs, I think, that echoes how you feel: 'Grief is the excess of wisdom: the more knowledge there is, the more sorrow.'" "I could buy that, on a bad day." "We all could. Ever read Goethe's 'Faust?'" "Not guilty," Penina admitted with a failing smile. "You should, sometime. It's my favorite. Goethe always carried a shovel around and he knew how to use it." The two women held each other's eyes appraisingly, before parting. "Come to my office, next time you visit. Please," Penina cajoled. Shira nodded.

For Penina it had been, completely overshadowing the reason she had wanted to speak to Shira. She went to emergency and studied the body of the man, lying in Yuri's bed. Although many Russian immigrants are of Jewish descent, but not Jews by Jewish law, she had always assumed that he was. Reflecting on it now, she couldn't think why she had made that assumption. When they had met in the army, she recognized at once that he was a special person, as a soldier and an officer certainly, but also beyond that. He had a sensitivity that was better picked up by women than men and at the same time he was heading an elite combat unit for deep penetration operations with a reputation for valor. A woman's man and a man's man in one. Penina recalled her meetings with him, some of which concerned a young lieutenant of Yemeni extraction, whose grandparents had come to Israel with the mass exodus of Yemen's Jews. He had been badly wounded in an operation in Gaza and evacuated by the helicopter rescue unit. It was too late to save his leg, which had to be amputated. His whole life had been shattered – his career, his marriage prospects, his social life and, at first, his spirit. He needed psychological help and Penina gave him all the time she could, guiltily robbing other patients. Whenever he could, Yuri visited the young patient. When he was operated on, he stayed at his bedside all that night, sleeping on a mattress on the floor. She remembered how his men loved him – not only because he was totally devoted to their welfare, but because of the man he was. In an oblique way, she fell in love with him through their love. It was love that unhesitatingly knew its object. There was no 'do I really love him?' 'Do I not?' 'Is he right for me?' 'Is he not'? His men believed he had nine lives. One of them once told her that if the Colonel was killed or seriously wounded, he would not be able to find the courage to cross the street.

She thought back to when she first met Shira, whom Yuri had brought to the field hospital one time. Penina, dissembling her true feelings, greeted her effusively and the two women got on like new friends. She did not want Yuri to think she was a bad loser. Shira had no idea that Penina was anything but a colleague of Yuri's. It was only when Penina got back to her room that she realized how much she had overplayed her hand with Shira and the corollary: how much she had underplayed it with Shira's husband to be. Reviewing the triangular relationship, then and now, Penina felt that she had come full circle. Admittedly,

Shira was now Yuri's wife. But no-one knew who, or what, Yuri would be, if he survived the coma. Might she be in for a second chance?

As Penina was thinking these thoughts, Shira joined her in the cubicle. She smiled weakly, and stood at the other side of the bed. Before Yuri had descended into full coma, the two women felt they knew how to conduct themselves in his presence. They believed they could be of help. The chances they faced were graspable: death or rehabilitation. There was always the possibility that the coma would envelop him completely, but it was impossible for each of them to realize what that meant. Even for Penina who had the benefit of having dealt with comatose patients, this case was made different by her emotional entanglement. It was like being held by the throat. Now that he had succumbed and the future stretched out in ambiguous endlessness, they were both emptied of their previous resourcefulness. Penina supposed they were thinking along parallel lines. "I hope," she said, "you will continue to read and sing and play music." "Yes, definitely," Shira replied. She was prevaricating. She had been thinking of giving all that up. The brief conversation left her with a taint of guilt. She wanted to deal straightly with Penina. Penina was struggling with the impossibility of being as straight in return. When Shira got home she rang her.

"Hi Penina, I've been thinking about our conversation. I mentioned Faust. Remember? It's one of my favorite plays. Faust studied just about all there was to know in his time. How does he put it? Just a moment, I have the book somewhere. Here. This is Faust speaking: "I've studied philosophy, the law and medicine, theology to boot, I regret to say, with vast effort. But now, poor fool, with all this lore, I am no smarter than I was before." Actually, that's a fairly free translation, but it'll do. The play is a tirade against the idea that our minds are capable of working everything out. Ultimately, brain kills spirit. Faust's way out is love. But he bungles that too, opening the door to tragedy. I can understand how things must seem to you, Penina. In short, there aren't many options. Either you must join a neuro-biological team at the cutting edge of research which will edge knowledge forward at a snail's pace, or you must move on regardless, using the tools you already have. There's a third option: Scream. Like a jackal. You know,

I've always wondered what jackals scream about. We have them in the kibbutz. I think I'm just beginning to understand. What I can't tell you is what the right Faustian choice should be. I don't think Goethe knew. He knew what the problem was. But he was a smart baby. He didn't pretend he had the answer. If I can be of help in any way, don't hesitate. You've got a damn good record and a brilliant career before you, according to people who should know. Don't spoil it, my dear. Shira.

"My dear Shira, thanks. The irony is that you're the only person I can talk to. I should be supporting you – not the other way round. Perhaps it's as you say. The human condition. I wonder. Those at the cutting edge of science do not intend to kill the spirit. They believe it is already dead. They mean to replace it or explain it away. They hope to prove that the spiritual is no more than a projection of the brain. In other words, it is the result of purely physical forces that were born in and of evolution. Morality and our values and our sense of right and wrong and even our belief in God (for those who have it) result from chemical reactions in our heads – like concocting a magic potion. The "spiritual world" has no life outside physical matter. For a long time, in my professional life, I've felt as if I bought a ticket to the wrong movie. I was misled by the reviews. Not that I am a great believer in religion. But I have seen the power of faith at work in countless patients. Tell them that their beliefs are based on some chemical reaction in their brains and not on God, or at least something spiritual which is independent, outside and reachable, you take away faith and with it, its power to cure. You quote Faust saying that after all he learned, he was no smarter. If the psycho-evolutionists have their way, we'll certainly be wiser but at a huge price – we'll be much, much sadder. Proverbs is right. We'll end up pulling the strings of our patients' minds as if they were puppets, But first we'll tell them that their physical bodies and evolution is all there is. We'll convince them that compassion is no more than a chemical process. That there's no God. The psychiatrist and the psychologist and the neuro-biologist will replace him, have replaced him already, for many people. A new trinity. Their offices and laboratories will be the new heaven and their pontifications the new encyclicals. And the sick and the incurable will be left without hope of divine intervention. I am not a religious person, although I believe that God exists. This is potentially a crime against humanity. You can call God an illusion, but I have seen what belief in him can do. To kill him would spell disaster. That is what all this is about – deicide. I wish I could have ended on a more cheerful note, but this is where I am at. May we live to see better times, Penina."

***

Having bared her soul, Penina felt the need to bare her body. Standing naked in the shower closet, she admitted, for the first time in her life, that she was in love. With Yuri. Not an assumption, not a maybe, nor a wish, as it had been in the army, but unconditionally. Her head suddenly felt clear, as after a migraine. There! She had admitted it. She was a woman in love. Each past relationship shriveled. But the knowledge that he, in turn, had been and might again, be fond of her, brought a flush to her face and a tingling feeling of physicality throughout her body, as if his hands were soaping her.

She did not often assess her physical attributes. She preferred to forget them. To look interesting, rather than good-looking, was how she presented her diurnal icon to the world." But now her eyes darted over her broad figure, taking in, with guarded approval, her swan neck, thickening waist, free-standing breasts, muscular back and the mild bulge at her stomach. Not a bad package, she confessed to her reflection. After all, she could not be expected to look like a freshly peeled post graduate. When she looked at her immobile face, it bore witness to a disaster zone. Only her aquiline nose won her endorsement. The rest she discounted. Her mouth because it was too thin, her ears because they were too large, her chin because it was too pointed, her forehead because it was too narrow and her eyes because they were an undramatic light brown. Couldn't she, at least, have inherited burning brown eyes like her mother and her siblings and her aunts? Only when she opened her mouth, was there something to be proud of. She had an enviable set of teeth. Two glistening rows of white incisors which she used both to enchant the world or threaten it. She felt her teeth accorded her the right to smile, or to snap, as occasion demanded.

She went to bed without reading, or listening to music, being enchanted by bells, or reciting the stations of her kabbalistic meditation. She lay awake for a long time, musing, between cool sheets, on her new emotional status. She dared not consider if there was a practical outlet for her love. Its object was in coma. He had a wife. Who wanted him back. It was Penina's proper task to restore him. To whom? His wife? A new career? Penina forced her mind back on its previous track. She was in love. At last. And with what a man. In recent years, she had lost track of her emotions. Perhaps, she wondered, she had spent so much of her life unraveling the emotions of others, that she had become alienated from her own. Circling her mind, like a bird, was the thought that she was thirty plus. Already. Where had her twenties' gone? She would wait for Yuri's re-entry into the world of communication, if it was to come, with anxious expectation. Would he remember her? If so, how? As colleague, friend, a woman? She could not expect any recollection for a while. Still, when he began to speak again, her real work with him would begin. She resolved to wear thinner tops that would outline her breasts under her open white coat. They were her best feature, her breasts. Certainly for the near to medium future. After that, she would have to rely on her teeth and her nose.

***

When can you justify pulling the plugs? It was a hard decision for the medical team to confront. The professor did not want to teach his students that the decision was virtually intractable, nor that it should be taken glibly. In time they would learn what was within the realm of possibility. He waited patiently to observe some improvement in Yuri's condition. But zero brain activity was recorded. On the two hundred and ninetieth day of full coma, he decided not to wait any longer. He would need Shira's permission to take her husband off life support. She was a secular woman, so there should not be an undue amount of discussion. Unlike a religious family who would consult their rabbi and then another and perhaps a third, before making a decision, Shira might delay her permission for a weekend. But she would give it. Standing by Yuri's bed, he consulted his diary and found a slot in the following day's schedule. He turned to the skull-capped religious intern accompanying him, trailed by a group of students. "We've come to the end of the road with this patient. See if Mrs Pozner can meet with me tomorrow, or even tonight. She's probably expecting it, but don't tell her what it's about. We'll do it the day after she consents, if the brother agrees. He's the one who might hold us up." "I've not been in this situation before, but shouldn't we give her a little more time?" "I think you'll find she's made her mind up already. She needs to be free and she knows it. If there was any chance of recovery, of course we would do all we could. But here is an able and intelligent, not to say attractive, young woman, married to a corpse. Both need to be freed." "One free to live and one free to die?" "All we can do for the patient, is delay his funeral." He looked at the intern's face, whose forehead was crisscrossed with lines. "I'm sorry, but isn't that for God to decide?" the intern asked, embarrassed about dragging God into a medical discussion. "He's decided already," said the professor, returning his diary to its pocket. In the professor's peripheral vision, the ghost of a smile settled for a split second on Yuri's face, then vanished. It must have been an effect of the light, the professor told himself, glancing at the opposite window, which the rays of the morning sun had just reached. "Unless the patient is suffering beyond endurance," he went on, "relatives always want to delay. Once you have their signature, you must act or all these beds would be filled with comatose patients and there'd be no room for cases we might actually be able to help. They may last for years but technically, they're dead men. It's not what hospitals are for. We have cemeteries for that. I've kept the Colonel for as long as I dare." "Did you ever think he'd make it?" the intern asked. "No. Not for a moment. I tried my best, but that doesn't mean I thought I would ever succeed." He began to walk away. The intern followed. "I've been watching him, professor. Occasionally his eyelashes flutter." "Did you stimulate him?" "No. Not at all." "That's an involuntary reaction. It means nothing." "Do you think we'll ever find a way of reaching these patients?" the intern asked. The professor heard the moral concern in his voice. "Reach what? There's nothing to reach. But you don't have to take my word for it. Write a proposal, find some funding and set up a research team to investigate. Just be prepared to look into it for the rest your life without result." "But professor, just as we use technology to maintain his body, might we not be able to do the same for his mind? Discover the technology to maintain it?" "And then it will be the turn of the soul, no doubt," the professor shot back. The other students grinned. The professor was glad to end on a light note. His students were being asked to confront a frustrating moral dilemma. In time they would learn the limitations of their calling. Now they were striving to save the world and have no-one die.

***

Shira recognized the intern's voice on the phone. She was sitting in a small patch of midday sun, on a small bench, opposite her house, facing an orange orchard. She and Yuri called the bench the contemplation seat. She could hardly hear what the voice was saying. It seemed that the professor wanted to speak to her. Her heart began to pound. Would the following day be convenient? She agreed a time and rang off. There was only one thing the professor could want to talk about. Shira had the sensation of being driven at high speed towards a point where many roads intersected and then narrowed into one. A line from one of Shakespeare's poems buzzed in her mind. "Love is not love / which alters when it alteration finds." Would Shakespeare have proscribed those words as the acid test if he had been confronted with a loved one in a coma? People did not survive coma for more than a short while in his day. Then, you were alive or dead – or dying. Or did he mean to include death in his judgement? Can you love the dead? Or can you only have loved the dead? When love passes into the past tense, what meaning does it have? As the sovereignty of love hovered between two tenses, she felt as if she had entered limbo.

***

Yuri's brother was waiting by Yuri's bed when Shira got there. "You can guess what this is all about?" he said. "I can guess." "And what's your choice?" "The choice is between admitting the truth or denying it. I'm ready to admit. What about you?" Shira looked straight into Akiva's eyes and awaited his answer. "I have to say, there's a discrepancy between what I am supposed to think and what I think. According to halacha, you never let go, if there's the remotest possibility of saving a life – to the extent that in certain circumstances you don't get a sick man to say his confession even when there is no hope, for fear that he might become convinced that he is dying and give up." "Clearly that's not what we've got here." "No, it isn't," Akiva agreed. "So I'm ready to say, let him go. But I have one favor to ask. It's the anniversary of our father's death in just a month. If some miracle doesn't happen by then, let that be it." Shira was irritated by his appeal to the possibility of a miracle. "If there was to be a miracle, why didn't it happen way back?" she said, scornfully. "The ricochet could have embedded itself in the wall, not in his head." The professor, in a hurry as always, accompanied by Penina and the Head Nurse, and one or two others, joined them. They gathered around the bed with the mourners-in-waiting. It was quickly agreed that the situation was hopeless. The professor was supportive of Akiva's plea to wait. He had expected worse. But Akiva was a baal t'shuva, a master of return, or born-again Jew. He still remembered common-sense attitudes from his previous existence, the professor reasoned. Shira took note that Penina had not participated in the discussion. She assumed that the clinical psychologist and the professor had talked it through before the meeting and agreed that time had run out. But she was wrong. Penina had argued passionately, and, in the professor's view, irrationally, for Yuri to be kept on life support. She had produced a file of long-term coma cases, logged from medical reports across time and the world, which reported on coma survivors, many of whom had been comatose for up to a year, occasionally a good deal longer, who had come out of it and begun a new life. She was herself in correspondence by e-mail with several such survivors. "How long do you think we should wait?" the professor had asked. "I can't answer that," she admitted. "But I have to," the professor said sternly. "We must let him go."

***

Shira spent all the time she could over the next few days with Yuri. She prepared lectures at his bedside, critiqued student essays, pondered over her father's legacy, played music and read aloud poems that Yuri loved in Russian and Hebrew. More for her sake than his. She no longer nursed the unmitigated hope that she was able to reach him. She was reduced to keeping herself busy and keeping her mind from wandering. In her mind, she listened to the rhythm of waves breaking on the shore. Without them, there was only back to back misery. Akiva came on two consecutive days. He sat on the opposite side of the bed, poring over large Talmudic volumes filled with columns of dense black print. They did not disturb each other. They even found each other's presence comforting. Shira absented herself whenever Akiva prayed formally, which was three times a day. She could not stand the swaying from the waist, the clenched fists, nor the words which betrayed a mental climate so alien to her own. He took a break whenever the stories and poems she read were sexually explicit or contained material contradictory to religious Jewish values. Little conversation passed between them. There was nothing much to be said. Two people, inhabiting distinct worlds, united for the moment, in mutual misery, barely tinged with hope. She had reached a point where she believed there was no more she could do but wait. He struggled to believe that he could still affect events by prayer.

***

One morning, Shira got to the ward early. Akiva had not yet arrived, or perhaps was not coming. She sighed with relief. She needed time with Yuri to say goodbye. She had brought some of his favorite things, including old family photographs, among them the only one of his mother in existence, a compact disc by the Russian folk singer Igor Talkov, a spare laptop computer and a rugged pile of essays by her students on the creative writing course. The opening bars of The Four Seasons reverberated from her purse. She had forgotten to switch off her mobile. Annoyed, she checked the caller's number. Her screen told her it was Menachem, the only person she was prepared to speak to. "I was getting worried about you," said his measured voice. "There's no need to worry. I'm fine." Awkward pause. "I wish I could believe you. Your voice gives you away." "Well, OK, there's a lot happening, but I'm coping." "Have they decided anything about Yuri?" Menachem would not have asked the question if he did not know a decision had been taken. How did he know these things? "Yes. If there's no …" she searched for the word she wanted. "Miracle?" he supplied. "Improvement," she corrected him. "If there's no improvement, they're going to let him go in a few weeks." "I see," he said. "Shira, come back to me if you need me." "Thank you." Awkward pause. "Let me rephrase that," he said, as if he had been dictating notes to a secretary. "Come back to me when you need me. I'll take your call, no matter what." He was gone. She thought for a moment or two. He was offering her a safety net. She was grateful. Then she remembered the unrecognized face she had seen hiding, at her father's funeral, all that time ago, before Italy, hidden among trees. It was his.

***

A nurse came to trim Yuri's fingernails, which still grew, the only natural process left. In the middle of the manicure, her pager sounded. She was called away to help with an emergency and forgot her scissors. A sudden impulse drew Shira to her feet. When she was sure no-one was looking, she cut a curly lock of hair from the back of Yuri's head. Whenever he was on a long leave from the army, he used to let his hair grow. Samson locks, as she called the resultant profusion of growth. She felt the strands between her fingers. How silky! How unexpectedly alive! Their softness brought back memories, like distant horses riding through water. Whenever they made love, she would grasp his pony tail as she orgasmed. The lock nestling in her palm reminded her of long weekends in Sharm el Sheikh in the Sinai and the highlands of Galili and the Taurus mountains in Cyprus and fishing villages along Turkey's Anatolian coast and England's Lake District and Ireland's Gael Techt. A memento that brought back memories of mutual wonderment and intimate sharing, of histrionic arguments and desperate reconciliations, of the silence of solitude and the passions of love, all given urgency by the knowledge that he would soon return to duty and constant risk, sometimes alone or with a few men, deep in enemy territory. She closed her eyes and imagined him on top of her, feeling the brunt of his need and the mystical latency of her own. And yet, she recalled, even in intense unity, there had always been division. How they had wanted to become one, without borders, without individuality, without ambition and career or personal baggage and previous relationships and fragmenting futures. But they always remained two people.

It bothered her more than she reasoned it should. In her first marriage she and Joel had been as close as twins. The kibbutz seldom celebrated a wedding between two of its members. Youngsters tended to look outside for a partner. There was something bordering on the incestuous about marriage and subsequent child-raising with people with whom you had been raised like brothers and sisters. She and Joel shared the same growing up pains, had slept in the same children's houses, received the same education, underwent the same political and moral indoctrination and generally occupied the same social and personal space. They had participated in the kibbutz's flourishing, summitry and decline. They viewed life from the same cultural platform. At work, they were often scheduled for the same or similar jobs in kitchen and field and fish-pond and kibbutz guest house and later in the plastics factory. They experienced the onset of puberty and sexual self-consciousness over a similar period of time. Not least, they were projected as if on automatic pilot, into an identical idealism. Not that they experienced the kibbutz in strict tandem. Joel was almost five years her senior, but they had gone through the same programmatic indoctrination, physical and mental. She first heard the English expression "Get with the program," from an American volunteer. It became a cherished motto.

In marriage, they hardly needed to speak. Each knew the other's thoughts. Friends saw it as a model marriage, the best that could be hoped for. They were everyone's darlings, role models and handsome to boot. Her sister, Limor, once told her that she envied her "seamless" marriage, contrasting it sadly with her own which she confessed was unraveling like a badly-knitted sweater. Shira believed all that people said of them. It was like receiving applause from an audience. She basked in her fairy tale. Her life and Joel's were almost mirror images before they went into military service, he to the air force as a career, she to military intelligence as a conscript. The threat of accident or war was always present, but formed a framework, which lent their relationship immediacy and purpose. A religiously observant colleague once told her that her marriage was a mystical union.

Her marriage to Yuri worked contrariwise. Everything had to be discussed because neither could predict how the other would react. It was stormy and passionate with long periods of mutual close down. It was a marriage that required constant care and repair. Neither doubted the other's love, both physical and emotional. Their physical relationship was more passionate than her first marriage had been. With

Joel, sex was a dream within a dream. With Yuri, it was sensational, self-assertive, even lurid. With Joel, culmination was like swimming to a beautiful island in the middle of a lake. With Yuri it was like climbing to the summit of a mountain. When she thought about it, she was astonished that both routes expressed her nature. With Yuri, she shared the same ideas but not the same attitudes. He was brash, she pensive. What had brought them together? Neither could explain it. But each had a thirst for the other and a familiarity which, in the end, temporarily over-rode their differences.

She looked down at his inert body. Was it still him? What did she feel for this abstraction of a man? Nothing, she admitted. All the feeling she had left was not for nostalgia, but recovery. Yes, she still loved him, but it was a contingent love, depending on him coming back. To her.

Her thoughts were not tidy. They chased each other around her head as she resentfully watched the mockingly motionless needles of his life-support system. In her confusion, she thought of Glinka. "Why, on earth, did I not think of him before!" she said to herself. He had written the opera, "Russlan and Ludmilla" in which a girl was thrown into a trance which could only be broken by her lover. Yuri had an immoderate liking for the piece. He loved the way Glinka had mixed folk songs into his score. She remembered Yuri telling her that in Glinka's day it was like using slang in a tone poem. But exactly how did the hero redeem his love? She sieved her memory for the answer. It was a ring. The magic ring that had been given to the hero by one of the good fairies that inhabited opera, at that time. She almost laughed. At herself. Were her problems to be solved by a good fairy? Despite herself, she began to wonder what she could use for a magic ring. She felt she was being driven against her will by an irrational tail-wind that had broken loose from childhood. On the morning of their wedding, in a civil ceremony in Cyprus, Yuri had disappeared for hours in search of a ring and had finally come back with one he'd bought from a goldsmith who made replicas of ancient jewelry. "With this magic ring, I thee wed," he had interjected into the service. Retrieval of the memory, required her to dive deeply into the archive of her mind.

She pulled herself together. She decided to go back to the kibbutz to get Yuri's copy of "Russlan and Ludmilla". She was about to leave, when Akiva arrived. "Blessed be God," he said, when she told him what she was doing. "And you're going all the way back to get a recording? Col ha cavod!" "Watch him carefully while I'm gone," she said. "I'll watch him as the night watchman watches for the dawn." At the door, she turned. Akiva was reciting psalms, rocking to and fro from the waist, to the rhythm of the words.

She did it in an hour, breaking enough traffic regulations to have herself banned for life. When she got back, the end of the ward was full of Moshe's relatives, sitting around, the youngest piled two or three high on the laps of mothers and elder sisters, waiting for the professor and a few senior staff who had drawn the curtain around Moshe's bed, to tell them the prognosis. She hadn't wanted this. She wanted a bubble, a padded cell, a spaceship. To be alone with Yuri. Moshe still droned on in intermittent bursts of seeming gibberish, as if in an animated conversation with a troupe of monkeys. Akiva was lost somewhere in Psalms. She heard a snatch of what he was reciting: "May the Lord answer you on the day of trouble/ May the name of the God of Jacob cause you to stand upright."

She brushed the words aside, like hair from her eyes. She put the earphones on Yuri, inserted the disk and pressed play. She watched his face intently for the duration of the piece. If he said anything, would she hear it above Moshe's drone, the chatter of his young relatives and Akiva's constant repetition of the same passage? If he did and no-one believed her, they would kill him on the day appointed. An execution! "Please Yuri. For pity's sake, show them you are alive! Or they might..." She did not pronounce the words, but heard them chase each other around her head. Still the needles mocked her, turning hope to technological ash. Akiva finished the psalm he was reciting. He had to pray with a quorum where his prayers would have more weight, he told Shira. He hurried off to the hospital synagogue for the afternoon service.

Shira could not explain what was happening in her mind. She sat back on her chair and fixed her eyes on Yuri. She began to feel nauseous. She had only eaten three sandwiches in as many days. She reached for a small fruit bowl from the bedside table and turned away from him, anticipating that she was going to throw up. As she held the bowl ready on her lap, she felt the nausea rise. As she raised the bowl to just below her face, she became aware of a sudden movement in the bed. The ruffle of bedclothes, as if its occupant had moved. She sat absolutely still, too agitated to vomit. The act of turning towards her husband, carried unimaginable risk. She might come upon something she could not handle. Slowly, she forced herself to turn her head. Yuri was sitting up, one hand extended in front of him, as if to shake hands with an invisible visitor. His long hair hung about his head in disorder. He looked like a Nazirite, who had taken a vow of abstinence. From what? From life? His eyes were shut. Was he dead? Was this rigor mortis confronting her? She struggled to speak. "Yuri, darling," she said. The sound of her voice sounded like an echo. "Can you hear me? Can you hear anything? Why are you holding your arm out?" His face was immobile, but not as before. The skin seemed to breathe. "Yuri, please!" She hated the sound of her voice. It was pitched too high. But when she tried again, it did not change. "Yuri! It's me, Shira. If you can hear, please make a movement. Any movement. Just so I'll know." The face remained impassive. She had to convince someone that he had moved. Otherwise, they would not believe her. They might think that, with just a short while to go before they unplugged him, she was desperate enough to try anything and had moved him herself. But the protruding arm, she couldn't have done that. Her eyes travelled across his face, searching for a sign. Was that a minute movement of the web at the corner of his left eye? Or was it an optical illusion? She studied the area intensely, adjusting her eyes like microscopes. Yes, his skin was pulsating in a minuscule motion, barely detectable. It was alive. Three fine furrows appeared across his forehead as if drawn by a child on a blank page. Then Yuri's eyes opened. Shira stepped back in shock. The eyes were unseeing, staring upward toward the ceiling, only the whites exposed. The thought crossed her mind that he was dying and that she was impeding his departure. But she moved as close as she could, leveling tear-filled blue-green eyes opposite the unseeing whites of his. "Yuri! Stay just as you are," she commanded. "Don't go anywhere! I want you to live! I love you." She almost laughed at her words. Yuri's eyes began to move. Like an antique astrolabe, the pupils began a downward trajectory and settled into their normal position. There, they stared, unseeing, at the wall opposite. "Yuri, can you hear me? Can you, Yuri?" The pitch of her voice was just lower than a shout. But he heard nothing. She caressed his hand, then his face. She put her vermilion lips to his and sucked like a honeybee. He did nothing. On an impulse, she loosened her top and guided his other hand to her breast. "Feel me,' she said. But his hand was dead weight. Was this all that Nature was returning after his ordeal, having taken the best from him? The best from the best. She must find witnesses. What happened must be recorded. Yuri was alive. In some weird way perhaps, but alive. There must be something somebody could do. She began to walk towards the nursing station, but immediately felt dizzy, as if the law of gravity had been reversed and the blood meant for her legs had flooded her head.

When she reached the nurses' station, she was greeted by the back of an Arab nurse on the telephone. She was having a private conversation. She turned and smiled at Shira and signaled with her fingers that she would be with her in a couple of minutes. Minutes? How could she wait minutes? In minutes Yuri's eyes might close. He could be dead! She spoke over the nurse's voice. "I am Mrs. Pozner. My husband is a prisoner here," she went on, unaware of her Freudian slip. "He has just woken up. He's been in a coma for three hundred days or something like that...." Still talking on the phone, the nurse flipped a switch on the console before her. A picture of Yuri appeared on a screen. His hand was no longer extended. He was leaning over as if he was about to fall out of the bed. The nurse cupped her hand over the phone and stared at the screen. "Allah, the Merciful," she exclaimed. She rang for a replacement to manage the desk, told the person on the line to ring back and hurried towards Yuri's bed, beckoning Shira to follow. For Shira, everything moved in slow motion, but sounds were magnified. Her breathing was like an approaching train, the rustle of her shawl like wind through bracken, her shoes like doorknockers on the plastic flooring. By the time she reached Yuri's cubicle, the Head Nurse, granddaughter of a Jewish doctor killed in the Hadassah hospital bus massacre, was taking Yuri's pulse. They had righted him in the bed.

His hand was no longer protruding. His eyes were shut. "Nothing," she announced, puzzled. She read his dials, spoke to him, scratched the back of his hand. "Nothing," she repeated, hardly believing what she said. She rang for the duty doctor, a Russian Jew, whose father had spent four winters in a prison camp in Siberia for teaching Hebrew during the Soviet regime, who went through the same procedures and rang for the consultant, a Christian Arab, whose grandparents were expelled from their village during the Israeli War of Independence, leaving behind an ailing daughter, his mother, who was too weak to make the journey. He, in turn, questioned everyone and rang for the professor, who asked Shira to re-enact exactly what had happened. She felt as if she was giving evidence before a skeptical jury, which included herself. "Our Colonel must be an expert at camouflage," Prof. Bondman observed, once he had taken stock. "Taking everything into consideration, I have to admit he may be hiding from us. That is not my medical opinion. It's what I think. I'm going to give him a last chance to come out with his hands above his head. If he is going to step out of his coma, he'd better hurry." "How long can we afford to wait?" the consultant asked. "It really depends on him. I hope he realizes there's a limit."

When Shira got back to her kibbutz, she could give herself no coherent account of the day. It had been a bizarre mix of reality and fantasy, in which the fantastic was the more real. Only Yuri's movements stood out with the vividness of events that had truly occurred. The rest, was as if it had not happened. Could she face more days like that? She did not think so, but knew she might have to. Had nothing really happened? She found it difficult to believe. How could she believe anything? She no longer believed herself. Perhaps it was her mind that Glinka's opera had stirred, not Yuri's. Had a scene from "Russlan and Ludmilla" produced results on the wrong cognitive apparatus? She made a number of phone calls to rearrange her schedule for the following morning. She wanted to move one of her lectures, but could not find a spare hall, until mid-afternoon. It meant she would only get a few hours with Yuri.

***

She noted that Yuri's bed had been moved into the farthest corner. When they pulled the plugs, they would not want it to be too public, Shira assumed. So they were expecting nothing, after yesterday's excitement. Yuri was lying on his side. She watched him for a while, but it was like watching yesterday and the day before. He seemed smaller. How was that possible in a day? Was he giving up? She felt an oncoming panic attack which she forcibly converted into a rush of energy. The compact disk, recorded in the Russian Federation by superstar Igor Talkov, shook in her hand as she slotted it into a spare computer and set it up on Yuri's bedside table. The music owed its soul to the Russian gipsy tradition and Jewish folklore. It was accompanied by explosive audial effects and a galactic fireworks display. Its running time was an hour, time that could be well used marking student essays. The ever-changing kaleidoscope of colored light and geometric shapes from the screen cast a vacillating glow on the pallid skin of Yuri's face, while the music wove oriental enchantment. She smiled at the sixteen-year-old, brown-eyed girl left to guard Moshe, her grandfather, hoping to allay the frown that sat high on the girl's forehead. Clearly she was nervous, perhaps frightened at finding herself between two comatose men who belonged neither to this world nor the next. She smiled back, uncertainly. Shira knew that the girl wanted to talk, but time was at a premium and she turned to the essays, making a show with her hand, towards the height of the pile, to indicate how busy she was. A few moments later, she turned back to the girl and asked if the program disturbed her. She offered to put earphones on her husband. The girl insisted there was no need and quickly became mesmerized by the music, which sounded to her, she called out, like a distant version of her grandfather's songs.

Shira turned to the essays. They were the first creative efforts of the course and the standard was high. Almost all her Jewish Israeli students had done three years military service, for men, and two-and-a half for women, had travelled abroad for a year or more as backpackers or volunteers and had experienced cultures and absorbed ideas that had broadened mind and character, so that by their early twenties, when they started university, they had witnessed more, read more and been forced to think more than the average student elsewhere. Their essays were a lightning tour of places, unknown or seldom visited, from Alaska to Patagonia, from Kashmir to the Tamil Nadu to Papua New Guinea. The only criterion linking them was a desire to visit the least trod places on earth. Her two female Arab Israeli students, whose societies did not allow them to travel where they pleased, turned to imagination, one describing a trip to mythical Arcadia, the other romancing a troupe of Dervish dancers in Turkey. Some of the stories, were fit to be published in modest literary magazines.

Shira was reading an account of a visit to a small town in the Argentinian Pampas, which had been settled by Ukrainian Jews, escaping persecution, in the late nineteenth century. The student based her piece on the white adobe synagogue that still stands, but is hardly used. By describing events that had taken place in the building, across the years and the people who participated in them, she caught the rise and fall of Jewish immigrant life of a community that had turned itself from a loose band of tailors, teamsters, rabbinical students and metalworkers into a flourishing community of Jewish cowboys, who lived life in the saddle. Some last-remaining, old-hands, are still in place, engaged in the preservation of memories, given that they no longer had a viable tradition. The writer had chosen one of them to narrate the story. Shira scanned it and put it aside. It was one of a procession of essays about remote Jewish communities from Alaska to Patagonia, from Shanghai to Cochin, from Birobijan to Assam where Jews had given life a try and which students couldn't get out of their systems until they had tracked down every last detail of how they came there and where they went afterwards. In her own mind she called it "ghosting." She would read it later. She aspired to finding something different and moved on to a piece by one of her Arab Israeli students, about an itinerant troupe of dervish dancers in Turkey "a thousand moons ago." This was Arab ghosting, she well knew, for the Arabs were devoutly fond of ghosts too. Interesting, she told herself after the first few sentences, how much both Jews and Arabs indulged their ghosts. There was a nostalgia, bordering on envy for old times and a feeling that the ghosts had axed out a better deal for themselves than the non-ghosts of contemporary society. The central character of the piece was the young son of the leader of the troupe who was being groomed in the thought and form of Semah, the dervish form of worship, in which dancers spin at great speed to realize communion with Allah. Neither knew that they were being closely watched by the boy's younger sister, who practiced in secret, all she saw them do. In time, she became more adept than her brother. When he caught her practicing, she told him that the thing she most wanted, was to be a Semah dancer. Knowing that their father would never allow it, brother and sister ran away to join another troupe in another country. She was dressed as a boy.

Some notes on the steps of the dance were included in the story. Shira, a natural dancer, drew the curtain and tried to master them in the narrow space. She was interrupted by Akiva. "I didn't know you were a secret dervish," he said. "I just like the idea of spinning. The religious part doesn't interest me." "I think you'd be good at it. You've got your arms and legs in just the right position. Some people never get it." "How do you know?" "I was quite good at it once. But that was like a thousand moons ago. In Chechnya. There were a few Alevi families on our base. They knew the tradition. A couple of us were interested, so they taught us. In the end I could go off like a rocket. I don't know if I still can. Let's find out."

He stepped outside the cubicle, took up a position, precisely as she had read, and began to rotate, standing on tiptoe of his motionless left leg, while driving himself in a circular movement with his right. Slowly, at first, he gradually picked up speed and was soon spinning like a dreidel. He stopped, a little unsteadily. "That's the trick,' he said. "Getting there is relatively easy, but coming back is like re-entry from outer space." "That was really impressive," Shira said, wondering what other mysteries her brother-in-law might be hiding. "You know, that dance goes a long way to explain why I am here, right now, as a Hasidic Jew." "You're kidding." "I never kid. You see, they taught me not just to spin, but to do it with the four Selams in mind. They are the stages of the dance, each expressing a different spiritual value, danced to a different musical rhythm. When they finished a session, they always recited verses from the Koran. I didn't like standing there in silence, waiting for them, so I asked another Jewish officer in the engineers, if he knew a Jewish prayer. He taught me the only verse he knew, but he didn't know what it meant. Of course, I didn't know either. It was a good ten years before I found out. He said that he always said it when he was in trouble, so I did the same." "What was it?" "Hear, O Israel, the Lord is our God, the Lord is One." "You couldn't have done better. But how did it make you a Jew?" "The first time I went to the Western Wall of the Temple, after I moved to Israel, I didn't know what to do. There were all these guys, praying as if the world would end if they stopped. Without thinking about it, I just started to dance. I was thinking about the Selams. I'd had a drink or two, lost my balance and crashed into some chairs. A rabbi came up and asked if I had been dancing. I said I had. He said that I should show more respect. This was a place of prayer. I told him that dance was also prayer. He asked if I had been to India. I said, not India, Chechnya. And then he said the most amazing thing. He knew a Jewish engineer officer who had served with the Russian army in Chechnya. He took me home and, that Shabbat, introduced me to the officer. It was the one who taught me the only prayer I knew. During the service, we recited it together. This time we knew what we were talking about."

***

Shira did not have a good night. How could she, with a husband on death row? Just two days to go. All she had been able to think of, between fitful bouts of sleep, was the series of nascent movements he had made at different times. She saw them over and over again, in painful close-ups. His eyelashes flickering, eyebrows rising, his mouth moving, a facial muscle pulsating, a hand protruding. They did not evoke hope, but misery, for she found no meaning in them. They belonged to the dark side. The mocking side. In the morning, she was only half alive. She did not even make coffee for herself. She climbed into the car and pointed it towards the university. What the hell was she supposed to be talking about today? Oh yes, she remembered, social realism in the nineteenth century French and the modern Hebrew novel. She could do with a high dosage of social realism herself, not just in the lecture theater, she told herself. When she took a call from Professor Bondman, she could not, at first, make out what he was saying. The voice was the professor's, but the message could have been Esau's. "I'm not hearing you," she said, slowing down. Her loss of speed was greeted with a chorus of car horns. "Israeli drivers!!" she fulminated, forgetting that she was one of the worst. She slowed down even more, to a crescendo of hoots. She heard the professor say: "Can you come? Now? There's been a …" She did not catch the end of the sentence. She was already eking her way, to make a left turn, through two lanes of affronted drivers, who objected to her maneuver vociferously with their horns. She honked back with egalitarian animosity.

***

The professor, Penina and the duty Head Nurse, were gathered around Yuri's bed. Penina slipped her palm into Shira's before anything was said. "I didn't think I would ever have good news to tell you on this case," the professor said, "but I have. Your husband regained consciousness just over two hours ago. Mazal tov!" Shira could not tell if she was in shock, awe, ecstasy or plain relief. She stared at Yuri. He was sitting, propped up by pillows. His eyes were open, but seemed not to see. "I've taken him through the basic neurological tests," the professor continued. "He passed." Yuri made a forward movement with his head, as if straining his neck to get a better sight of something. "He did this before," the Head Nurse said. "We don't know what he wants." Shira followed his eye line. "I do," she said. "He wants to see that bird." Everyone turned. On the window ledge, where the old building and the modern extension met, an opalescent male Palestine songbird was hovering. He had the ability to stay airborne on the same spot for short intervals, held aloft by the almost subliminal fluttering of his wings. "Is that what you are after?" the professor said to Yuri, pushing the bed towards the old-fashioned window that could be opened and closed. Penina forced it open. The birds fled. "They'll be back soon enough," the professor assured everyone. "Back," repeated Yuri. The word stuck in Shira's throat, as if it was she who said it. She wanted to cry. It was like hearing a baby say its first word. The professor had been right. A few moments later they were back. First the female, a dull, tweedy grey, resumed her position on the ledge, scanning the sky. Then the male, an iridescent, turquoise-black, began to flutter above her, like a tiny helicopter. Shira recognized the high-speed, intense chatter of the birds, punctuated by mechanical-sounding, low-register, pops, like flash bulbs going off at a celebrity photo shoot. Yuri leaned forward for a better view. His eyes bulged with effort. The head nurse slipped two pillows under him. Obligingly, the glittering male bird opened wide his beak, curved like a crescent moon, designed for drinking nectar, to demonstrate his incomparable songster skills. Shira remembered times she had sat with Yuri, listening to the romantic conference of these birds, up to half a dozen pairs, among the branches of the white Syrian bougainvillea that grew around the trunks of palm trees on their kibbutz. Had Yuri remembered them too? She almost said thank God.

Prof. Bondman interrupted the reverie. "Beauties aren't they? If I wasn't a doctor, I think I would have been an ornithologist. We've only had these birds in Jerusalem since the early Fifties, when we planted gardens and laid out parks, for the first time, in the holy city. The songbirds were a bonus we did not expect." He smiled at Yuri. "This man may yet surprise us all," he repeated, before leading his party away. Shira stayed. Yuri had remembered the Palestine songbirds. Did he remember her? She moved towards the bed, until she was as close as she could be. He turned his head slowly and looked at her. But there was no recognition. She was like any other object in the ward. She smiled, but there was no response. She felt she was waiting to have her photo taken by a broken camera. She held the smile as long as she could, then turned away sharply, refusing to let him see it die. As she did so, she became aware of the smallest tightening at the corners of the lips and a slight enlargement of his cheeks. She encircled his upper body with her arms and kissed the neonate smile. When she pulled back and looked at his face, his eyes told her that her action had been pleasurably inexplicable.

***

Shira was severely disappointed that she had not been present at the exact moment when Yuri came out of coma. Her prime reaction was existential relief interlaid with a thankfulness that knew no address. The next day, full of wonder and apprehension, she drove slowly to the hospital, aware that she was taking her time, like drawing a long breath. Yuri seemed as comatose as before, but his monitor needle had a steady rhythm. She kissed his head and caressed his face repeatedly, read a poem and sang a song. She found a recording of Naomi Shemer's

"Song of the Weeds," on his cellphone and securing his earphones, pressed play. She kept her eyes more on the needles than on Yuri himself. She gasped in wonder as the graph performed a nifty dance. She was glad no-one else was there. She no longer needed evidence to prove he was alive. It was a shared moment of intimacy, pointing towards a recovered past and an admittedly overcast future that could only be illuminated by the torch of hope.

***

The professor, two of his senior staff, the Head Nurse, and the Head of Clinical Psychology and a batch of students, were gathered around Yuri's bed. "Why do you all wear white, always?" Yuri asked, inspecting them as if he was taking a parade. "We have come to see how you are getting on. Do you know who I am?" asked the professor. "Yes. You are Lieutenant Colonel Pozner," said Yuri. "And who are you?" the professor asked. "I am Professor Bondman." Some of the students giggled. Yuri scowled at them. "You mean I am the patient and you are the doctor?" asked the professor. "Yes. And I'm very pleased with your progress, Colonel." "You have been here a very long time, professor," said the professor. "It was only possible because we had a spare bed and you are an unusual case. Do you think you are ready to leave here and go into rehab?" the professor asked. "A different place? I do not like different places." "He's made remarkable progress," said the professor, turning to the others, "but we can't afford to make a mistake." "Mistakes are made in heaven," Yuri interjected. "Verbally, he's already out of here," said the Head Nurse." "He can joke and that puts him streaks ahead. He's playing with us. That's the very best sign." She bent to pick up Yuri's earphones which had dropped to the floor. Yuri seized the opportunity to caress her buttocks. "And that's another good sign," she said, rising, un-phased. "His libidinal drive is alive and well. He must simply learn how to use it, appropriately." Natalie, Head of Clinical Psychology, turned to the students. "As coma patients recoup their minds, the libidinal drive, which usually returns no matter what, can get out of control. They'll sometimes grope any female within reach or make lurid remarks or even, in some cases, masturbate openly. It's a stage in their progress – so long as they eventually relearn the norms and some degree of social responsibility.

Meanwhile we try to keep them moving forward slowly. And we can. But it really depends on how the brain mends. That remark about mistakes being made in heaven, clearly a rewording of the saying that marriages are made in heaven, was a clever recognition by him that there is something beyond behavior. I don't know why he said it. But it's a sign. Perhaps he is trying to re-understand what marriage means. What wife means. Perhaps his relationship to his wife puzzles him. That's my guess, anyway. I'd say he was almost ready for rehab and not far from going home. But the cleaning lady will have to watch out." Shira arrived after the professor's rounds were finished. She walked to her husband's bed. He was asleep. "We're going to get through this together, Yuri. What do you say?" she asked the sleeping figure. Shira walked away, debating what his answer would have been, if he had been awake.

Chapter Two

As Yuri inched his way out of the coma, he lived in a land of shadows. He could not tell the difference between memory and present, between possibility and event. He was to claim, despite the categorical denials of his doctors, that he had experienced mental states, if abnormal ones, while he was still comatose. His recall was too strong for him initially to believe otherwise. He claimed to have experienced other forms of existence, which he termed "presences." The medical team and visitors heard him out as if he was a child suspected of not telling the truth.

Throughout the days of coma, Shira was confronted by a shadow of a man, almost a ghost, who could do nothing for himself. Now she faced a ghostly apprentice painstakingly learning how to be human. Could he be likened to Adam Rishon, the "First Man?" Not that she believed there had ever been such a creature. That was metaphor. She believed there may have been initial groups that jumped out of the trees at about the same time, but there must have been a gap between assimilating their new physical reality and forming a new consciousness to cope with it. Was consciousness innate in their chemistry? Or did it require something religious Jews mean, when they talk about God breathing his spirit into Adam? It didn't mean that literally, of course, since there was no God in her firmament. So what did it mean? What turned the "First Man," from 190 hairy pounds of flesh and bone, into a human being? Was that what she was waiting for? For Yuri to perform the pristine act: to attach consciousness to physical reality? Without God's help, but with Evolution there to back him up ?

She continued to read to him from his favorite novels, played messages from friends on her mobile, and DVD's of music he loved, donated by army buddies. Sometimes she sang in her soft soprano. She spent hours at his side, watching over him, drying the spittle from his lips and the mucous from his eyes, helping the nurse bath him, holding his hand, kissing his forehead and sometimes his lips, and spoon-feeding him with the grain less liquids that his frail digestive system would tolerate. It had been easier to "deal" with him when he was comatose, when she depended on hope. The idea that one could be alive and virtually dead at the same time was obnoxious to her. She had been raised on the belief that life meant hope and hope was everything. If you could not hope, you were hardly human. One of her father's favorite sayings was the Roman adage: dum spiro spero, dum spero spiro – while I breathe, I hope. While I hope, I breathe. She often heard him proclaim it, in later life, in his rasping tenor. But now, as she watched her husband's laborious return to the cognitive world, hope was less a requirement than dogged determination. She was running low on fuel.

***

In those days of "coming out" when his brain began to put on new clothes, he had to remember to relearn everything. Sometimes he astonished, leaping ahead of himself in comprehension or recall. Shira felt that her limited contribution was best achieved by stimulating memory, sharing soul intimacies, enticing the re-conquest of small things. It would have helped if he could remember that she was his wife. But that turned out to be a long process. At first she existed only as a voice. A voice buried within a person without identity. No-one had identity. There were no such people as nurses, doctors, visitors, old friends. He saw them but did not know who they were nor why they were there. The person whom he later identified as his wife came and went to no particular purpose or schedule. The constant disappearance and reappearance of people, disturbed him. Others shared the same space that he did, but he would have been astonished if the point could have been made to him, that they mattered. Nothing was certain or firm in his ethereal world, which was like darkness lit by fireflies. Shira passed in and out of his existence as a mother appears and disappears in her baby's perception. The substantive difference is that a baby is aware of its mother's absence. For a long time, he was not aware of her when she was not there. She existed only when she was present. As time went on, the voice developed a rhythm, and pitch which he could differentiate from others. It was cooling, like a fan on low. Finally, he recognized its owner as someone more than a pleasant outline that made solicitous sounds. That was a major breakthrough. He understood that she did things for him that other people did not. It was the birth of the concept of relationship, which he consequently extended to nurses, volunteers, doctors and medical clowns, in a variety of ways. Once he could see and hear them in relationship to himself, he could accord them a shallow identity.

The environment he lived in was bizarre and illogical, but there was a logic in its illogicality, and a kind of autistic rhythm in its daily repetitions. An account of his fantasies would add little to the sum of human knowledge, but two in particular were bridges. The first provided him with a rickety return to material reality, the second was instrumental in rebuilding relationships based on past events, not merely what went on around him on a daily basis.

Both were brought into the open, thanks to a visit by Penina. Yuri had been moved to rehab, in a separate but neighboring building, since his condition was no longer considered life-threatening. The professor had misgivings about his decision, but could no longer justify Yuri's occupancy of a bed in emergency. After wading in a lake of bureaucracy, he negotiated the transfer, with the proviso that Penina would visit whenever she could fit it into her schedule and Natalie, her boss, would cover for her at the hospital. Penina, being Penina, generally visited in her own time, early, before the rehab medical staff did their rounds, when the Colonel was just waking up. She reckoned it was the best time to catch him, between two worlds. No-one believed he was making sufficient progress, given a breakthrough start. If anything, he had suddenly begun to make inverse progress.

At the beginning, she found him guarded and monosyllabic. Words were an obstacle, not a means. That had to be reversed. She began to talk to him, watching carefully for reactions, as if she was training a reluctant parrot. He listened with what appeared to be interest, but nothing more, preferring to remain silent, or, perhaps worse, unable to express thoughts he might have had. His eyes watched her knowingly, but otherwise, he gave no clue that he understood. She had begun to tell him a compote of a tale of events spread over a recent weekend in Tel Aviv, with friends. What they did, the things they said, places they went to, people they met. He was listening, she could tell. But did he hear? She glanced at her watch. She had been speaking almost an hour. She had drawn no verbal response. She felt exhausted and helpless. "Go on," he said. "Why?" she asked. He didn't answer. "Why do you want me to go on?" "I see what you say. I see it, in pictures." She made a call, asking Natalie, to cover for her for another hour. "You and your Colonel," Natalie answered in a despairing tone. "Emergency is packed with cases you could really make a difference to – and you want to spend a day talking to your Colonel Fantasist! They should have put him in an institution and left him to his destiny. If he normalizes to some degree, great. Look, this time I'll cover. OK? But, let there be no mistake, the hospital is where you're really needed." Dispirited by Natalie's reaction, she carried on talking to Yuri, diligently milking situations for far more than they were worth, without eliciting a response. She kept telling herself something she had learnt at college: speech liberates. She had to get him to speak, to converse. She would have screamed at him, if she thought it would help. "Oh, I almost forgot," she restarted, launching into an episode that had escaped her. "One of the most fun places we went to was a new boutique pub. Not like an English pub. More a restaurant cum pub. Maybe a bistro would be more accurate. I've never been that much into beer, but this was something else. I know we've got some great beers here, but I had no idea that we'd also developed a specialist beer market. We went to some place that's just opened which has beers like you never tasted. I, for one, got hooked. There's one called…." "You are making me thirsty," Yuri told her. His response had taken ten minutes of one-way oration. She plunged on, describing the place in meticulous detail, the owner, an Israeli from Holland, who studied the beer industry in Europe, the Caribbean-style décor, the furnishing, the design of the glasses, the low-key lighting, the international clientele, the headscarfed African barmen (probably illegals), the taste of three different labels she had ventured to taste while a hail of conversation raged around her. "There was one called… oh shit, I've forgotten, but it's a smoked stout and you know, if I had drunk a full bottle of that, they would have had to carry me out." "What was special about it?" Yuri wanted to know.

"Well, it was lightly smoked, for a start. I didn't know you could do that with beer, or even that anyone would want to. At first I didn't want to try. But it smelt so good, an aromatic mixture of chocolate, roasted malt and espresso, I just wanted to smell it. But when I did, finally, sip some, it was like a liquid bouquet. Caramel, figs and dates. Wow!" She broke off and looked at him. He did not seem impressed. She was getting weary. She had been speaking for two hours.

To her relief the lunch trolley arrived. "Pea or mushroom?" the gray-clad volunteer manning it, asked expressionlessly. "It matters?" Yuri replied. "Oh! Talkative today, are we? Which then?" "It's all the same. Pea is mushroom and mushroom is pea," he said. "Very interesting. So which do you want?" "You tell me," Yuri told her. "Well, you had mushroom yesterday and the day before. Have the pea for a change." "Yes. Give me pea for a change." She ladled two scoops of a pale-green viscous liquid into a soup plate and placed it on the folding table attached to the bed, with a few rice crackers. "Eat it all up this time." she advised. "It's very nice. I had some myself." Yuri stared at his lunch. Penina seized the opportunity to get an insight into his mental geography. "Do you like soup?" she asked. "I don't remember." "Don't you remember the soup you had before you came here? Did you like that?" Yuri was silent for a long time, as if he wasn't going to answer. Then he spoke. "Yes. When I was a young boy, we had pea soup with peas. This pea soup is without peas." "It has peas, but they're blended. Do you remember the taste?" "Yes. It was rich. Hot. You could smell it." "Do you remember what the smell was like?" "It smelt of the garden. We put things in it to make it strong. This pea soup has no smell and no taste. It is joke pea soup." "Are you going to eat it?" "I'm not hungry." "But you must eat. It will help you get well." "When we had pea soup in Russia, the smell made you hungry. If you were not hungry, you felt hungry," he said, spooning the liquid resentfully. "I feel like I used to when I had too many sweets before supper." He fed some of the liquid into his mouth and swallowed with a pained expression. "This pea soup doesn't make you hungry. It makes you not hungry." Despite his comments, he continued eating in a waywardly manner. Penina smiled, delighted, not at his culinary performance, but his new ability to compare a past event and a present one, using two of his ten senses, taste and the memory of taste. Hope renewed, she chatted about everything she could think of for the rest of the afternoon

***

Rehab was a new experience, devoid of faces he knew or half-remembered and of sounds and colors and lighting that he had become used to and of a routine to which he had become naturalized. The world had to be reinvented. He responded by closing down. He slept most of the time and surveyed his new environment with suspicion when he was awake. He stopped having revelations of previous life experiences, stopped dreaming (if there was a difference) spoke little, ate little and asked for little. He was still on a catheter and still required the bedpan and only pressed his bell when in some need connected with either. After a while, he had begun to listen to music again. Popular songs, mainly Igor Talkov in Russian. Naomi Shemer in Hebrew. Elton John in English. Penina approved. The combination of music, rhythm and words could only help the restoration of thought and speech.

***

Penina was about to go home when Yuri asked if she wanted to hear about his dreams. Her head was by now empty of ideas. She agreed. By the end of his recitation, she was thankful she had.

"In the first dream, I was on my back. I was on a cloud, facing the firmament," Yuri recalled. *"The cloud was very high in the sky and was lit by the sun and the moon."* He stopped abruptly. *"Sorry, Penina. I just can't get back into it. It's pretty stupid." "It might help if you lay on your back, closed your eyes and told me the content of your dream as if it was happening now. Just let it come."* Yuri rolled onto his back and closed his eyes. He began to speak sooner than she expected. *"The western sky is full of streaks. Silver, gold and red. An Aztec god has been sacrificed. The streaks are his blood. The eastern sky is deep violet. Awesome. Dramatic. Beautiful. The cloud I am on is giving way. I am falling. Falling. The downward motion makes me want to sleep. I force my eyes open. I must discover — where I am. I am in a glass elevator, descending slowly, through the center of the earth. All around is awesome. Beams of light strike glass mountains*

which are like giant prisms. They split the beams into great multi-colored shafts. Each mountain produces a different spectrum. Huge green flames leap high in the sky and die down to become fields of smoldering embers, the size of small lakes. Their light is cold. There is nothing on this planet to sustain life, nor the hope of life. The only thing to do here is die. That is why I am here. Here, in the middle of nowhere and nothing, where no-one has ever been.

"Not to resist. That is the only answer. Is it wrong to accept what you can do nothing about? Doesn't "inevitable" mean that resistance has no point? I do not mind. I am not frightened to face death. My concern is that nobody will know what happened to me. Why is that painful? I am about to vanish forever. Will some part of me survive? I feel great sorrow, not for myself. My sorrow is for existence. I am getting weaker. It will be over soon. Something is flickering inside my head, like the final seconds of a Sabbath candle. Slowly, the flame departs through the top of my skull. The thinnest smile forms on my lips, like the condensation of breath on glass. I watch it, carefully. What is there to smile about?"

Yuri stopped speaking and remained quite still. Penina was in awe at what he had said. She had made some notes on his phraseology. She read them through, then tapped his arm, but he did not wake. She took his pulse. Not much off normal for a man his age. Had he dreamt the original dream again, or was he dreaming its memory? She played a few sentences back to herself. Why was the descriptive power of his dream so much greater than his still-limited everyday conversation?

Over the next few days, he recounted other dreams, all to do with death. He died, usually alone, never knowing why or where, surrendering to inevitability without a whimper. Was that how he survived? Something inside him was fighting the very death he had accepted as inevitable, as if he was calling inevitability's bluff. How to explain that? Was the secret of life, the threat of death? The stronger the threat, the stronger the will to live?

The dream was a watershed. Previously, reality had been ephemeral, unstructured, ill-grasped and meaningless. Somehow, this dream made him conscious of his environment. Objects had purpose. They were not just there. Without them, he did not exist. His bedside table, for example. It went some small way to define who he was, or at least, where he was. Who he was and where he was, were inextricably linked. By changing one, you changed the other. He began to examine things around him. Only by doing so, might he discover who he was, or might be. The second dream which Penina considered a break-through, was what she named in her file, the Banana Dream.

I was inside a banana hanging from a tree on a large plantation. There were five other bananas in my bunch but they were all of the standard variety you can buy in a shop. I was fully human but miniaturized. I was about 12 years old. I don't know how I knew that, but it was a fact. As far as I could see I was the only human banana. A woman who was attractive enough to be Shira was walking through the plantation. She was barefoot. She wore a flowing skin-colored dress which made her look as if she was not wearing a dress at all. I followed her progress with my eyes, wanting her to see me. She was about to pass the tree I was on without noticing me when, on an impulse, she stopped. I wanted to shout to her that I was not a banana and that I didn't know how I had got here. Someone had made a huge mistake, I wanted to say. But I understood intuitively that words would be useless – who ever heard of a talking banana? I remained silent. She stood beside the tree and studied me closely, shielding her eyes against the sun. I thought: wasn't it a pity that she wasn't a banana too. I could not tell what she was thinking. Did she like me? Or did she think I was weird? Then she smiled a strange smile and plucked me with soft, warm fingers. I was free. She studied me as she walked, as if I was carved ivory. We came out of the plantation into a field carpeted with wild flowers. She bent down to gather some cyclamens. Needing both hands, she placed me between her breasts. Flesh rippled around me like warm waves on a tropical beach. I got an erection and reached down to make it less obtrusive. But I had no penis! How could I have an erection? Was there such a thing as a mental erection? In panic I felt the rest of my body. No legs! No chest! I was pure banana. Did I have a face? I ran my hands across the place where my face should be. No lips, eyes, mouth, nose! If I had none of these, how could I have hands? I lurched forward and stared eyelessly. No hands, no arms! I was trapped inside a banana. How was that possible? Would I ever get out? Why had she chosen me, if outwardly

I was no different to the others? She sat on the grass and unpacked a small picnic – sandwiches, a tomato, a piece of cake, a carton of juice and a large book without title or author. I knew at once I was on the menu. I shouted with all my might: "wait a minute, there's someone in here!" My voice was deafening but she didn't hear. She dispatched her sandwiches with pitiful unconcern, then picked me up and began to peel me. I screamed at her but she did not hear. "Hellooo! There's a person in here. Don't eat me! I'm not what you think!" For a moment, she looked as if she might have heard me, but didn't stop. She opened her mouth slowly and took a deep bite. I felt myself being churned to a pulp in her mouth. Teeth, tongue and digestive juices made quick work of my soft flesh, reducing me to a semi-liquid squirt. There was no pain. Just a pulsating fear of the cavernous darkness as I passed into her womb. Yes, her womb. Not her stomach. At least I was spared the process of digestion which would have reorganized me into a thousand tiny packages. How will I ever get out of here? My God, she's not going to give birth to me, is she? If so, what as? Please God, not a banana!

The Colonel's odyssey of return to the world of identity began with that crazy dream. Shira had materialized in his subconscious, which meant he was ready to recognize her in reality. He continually lurched in and out of consciousness and fantasized generously between splutters of cognition. But the groundwork was being laid in the fantasies which filled his mind and gradually fell away. Shira existed as a woman again in his subconscious, the antechamber to reality. Penina told him later that the banana episode graphically illustrated his need of, and affection for Shira and his pristine fear of her. It illustrated the formidable agenda that had to be resolved between them. The truths of their relationship were hidden in the dream, like treasure that pirates have buried, intending to return. The important thing was that the process of recognition had begun. His subconscious was functioning and trying to come to terms with reality, present and past. The constituent elements of his brain were still at war. If one of them won an outright victory, he would not regain his mental balance and death might not be far away. The outcome was still in doubt. Penina thought it was significant that, in the banana dream, he was unable to speak and that when he did, Shira did not hear. His mind was reaching out, but was impeded by the fear of being misused or misunderstood by others.

***

Shira came and stayed by his side for as much time as she could afford, but for him there was as yet no continuity in her appearances. Each time she left, he forgot her, unable to open a mental file on her existence. Only when he would be able to remember past visits would he be able to predict future ones. That would come, yes, it would come, Penina assured everyone. Except herself. She was the one person who knew the nature of the war being fought within his head. Would the "good" side win? Or the dark side? Or might the outcome be 'guaranteed mutual destruction?' She kept her doubts to herself. Only she knew what the pitfalls were. It would be counter-productive to share, and self-damaging to pursue alone.

Yuri's brain knew how much it could take and prescribed its own remedies, summoning sleep when things became too demanding. Apart from his dreams, where reality and the world of fantasy met in a series of sometimes deadly, sometimes inconclusive clashes, he began to recall distant memories. He was opening a file on himself. Often the things he recalled came from army life but more frequently from his boyhood in Russia. As the sun peeked through the shutters of his hospital space, he would be transported to a different space in the Crimea, almost forty years earlier, where the same sun peeked through the shutters onto a different scene – his parents waking in the ancient double bed on the other side of the room, their tangled limbs protruding beneath the cotton sheet to catch the faint breeze, while he squinted his eyes, pretending to be asleep, as he waited for the mysterious, proselytizing ritual with which days were inaugurated. The dream clips of that period were like still photographs, slices cut from life. Or like sliced salami, which he kept in some refrigerated archive in his brain.

Chapter Three

Shira had to be reconstructed from scratch. There was no sudden moment of recollection, when she and Yuri threw their arms around each other in emotional restoration. For one thing, that was not the stop at which they had got off. The last time they parted had been in crisis. They had reached a crossroads, after an adventurous journey, which beckoned them in separate directions. They did not acknowledge it to each other, but they each knew, and each knew that the other knew. They had ridden the heady merry-go-round of love and hate and apathy. The music had stopped. The ride was over. There was no winner past the post, but two losers who had failed to complete the course. They were like a couple who couldn't afford some object they both desired. Divorce requires a great deal of emotional outlay. At that point they didn't have it. At the time of his injury, they were adrift. It was a long time before he recalled all this, and much longer before he could face it. She too.

For weeks Shira sat there almost daily but he couldn't attach any meaning to her. When he awoke, he did not notice if she was there. He did not look to see. He might discover her accidentally while turning his body to a more comfortable position, or by her deliberately attracting his attention. Even so the feel of her fingers on his face had no reference, pleasant although it was, now and again, even stirring. But for the most part, it was like an unknown person accidentally brushing against him in the street, an act without purpose. The memories he needed to rebuild her image in his mind, were unavailable. Hence the gap between them and the woman who sat at his bedside was like a broken rope bridge, across a chasm. A conventional marriage, for which memories were a replay of mundane worries, joys or woes, was more readily retrievable. But a span of eighteen years, which included their first meeting, when they both felt they already knew each other, a teacher-student relationship without impropriety, a brief affair – lasting little longer than a proverbial one-night stand – which led, after years of no contact and little reciprocal thought, to ten long years of matrimony, sustained by two unlikely people, neither of whom had any trace of ideological belief in the institution of marriage, nor a firm commitment to what it might mean, is a prestigiously long time. Yet that was the backlog that he (and she) had to work through. The relationship he was striving to recall was rendered the more irretrievable, given that when he was wounded, they were facing the descant of their life together, no longer the main theme. He did not remember the Shira he was trying to remember, because at last remembrance, there was little that was memorable between them. "It was like looking" as he later put it, "through a fog on one side of a river, for someone lost in deep mist on the other – if that is meteorologically correct." Their subsequent affair, which began during his first leave, like their ten-year marriage, remained irretrievable, except for a few tantalizing memories which seemed to belong nowhere, inconclusive fragments. He sensed more than he knew that they had had a meaningful relationship in common. But the expression "Yuri's wife," by which he heard other people refer to her, meant nothing.

Coming to believe that she had the ability to return was a major step in his recovery. He began to grasp that some events were predictable. It was also an important moment in his reconstruction of her as a person. It would be a long time before his memory of past times began to flow like an unblocked drain and he would be able to connect her with things that had happened long ago. For the moment, she was a person without past or permanence, who unpredictably sat on the chair and read or chatted.

***

One late summer afternoon he awoke with a start. Something had changed. At first he could not tell what. There was a sense of wonder in the air. He realized he had returned from nowhere – neither from a dream, nor a fantasy. He had been asleep, nothing more. A stream of low energy flowed into his emaciated muscles. The sun was nearing the end of its day's journey, leaving the stone, with which much of Jerusalem is fronted, in darkening shadow, its departing shafts highlighting domes, minarets and church towers, deepening the pink of the Western Wall of the onetime Second Temple of the Jews, seeking out ancient wooden doors and window frames, lending grace to newer buildings, courting larch trees and covering the old city in a golden haze – yet all he actually saw through the half-shuttered window was the east wing of the hospital building against a sweep of saffron-blue sky. It came to him, as an important fact dawns on a researcher, that what he had seen was inside his head. A montage of Jerusalem, culled from images he had witnessed in the past. He sat on the edge of his bed, nursing his revelation, for a long time, unsure of what it meant, but convinced that it was an important clue in the crossword of meaning. Time had meaning. As he remembered Jerusalem, other memories were being marshalled in his brain. In that instant, he had an inkling of an idea. The past existed. It could be thought in the present. Rediscovering that the past was alive inside his head, that it referred to real events that had once taken place, was like rounding a headland in a rickety boat and seeing the ocean. He had only a frail grasp of what he had discovered and it would be long before he could wring out the implications. At her next visit, Penina recognized that Yuri had found the key to a locked room. The lock was rusty and the door frame out of alignment. What would he make of the room when he had free access? And what would he make of himself? And others? Others would be some way down the line, Penina opined, and resolved she would not be last.

***

A few mornings later, Yuri woke up, wondering if the woman who sat in the chair, was there. As the thought evolved in his head, he realized that his mind was taking a step forward, that the enquiry was more important than the result. He turned his head slowly, prepared equally for disappointment, or epiphany. There she was, asleep, breathing. Not only did she exist, she had come back. He felt like a tortoise who smells something good. He was surprised when he realized that he was pleased. He was pleased that he was pleased. Was she? Was she there because she chose to be? Was she there for him? Why him?

She looked and smelled very nice, he had to give her that. Penina maintained that he could not have thought 'why him' at the time. He had too primitive an understanding of himself. More likely, he was overcome with a feeling of pathos, set off by the way Shira's head touched the back of the chair, exposing her broad white throat and her innocence. She opened her eyes slowly and he closed his. He was afraid of what she might expect of him. He could not have described to her the whirlpool in his head. He had not been closer to crying since he was a small boy. But boy vanquished man. He wept, silently, hiding his tears, suppressing the sound.

Over the next few days, he saw her as a person with the will to come and go, to choose. He compared her to himself, and realized his powerlessness. He could only allow things to happen. He was rooted like a tree. He recalled a Hebrew song about man, who is described as a tree in a field. The lyric, he had supposed, was meant to show how man was rooted in Nature, but for him it was a cruel reminder of how he was chained to his bed, which was the nature he was rooted in now. Self-pity rose like a wall between them. In the preceding weeks, he had fantasized much and felt nothing. He had witnessed the most beautiful of things and the most awesome, but they were equally emotion-free. He had cruised through them without involvement. The fearful was not fearful, the erotic not erotic, the beautiful had no criteria. Now emotions were back in play, raw, crude, merciless as a shoal of sharks. He was no longer a dispassionate passenger visiting strange worlds. He was a man who had missed a rung on the ladder and was fighting for a foothold, lest he drop to the depths. He knew the depths. He had been there. From somewhere deep inside him a yearning and a deep fury formed like twin whirlwinds that seemed to burst through his skull. He could not know it, but they were symptoms that he was getting well.

Recovery would finally depend on the rediscovery of himself. Until he awoke that afternoon, aware of his first composite memories since he was wounded, his mind had been like jelly that wobbled with the impact of each catalyst. Progress depended on his reaction to stimuli from outside and the resurrection of memories from somewhere inside. To understand himself, he had to understand others. The first person to whom he might have been expected to turn was Shira. But in one of those mental maneuvers which we execute without precisely knowing why, his attention focused on Moshe, the Kurd, who had also been transferred to rehab where he was achieving brief moments of clarity. Might he be the Colonel's guide and exemplar on the road to recovery?

***

A few days later, Shira brought with her more Russian gipsy music. As she was arranging her husband's earphones, she thought she heard him say, "Kiss me." She examined his expressionless face and closed eyes and thought she must have imagined it. His lips parted slightly. She placed hers on his and felt a detectable response. As she drew back, she saw the ghost of a smile creasing the corners of his mouth. She felt elated for a few moments, then her spirit dropped. Had he really asked her to kiss him? It was the last thing she might have expected. But wasn't that just it? It had to be true because it was so damned unlikely! She leaned over and kissed his closed eyes. He opened them and she said: "Do you want me to kiss you again?" He smiled a cracked smile. She opened his mouth with her tongue and kissed him with all the passion she felt was permissible, plus some, in a busy public ward in a rehab unit.

He remembered that kiss. It was the first time, since he was wounded, that he was able to hang a memory, like a hat, on the back of a peg and retrieve it whenever he wanted. Not long after that, he began the process of reconstructing Shira, assembling, at first a fragmented collection, then a swelling wave of memories. It was not a matter of chronology. He did not, at first, rebuild the progression of feelings and events as they happened. She came back into his life out of a fog, unclear, barely recognizable. He had to screw up his eyes to identify her in memory – by shape and smell. And when finally he recognized her, his mind played a curvaceous trick. The person he recognized was not the person he had known. The Shira who now formed in his mind was a bundle of possibilities, of hypotheses yet to be tested as if they stood, once again, at the beginning of their relationship, as untapped potential. The years of heady happiness, of grim strife and debilitating disillusion – the true history of their marriage – coagulated into a single account which could not be separated, and was hence incapable of being analyzed. He saw what might have been, not what subsequently happened. He saw her innocence and his needs. He saw her fear of coming out of her shell – and the elaborate camouflage behind which she hid. He saw how hard it was for her to love and how easy it was for him to take advantage. He felt the centrifugal energy which drove him outwards and the centripetal forces which drove her into herself. And he recognized the arbitrariness of how things come to be. There was a painful innocence about the Shira of his mind, unformed, more intimate than her naked body. He felt something like compassion for them both. But there was nothing either of them could do. Their subsequent life mocked their beginnings. They had never understood each other – although they would both have denied this, even at the worst of times – and had hidden from themselves. From the beginning they looked to each other for the wrong things. If a person can be likened to a text, they had misread each other, as one might misread the meaning of a letter. Astonishing in that she was a teacher of literature to whom the text meant everything, and he, educated to analyze text and sub-text, to let no detail escape.

He watched her surreptitiously as she sat on the uncomfortable chair beside his bed, reading aloud to him, or quietly to herself, shifting her weight, looking up suddenly with concern, smiling probing smiles, her face dropping in disappointment, chatting urgently to nurses, doctors, psychologists, volunteers, cleaners, drifting into sleep and back again, waking up with a jolt of guilt. She still possessed a dreamy quality that was hard to quantify. She must have had this even as a girl. He was sure that by the age of eleven or twelve, she was already a mistress of hiding her feelings and projecting their opposite. A chameleon around the kibbutz. He imagined her changing to light green as she lay on the grass, or to sage as she climbed an ancient olive, or gilt before sundown. She used camouflage to protect an inner core which he never discovered. If you observed her closely, you realized that she was with you and somewhere else at the same time. That there was some other place, perhaps more real and in some way more desirable, a hairsbreadth away, where she habitually hung out. At first, the Shira who began to swim into his thoughts was not the Shira he had known. He pictured her when she could not have been more than 12, and he still a toddler in another country, when the astrological odds against them ever meeting were hopelessly high. He had very little to go on apart from intuition and scraps of information she later told him about herself, released irregularly during the course of their relationship.

He remembered, or imagined, a lithe, teenaged creature, with a mass of red curls, her eyes green-blue, her skin, which she kept religiously out of the sun, was alabaster-white punctuated with colonies of red mottles. Her inability to tolerate direct sunshine would have a direct affect upon her future. She avoided beaches and the kibbutz swimming pool. Whereas her friends knew every cove and current along the shoreline and the vagaries of the sea wind, she became mistress of the quiet places of the woods, walking barefoot among the panoply of wild flowers that sprang up to cover the land in spring or the bowed fruit orchards at the height of the season. She visited such places alone, armed with a novel which she read with rapid eye movements and projected every detail onto a screen in her mind. In this way she acquired an unusual depth and insight of modern Israeli language which won her top marks in her school-leaving exam and set her on her way to three university degrees in Hebrew, English and Arabic literature. If she did not have to avoid the sun, she would probably have studied science. Whether her predilection for intimate quiet places helped form the cocoon of mystery which she wove around herself, is not something Yuri was sure of, but something he suspected. It did not make his reconstruction of her, any easier. "I unraveled her as what she might have been," he told the professor. "I'm not sure that I know who she really is."

***

It was the first PLE that Yuri had produced since his coming out. Penina eagerly pressed play. The voice she heard was quiet, unhurried. *"I see myself reflected in the water of a pool. There is a feeling of calm and well-being, of things as they ought to be."* The speaker sucks his breath in before he goes on. *"But the man reflected in the water is ill at ease. Can he really be me? I hear a woman's voice from behind a screen on the far side of the pool. It is lamenting the lack of decent eye-makeup. Only the Syrian stuff is any good and you can't get it, she says. She will have to go to Rome at the next opportunity. I smile at the thought of making the arduous and sometimes dangerous voyage to the world's capital, a five days journey, for the sake of some decent kohl but I know it would not be the chief reason for the enterprise. "And I'm almost out of Dead Sea mud," she shouts in mock despair. "What am I to do?" "I could go into Cadiz and get some from the gladiator manager for sure," I say. "It's a scandal" she replies "that they can buy up the entire supply of the stuff. It comes all the way from the Dead Sea and they use it to heal the wounds of those stupid gladiators, or massage their bodies when they will only kill each other anyway! What about women's faces?" "I think it's more important to save a gladiator's limb than a woman's face. The face will wither on the vine." "No! A woman's face is more important. I can prove it. A gladiator will give his life for a woman's face!" She comes out from behind the screen, trailed by the Persian slave responsible for her makeup. "Well, how do I look?" she asks, confident after three hours of bathing, oiling, massage and facial care. She is half-dressed in a blue linen strophium wrapped around her breasts six times to give maximum support and a beige under-tunic. She smiles. Life has been kind to her. She has most of the things she wants — wealth, a position in society, control of her life, a palatial home, the respect of the merchants of Cadiz and the retention of her good looks at an age when most women are abandoning the fight or taking desperate measures to hide its scars. Since the death of her husband she has clawed her way to success in her own right, determined not to be seen as an empty-headed widow. She has swum through the breakers and is now floating without a care — other than the annoyance of not being able to obtain her favorite toiletries - in calm waters. Her life is a predictable mosaic and I am one of its pieces. She cannot see how the arrangement might be less than satisfactory for this particular piece at this moment in time. "My mother, God rest her soul," she says, "used to say you should never show a fool something that is half done. There will now be a short interval followed by the finale when I shall present the finished article. In the meantime my dancing girls will provide some appropriate entertainment." She claps her hands and disappears behind the screen. Three of her best dancing girls enter from the ante-room and begin the sensual acrobatic routine that has made them famous throughout the Mediterranean. What am I doing here? I search for an answer but find none, beyond the fact that, by a miracle, I am still alive."*

***

At this time Penina and Shira were not seeing much of each other. Penina wanted an opportunity to meet and tell Shira about Yuri's new previous life experience. They fixed a meeting in the rehab restaurant. She thought that Shira, wearing a dark blue business suit, looked older and that her self-confidence was on a lower key than when she had last seen her. But the most striking thing about her was that she had cut her hair. Those thick blonde locks were gone. Instead, she had a semi-gamine hairstyle. Penina couldn't make her mind up if she liked it or not. "Great hair. It really suits you," she observed. "I so much needed it. The way I had it was way too much. It was overheating my brain." Neither reflected on the way Shira had changed her image by going for a new style.

Shira listened to the poolside tape several times. "Who is this woman? Any idea?" she asked, and added, "maybe she's the mysterious Julia." "I hope not. Yuri keeps calling me Julia. This woman has three hours of body care and makeup before she even gets dressed. I barely have time to dab my face. I don't think she's me." "I hope he'll get back to the main story soon," Shira said. "If he only gives us bits and pieces taken from anywhere, we'll never be able to put them together in some kind of format." Penina waited for her to go on. Perhaps the PLE would strike a chord in her memory. Shira stretched her legs and arched her back. "He always had a vivid imagination," she said finally. "It was imagination that brought us together. I live in my imagination more than is healthy." "You dream of past lives?" "I wish I did. I never have dreams as clear cut as Yuri's. I never know where I am. There is nothing to describe. Nothing happens either. My dreams are pure mood. Beautiful, or frightening, endless or short-lived. Sometimes, I am in a place I must get out of, for one reason or another. Sometimes, I'm in a place I like, for one reason or another. But I never know what the reason or another could possibly be. No action. No scenery. And very often, no me. I am not there as a physical presence. It's just an impression of me, a shadow.

"In one bizarre respect, I'm like Yuri's mother," Shira admitted. "I know so little about her. I really need to know more," said Penina pensively, inviting her to go on, with her eyes. "As far as I can put her together from the pieces I've heard, she lived a robust life in her dreams and imagination and a thinly veiled one in everyday reality. Everyday life crucified her. The life of imagination, of inspiration was what she yearned for. For me, that other world, the world of imagination, is a world to escape to. It's a place to be, not to be imported into mundane existence. When I am ready, I come back. Relatively, happily back, despite the inconsequentiality and vulnerability of everyday life. But she wanted to live her everyday life as richly as her imagination allowed, through art. She condemned herself to death, meaning herself as artist – and committed suicide. Yuri knows this, well enough. Yet, in a way, he doesn't, because he won't accept it. It's the one thing, he can't face." Penina's eyes dilated. "Are you telling me, his mother committed suicide?" "There are two schools of thought. According to Akiva, and Yuri's father, whom I never met, she did. According to Yuri, she didn't." "But she no longer exists?" "Correct. Except in his mind."

"I have this idea that he is looking for her. He assigns some part of his life, when he is dreaming, day dreaming, meditating, whatever, to finding her. He keeps it very secret. He told me once and never referred to it again." "When did it happen?" "Before he came to Israel. It must have been when he was about ten, or perhaps eleven. He came with his father. He didn't know then it was a case of suicide. He believed his mother died in a swimming accident. They were on an archaeological dig, the whole family, him, his parents, his elder brother. They went to the Crimea almost every year, since he was a baby, to participate in the dig. Other families went too. It was in summer, a working holiday. No-one worked too hard, but over time they excavated the greater part of an admittedly not very important Greek trading post, going back to the first century BCE. His mother was an excellent swimmer. She loved to swim in the moonlight and twice swam across the Bosphorus to the Russian side. The second time, she did not come back. A massive search, with every boat, they could find, was mounted.

Volunteers combed the nearby shore. But the search was hampered by the security cordon drawn around a former Soviet base for nuclear submarines, which still functioned under an independent Ukraine. The prevailing current would most likely have carried the body ashore. One of the top secret sites in the onetime Soviet Union, it housed Russia's major riposte to a first American or NATO nuclear strike, by dozens of nuclear subs that would be released into the Black Sea, with the capability of devastating any target in the world. A large part of the surrounding coastline was out of bounds to anyone but the military. The body was never found. A verdict of death by misadventure, was recorded. That was the official version that most people believed – except Yuri's father and Akiva. They knew her depressive states.

"She had tried suicide in Moscow three times. Two of them coincided with exhibitions of her work, which the critics praised and she despaired of. The last time, when her husband was carrying her out of hospital, she said that Moscow was too depressing a place, to commit suicide. That's why she kept getting it wrong. She was particularly contemptuous of suicide notes. Banal, she called them. No-one needed a note, she used to say, the misery of their lives, was the note. But the night she drowned, Yuri's father found one under his pillow. It was a shopping list for the following morning. She had never written one in her life. She scorned that sort of thing. She hated shopping and usually came back with far too much, or nowhere near enough. Her last word was this shopping list for a few mundane household items, like toilet paper and beetroot. At the bottom, she wrote: 'that's the best I can do. Add whatever is missing, sorry.'

Leonid, Yuri's father, alone knew what it meant. She was taking a permanent rain check on the everyday, on all those moments in time which go on and on, which cannot be lived to the full – to her full. A shopping list! How apt. She wanted to live a life of imagination in the commonplace and through her art to idealize it. She was a success in other people's eyes. But not in her own. She saw through herself. Leonid told no-one, least of all his younger son and let the world think she had drowned, tragically, while swimming. But it was a tragedy, not an accident. The one person Leonid couldn't fool was Stas (now Akiva), his older boy. He must have been in his early twenties. He had just come back, disillusioned and badly wounded, from Chechnya, and a drug addict. He remembered one of his mother's attempts and had heard rumors of others. Leonid kept Stas' curiosity at bay, sometimes buying him off with cash which was quickly turned into heroin, but on the eve of his departure with Yuri, for Israel, he could not hold back. He met his older boy in a restaurant at the airport and while Yuri slept, allowed the facts to be slowly drawn out of him. It must have been like extracting wisdom teeth. Years later when Yuri visited Russia, he met his brother, now a transformed character who was tinkering with Buddhism, who told him the truth. It was too much for Yuri. He refused to believe it. He preferred to think she had got into difficulties while swimming, perhaps been thrown against rocks, perhaps been swept away, but for whatever reason, had begun life over again, in another place. He had been a bit of a mummy's boy and it was too painful to believe his mother did not love him enough not to kill herself. He still believes that. He still believes that she is alive somewhere and dreams about him. Once he dreamt that he met her. He also believes she may have lost her memory of everything, except him. He has no problem in holding conflicting opinions simultaneously. We all do it."

"But in his heart, he thinks she's still alive?" Penina asked. "How can I know? I'm only guessing." "His brother, Akiva, could have been more help in solving his torment," Shira continued. "As you know, the brother joined them in Israel, became Jewish. Joined Lubavitch. Yuri and he met just once, and could not agree about anything, least of all religion and their mother's fate. Religion has become the big divide and they seldom meet." "What do you mean, his brother became Jewish? Was he a half-brother?" "You don't know? My husband's not Jewish. His mother wasn't. He was officially regarded as Jewish in Russia because his father was a Jew and there they go by the father. But here, obviously he can't be. It doesn't bother him. He says he was brought up to think of himself as a Jew, his Russian passport says he is a Jew and he regards the fact that the Jewish religious authorities only concede Jewish identity to someone born of a Jewish mother – or someone who converts to Judaism – as an aberration. I agree." She smiled at Penina. "We couldn't get married here. We went to Cyprus for it. You know what, Penina, I think I should leave you to get over all this. It's a lot to take in." "It has been," Penina agreed, with a frown. "You know something," Shira added. "I've often wondered if he was marrying his mother when he married me. I've often had this idea, that he believed he was marrying not me but someone else. What do you think?" Penina pursed her lips. "You really ask them, don't you Shira?" The two women parted with smiles of reciprocal puzzlement.

***

Although the majority of Russian immigrants are Jewish beyond dispute, many others are not considered to be Jews under rabbinic law. Penina had always assumed that Yuri was a Jew. When they had met in the army, she recognized at once that he was a special person, as a soldier and an officer certainly, but also beyond that. He had a sensitivity that was better picked up by women than men and at the same time he was heading an elite combat unit for deep penetration operations with a reputation for valor. A woman's man and a man's man in one. Penina recalled her meetings with him, some of which concerned a young lieutenant of Yemeni extraction, whose grandparents had come to Israel with the mass exodus of Yemen's Jews. He had been badly wounded in an operation in Lebanon and evacuated by a helicopter rescue unit. It was too late to save his leg, which had to be amputated. His whole life had been shattered – his career, his marriage prospects, his social life and, at first, his spirit. He needed psychological help and Penina gave him all the time she could, guiltily robbing other patients. Whenever he could, Yuri visited the young patient. When he was operated on, he stayed at the young soldier's bedside all night, sleeping on a mattress on the floor. She remembered how his men loved him – not only because he was totally devoted to their welfare, but because of the man he was. In an oblique way, she fell in love with him through their love. It was love that unhesitatingly knew its object. There was no 'Do I really love him?' 'Do I not?' 'Is he right for me?' 'Is he not'? His men believed he had nine lives. With him, however perilous the mission, they felt safe. He was beyond being their commander. He was their totem. One of them once told her that if Yuri was killed or seriously wounded, he would not be able to find the courage to cross the street again.

***

If Shira had been asked if she felt closer to Yuri, now that he was well on the way to recovery, than when he was in coma, she would, in all honesty, have had to say, no. She had felt an almost umbilical connection with him under threat of death, a relationship in which she breathed life into his lifeless body. He lived, not only by dint of state of the art technology and medical expertise, but through her will. She knew that was not strictly true, but believed it nonetheless. They had never been so united. But the more he improved, the looser the relationship grew. She had not found time to visit him for a few days. One morning Shira could tell, the moment Yuri looked at her, that he wasn't sure who she was. His face wore the quizzical look of someone trying to recall where they had met. Feeling she had to make some claim of familiarity, she walked boldly up to the bed and bent to kiss him. He responded by encircling her with an imprisoning arm, forcing her lips with a thrust of the tongue and slipping his free hand inside her skirt. She had to fight her way out of it. She felt nauseous. Was this her husband, restored from the dead? Would there be more of the same when they got home? Would she be able to handle him? He thought she was just another female. And she? What did she feel? Her overriding thought was that this man, whoever he was, was not her husband. The thought of being in the same bedroom made her tremble. She was never the kind of woman who responded to smash and grab sex. Passion, yes, rape, no! She could not tolerate the "help yourself," attitude to sex, as if she was a meat chop at a barbecue. If there was to be sex, she had to agree, be in the mood, sometimes initiate. But how do you initiate with a man who was always ready? How would she be able to minimize contact when she wanted to? And for how long? He would have to have his own room. She may have to sleep at her sister's. Yuri was grinning at her like a naughty boy who had been caught doing something outside the canon of acceptability. The moment could not be allowed to pass, she told herself and faced him. "Yuri, don't you know who I am?" The grin intensified. "I'm Shira. I'm your wife." The feverish glint in his eyes began to subside. "Do you know what that means? It means we're married. We have a special relationship. Don't you remember us? We loved each other. Doesn't that mean anything? Remember? You were an officer in the army and I a lecturer at the university. We lived on a kibbutz. You remember the kibbutz, don't you? Chicken pens and dairy herds and orchards and a recycling plant and an optical center and citrus. You loved working in the orchards. We used to read poetry together. Don't you remember? Emma Goldberg and Naomi Shemer and Yehuda Amichai and Rimbaud and not to mention the Russians, Boris Pasternak and Marina Tsvetayeva. You've been very ill and now you're coming home. Yes, sooner or later. We're going to start over again. Just you and me. We'll have to get used to each other. We've got to make it work, Yuri. But you have to remember that I'm your wife, not a piece of female haunch." She spoke in a rush. Yuri's grin became a grimace which retreated slowly, replaced by a look of profound grief, as if he understood her words but could not cope with them. She was unable to stop. She had made up her mind to say what she had to say. Finally, he looked down, avoiding her eyes, as if her words evoked painful memories or none at all. "Yuri. Yuri? Did you understand me?" He looked up with the expression of a beaten whelp. Her skin reddened and tingled. She felt a wave of sympathy rise like a breaker at high tide and wanted to stretch out her arms to enfold him, but feared his response. She recalled a poem by Leah Goldberg, who once wrote, perhaps in similar circumstances that what was between her and the person she was addressing was not the ocean," she said, paraphrasing the words slowly, as if they were painful to remember. "Nor the depth, nor time..." She could not go on. He was staring at her, blankly. "But what we are," she said continuing the poem as if she was speaking her own words. "That's what's between us, Yuri, "what we are is between us." She wanted to cry but feared driving him into melancholy. She squeezed his wrist.

There was nowhere to go. She dreaded walking through interminable corridors or riding with other people in the elevator. She vaguely remembered using a rest room on a lower floor and took the stairs. The rest room was in two parts – a small outer room with washbasin and mirror, adjoining a toilet. Glancing at the mirror, she caught the reflection of a woman she barely recognized, something like a decade above her chronological age. Fearing tears, she locked the outer room and squatted on the toilet. She persuaded herself not to cry. Argued herself out of it. Wasn't it just too bathetic, crying on a toilet seat! She forced her tears into retro and her mind to dwell on the bright side. Wherever that was. She had over-reacted. At least that is what she finally persuaded herself. They had warned her that her husband could not control his libido with regard to women. She was a woman. Ergo, nothing surprising. Certainly, he had shown remorse. Never more so. And if he did not recognize her, so what? He had only just come out of the land of the half-dead. She had hurt him deeply. Should she go back and make up? No, she would come back tomorrow and pick up whatever pieces had not blown away.

***

In the morning Penina went straight to Yuri's bed. He was awake, listening to a tape. He took off his earphones when he saw her. "How are you today?" she began. "Tired," he said. "What are you listening to?" "Tchaikovsky's Sixth. The Pathetique." "I see you like Tchaikovsky," she said, noting several tapes of the composer's orchestral works and songs littering his table and bed. "Is this a favorite?" she asked, holding up the 1812 overture with its cover of a huge canon superimposed over the embattled armies of France and Russia. "Everything he ever wrote is my favorite," Yuri said, pronouncing the words slowly, as if he had a marble in his mouth. "The tragedy of his life is right there in his music. It speaks to me. Beneath the notes." He held up a small brochure in Russian. "This brochure came with the disc. It says his mother died when he was 14. My mother died when I was younger than that. His mother is present in everything he wrote." "I understand that," Penina told him. "It must be a solace to you." "Solace and pain. There is pain throughout his work. But it is always coupled with its opposite. The pain and the triumph. The pain of the inevitable loss of comrades, the pain of being wounded and of recovery. The pain of victory. The pain even of beauty, as in Swan Lake. The pain of life, as in his Sixth. Pain from the death of his mother. I hear it even in the famous finale of the 1812, for which he uses battle cannons, on stage, to augment the joy of Russia's triumph over Napoleon, when pain threatened glory.

"There is no victory worth having, without pain, he is telling us. But there was more tragedy to come. When he discovered he was homosexual, he tried to drown himself. His mother was no longer there to comfort him. To convince him that someone loved him, whatever his truth. Today he would be conducting gala concerts for AIDS charities in Los Angeles. Then things were different."

Penina's emotional response was divided between sympathy for his confessional and astonishment that he could read. It was a stage he was not expected to reach for some time yet. She wondered if he could also read Hebrew. She wondered if he was ready to read his own text. When should she try? She picked out a Hebrew disc from his collection. It was a series of songs sung by David D'Or, the international Israeli countertenor. "You like D'Or? Then, we've something in common," she said. "I don't like him, I love him" Yuri replied. "I've heard him many times. But I never knew much about him. He sings everything from opera to pop, religious to rock, klezmer to baroque. I was just reading about him." He handed Penina a flyer in Hebrew. She scanned it as he spoke. "You know he has this extraordinary high pitch, don't you? His voice spans four octaves. The brochure says that when he felt his voice was breaking, he was utterly determined to hang on to whatever high notes he could and trained himself to do so. When he studied at the Jerusalem Music Academy, he chose the soprano, Miriam Melzer, as his teacher. He has two voices. One, a straight chest voice, as it says there. The other, alto. He bridges western and eastern music. His family came to Israel when the Libyan Jews were kicked out of the land they had lived in for many centuries longer than the Arabs, in the 1950's." "My mother's family came here at about the same time, when the Moroccan Jews were thrown out, "Penina said. "We share a musical tradition similar to his. It's pure soul. Whenever he performs, there is certain to be a member of my family in the audience, usually me. I'll leave you to enjoy. My favorite is 'avinu malkenu.'" "I'll have it ready, next time you come by."

As soon as Penina got down to the lobby, she made a call to Shira. "I've made an unexpected discovery," she told her. "Your husband can read. Hebrew and Russian. I really think now is the time to get him to read his own tapes. I'd like you to be there." "Great," said Shira, unconvincingly. "When?" "Tomorrow morning." "Count me in." Penina sensed that Shira was less than overjoyed. Her voice sounded as if she had pressed her foot on the accelerator but was braking at the same time. Why should she be ambivalent about her husband's progress? On the other hand, why shouldn't she?

***

The Colonel was awake. He looked tired but pleased to see them. He studied his watch for half a minute and irritably asked Shira what the time was. Shira was shocked that he couldn't tell the time. She kissed him formally on the lips. He held her face in his hands to return the kiss. "Can't you sleep?" she asked, drawing away, slowly. "It's more peaceful to be awake. I wish I could be like him," he nodded towards Moshe the Kurd, in the bed opposite. "He sleeps like a baby." "Do you know that you talk in your sleep? A lot. You talk a lot," Penina said, studying his expression before checking his notes. "If I do, it must be as incomprehensible as my dreams." "It's not. It's very clear. Would you like to read some of the things you've been saying? I recorded it and had it printed out." He looked at the sheets of paper in her hand disbelievingly. "Let me see," he said, reaching for the print-out. Penina gave him his first statement about being taken prisoner at the Battle of Beitar. He began to read slowly, chewing the words as if he was masticating his breakfast. His forehead furrowed. Twice he stopped and stared into space, as if visualizing the events described. He shook his head this way and that. "Who wrote this?" he asked. Penina did not answer. "Did you find it interesting?" she asked instead. "Yes. But why did I have to read it?" "Is there anything you don't understand?" "How would I know? What the hell is going on?" He handed the sheets back to Penina. She hesitated, then said. "This text is part of a story you recited over many nights. There is a lot more." He smiled, disbelievingly. "You're mixing me up with someone else, Julia. I'm no writer." Penina pressed on, ignoring the clue. She would see to that later. "It's not that you wrote it, Yuri. You spoke it. When you were reading, did it seem familiar?" "Familiar? No. What do you mean, I wrote it?" "Yuri, you remember you were wounded in an action on the West Bank and that you were rushed to hospital in a critical condition and after they operated, you went into a coma, a long sleep, from which you have only recently come out?" "I was shot, sure. But now I'm fine." "Well, when you came out of the coma, you began to talk about things in your sleep that happened long ago. The piece I showed you was one of them." He looked at her in silence for half a minute, snatched the sheets out of her hand, and scanned through them at a fast pace. "Are you saying that this 'I' here, in this whatever it is, is me?" "We don't know that. All we know is that it's what you said in your sleep. You recited it." He looked in puzzlement from the text, towards the two women and then at the microphone rigged above his head. "So that's it. I thought that that thing was there to check on me during the night, in case I stopped breathing. But now, I know what it's really for. It's a spy machine. How much of this stuff is there, Julia?" he demanded, brandishing the text under her nose. "Why record it?" he asked sharply, his anger rising. "It's a very interesting account of life at a crucial point in our history," Shira said quickly. "Penina has had it checked. It's accurate as far as they can tell." "Shit! Julia," Yuri exploded, ignoring Shira. "I'm going to look like a true nut if this gets out. The Army will never have me back. This is my death warrant. You're a shrink, right? Well, listen shrink, I want you to get every page of this crap, everything there is, and give it to me." As he spoke he tore the pages into shreds and flung them across the floor, before reaching up to rip the microphone from its site. He hauled the recorder off his bedside table and crashed it to the floor. A procession of wires springs and batteries spilt out. "What do you think they're going to say if they think that I think I once lived in ancient Rome? For God's sake Penina, I wouldn't stand a chance. Have you ever met an army shrink? They're formidable." "I know, Yuri, I was one, once." He looked at her in surprise. "Tell me, Penina, have you ever had to escape from stone? Have you ever been imprisoned in stone?" "Not stone." "Well I have. I am still. There's more in me than what you see," he shouted in a voice that proclaimed his disbelief at the possibility of being believed.

They were interrupted by the Administrator of the Rehabilitation Center and a small delegation of duty doctors and nurses. The latter began clearing up the mess. The Administrator faced Penina with combat eyes. "Can you explain what's been going on?" Madeleine was a tall woman, black hair tied in a rigorous bun, used to giving orders and demanding explanations. By reputation, mercilessly efficient. "Yes, the patient, Colonel Pozner, became over-stressed." "For what reason?" she asked, running her eyes over the torn pages, now piled up on the bedside table, cracked recorder and microphone hanging limply from its coupling. Penina knew of the woman, but had not met her. She had been told that in the Air Force she had a legendary reputation for analyzing aerial, including satellite photography. "I gave him a transcript of some of the material we have recorded from him at night. It distressed him because he thought it would prejudice his chance of resuming his army career." "Was your action necessary?" "We need to know where his revelations come from and whether or not he recognizes them when conscious. It's an essential part of his treatment and recovery." "It's clearly not helping, as can be seen. I'm banning him from having sight of any more transcripts, at least temporarily, until I've had a chance to go into this matter at the highest level, after taking appropriate medical advice. I think I have the right to insist we all paddle in the same direction, if we're to continue working together." She shot a commiserative look at Yuri. He had got back into bed during the short altercation and was listening to his music. She removed his earpiece, without making her action seem overbearing. "Sleep in peace, Colonel," she said, speaking into his ear. "Fear neither the sun that strikes by day, nor the noon by night." The Colonel grinned at her as she replaced his earpiece. She took a few paces from the bed and indicated that Penina and Shira should join her. "I am strongly of the opinion that you should make it known to the Colonel that he will never return to the military," she told them. "This man is a soldier. He cannot be expected to adjust until it is made clear to him. And I'm sure this is an area where you can help," she added, turning to Shira. "A wife may enter, where angels — and psychologists – fear to tread." "Of course," Shira replied, inwardly recoiling from the task. "From what I've learned, he was one of the best. How have the mighty fallen," Madeleine said, before leaving. Her entourage followed, keeping a respectful, if not fearful, distance.

"That's a piece of homework that I'm not looking forward to," Penina admitted. "He'll never take it, if it comes from us," Shira said. "It's got to be the army that informs him. Luckily, I know the right person." "It's not something I want to get onto right now," Penina said. "It makes more sense to find out if he can continue the story from where he left it." "How can that be done?" "Hypnosis." "Aren't there risks?" "There are risks if you do it, there are risks if you don't." "On a scale of one to ten." "About five and a half." Penina expected Shira to want to think it over. Instead, she said: "Let's go for it." She watched Shira walk back down the ward at a business like pace, head in perfect alignment with her spine. There was something bordering on ambivalence about the speed with which she had made her decision. Was she secretly hoping that Yuri might regress, be confined in a home and save her the onerous duty of having him back? Penina had been forced by her job to live in the minds of many patients who could not distinguish their true wishes, but swung from branch to branch and back again, as the moment or the jungle rhythm dictated. If Shira's head and shoulders had sloped forward just a fraction, as she left, Penina would have dismissed her speculation. She also had to admit to herself that she had a vested interest in the relationship between Shira and her husband. Was she letting her own wishes affect the way she colored the picture book?

***

Yuri's recovery was not a straight line. It was like a war with advances and retreats, healing and casualties, victories and defeats. After making spectacular progress, he descended in a depressive spiral. He was trapped in his own thoughts. Ideas hurtled through his head like tiny meteors, but because he could not express them in words, they remained shadowy, ill-formed, unrealized. He remembered a saying once common among Russian immigrants, seeking to explain to people their initial inability to speak Hebrew: "You must regard me as a dog who understands, but does not speak." Was he one day going to come out with a river of nonsense like Moshe, who still twittered merrily like a bird, two beds away? What went on in Moshe's mind? Did he have dreams and memories and things he wanted to tell his family, which surfaced only in his incomprehensible post-coma jargon? Did he think he was talking coherently? Was he recalling life in Mosul in the 1940's? Did he dream about its great synagogue? Did he dream of living during the Roman Empire, or as a Jew under the first Caliphate of Baghdad? Was he destined to a life without speech? And would he, Yuri, follow him?

***

"Did you have a good night, Colonel?" "A disturbed night." "Disturbed?" "Dreams. They exhaust me." "What did you dream about?" "A lot of nonsense. "I'm interested, tell me." "Well the main one was erotic, in a morbid sort of way." He stopped like a toy soldier that needs to be wound up. "Go on." "I've no idea where or when it was. It was a war situation. I was escaping with this woman. She was beautiful but almost dead.

"I was helping her to walk, she was so weak. We were in the hills. It was dark. She collapsed and I had to carry her on my back. I knew we were both going to die. I thought, why use my last strength to carry her another hundred meters for no purpose, when I could use what strength I had left to make love. So I lay her on the ground and ..... Not a very moral tale, but one can see the point." "Did you have an emission during the night?" He smiled, but did not answer. Penina felt herself blush.

"Look Yuri, you keep telling me about unrelated dreams that you have, like the one about this woman that you made love to. But these are dreams such as anyone might have, woven out of the events of the day before, or concerning something on your mind. Yuri, I want to take you back to where you stopped in the transcripts, which was when you were on the way to Rome as a slave. There is a story in you that is waiting to come out. You owe it to yourself to give it space. " "I don't know what you are talking about, Julia" "I will record you and you will read the transcript when it's finished. But, please, no violence." He looked doubtful. "Your wife will be here," she added. "How will you get me to the place I'm going to?" "I won't get you there. You will. I'll only make it smoother. By hypnosis. What do you say?" A deep vertical furrow formed from his lower forehead to the top of his nose. Penina readied herself for a negative answer. "Let's try," he said, renouncing his previous adamancy. Had Madeleine had a word?

***

After lunch the following afternoon, Penina met Shira in the rehab lobby. They took the stairs to the ward, which was almost empty of visitors. Even Moshe had only three. The two women and the Colonel were all tense. Penina tried to lighten the atmosphere. "Remember what we're supposed to be doing?" Penina asked Yuri. "You think I'd forgotten?" "No. But we'd better get going. In a couple of hours, it'll be visiting time for everyone and this place will look like outside Beitar Jerusalem football club, after a match." She looked around. She had established her authority, lightheartedly, but she was in charge. "Let's get you comfortable." The Colonel made to stretch out on the bed. Penina told him she would rather he half sat. Shira puffed up the pillows behind him. "We're going back to before you were born. Many, many centuries ago. When I wake you, you will remember nothing, you will return to who you are now. Are you ready?" He didn't answer but leaned back on the pillows and closed his eyes." "I'd like you to keep your eyes slightly open, like a door slightly ajar. Shira could you put his bedside light out." Penina steadied her mind in the semi-darkness. The next time she spoke, her voice was deeper, richer, perfectly even. Shira studied her. She was sitting bolt upright, in complete control, hermetically sealed from everything outside. Shira sensed an intimate, almost umbilical, connection, between her husband and Penina. She had to fight off envy.

"Imagine the sun," Penina began. "It's a ball of fire. High in the sky. It warms the whole earth. It is very powerful and very beautiful. It is late in the day and the sun will soon set. Over the horizon. It will drop like a ball, slowly and you will go down with it. The sea is very calm and the sun is beginning to go down very slowly. Very slowly. I want you to hold your arms above your head and as you watch the sun go down, I want you to lower them. Your arms will follow the setting sun and come to rest by your side. I am going to watch your arms and count slowly from 10 to zero and when I reach zero, the sun will have set. And as the sun goes down, I want you to relax every part of your body. Just think about the sun going down and every part of your body relaxing at the same time. The sun will go down and you will go down. Are you ready?" Yuri nodded.

***

"Ten. Nine. Eight. Seven. Six. Five. Four. Three. Two. One. Zero. The sun has disappeared beneath the sea. Only the sea is left. It is beautiful. Vast. Calm." Shira was almost mesmerized herself. She looked at Yuri. He was transformed. She remembered when he would come home from an anti-terrorist operation and sleep so deeply for a day that nothing could wake him. But he was never as deeply asleep as now. He did not seem to breath. He exuded peace. It was uncanny. The bottom of her spine felt as if it had been touched by an icy cold hand. Penina went on: "Keep looking at the sea. Vast. Calm. I am going to count you down again. I want you to go back through time. With each count, you will descend more deeply into the past, into the long-ago. Keep looking at the sea. You will descend in time through the sea. The sea will let you. It welcomes you. I want you to descend through the sea until you reach the period of the Roman Empire. To Rome. After the last revolt of the Jews. You are a prisoner." She began the countdown anew. At the end, she waited a full minute in silence. Then she asked: "What do you see?" There was a long silence, as if he saw nothing. He seemed more lifeless even than when he was in coma. The blood was drained from his face. Shira's breathing speeded up. She glanced at Penina, who looked like a sculpture of herself. A sculpture that exuded powerful vibes, like electrical currents. Shira's pulse dropped, as she picked them up. Yuri began to speak.

"The sun is rising above the horizon. It is not yet hot. It is gathering its strength to mock us. I am with others, but they are not people. None of us are people any more. We are in a camp near the barracks of the Ninth Legion. We have been here for almost a week. Tomorrow we will be sold in a huge slave sale that will take place in the center of Rome. When we were brought here, our first thought was escape. But escape to where? Escape means nothing. Besides, we are shackled day and night. Some of the women, who are expected to be sold to rich homes and who must be without blemish, are allowed to walk freely, but even for them, escape is impossible. Any Roman citizen can earn himself a few coins by returning an escaped slave. A worse threat is the gangs of professional slave catchers who throng the area. They are efficient and ruthless. This morning they caught two Jewish women who got through the gate pretending to be interpreters. They did not get far. They were picked up by bounty hunters

while trying to persuade a ship's captain to take them to Tyre in Lebanon in return for sexual favors. From there they hoped to get back to Samaria.

"Most of the time is devoted to sorting us out by skills. Adult males suitable for the arena. Beautiful children, below the age of puberty, for private homes, temples or high class brothels. Women with the best bodies destined for the houses of the elite. Men and women with special skills like doctors, midwives, scribes, singers, butchers, carpenters, musicians, dancers, potters, embroiderers, security guards, spinners, beauticians, hairdressers, stone-masons, cooks and herbalists are all expected to raise a good price. The mass of unskilled captives, simple villagers and the hoi polloi from the cities, will not be auctioned, but sold for a fixed sum to ordinary homes and workshops. In Rome, even poor families have at least one slave and every workshop, no matter how small, has one or two to do the heaviest and dirtiest jobs. The slave trade represents a large part of the empire's economy.

***

"The vast majority of us are Judeans, but there is a strong contingent of British and Germans, plus Syrians, Nubians and Scythians. The others have been in the camp some time. The slave traders have been waiting for a major influx so that they can hold a grand auction at which bidding will be brisk, with few leftovers. We have been ordered to assemble on the square to witness the punishment of the women. We stand in line, naked, waiting. Men and women are separated. It's mid-afternoon. The sun is still high, burning our shoulders and buttocks. Guards circulate casually, as if they know no-one will risk making a run for it. A group of slavers come out of the office, led by Vertigo, a huge man who moves slowly as if he knows the world will wait for him. He wears heavy military sandals and a short, domestic toga emphasizing his immense thighs. He is bearded in the Greek manner, following the fashion the Emperor Hadrian has introduced. People talk about him in a mixture of awe and hatred. He is the biggest trader in Rome today. They say that he is the agent of a group of senators and knights who have made a fortune from the sale of humanity. Over 100,000 slaves have passed through his huge hands. He keeps to the law, so as not to compromise his backers, but swims like a whale among its anomalies. The traffic of slaves from the slave market directly to brothels *has been banned by the emperor, but Vertigo gets around the new edict by having suitable women and children sold to third parties who resell them to the trade.*

"The two Jewish women, mother and daughter, are brought out from the women's prison on the far side of the square to face Vertigo. He makes a sign that they should turn towards us. They wear grimy male togas – a sign of disgrace – ripped from neck to midriff, exposing their breasts. The mother is in her mid-twenties, the daughter perhaps eleven or twelve. The younger one is trembling, her eyes fixed on the ground. Her entire body shakes. Her mother holds her head erect, refusing to acknowledge the shame of her nakedness. I can guess how such a woman must feel. I do not to look at her body. She fixes her gaze above our heads. Mother and daughter are dwarfed by Vertigo's huge frame. Beside him, they both look like children.

Vertigo ignores them. Instead, he speaks to us. "Tomorrow morning, you will all be sold by public auction." Vertigo's deep voice surges over us like a wave, while his hooded pale gray eyes slowly scan our ranks. "What you're fate will be is up to the gods. But I'll give you a few words of human advice. The good citizens of Rome want the best. So make the most of yourselves. When your turn comes, get up on the platform and don't flinch. No-one wants a cringer or a mouse in their service. If you're asked a question, answer promptly and truthfully. There'll be interpreters. If you've got tits, make the most of them. If you've got muscles, flex them. If you've got a skill, look intelligent. It will be over quickly. Judgment will be made in the batting of an eyelid – whether you are sold as this or that, to this master or to that one. And it will make a difference to you, believe me. We have gone to a lot of trouble to find out as much as we can about you – your physical condition, your skills, your background. They have been recorded on documents which you will wear round your necks. According to Roman law, I am responsible for the truth of what the labels say. So if you've been telling lies or there's something you've held back, now is the time to tell us while it can still be corrected. If your new master finds something is untrue and demands his money back, I promise you a warm reception when you are returned to me.

"A good slave is like a pool of clear water – transparent. Muddy the waters and your value muddies with them. And just a word about my *customers. Some of them were once slaves themselves. Now they are freedmen. They know every thought you are thinking. Indeed they know thoughts you haven't thought of yet. As for the freeborn Romans, they have been associated with slaves all their lives. They know more about the life you are about to start than you ever will. Never lie to them or it will cost you dear. There is a saying – truth is in wine. I say it is in fear. Fear your masters and it will go well with you. Forget whoever you once were, or think you were, or hoped to be. From now on you are merchandise. See that you get a good price for yourselves. Look keen. The more the client pays the more he'll value the purchase. No-one values what he buys cheap."*

"He turns towards the escapees. "And what about you two Hebronites? Apart from murdering your master, or setting fire to his home, or sabotaging his possessions," Vertigo bellows, although he is within a foot of them, "running away is the worst crime you can commit. It's the worst form of theft – it's stealing yourself. There are a few simple things you must learn. When you are bought, you belong to your master or mistress, body and soul. If you run away, abscond or flee, you are stealing your master's property. Because all a slave is, is his master's property. Learn that. No-one has ever taught you a more important lesson." He waits for the women to absorb his words, as if he had outlined a difficult theorem. The women flinch, under his impatient scrutiny. "I am not going to beat you. You wouldn't survive if I did and I would have nothing to sell. No. I shall write on your scrolls "tried to escape." What that means will become apparent in due course. I promise you will regret your rash stupidity for what remains of your miserable lives." Vertigo looks away disdainfully as if they had taken up too much of his invaluable time.

"He turns his gaze like a low flame, back to us. "I remind each and every one of you – Rome is the greatest power the world has ever seen. Don't trifle with her. And don't trifle with your master." He stops speaking. Everyone remains still. The silence is absolute. My mind races back to the wadis of Galili in spring when a million flowers nudge and jostle each other, reaching for the sun in the short season of their lives.

"Every one of us looked into the abyss of their soul and found it empty. Only my brother, Matitiyahu, and a few others did not see a bleak vision. Our onetime power was no power. It was transitory, ephemeral, a puff of *smoke. I felt the power of Rome, tangibly, like a rock. It weighed down between my shoulder blades, forcing me to my knees. Lord God of Israel, do not desert me in my weakness, but give me strength. Not the strength I needed in battle, nor the strength that was necessary to live under occupation, but a new strength – to survive – and one day possess the gate of my enemies."*

The Colonel stopped speaking. He showed signs of distress. His back arched, and his fists clenched, as if he was about to have a fit. He began to sweat profusely and broke into a hail of sobs. Shira was horrified. Penina remained clinically cool. "Yuri, I want you to raise your right arm as I count," she told the patient in a firm voice. I am going to count from one to ten. When I reach ten, you will be back in your hospital bed. You will remember nothing of what you experienced. Very slowly. One-two-three- four. You are rising through time. "Five… six..seven…eight. Rising through the elements."

Before she could finish, a duty nurse appeared, her mobile phone close to her lips as she reported a patient in distress. She gave Penina a withering look and tried to check the patient's pulse. Penina blocked her hand and continued with the countdown. "Nine...ten. You are back, Colonel. Your wife is right here." The Colonel's sobs slackened off, as he returned to full consciousness. He opened his eyes and smiled at us casually as if he was re-joining his friends after a short visit to the toilet. As Penina turned off her tape-recorder, Madeleine, the administrator, accompanied by her usual entourage, plus the duty doctor, surrounded the bed. "What is it this time?" she demanded of Penina. "The Colonel was having a previous life experience. At one point he became distressed." "How are you Colonel?" she asked, turning to Yuri. "A bit tired," he told her. "I shouldn't wonder. The nurse tells me that the patient's blood pressure was 168 over 110 and that you were using hypnosis," she said, turning back to Penina. "I sincerely hope you had permission to do so. Even so, you should have notified my office. I have spoken to Professor Bondman. He will come if he can." The professor arrived a few minutes later and took charge. "How are you feeling," he asked the Colonel. "Bad dreams. I have them all the time." "What do you remember?" "Nothing. Just a feeling of menace. Of tragedy." The professor checked his heart and took his pulses at wrist and neck, he instructed a nurse to give him a light sedative. When he was satisfied that the crisis was contained, Prof Bondman took Penina aside. "Were you using hypnosis?" "Yes. It was going well until…" "Until! This is exactly what we have to avoid. We've discussed this and you have deliberately gone against my express instruction. What exactly brought this on?" "He was giving an intensely vivid and detailed account of being in a slave camp in Rome before going on public auction. He became distressed while reflecting on his new lowly status." "I don't see how any of this can be doing him any good. Do you?" "As I've said before," Penina answered, "if it's in his mind, it's better for it to come out." "Is it really on his mind, or is he making it up as he goes along? Perhaps the wisest thing we can do is increase his sedation and see if that gives him better nights. What he needs above all is rest for recovery and just now he is not getting it, thanks in part to you. He looks as haggard to me, as he was at the beginning of this unfortunate saga. One of these outbursts could lead to a hematoma." Only now did he release Penina from his gaze. She felt freer to speak. "I'm not sure I can agree. These images, although we do not know what prompts them, or where they come from, may be an important stage in his recovery. Maybe there is something troubling him which he needs to work out. If he doesn't, it may have serious consequences later. I can see that these episodes are potentially dangerous. He needs careful monitoring when they occur. Perhaps we could arrange for me to be called at night whenever he has them. I can be here in twenty minutes. There must be a way of minimizing risk and still letting him express whatever he must. If all we can do is suppress the symptoms, we may be doing him untold harm."

"I think you should talk to Natalie. Put it all before her. See what she advises. Whatever she says, hypnosis is out." "I've had several discussions with her." "And?" "She regards the Colonel's revelations as little better than the patients we admit with Jerusalem syndrome." The professor shrugged his shoulders as if to say 'she may be right.' "This is not some sad case of a demented man who believes he is the reincarnation of Jesus of Nazareth," she went on. "I've had several of them under my care. This man is rational, recreating a lost world in plausible detail. Jerusalem syndrome patients can't tell you anything that's not in their scriptures. Our patient writes his own." "Penina, we cannot have another incident like this, in rehab of all places. Hypnotism can be a two-edged sword. It can be highly dangerous. You can't afford to make decisions in a vacuum." He was interrupted by Shira. "I think it is only fair to Penina to point out that she had my permission, in writing, to hypnotize my husband. I think she is right that it is better for this material to come out rather than let it simmer in his mind." "With all due respect, Mrs. Pozner, it is my signature she needs, and if I deem it life-threatening, then yours. We have certain protocols which must be maintained. They will not keep the Colonel here much longer. He needs to be de-institutionalized and to learn to cope with the real world. Once he is back home, you are free to deal with him as you see fit. But I don't advise any more experiments." "I couldn't agree more," Madeleine put in. The professor pressed play on the recorder and listened to a few minutes of playback, through headphones. "As for you, Penina," he said, as the rehab administrator and her entourage moved off, "I must be honest. I don't know whether you should be led away in chains or given a medal."

***

"It would be an understatement of historic proportions if I said, I don't need a drink," Penina told Shira. "How bad is it, do you think?" Shira asked. "I'd say the shit was about up to here," Penina replied, indicating her chin. "Know a good place?" "Yeah. It's called Lilith's. That's not its real name, it's the name of the owner. I don't know the name of the street either. See you at the gate." The two women went to their cars and drew parallel at the exit barrier. "Follow me," Penina shouted through her open window. "When I stick my arm out, park anywhere." Shira grinned and soon discovered that Penina was as crazy a driver as she was. Crazy, but safe. The phrase appealed to her. She repeated it to herself in a low voice.

***

Shira had never been to, nor heard of Lilith's. It was a low lit, low ceilinged, low life type of hangout, in the shape of a parallelogram that had once been a refrigeration store for meat. Thick gray pipes adorned the walls which were insulated with black. Tables and chairs were made of different materials, plastic wood or metal. No two tables were the same shape, no two covers of the same pattern or color. A very large waitress, wearing a T-shirt, which read "Don't push me! Or Else!" took their order. Penina opted for an arak. "That's for starters," she told Shira. "How about we share a bottle of Golan Gewürztraminer?" "I'm surprised they've got it here." "They've got everything here." "OK, I'll have the same as you're having." A tall, exaggeratedly slim woman, of indecipherable age, dressed in a calf-length, narrow-cut, black dress, replaced the waitress. To Shira, she did not seem to have any figure at all. She looked like a cartoon. "Is this your friend?" she asked Penina, who nodded acknowledgement. "Welcome," she said with an engaging smile. "Choose your drink, choose your music, choose your friends. We're one big, happy family here." She withdrew as quickly as she came. "That was Lilith," Penina said. "Her mother called her that after Adam's first wife. You know the legend, I'm sure." "I'm not good on it." "If you read the creation of the world verses in the Hebrew Bible in a certain way, there's a way of deducing that Adam had a wife before Eve. This wife was Lilith, born as he was, of the earth. Because she was born at the same time and from the same material as him, she felt absolutely equal and gave Adam a hard time. She became a demon and Adam got a new wife, Eve, taken from his rib – who would be more amenable. Lilith's mother – I mean the woman, who owns this place – was a big noise in the feminist movement in Israel and named her daughter Lilith, in the hope she would champion women's rights and give men what they've got coming to them. I've got a cousin who goes into all this, from Bible, through midrash, through Talmud, through Zohar, through Kabala, through medieval mysticism. He's obsessed with the legend." "He thinks men should be given a hard time?" "No. He thinks men and women should remember the Lilith story, start all over again and work together in absolute equality." "That would be nice." "It's all in the Book, you know. All you've got to do, is find the place." Shira looked at Penina with new interest. Her exposition had lent fire to her eyes. Shira had never had a chance to look at her on her own terms. She had studied her face often enough, when she was telling her something to do with her husband. But that was a judgment of words against professional poise. Shira had invariably seen her in terms of her own self-interest. She thought of her as plain but vivacious. Now she saw an epiphany of gracious good looks, breaking through nature's miserliness. Her words had brought her to life. As a professional wordsmith (of other people's words), Shira liked that. There was a barely discernible beauty attached to her, not only in the eyes, but hidden beneath the skin, unobtrusive but undeniable. Penina was communing with the wine, lost in her own internal soundtrack. It was a unique moment to study her. Shira thought of a painting by a great master, before and after restoration. Like a masterpiece, once hidden from view by another painting's overlay and the grime of centuries, it was now on display. But temporarily, because, unlike the restoration of a painting, it did not hold fast. There! Penina's expression had returned to ambiguity. "What did you think of the professor's performance?" Shira asked hastily, not wanting Penina to think she had been spied upon. "Oh hell. If we're going to talk about that we'll need another bottle. I'll pay." "The one after that's on me," Shira quipped, without conviction. "The one after that will have to be another time – we're both driving," Penina said, summoning the huge waiter, but it was Lilith who came to take the order. "Same again?" she asked. "No, I think I need something sweet. Could you stand a Muscadet?" "No," Shira replied. "You go ahead. I'm not bothered." Lilith intervened: "We've got a great Bordeaux, a prizewinner, but it comes from the Territories, if that bothers you." "Not me," Shira said, "I don't believe in boycotts. I believe in peace." "To seek peace under a boycott is like negotiating with a noose around your penis," Lilith said. "It doesn't worry me either," said Penina, laughing. "The soil this wine was grown in most probably belonged to the tribe of Benjamin, anyway. Who am I to say I won't drink it?" "This particular wine is called Edom. You won't be disappointed," Lilith told them before she returned to the well-stocked bar. "I thought she would be anti-penis," Shira observed. "No! She's very pro penis. She is a champion of equality, not castration." Lilith produced the bottle almost immediately. She must have divined that was what they would choose. They watched the ritual opening in silence. Lilith poured some for Penina to taste. "She's right," Penina said, "we'll be a long way from being disappointed." She took a long draught and nodded her appreciation. "You remember my problem" with the department over your husband reading the tapes?" she said to Shira. "Well, this new business could dwarf that. That time they only had to clean up the debris. This time they had to call out an emergency team. Both incidents have been noted on my record. Did you see Madeleine taking snapshots, both times? They're probably in my file now. This whole business is going to bolster any lingering doubts the hospital authorities may have as to my lack of competence."

"But Professor Bondman seems to understand why you have to do what you have to do. You knew you were on thin ice." "There's nowhere else to skate without bumping into people. I get so pissed off with the plod, plod, plod of things. I used to spend all my time hunting for certainties. Now I say fuck certainty. In any case, most certainties are uncertainties in disguise." "But uncertainties have a role. You can learn from them," Shira observed. "Does that matter? Look, this is my throw. Caution was created to be thrown to the winds." "I can't believe you mean that," Shira challenged her. "Maybe I don't. Maybe that's the Gewurtz stroke Bordeaux, speaking. But why shouldn't they be right? Sitting on your arse isn't Jewish. Jewish means to argue things out, ad absurdum, then go for the two most contradictory objectives at once." Penina was aroused, adversarial, passionate. Her brown skin shone noticeably, across her shoulders and forearms. The lightly toned makeup on her face and lips seemed to darken. "So what will you do?" "What will I do?" Penina repeated, pausing to consider, as if a total stranger had asked. "Start packing my bags, I suppose. What else?" "Why not wait and see?" "Because there's nothing to wait for and nothing to see. Look, Shira, at best the matter will be debated, and no action taken. I'll just get a warning and they'll expect me to carry on as usual. Except that there will be nothing usual any more. When Natalie retires, I won't get her job. They'll bring in an outsider, probably with less experience than I have. And all the time I'll be watched, unobtrusively perhaps, but watched. I have to look for another lake. The water level in this one has gotten too low. It wouldn't be high enough for a medium-sized frog." "What about my husband and his PLE's?" "He'll be out soon. He'll go home to your care and hopefully begin laying golden eggs again. He won't be my responsibility." "So what are you going to do?" "Either a different hospital or go private."

"Which would you prefer?" "Oh, private. Be my own boss. I'm far too bossy to be anyone else's." "Don't you think you should sleep on it?" Shira asked. "I slept on it in the car on the way here. I almost crashed. And I wrote my resignation in my head about twenty minutes ago – while Lilith was opening the Edom. Come to think of it, this is my farewell party. Aren't you going to wish me luck?" "I would, if I didn't feel I was talking to two bottles of boutique wine" "Wine speaks truth. The Romans knew that." "So, if we were all drunk all the time, the world would be a better place? I'd find that hard to take. I'll tell you one thing I've learnt: truth kills," Shira railed, her natural cool drowned, temporarily, in alcohol. "Right. Half truths are about the only form of truth we can handle. And even then we have to bolster them with lies." "I never guessed that you were such a cynic," Shira answered, suddenly picking up the bottle, to examine the label, perhaps as a way of shunning eye contact. "It says Psagot Heights. How apt." "Tell me, what good is there in my not sending in my resignation?" "Penina, you have crossed the red line twice, over my husband reading his tapes and now hypnotism, and because you think you've gone too far, you want to overturn the apple cart. That sounds like a spoilt brat, if I'm to be as blunt as you deserve." She sensed Penina bristle. "You'd go on pushing shit up the mountain, right?" Penina demanded. "Yes, I would," Shira replied, "and at the same time, I'd be fighting to prove that I was right in crossing those red lines because that is what red lines are for. I wouldn't stop until I had proven to everyone that crossing them was good for Yuri." Penina's eyes met Shira's, her head held at a slight tilt. She glanced at her watch. "It's late, I've got to go. Coming? Or do you want to finish the bottle?" "I'll stay," said Shira, "I hate leaving things half done." Penina leaned forward for the socially-sanctioned twin-cheek kiss, brown eyes gleaming, perfect teeth shining in a becoming open-mouthed smile. As Shira kissed the air on each side of her face, her cheek caught the ripe softness of Penina's brown skin. It was like a pleasurable electric shock. Penina left a sensual memory – like a lingering Middle East perfume.

Shira did not feel like leaving. There was nowhere she wanted to go. The barn of a place was almost filled with customers speaking a dozen languages beside Hebrew. It was as if a hand had reached into the street, cotton picking Jews from half the world and placing them at these tables. She went to the toilets, which were decorated with graffiti. None of the four or five she read was obscene. They were philosophical, literary, or comic. Cartoons too, mostly political. As she squatted, she ran her eyes over a cartoon crayoned on the door in front of her which must have been drawn by a graffic artist of no mean talent, depicting Israel's national bird, the duhifat or hoopoe, listening attentively, from its perch, to a small lapdog telling her that back in Lithuania, it used to be a Rottweiler. A small smile gathered about her lower face, as she thought of the way we furbish and refurbish our narratives and how the artist had captured a compellingly revealing moment. She was in no hurry to get back to her table, which is how she came to take one of the most important calls of her life, on a toilet seat. It was the head of her department, just back after a long bout of absence. He suffered from a wasting disease that kept him at home or in hospital for long bouts. "Congrats, Shira, I hear you made a stir in Italy. I've had mixed comments about your performance, mostly positive." "I think I did what I went there to do. It wasn't easy sailing. The Edward Saidists, and there were a lot of them, were waiting in ambush. They went for me for supporting what they saw as George Eliot's unblinking colonialism, you know, the whole Orientalism spiel. Then there were the post-moderns, or should I say post-post-moderns, or even post, post-post-moderns. Literary critics who thought I was skimming Joyce's text and not contextualizing enough. One of them said I had simply hung my interpretation on the book like a door number without proving anything scientifically. Getting back to Eliot, do you remember, that in my proposal, I postulated that the way she championed the Jewish voice in English society could be taken as a prophetic endorsement for taking greater regard of immigrant societies in Britain in this day and age? I thought at the time, that that was just my reading. But, just before I presented, one of the other participants showed me a copy of a letter to Harriet Beecher Stowe, in which Eliot decries the attitude of her contemporaries towards the Jews. She infers that she wrote "Deronda" as 'a corrective to the impious, not to say stupid pervading view of them.' She insisted that this prevalent attitude extends to all oriental peoples, and is a national disgrace. Then she says, and, mind you, I'm quoting from memory: 'there is nothing I should care more to do than to rouse the imagination of men and women to a vision of human claims in those races of their fellow man who most differ from them in customs and beliefs.' I was so excited to have my deduction confirmed in Eliot's own words. Did you know that such a letter existed?" "Yes, I've read it. And I expected that you had. It should have come up in your research." His voice was bone dry, in contrast with the breezy notes of his greeting. She was under attack. "Well, the good news is that the representative of an American university press was there and said that if I developed my ideas as a book, she'd like to publish." "I'm sure she meant it. And of course you are free to publish whatever you like, whenever. But you also have a responsibility to the department. A book of this type must present all sides of an argument. Intuition and textual analysis are no longer everything. If I may make a suggestion: be editor, not author. Write a long introduction which places "Deronda" and/or "Ulysses" in historical context, as you see fit. But get experts in various fields of literary criticism to put their views, some of which naturally will clash with your own. Certainly, the Deronda part should include at least one contribution that puts Edward Said's viewpoint on the colonialist perspective. And as for the Joyce part, it must include someone who sees Joyce's work in terms of his dissatisfaction with the reactionary past while glimpsing a radical political future. In fact, revolutionary, although I hate that word. If it comes from Israel, scholarship should combine every view, not like the biased nonsense much of the academic world likes to trade in. You have the ideological background to do it yourself. But to be frank, Shira you still tend to deal with literature, however perceptive you are – and you are – as if novels were meant to be 'a good read,' however elevated their level. That's good for the airport bookshop crowd. What we are looking for is a sociology, a philosophy, perhaps an anthropology of the novel that places it in its cultural context, whether as intended by the author, or not." "I'll have to think about it, Norman." "Of course. Best thing is to meet. For you I can always find time, Shira. Ring me when you're ready. In the meantime, all the best. You made quite a little splash at the conference. Dust yourself off. I've heard complimentary things from people who were there, or, more importantly, who sent the people who were there." He rang off, in a hail of coughing. She flushed the toilet. "Editor!" she barked aloud derisively. "You can forget editor, Norm. I'm author or nobody!" she added, hardly allowing the last word to get past her teeth.

Almost immediately, her phone rang again. She cursed. It was the General. "Oh, General, I was thinking of ringing you." "Good. Perhaps we could meet. Where are you?" "At this moment in time, I'm sitting on the toilet at a bar I don't know the name of, nor the address whereof." "Nice of you to think of me under the circumstances." "This is an important moment in my life. I've just flushed my career, along with some great Israeli boutique wine, down the sewer system." "Careers are falling like leaves, these days," the General remarked. "Penina, just a while ago, told me she's thinking of resigning," Shira told him. "And there's me," he came back, "my career in the military has shuddered to a halt. It's called retirement. Tell me more." "Oh, General, perhaps we had better meet. For the second time in my life, ideology has ruined everything. First the kibbutz, now, literature. And if you believe the novel is dead, as many do, what we're doing in literature departments can only be described as literary necrophilia." "So what has it to do with your career, Shira?" "My brilliant career? Look, fundamentally, I believe…no, wait a minute, I can't concentrate while I'm sitting here. Toilets were created for a different, if analogous purpose. Hold on." He listened attentively as various sounds emerged from his state of the art phone – the impatient zipping of a zip, a door angrily unlocked, then slammed, a sudden gush of water, the low buzz of a dryer, another door, screeching on its hinges, a long pause and finally, she spoke, to a sub-Saharan African musical accompaniment. "That's better. Literature for me is what religion is for the believer. It tells me what the world is about, what to take notice of in life, what people are really like, what relationships are based on, how they work, or don't, where we, as human beings, might be going. Except, it does not lay down laws. It does not hand out thou-shalt-nots. It does not claim that what it says comes from heaven, unless, maybe, it's science fiction. You do with it what you will, or what you can, not what you are told. You make your world and derive your responsibilities from it. It's explorative, not exploitative. I know secular people who would not touch a religious dogma to save their lives, who live perfectly moral lives that could not be challenged by the most pious rabbi. Non-Jews too, both secular and religious. Why? Because they know what it is to be human. They don't get there by analysis, or faith, they just know, feel, believe, touch. In most cases literature helps them. Choice. My God, if being human means anything, it means choice. Ideologies remove your right to choose. And I think I know something about ideology." "I understand Shira, but..." "No, let me finish. You know, there's one thing from religion classes that always stuck in my throat. Of course I mean religion as taught in a doctrinally-secular kibbutz movement, as part of Jewish history.

"You know that when the Jewish people were supposed to have been offered the Law at Mount Sinai in the Bible, they accepted it by saying we will obey and we will hear, meaning that they agreed to obey – in advance – whatever it demanded. That was free choice. Even I might have said yes, if I had been asked. Great. Based on blind faith and ignorance, perhaps, but it was free choice. But later the sages came up with another idea – that God actually held Mount Sinai over the heads of the tribes of Israel, and told them that if they didn't accept the Law, they would be obliterated. Unsurprisingly, they agreed. What interests me is why the second version was needed. I think it was because exercising free choice on an issue as huge as the Law was seen as an insult to the majesty of the Law. The sages could not believe that God would let man decide the answer for himself. They would rather we were threatened by being crushed under a mountain than exercising our own minds. What they yearned for was ideology, not free will. If we accepted the Law freely, we could throw it away freely. That terrified them. For me, great Literature is free choice without the threat of a mountain being held over my head. And I don't care if it's God holding the mountain, or the Literature Department. Sorry I took so long. Are you still there?" "Just about. Look, Shira, this is stuff that has been argued backwards and forwards for two thousand years. We're not going to solve it. I admire your impassioned advocacy for Literature. But you can't base the constitution of a nation on it. You have to have laws, which every country has. You must either go for total utopian conformity, or for punishment and crime. You can't defend a divorce action where adultery is involved by saying I only did what Madame Bovary did." "Oh did I say that? I would never say that.

What I do say is that while you are forming your attitude to life, you could do a lot worse than read Flaubert's Madame Bovary or Tolstoy's Anna Karenina and say but for the grace of God, go I. Flaubert does not moralize, but he does spell out illusion and possible consequence. The seventh commandment tells you nothing. It just says: wear a long skirt."

"Shira, you are superb. You are a religious animal without knowing it. Don't deny it. Put simply, you believe in Literature, instead of the Bible. It's your secular canon. Your holy secular canon. It's your Midrash, darling. And isn't the Bible also Literature?" "Of course it is," Shira came back breathlessly. "But it's not normative. I must be free to take or leave its predilections as I wish. Example: I think not murdering others is a damn good idea." "We could go on forever like this. Find out from somebody in the bar, where the place you are speaking from, is, and I'll come over. I must confess I've never read "Ulysses" and never heard of George Eliot. When you referred to him as 'her,' I thought it was a typo. But I looked it up and found that she used the name George because she wanted to be taken more seriously than she might have been if she had tried to publish her intellectual arguments as a woman. People like Jane Austen did not have to do that. What she wrote, could only have been written by a woman. Happily we've seen the end of the need for that sort of white deception. I'm glad you made me aware of her." "I'm glad I did too. George Eliot is a writer with no sell-by date." Look Shira, shall I come round. I can tell from your voice that you are in crisis." "General, I'd love that. But not this time. This time, I must do it alone."

Shira still didn't feel like leaving. She still couldn't think of anywhere to go. She had noticed that at the end of the bar was a large wooden table strewn with CD's and discs, which customers inserted into a player at will. The resultant music, which provided quality background noise to cancel out the banalities of, and gaps in, idle conversation, took the patrons of the establishment on a world tour, featuring Middle Eastern, Indian, sub-Sahara African, Russian and South American stopovers. Shira sorted through the assortment of singles. Albums were absent, so that time could not be monopolized by aficionados of a single artist or group, she guessed. She spotted something she once loved but hadn't heard for a long time. As she slipped it into the open player, she noticed a microphone on a shelf above the table. Without fully appreciating what she was doing, she picked it up, found it was live and without hesitation, began to speak: "Hello everyone. I'm Shira. I just wanted to say something about a single I am about to play. Some of you probably think you know it, but you are mistaken. Because every time one hears it, it means something else. It's a song, perhaps a psalm, even a prayer, written about the work and philosophy of an Israeli ceramics artist called Rayah Redlich. It's called 'Beauty of Incompleteness.' It was written by an ex-student of mine. I'm in Literature. He was looking forward to a career as a song writer, more precisely as a troubadour. It's addressed to a broken world. And all the incomplete and broken hearts in that world. And it's true. For what is whole? What isn't broken? Whose heart isn't broken, somehow, some when? It's not a plea for healing or repair. Rather it advises us to take the incomplete as intended, as meant, the only true perfection. Because what we usually mean by completion just isn't possible. The title of the piece was taken from the inscription on Rayah's gravestone. It is the message she wanted us to remember her by. Here we go. 'Beauty of Incompleteness.' Make time for it – you won't be sorry. She pressed play and sat on a seat away from everyone. Her ex-student's plaintive voice filled the room with hushed boldness.

"Give me your broken, give me your tainted, give me your uncompleted. I promise I won't mend them or blend them into harmony.

I promise not to make them be what they were not meant to be.

The most beautiful sound I ever heard was half a scream; the most beautiful thing I ever saw was a ceramic bird with a broken wing.

The world is a broken place. Broken space. An emporium for the broken-hearted. If there is a God, he must be broken hearted too. If he is not, he cannot be true.

The stampede for completion brings but one result: woes of disappointment, wounds rubbed down with salt.

I am not complete, nor are you, nor are they.

The desire to make us so is the greatest incompleteness there can be.

Let us accept ourselves for what we are – broken vessels chasing a star. That never stops, is never caught.

Nor can we, in our short itinerary, solve every problem, repair every crack.

All we may seek is our reward for passion unspent, for the curtain rent, for the beauty of incompleteness."

Shira returned to the table where she had been sitting. It was deserted. Lilith appeared from nowhere, like a stealth bomber, and sat beside her, startling Shira out of her contemplation. "It's because she's so thin, you just don't see her," Shira reasoned. "That was beautiful, the way you introduced it," Lilith told her. "Rayah Redlich reminds me so much of the Canadian Jewish singer, Leonard Cohen. I mean his "Come Healing." You know it?" "I'd consider myself a lot poorer, if I didn't." "You know, I've never known what one line in it means. He talks about the heart below, teaching the broken heart above. Do you dig that one, Shira?" "The last time I heard it," Shira replied, "I reckoned that the heart below was the human heart and the heart above is God's heart – which is broken, like everything else. Human beings – who Cohen calls 'troubled dust' – are supposed to mend God's broken heart. I don't remember him saying anything about the other way round."

Shira became aware that Lilith's attention was divided. She suspected that the cause was the entrance of two personable women, who could have been mother and daughter, who had taken a table at the far end of the establishment. After a few minutes, Lilith asked to be excused. "Those are two of my most frequent customers, not to say friends. I must say hello. Why don't you join us?" Shira would have preferred to continue the conversation as a one-on-one. Failing that, she preferred to be part of a new conversation than to be alone.

"This is Shai and this is Emily," Lilith announced. "Shai is a student of social work and Emily is a professor of laughter." "That's what Lilith calls me," Emily intervened, with a straight face. "Actually I've got a diploma in stress management, stroke laughter." "I didn't know there was such a thing," said Shira, "but I can see why it's necessary." "Oh, it's necessary for sure," Emily said earnestly and went on as if addressing a class. "Do you know how many people have stress related disorders? You don't want to, it's frightening. And it's getting worse. I think it's a terrible joke that ten thousand years after men discovered there were more possibilities on the ground than in the trees, our stress factors are winning over our fun factors. And with unprecedented leaps in technological invention, we are allowed to be in any two places, or more, at the same time, and communicate with more people in a day than we previously could in a decade, more or less. We just have to laugh, it's our ultimate line of defense. Laughter is a human invention after all. It may well be the one and only thing we worked out for ourselves. Animals don't laugh. But they all cry. So my take on this is that if you don't know how to laugh, you are not fully human. You might as well have stayed in the trees." "Perhaps we should all go back. But seriously, you must have a really funny time. Do you laugh all day?" Shira asked, with a smoldering grin. "You already know the answer, I think," said Emily, retreating into a friendlier voice. "That's why you asked the question. In fact, I don't have a sense of humor at all, which is what made me interested in this subject. We never laughed at home. And when I realized that there were people who laughed – for all sorts of reasons, I just had to know why they did it. I decided to find out." "But why didn't you laugh?" "It just never occurred to us. I could never understand why kids at school laughed their heads off. If something went right they laughed. If something went wrong, they laughed. If nothing happened, they laughed. If you take a group of small children and sit them on the floor and leave them there, sooner or later one of them will begin to giggle and the others will join in until they get hysterical. Or they'll fight and then they'll cry. I knew perfectly well how to behave in the second set of circumstances, but not in the first." "Not even by example? Surely laughter provokes laughter." "In some, but not in others. There are many people in the world who never, or rarely, laugh. They have to be taught." "How can you teach it, if you can't do it? Don't you need a sense of humor? Surely!" "Not at all. I know what is supposed to be funny, what sets people with a sense of humor off. I feed stuff to them like you might feed fish in a tank. You don't have to eat it yourself. But I mainly teach artificial laughter." "What on earth is that?" Shira asked.

"Perhaps I can be of some help here," Shai interrupted. "Artificial laughter is for people like Emily and me who don't see the funny side of anything. She teaches us to laugh as an exercise, like going to the gym to develop your body. Laughing is a physical exercise, just like push-ups. As in that case, you have to learn it. You don't walk into a gym for the first time and start pushing one hundred and twenty pounds. So, in a laughter class, you sit there in a group of say, twenty or more – actually the more the better – and Emily will say 'something funny has just happened' and we laugh like mad. I've just come from a class. I laughed myself sick. Not at any particular joke. It was just an exercise. I feel like a new person. People like us love going to comedy shows or hearing stand-up comedians perform. We wait until other people laugh real loud and join in – it's like choosing a wave to surf on." "But what's the point, if it's not prompted by a genuine experience?" "To start with, it makes you feel like everybody else. There's nothing worse, when everyone is laughing, to sit there staring into space because you don't see the joke. People wrongly think you disapprove. Or that you're a freak. But there are great physical benefits to laughter. Why should people with no sense of humor be left out? Did you know that each time you laugh, you use fifteen important muscles in your face? You're also exercising your diaphragm. Your neck muscles. It's very good for the cardo-vascular system too. Why should we be denied all that, just because we don't think anything is funny? Boy meets girl. What do they do? They laugh. It's a way of growing closer." "But if they are not laughing for the same reason, what use is it?" Shira had to know. "They are still sharing, even if the cause is different. 'Normal' people, often put on a false laugh or laugh louder than the occasion demands. They do it, because it is attractive to laugh. Or because they want people to think that they got the funny bit. They also want to show their face at its best. So do we. Very much so."

"Speaking personally," Emily contributed, "I have no problem faking it – I mean laughter – in a mixed group. I have no idea what I'm laughing about, but I may have a better understanding of why I'm laughing than the others." "Then there's no point asking you which kind of humor you prefer, Emily. If you appreciate Jewish humor, or American Black humor, or whatever humor. It makes no difference, right?" Shira observed. "Oh, I'm very conscious what makes different people laugh. I've got a long list of subjects. I don't really have a preference, because basically, I don't think any of it is funny. I'm not Jewish, by the way, but if I had a preference, I think it would be Jewish humor." "Why, on earth?" "I think it's because Jewish people laugh more than anybody else. And because their humor is always part serious. I get that bit. That's why I love working in Israel. Israelis laugh like drains after a downpour, and yet they still accept me, even though I'm someone who just doesn't get it. I get more sympathy and understanding here than anywhere else. I suppose I'm just another addition to the creative turmoil that goes on in the place."

"I found that terribly fascinating," Lilith said to the others." "Thank you," said Emily, as if taking a curtain call. "Do you know all the stuff about humor and the Holocaust. How it saved sanity, even lives?" Lilith questioned the others. No-one did. "Oh, you must. There's a book. Now what's it called? Ah, yes: 'Laughter in Hell'. And there is another one. What I'd like to know is: were they really laughing or were they going through the motions. Either way, it worked. But that is the test case, isn't it: the Holocaust? Laugh your way through that."

Lilith accompanied her to the exit. "Hurry back," she urged, "you know, like service station attendants once said on Route 66, to people on their way to start a new life in California." "I've been to California," Shira replied. "Been there. Seen it. Done it." Lilith looked at her quizzically. She detected a certain underlining in Shira's words that rescued them from cliché. Shira loitered her way to her car, welcoming the departing heat of the late afternoon sun as it embraced her supple skin. She felt she had been reborn. What as, she did not know. She would have to find that out, she told herself, as she laughed a trial artificial laugh. Like a partially inflated balloon, it quickly sank. Next time, she would have to blow harder.

***

Shira was every bit as discomfited by Yuri's unpredictable redemption as she had been in face of his presumptive death. It left her even more restless and apprehensive. She would flit from friend to friend and library to library and book to book and lane to lane. In the early hours, she would drive back to the kibbutz, talking on the phone in the dead of night to her fellow-owls, or receiving an occasional call from the General. His were usually single paragraph calls, often jokes, whose pay-off line was followed by the electronic gurgle of the provider, the General having rung off. One time he rang to say that he had been reading some transcripts of Yuri's PLE's she had given him and that they reminded him of a saying by the Eighteenth Century mystical rabbi, Nahman of Bratslav, that God created man because he loves stories.

Another time she rang the General, to get some much-needed balsam to heal the criticism of her conference paper by colleagues and students. All he said was: "My advice is to bear in mind a World War II maxim of the British Royal Air Force, that if you're not catching flack, you're not over the target." She would get home and doze or sleep almost immediately, or lying in bed thinking unwelcome thoughts. That was what she dreaded. Apart from her one-on-one late night chat shows, she doodled poetry in SMS format, as she drove. This was straight off-the-top-of-the-head stuff in which she indulged in tremulous times, when stress and time were twin pegs on which her day hung. Shira was better in a crisis than under looming uncertainty. Responding to an immediate threat was in her nature. Doodling was her riposte to helplessness. But it had rules. No re-writing. No looking things up. No embellishment. No quotations. It had to come, like a baby, the way it was born.

She began the one she called "He/She," the night after drinks at Lilith's, when she was stuck behind a small convoy of three tractors being driven from one cornfield to the next. Watching the dimly-outlined back of the Thai driver in front, she began. The first part was written in the time it took to slow down for and eventually overtake the convoy. She finished the second part the next morning, at home, at breakfast, to prodigious sounds of early morning lovemaking, coming from the bedroom of her son, who was on a week's leave. His current girlfriend, a shy young athlete, was conspicuously noisy in bed:

"He desires to separate war and peace /milk and meat / bullets and votes / politics and faith / prostitution and love / propaganda and truth / Arabs from the land of the Jews and Jews from the land of the Arabs. But how do you tell Which is which? Who is who? What is what and When is when?

She desires to bring together hearts and minds / bodies and souls / history, present and future / right hands and left / earth and rain / hunger and food / tears and laughter / hope and fear / parents who think they must be wrong and children who think they are right. But how do you tell Which is which? Who is who? What is what and When is when?"

Shira read it through, momentarily annoyed, because she couldn't fathom its meaning. Then she remembered one of her self-imposed rules of doodling: never explain a doodle to yourself. They are meant for other people. Wait and show.

***

"Your husband's recuperation is inexplicable. Mental alertness and verbal capacity "normalized" far quicker than anyone had expected, if his motor neurone responses are still spasmodic. He certainly cannot drive a car yet, if ever." Madeleine looked up from her computer file and faced Shira. "I have discussed his case with the medics. He is ready for release." "When?" "At the weekend." "Are you sure he's ready?" Shira asked in a faint voice. "There is no more we can do for him. He needs to be out of here for his own good." "A nurse told me he can be difficult." "I won't deny he can be a liability. He still gropes at females, including visitors, exposing himself, making lurid remarks which are interlaced with insights possessing high cognitive value. But once he is home, in a normal situation all that should end." Beads of sweat adorned Shira's forehead and shoulders. Madeleine lacked the gift of putting people at ease, even when she would have liked to. She wanted to respond to Shira's concerns. The best she could offer was to look less severe than usual. "As I was saying, what he needs most is his natural environment which he can grow back into, over time. I'll be in touch with social services about home care. They'll cover the days but nights will be your responsibility. You may have to get help privately, but the army should take care of it. Sometimes they don't. If that's the case, get in touch with me. I may be able to pull a few strings."

"If you're letting him go, what does that mean? What can he do for himself?" "I think a lot of resources will come back quickly once he's in his home environment. He can dress himself, but he makes mistakes and can get very angry about them. He still needs to be fed. He eats as if knives and forks haven't been invented. To be on the safe side, I wouldn't leave anything sharp about." "Meaning what?" "I don't mean suicidal but he can get furious with himself and he might harm himself just to spite himself, or someone else. Better not chance it." "Am I in danger?" "The professor thinks not." "Can I see Professor Bondman?" "Impossible, he's working round the clock with the stabbings. He did seventy two hours at the hospital until his wife came and insisted on taking him home." "Does this mean my husband needs round-the clock monitoring?" "Yes. That's so. Look, I know you're working and it will be hard. But I'm talking about extreme possibilities that will probably never happen." Shira was feeling faint. "Are you sure you can't keep him here a bit longer?" she asked with a slight tremble in her voice. "Am I sure I can't keep him here?" Madeleine repeated in a lower key. "Yes, I'm sure," she added firmly. "The best I could offer is another institution a couple of pegs down from us. He'd be much better off at home." "I'm not sure that I will," said Shira, between a confession and a plea. "You will find the strength and that will be the best help he can get. I've seen women almost crack under the load they are asked to bear, but somehow they find the strength. It's a strength men don't have. In situations like this, our hearts flutter but we get down to it. Their hearts don't flutter but they stay rooted to the spot." "I think I know what you mean. I think." "Of course, there are other situations where the reverse is true. I've spent a lot of my life in the shadow of men. They answer to a different call. You are, one might say, in a privileged position to help your husband remake himself. The mind that is best for him is not necessarily the one that was damaged by a bullet. He was about to be made up to general – I know, I have my contacts. So it's a big responsibility. Are you going to help him reconstruct a lost past whose purpose is over, or lead him into a future which he may be reluctant to discover?" "What would you do?" "I've never been asked that question and often wondered why. "I think I'm being as honest as I can be when I say: I would leave the past to the pigeons. Nor would I reconstruct at all, but construct. I say that with all the wisdom of a woman who has never been in your situation." "Have you read a French poet called Rimbaud?" "No." "Or a novel by a modernist Chinese writer?" "Another 'no' I'm afraid. What am I missing?" "Only the working out of what you've been saying, the rejection of the past." "What were their names again?" Madeleine asked, brandishing a gold-tipped pen. "I wouldn't begin with them. Look up 'Theater of the Absurd' to start with. Brilliant dramatists writing all too often for empty seats. That's the greatest absurdity of all. A computer is all you need." "You know, Mrs Pozner, I almost envy you." "If Yuri comes out of this recognizably himself, I think I'll envy myself. One last thing: is this the end of medical services? No more help on that front?" "He'll be invited in for checks. He doesn't have to come. As for his mind, they've been looking for a psycho who would visit once a week. Penina Frydman has volunteered. It's unusual for a full-time hospital psychologist to be released for home visits, but they may let her. She knows his history. She also has the physical strength if he gets too frisky." "Is that going to be a major problem?" "I'll confess: as far as the female staff here are concerned, he has outstayed his welcome. But you should be able to handle it." "I'm not that sure Madeleine. You see, I don't know who he is any more. Nor am I sure who I am."

In the three days before Yuri came home, Shira plunged into her work. She fiercely prepared everything. Her students barely recognized her new style which emphasized brute fact and discounted intuitive reason. She over-filled their minds with more information than they would ever remember. All the time, a ghostly debate resounded in her mind. It was something that Lilith had mentioned when she talked about the difference between Adam's two wives. Primeval Lilith, who saw herself as his equal and came to rue it. And Eve, who was his helpmeet, taken from his rib, which Shira had always considered the ultimate identity theft, which tried to divest women of the original act of propagation. She had been Lilith before Yuri was wounded. Was she expected to be Eve now? To help him mend? To attend to his wants? To be his helpmeet? The role did not fit her temperament nor her reality. Only her sense of duty and compassion. She would never have applied for the job, had it been advertised. Was it merely temporary?

Or permanent? Was she capable? Thoughts chased each other around her head like monkeys in a temple.

***

Yuri had an exceptionally fraught night. Nightmares on horseback. He forced himself to stay awake. Moshe was supposed to be released that morning. He wanted to see his exemplar, competitor, opponent and rival go back into the world from which he had been plucked. Moshe had helped to keep Yuri alive as much as the technology to which he was attached. Merely keeping up with the carousel of Moshe's progress had extended his mind to its fullest. He had watched him with the abject attention of a Roman priest studying the behavior of holy chickens before a battle. And he sensed, all along, that his own return depended in some wise, upon Moshe's. A young Arab nurse was giving Yuri a blanket bath when Moshe's family arrived to claim him. They came when they liked. Virtually uncontrollable. It would take Madeleine to get them into line. They were in jubilant mood, irrepressible, making even the most serious cases raise their heads to watch. The grandmother, dressed in black and gold, walked the ward accepting smiles and congratulations from patients and visitors. She hugged her son for a long time before leading the procession towards the exit. As it passed Yuri's bed she called to Moshe: go in peace and live in peace. Moshe, sitting upright in a wheelchair, stopped the procession and asked to be given his oudh. "No-one has heard this yet," he called out to Yuri. "I want you to be the first. It is about the land that gave me flesh, bones and a language. It is about my blessed Kurdistan. A land where great things are going to happen." Moshe played a few introductory chords on the deep-bowelled instrument that he cradled in his lap like a baby.

"Kurdistan, Oh Kurdistan," he sang. The sound traveled up Yuri's spine and seemed to settle at the nape of his neck. "Only the beauty of your women fighters / rivals your mountains. Only the spirit of your young men / rivals the task before them. Emerging from the womb of the world / a late child. But ready to take its place / beside the firstborn."

There was not a dry patch on any cheek. No-one stirred, until the grandmother threw her arms around her son and showered him with kisses. The others, men, women, children followed, in an outpouring of their shared origin. Moshe's eyes gleamed. He pulled away from the last embrace, held his oudh high and broke into the song again, this time at a faster pace, a higher pitch. His first rendering had sounded like an anthem, the second was like a wedding dance. His family took up the chant in Kurdi Arabic as they moved off, dancing between patients' beds, to the exit. Yuri noticed that the Israeli Palestinian nurse was singing lustily along with the others. "Wasn't that just beautiful?" he said to her. "I love it. I love it," she replied and continued singing the words to herself. "But I made one alteration," she confessed. "It's a secret but I know I can tell you. I changed Kurdistan to Palestine. I'm sure they wouldn't mind."

***

Shira stifled apprehension and force-fed hope. She insisted, in short, sharp debates with herself, that she was happy to have her husband back. The long holidays were at their most boring or most remunerative, depending on circumstance. She needed time to pick up where things had been left. Whatever that meant. Sexual "normalcy" was quickly restored between them. But she could never relax. She had to monitor him constantly. The pitch of his voice, the time he got up, the time he went to bed, the things he ate, the way he ate, what he read, what he watched on television, how he moved, when he moved, how he dressed, how he related to other people, how he sat, how he sounded on the phone, the opinions he expressed and what music he listened to were all signs of the shifting sands of spasmodic recovery. She quickly learned how to evaluate variations of whatever 'norm' he was wearing on a particular day. They signposted moods and needs which she could only see in terms of their riven personal history. The past stood in her mind like a yardstick against which she measured every action. She knew that it was counter-productive. She knew that she should jettison the past as the pilot of an aircraft dumps fuel before an emergency landing. She had to accept him as he now was, not according to an outdated inventory.

She saw what she was doing as a visual construct: like reassembling an old book that had lost many pages, her only guide being its page numbers. But Yuri had forgotten whole tracts of the text. Was he writing a new one?

On one occasion they managed to talk about it. She planned a special dinner for his forty-fourth birthday. Once, they would have gone out to a restaurant. But his behavior was still unpredictable. She prepared everything ready to be cooked and took him for a warm-up drive through the valley of Jezreel where history, beauty and the uncertain future met head on. On the way back, she took an unmarked path into the Ramoth Menashe forest, a Unesco biosphere reserve, known as the Tuscany of the Middle East and one of the most beautiful sites in Israel. It was a site they both knew well – it's streams and springs, its basalt hills and gall oak trees, its towering dill bushes and lowly willows and the string of kibbutzim nestling within its embrace. Eighty thousand dunams of ancient and modern Nature, in the heart of the country, protected from incursion and misuse. There was no time to explore, only to recapitulate on memories. Shira stopped her car near a clump of centuries-old gall oaks and stood among them in silent vigil. Yuri was fixated before a basalt hill. Was that the one they called the volcano? His memories were not cognizant with hers. He had done special forces training here, long before the site was declared a natural wonder. For him, the place had two facades: beauty and the beast. He was surprised at the way he envisioned it. Shira remained sequestered for something like twenty minutes. He walked slowly to where she was. "A shekel for your thoughts," he said. "I was just thinking of some words of Wordsworth's." "Tell me." Shira took a few steps forward, as if she was on stage and stretched out her arms in acknowledgement of the scene surrounding them. "Nature never did betray the heart that loved her," she proclaimed. Then she took his hand and tossing her head as if she still wore her hair long, she led him to the car.

***

"That was delicious, Shiraleh," he said, draining his third glass of Golani Cabernet Sauvignon at their house the same night. She had not heard him use her diminutive name for over a year. "What was it?" he asked. "Don't you know?" she teased. "It's what I do on special occasions. It's the only thing I can do. Baked fish steak. It should have been halibut but all I could get was Nile perch. It worked though, I think, except that I overdid the ginger. It used to be your favorite." "I must have had good taste in those days. I look forward to many more special occasions," he added in a nondescript voice that did not match the temper of his words. She waited for him to go on, to give her a clue to how he was feeling. He kept his eye on the wine in his glass. She did the same. It comforted her, despite his ambivalence. For the first time since his homecoming, she felt responsive. She had no complaints about their new-old sexual encounters, which ran the gamut from routine to hunger. But now she felt something more than either. She felt it was safe to come out. To leave her secret retreat, at least temporarily, and meet him on equal terms as one of a pair of lovers. Then, she told herself, she could hasten back to her secret abode, her secret pond and its golden fish. "I need to speak to you, Shira," he said, a touch officiously, as if about to reprimand a junior officer on a disciplinary charge. "When we met, we both had this overpowering feeling for each other, inexplicable at the time. Since then a lot of water has passed under many bridges. Is it still as inexplicable as it was?" She studied the golden hue of the wine, but said nothing. The question was too big. Answering it would be like opening an old trunk, full of forgotten things. "It is for me," he answered, after a long pause. "If I thought you were the person I was looking for and you felt the same, perhaps that would make us believe we had met before. We must have imagined, before we met, what he or she would be like and suddenly there he/she was. That is the closest I can get. What about you?" She had to join him. It was like walking in heavy rain. "How did we imagine this other person? Did we each have a physical image in our mind? Surely you don't have a detailed image of the person you feel destined for, but a type, an impression, a possibility. The first time I saw you, I remembered you. You were not someone who just happened to walk into my life, whose looks I liked. It was recollection, not a reflection. When we talked, nothing surprised me. Whatever you said, I imagined you would say. It was like a homecoming. Explain that." "I can't deny it," Yuri said, reluctantly.

"But what is there to make of it now?" she asked. "What's changed? I have to know," she said."

Yuri's mood changed immediately. A sudden storm gathered on his forehead. "What's changed?" he exploded. "Shira, can you seriously ask that? I have been to hell and back. I have had revelations from the past that are too vivid not to be true. They conform to the yardstick of history. Ask Penina, who has sent some of them to a classicist, who says they are authentic, correct in all detail. If they are not memories of past lives, what are they?" "You cannot, Yuri. You cannot speak of past lives. First, you must ask if such lives are possible. Do they conform to logic, to science? Once the brain is dead, the brain is dead. It's useless shouting 'Long live the brain.' How can it pop up, decades or centuries later, like buried treasure. Life isn't archeology. How can you entertain this – I'm sorry to have to say it – crap? How can some former personality, long dead, invade another person already born with their own DNA? Do the two DNA's fight it out? Do they use foils or pistols? Is the DNA inherited from present day parents somehow negated? I could go along with religion easier than this, although the very idea of God guts my mind. I cannot see how anyone can believe in what's ironically called previous life experiences. I'm sorry. I don't see how you could. You're not a yeshiva boy who knows no better. You've had an education." Neither knew how to go on. Each tried to form a sentence that would not antagonize the other. "Tell me, Yuri," she said in a low voice that broke the brittle silence like the snap of a papadum, "have you really thought this through?" "Thought! I don't think about anything else. What am I Shira, a reincarnation or a freak? Look, listen to me. I've no idea where all this stuff comes from. When I read it, it's like reading a novel by someone else. I can see there's meaning. I can see there's passion. I can see that it's about people who might have existed, but it doesn't touch me. None of this happened on my watch. And I'll tell you something, my present life doesn't touch me either. Whatever I do, whatever I say or think, is not me. This is not me speaking to you now. The person you are listening to is someone else. I don't know who he is. I don't know who you are. I only know who you are supposed to be. You are a thought. I have memories but they don't have substance. They don't have substance because they don't have meaning. The only meaning I can still experience is the memory when we first met in a kibbutz classroom. That makes me feel something. But everything that has happened since and everything in these so-called past lives is no more real to me than the son of a shadow." "This is hardly believable Yuri. You express yourself analytically. You must have understanding. If you have that, you have meaning." "I wish, I wish. But Shira, these words have no meaning for me, because, yes I understand what I am saying but I do not feel it. It is feeling that matters. I've lost the ability to feel. I can remember only. But the pieces of my life with you and the so-called PLE's I've had, float in my mind like plankton in the sea. I understand myself only as a formula. Emotion left the building with the night staff." "But Yuri, if you understand there is such a thing as feeling, how is it you can't feel? Isn't that a contradiction in terms? And what about love?" He looked at her with a forlorn look. Slowly the light seemed to drain from his eyes, until they were like pale disks. She shuddered. She wanted to scream but managed to block the sound before it left her throat. Then the tears. Not hers, his. For a brief moment, she was horrified. She had never seen him cry. She never imagined he could. And here he was, a combat officer who knew what it was to court death as a way of life, weeping like a child. Shira felt a wave of emotion rise in her like a whirlpool. "I love you, Yuri, I love you heart and soul. Do you understand?" "Yes Shira, I think so." "Oh Yuri, if I believed in God, I would thank him for this," she said, leaning across the table to find his lips. He took hers gently at first, as if he was sampling new wine. Then he drew her across the table and lay her down upon it to the music of bouncing cutlery and spinning plates. As he entered her, she proclaimed, in a whisper, her one dogma: "Whatever I understand, I understand only because I love. Leo Tolstoy: "War and…"

***

"I rang to know how you are doing," said the General. "Well, today was a watershed day," Shira told him. I was out, and when I got back, Yuri was nowhere. A neighbor told me, he had gone to the pool. That was like ice down my spine. I drove like a maniac to the pool, privatized now, of course, and searched for him. He was on his back, reading, wearing the brightest red shorts that he insisted on buying soon after he came home. Totally inappropriate. I made my way towards him, slowly, stopping to chat with friends and dreading what I might hear. You know what the pool is like this time of year, crowded with nubile young girls and half-dressed women everywhere. Like the South of France. But no-one was embarrassed or appalled or spoke to me in whispers. If Yuri had misbehaved, someone would have told me. It was the perfect environment for a groper, or worse, but apparently he'd done nothing awful. I can't tell you how relieved I was." "I can imagine, after some of the things he's done, the General put in. "But it was a watershed in another way," she said. "I can't explain, but Yuri has this way of looking at me sometimes that makes me want to scream. His eyes drain until there's no light in them. It's like some people, when they're about to pass out. Impersonal. Robotic. When I got to him, he held the book I thought he was reading down and looked at me. He had those eyes. My mind went blank. I managed to say that I'd been looking everywhere for him and only found him thanks to those crazy red trunks. It would normally have got a smile. But nothing. So I asked if he wanted a Macadamia chocolate ice cream. It was his favorite. He looked at me as if I hadn't spoken. Then I noticed the book I thought he had been reading. It was in an oriental script. I asked what it was. "Ancient Sanskrit poetry," he said. He admitted he couldn't read it, but liked looking at the letters. "I read the letters, not the words," he said. I just smiled, as if it was the most normal thing. But it was getting too Kafkaesque, even for me. It pointed up how totally bizarre our life has become. We are totally separate entities. Everything in marriage is done on credit, but when there's nothing left in the account, you have to take a massive loan. What if you can't afford the repayments?" "What keeps you both together?" "We relate through sex." "And how is that?" he ventured. "Great mechanically. Threadbare emotionally. Sex can keep an affair afloat, not a marriage. I can't face this situation for ever. I just can't. And I actually thought, a couple of nights ago, that things were improving." "So what are you going to do?" "I don't know. Perhaps he'll change. I can't. I don't know what to change into." "You'll do what we all do – change into what's possible."

He rang off with his customary lack of ceremony. Reflecting on the conversation, Shira could not believe she had discussed her marital sex life with a man with whom she had committed adultery. She knew the General had, at best, a highly myopic recall of his sexual exploits. Had he forgotten their second relationship already, as he had forgotten their first? Certainly, he had made no further advances, since her post-Italy submission, not even as conversational innuendo. Not that she would have welcomed an approach. When she considered Yuri's odyssey, haunted by tragi-comic encounters and Penina's crisis in life and career, and the General, uncertain for the first time, as he faced, not the enemy, but retirement, and her own perambulations across a narrow but precipitous platform, which might as well have been on the moon, she wondered what Emily, the professor of laughter, would have made of it all. From deep within her throat, a peal of laughter surfaced. It sounded like the real thing, but was artificial to the core. Still, it brought a smile to her face and made her feel a whole lot better. As she went through her cosmetic ritual, that morning, which translated brooding potentiality into public confrontation, she told herself she was ready for anything – and laughed.

DURING YURI'S LAST DAYS IN REHAB, he had recited a flow of past life experiences, un-induced, based on life as a slave in Rome and Italy and his escape to Palestine, via Egypt, almost a decade after he had been deported in chains. Madeleine, realizing the historic significance of his "reminiscences" instructed her staff to record everything he said, while he slept. She did not tell anyone, other than the professor. They both thought that Shira would have enough to cope with, after her husband's release, without adding the role of amanuensis. He stopped having PLE's three days before he was released, for good reason, as the text makes plain. She presented the tapes to Penina for processing.

Made in the USA
Middletown, DE
21 May 2019